Where the rich and beautiful play.

THE CLUB

JACKY MELLON
She's a dazzling star like
her mother. And speeding on the same
downhill skid to self-destruction.

EDDIE BERNARDO
Jacky's sexy Italian live-in
director. He's man enough for ten
women. Almost enough for Jacky.

ELLISON
America's coked-up king of fashion.
Jacky amuses him, and he'll be there to
pick her up. As long as she matters.

GLESNEROVSKY
The Russian ballet stud.
Jacky wanted his body and took
it without even asking.

STUART SHORTER
The beautiful people let him
play with them. Because he decides
who gets into The Club.

THE
CLUB

STEVEN GAINES and
ROBERT JON COHEN

This is a work of fiction. The characters, names,
incidents, places, and dialogue are products of the authors'
imaginations and are not to be construed as real.

This low-priced Bantam Book
has been completely reset in a type face
designed for easy reading, and was printed
from new plates. It contains the complete
text of the original hard-cover edition.
NOT ONE WORD HAS BEEN OMITTED.

THE CLUB
A Bantam Book / published by arrangement with
William Morrow & Company, Inc.

PRINTING HISTORY

William Morrow edition published March 1980
Bantam edition / August 1980

ISBN 0-553-13746-8

Published simultaneously in the United States and Canada

For those who couldn't get in

SUNDAY

1

Jacky Mellon always believed that the only way to see New York City at night was through the amber-tinted windows of a limousine. During the day, when she felt that limousines matched neither New York's lighting nor tempo, a taxi would do. But at night, with the city ink-blue-on-blue, the skyscrapers twinkling malevolently around her, the sleek black car and privacy of tinted glass seemed appropriate. Particularly if she was going to make an entrance at The Club.

Jacky Mellon's limousine turned onto Fifty-seventh Street and abruptly pulled to a halt in a line of traffic. A row of Cadillac limousines, Bentleys, Rolls-Royces and taxicabs stood in line, waiting to pull up to the marquee at the east end of the block. Jacky stared absently at herself in her reflection in the tinted window and wondered if she had enough time to put on new makeup before her car arrived at the entrance. She was ten minutes fresh out of bed with Eddie Bernardo, with whom she had spent a blissful hour in carnal embrace. Even now in the limousine his smell was stronger than that of the rich leather. When they were through, she had managed to fix her hair a little before she left the house, but that was all; she was sure she at least needed some fresh lipstick. At the rate the traffic was crawling her limousine probably wouldn't get near the entrance of The Club for another ten minutes anyway; from down the block the crowd under the sparkling marquee looked enormous, spilling out onto the street and fouling up traffic in both directions. A police officer next to a parked patrol car with a flashing beacon was unsuccessfully trying to unsnarl the tangle of waiting automobiles. It was nearly two in the morning on a Sunday night, the rest of the city was practically deserted and this one block seemed like the vortex for all the activity in New York.

Without fail there were hundreds of people in front of The Club every night, waiting anxiously to be admitted, in the summer heat, in rain and snow. They came from small

3

towns in the Midwest, from London and Beirut or from just around the corner, ineluctably drawn there to be part of an international phenomenon, a discotheque so narcotic in its pleasure-giving ability that it had become the most famous nightclub of all time.

Yet most of the people waiting hopefully behind police barricades under the black Art Deco marquee would never be given the nod of admittance by Stuart Shorter, the tall, nervous owner of The Club, who indicates to the formidable array of bouncers who will venture past the red velvet ropes and inside. Fame and fortune are helpful credentials but no guarantee that you will be included in Shorter's whimsical formula for that evening's proceedings. White House aides have been left cooling their egos in police-escorted limousines at the curb. The shah offered to buy Shorter a house in Barbados if he could guarantee the admittance of his visiting sister. Jimmy Carter's son Chip was denied admission for his fifteen Secret Service security escorts because they were too shabbily dressed. Even the secretary-general of the United Nations phones ahead to make arrangements at the door for members of the Security Council—often to no avail.

Paparazzi buzz up and down the street, snapping photos like nervous fireflies. They leap after people who bolt from their limousines, flashbulbs exploding. From out of the noisy crowd emerge the rich, the famous, the young and the beautiful. The glitterati. Mick Jagger pushes his way through with Terry Southern tagging along. Jerri Hall is not far behind. A dowager empress is admitted with a handful of uptown hustlers. Princess Grace of Monaco is given red-carpet treatment. Caroline Kennedy and two college girlfriends wait impatiently at the ropes until she is recognized. Warren Beatty, tousled hair falling across his forehead, slips in alone. Andy Warhol floats past with an entourage of followers. Catherine Guinness holds tight to Robert Hayes so as not to get lost in the crush. Two handsome young men, Brazilian playboys on the Rio-New York-Paris circuit of women, push their way through the crowd. Truman Capote in sunglasses, hat and scarf. This year's top male model. Last year's socialite. Mistakenly, Yves Saint Laurent is left standing at the ropes, a cape thrown over his shoulders, crying to the doorman, "But it is *me*, it is *Yves*!" Farrah Fawcett is rushed past the crowd with her boss at Fabergé, Cary Grant and two bodyguards. Burt Reynolds, bashful without his toupee, holds his face down away from the cameras. Also passes the elite of photographers, newspaper columnists and those with access to a rented limousine or a designer sports jacket. Perhaps, for a touch of Fellini, a fairy princess drag queen in an antique wedding dress whizzes in on roller skates. And still the others wait, restlessly, calling Stuart Shorter's name like a chant. The bouncers menace back those who would intrude beyond the velvet ropes without an invitation, while out on the street the long procession of glittering automobiles continues to expel passengers at the curb.

Jacky felt a rush of anticipation. She loved going to The Club. It never failed to make her feel good. She felt safe inside, secure. It was so overpowering, the frenzy of sound and light. A glamor inferno. There was very little chance to think of anything too serious. It was what going to the circus should have been but wasn't. It was as breathtaking as a roller coaster, as bizarre as an LSD trip, as relieving as coming home. And the pops of the *paparazzi's* flashbulbs were fuel for her very being. Under the glowing pastel-colored lights of The Club Jacky was continuously reassured that few women in the world were as celebrated as she. It was confirmed by the way people stared and by the way other women enviously examined her clothing and appraised her dates. At The Club each of Jacky's smiles and frowns was subject to comment in tomorrow's gossip columns. And she loved it. She ate it up.

Jacky Mellon needed every bit of it.

All alone in the back seat of her darkened limousine, she slouched down on the large leather seat and knocked two little white mounds of cocaine onto the top of her right hand. She held them up to her nostrils on the back of her fist and snorted in strongly. The stinging brought a rush of tears to her eyes as the cocaine was instantaneously absorbed into the nasal membranes. Her face flushed a bit, and then she felt light and good.

Liz Smith may report that Jacky Mellon shakes her way around the dance floor of The Club every night, but underneath that public veneer of fun and success, Jacky Mellon was running scared. She pinched her nostrils together between her fingers and inhaled sharply. Why did she have that frightened feeling all the time? she wondered. Was it the cocaine that was making her feel so paranoid?

The limousine came to a sudden stop, and Jacky sat up.
A group of people walking down the street tried to peer
into the car windows to see who was inside. She pretended
not to notice them and fiddled with the radio tuner hidden
behind a leather panel. She turned to a disco station first,
grunted in disgust, then turned to a rock station. When she
finally could not find a song that pleased her, she impatiently snapped the radio off and hoisted a large portable
cassette player onto her lap from the floor of the car and
turned it on. Her own voice singing "Love in My Life"
filled the back of the car.

It didn't sound so bad to her. She wondered why it
never sold, why none of the records ever sold.

There was something wrong with her career.

She was teetering on the edge of disaster. She was a
much acclaimed actress and singer, but her talent seemed
to be of a very narrow range. There was one performance
she could do brilliantly, but only one performance. Over
the years she had become a caricature of herself; by now
her every eyelash flutter and facial tic had become so
predictable that she was a staple in the repertoire of every
female impersonator in the country.

No matter that her appeal as a performer had worn so
thin; she was still the gossip columnist's delight. The
National Enquirer and the *Star* had sold millions of copies
with Jacky's face on the cover. But as was pointed out only
the week before by one of Jacky's prime critics, New
York's famed syndicated columnist Addison Critch,
"Jacky Mellon's fame is not only ill-deserved but an
embarrassment in the entertainment business. She has no
purpose except that as an object of personal derision and
gossip. And if she still has a following, her audience is
comprised totally of a narrow cult audience, predominant-
ly homosexual, who would worship her even if she were to
evacuate her last night's supper on the screen. Enough
attention has been paid to Jacky Mellon in payment for
her mother's talents. Now it is time to give her the
hook."

Indeed, Jacky was a cult figure, and she hated it. She
wished all those screaming fans would just disappear. She
thought it undermined her credibility as a star. For that
very reason she had no respect for Barbra Streisand. Or
Bette Midler and Liza Minnelli. And of course, there was

the worst offender of them all, the queen mother of all cult figures, her own mother, Angela Mellon.

Angela Mellon, the rosy-cheeked, blue-eyed girl next door, was one of America's most beloved movie stars. As a young actress during the Second World War she became a symbol of American wholesomeness and determination, a particularly indelible image in the minds of the public, ironically so because these traits were hardly true in Angela's personal life. Away from her career Angela Mellon was slothful and often selfish. She lived and died a frightened woman, haunted by ghosts and demons of her own devising. Dependent on pills of all sorts, she lived with a string of men who abused her, both personally and financially. Jacky's mother danced her way quickly through life, like a spinning top, and little Jacky was often carried along as an afterthought by the centrifugal force.

As a professional, no matter how successful Jacky became, she felt she always walked in her mother's shadow, expected to succumb to all the same pitfalls: booze, bad drugs, bad men, bad luck.

Eddie Bernardo was going to change all that. Eddie Bernardo would straighten out the kinks in her life and elevate her career. Eddie was going to direct Jacky in a masterpiece that would forever confirm her as a star. In the circle of people in New York and Los Angeles who concern themselves with those things the show had been the number one topic of conversation for months. It was called *The Performance*, a name which immediately made it privy to a million vicious jokes, all of which got back to Jacky. It had been touted to the media by its press agents, Mary and Elliot Gavin, as the most lavish show ever mounted on a Broadway stage. It was an epic show business drama, tracing the dynasty of a singing family, including a matriarchal grandmother who was a star of the Vienna Opera, her daughter, who became an American pop singing idol, and a great-granddaughter, who headlines in Las Vegas. Jacky played all three roles in what was promised to be a *tour de force* performance. *The* performance.

Naturally the show had turned into a potboiler for the gossip columnists. Jacky's affair with Eddie had turned out reams of newspaper copy. Eddie was something of an item himself. He was Hollywood's hottest young director, a sexy Italian import who had been in the States for only five years and was already part of the new Hollywood elite. He had directed four highly successful yet artistic films, all of which managed to lift a supporting actress to starring status. Two of his leading ladies had won Academy Awards for "Best Actress." His movies also offered a deep understanding of women in difficult transitions, while dealing with them on a frank sexual basis. His work was regarded just as rich in entertainment value as it was in social comment.

Eddie's reputation was also rich with tales of his sexual adventures. Half the women in Beverly Hills were claiming him as a triumph, and the other half were trying. Even Warren Beatty felt his champion's title threatened. Eddie's most publicized tryst had been with Suzanne St. Jacques, a beautiful but talentless TV star who dumped her husband of eight years to live with him. The relationship went on for another six months until they had a violent argument in La Scala on Little Santa Monica Boulevard and Suzanne went back to her husband—who didn't want her anymore. A few months later Jacky came into the picture, and what Eddie Bernardo found so compelling about Jacky, none of the spectators could figure out.

There was one curious point about *The Performance;* Eddie had never directed on the stage before. Ever. And he was determined that Jacky would be nothing short of brilliant in it. Eddie considered himself a creative perfectionist. He had zest for his work and love and ego. He attacked his projects with a fiery Sicilian spirit, just the way he ate his meals and fucked his women. And while a good meal depended on the chef and a good woman depended on the moment, a man could always depend on his work. *The Performance* would be like nothing Broadway had ever seen, and then he would show everybody, including the cynical New Yorkers.

To make sure that *The Performance* would be a triumph for them, they had just toasted a new master plan for Jacky's life with an hour of fucking in her apartment in the Olympic Towers. They had agreed that beginning the next day Jacky was going to start a brand-new regimen. Up at nine, then a half-hour jog with Eddie through Central Park every morning. Then there was a diet that would strip away fifteen pounds from her middle so she could get into her expensive Ellison costumes without having them refitted. There was also a supply of vitamin pills that she was to take every four hours to help build her strength, pills that she had never heard of before, like kelp and lecithin and enriched bone. And from now on she would be in bed every night by midnight, preferably with him.

And *no* cocaine.

And no more café society until after the show opened. She'd have to drop her pill-popping friends temporarily, he said.

And The Club would be off limits until the opening night of *The Performance*, when they would go there together for the big party that Stu Shorter was throwing for them. Eddie saw The Club as the scene of the crime, so to speak. It was Jacky's biggest downfall. She went there three and four times a week, and it left her bleary-eyed and exhausted at rehearsal the next day. Not only did it encourage her to stay up late, but in turn she took more drugs to give her the energy. So no more Club.

In fact, she promised him when he left her apartment that she was going right to sleep, but instead, she called a limousine service and got dressed. After all, she deserved one last farewell visit. She didn't even stop to shower. She immediately phoned Ellison and asked him to meet her there. Ellison was her best chum, and he, no doubt, would have a fresh supply of what he called nose candy to refill the diminishing amount in her own bottle, which she dug into in the back of the limousine, scraping the small metal spoon around the sides. She dug off bits of caked powder and snorted them quietly into her nose.

If Eddie had decided to live with her in the first place when they had come to New York, none of this ever would have happened, she reasoned. If Eddie was so concerned about her health and her habits, why had he insisted they have separate apartments in Manhattan? When she said she was ecstatic about going back East to do a show together, she meant together. They lived together in Los Angeles. Of course, Eddie kept his own house. But in New York having separate apartments was kind of creepy, and she was glad he had called it off.

Tomorrow night he was moving in with her.

And then she'd *never* be able to go to The Club.

The limousine inched its way up under the marquee, and Jacky could see the faces of the people clamoring for the attention of Elliot, the blond, unruffled doorman who helped decide who was admitted. She looked around for Stuart Shorter but couldn't find him. She guessed he was probably inside. It was Shorter who had developed the rules about who was admitted. One night he had recited the rules of the door to her: They did not allow people who wore gold chains or shirt collars outside their jacket lapels; nobody wearing a cheap sports jacket or a plaid jacket; no "BBQs," by which he meant people who looked as if they lived in Brooklyn, the Bronx, or Queens; no "B&Ts"—bridge and tunnel people; no "Harlem niggers in leather topcoats"; no "folks from New Jersey"; no "Qiana from the Americana," by which he meant the rich South Americans who often stayed at the Americana Hotel and wore polyester blends of Kodel Qiana; and the Bagel Nosh crowd wasn't welcome at The Club either. Shorter went so far as to tell one man that if he allowed him to burn the lapel of his polyester suit with a cigarette, he would admit him into The Club. The man declined, but only at his wife's insistence.

And once a young punk came up to the door with his jacket thrown over his shoulders like an Italian director with two cheap-looking girls on either arm. When they wouldn't let him past the velvet ropes, he spit at Stuart Shorter. Shorter stopped his bouncers from pummeling the boy, but the angry youth wasn't scared. He yelled, "Do you know who my grandfather is? My grandfather is Tony Pallante!" and stormed off. A half hour later two limousines pulled up, and seven mobsters piled out of the car with the offended grandson of mobster chieftain Tony Pallante. They proceeded to beat up Shorter and his bouncers and spent the rest of the night happily inside The Club with their young ward. Shorter wisely never pressed charges but sported a black eye for a week.

Jacky certainly hoped there were no incidents like that tonight at the door. But people were likely to do anything to get inside. One night she heard a crying woman insist that she was pregnant and miscarrying and that her husband was inside The Club and she had to go in and find him. She was not admitted. Another man brought three changes of clothes in his car trunk and kept changing till Elliot liked what he was wearing. There was even a limousine and driver that waited at the corner and charged people twenty bucks to drive them up to the door, claiming it would improve their chances of being admitted.

Some people claimed to know somebody important, often Stuart Shorter himself. There was the time that a gentleman who appeared as a guest on the Jim Martin late-night TV show had asked Martin for a letter of introduction to Stuart Shorter, who had also once been on his show. Martin wrote a note for the man, who dutifully presented it at the door. He was laughed at and shoved aside. When he persisted, he was shoved so hard he broke his ankle. Jim Martin paid the man's doctor's bills in embarrassment. Other people have been less fortunate. One stubborn twenty-six-year-old man became embarrassed and insulted that he and his new wife were denied admission. He tried to pass by the velvet ropes forcefully, and a bouncer ruptured both his testicles with a knee to his groin.

Some people were purposely snubbed as insults, like Edgar Roman, the pudgy pop singing star who threw himself a birthday party at The Club and never paid the bill. Shorter shrewdly never made a fuss or told the papers. He just kept Edgar Roman waiting at the door a few times, and the check was forthcoming.

But most people simply claimed to know The Club's front lady, Sylvia DeLaGrecco. Jacky *loathed* Sylvia De-LaGrecco. She was a walking Rolodex of the rich and important in New York. A wealthy widow of a Greek-Italian shipping magnate, she had some dubious title of royalty and a brand-new twenty-two-year-old husband in tow named Toddy, whom everybody at The Club seemed dying to fuck. Sylvia was a stunning woman in her early fifties whose formula for fame was that she liked to dance and liked fashion designers, two amusements she put together by becoming a New York tastemaker. Wherever hot-blooded, fun-loving, beautiful Sylvia DeLaGrecco went, a trendy New York crowd followed. Naturally Sylvia would have languished with embarrassment if anybody had known she was still on The Club's payroll; Shorter had given her $25,000 in cash to send celebrities to The Club when it first opened. And the people she brought gave her things in return, more money, jewelry, clothing for her and her young husband. She dined out on her power at the door every night of the week, and her fame spread far and wide. She would no doubt be at The Club tonight.

When her car finally stopped, Jacky felt a tingle of anticipation travel up her spine. The people nearest to the curb leaned against the windows and stared at her. A woman in a garish silver lurex outfit recognized her and shouted her name loudly. Then the name was repeated excitedly several more times as word spread through the crowd that it was Jacky Mellon in the limousine. She straightened her suit, a tawny beige cashmere outfit that Ellison had made for her just last week for $900 with a fluffy tunic top, waisted with a thin brown belt and Anne Allegretti gold clasp, and took a final glance at herself in her reflection. She thought for a second she looked tired and old. And then she realized it was her mother's face she was seeing.

Maybe Eddie was right. Maybe she should go home and get some rest. But in another moment the chauffeur was around to her side of the car and the door was opening and the oohs and ahhs of the crowd greeted her ears. She put a public, frozen smile on her face and got out of the car, waving languidly at no one in particular. From everywhere they were calling to her, shouting her name, "Jacky! Jacky!" A dozen strobe lights went off in quick succession. Two of the bouncers from behind the ropes quickly pushed their way out to where she was standing. The people on the street separated in waves as they flanked Jacky on the short journey up to the velvet ropes. An old woman who collected autographs proffered an autograph book in front of Jacky imploringly. Jacky tried to take it from the woman and sign her name, but one of the bouncers got in the way, and the woman was roughly brushed aside and swallowed up by the crowd. Jacky was about to complain when the excited mob began to crush in on her, chanting, "Jacky! Jacky!" She was a little frightened for a moment until the velvet ropes mercifully parted and she was whisked into The Club, away from the screaming people on the street.

2

Once she was inside The Club, like slipping down the rabbit hole, nothing seemed very real to her. She could never remember what the space used to be. It had been explained to her many times, but she always forgot. It had been either an old movie theater or a grand department store. In any event, the whole thing had been gutted and rebuilt as an opulent, decadent circus. The psychological premise was visibility. You could see everyone and be seen by everyone. There were no tables and chairs, only a stream of long, low suede banquettes at odd angles to the walls. The major part of the seating was provided by a semicircular balcony that overlooked the massive dance floor. Hovering above, the domed ceiling was covered by a hand-painted tapestry of gold-leaf lightning rods, which gracefully fell to earth on fluted columns that held up the balcony. In the three lucite and chrome carousel bars decorated with stacked crystal block centerpieces like mountains of ice, an assortment of muscular bartenders, their biceps banded in brass, twirled and danced as they poured drinks.

The dance floor seemed to have a life force of its own as a thousand people writhed and squirmed with the joyful abandon of a religious experience. It pulsated and throbbed, changing shape and direction, sometimes splitting off in little clutches like an amoeba reproducing. The dancers were a sea of arms and bodies swirling and pumping around each other, the colors painting them red, blue, applejack green. The flashing pastel lights glinted off the dark richness of the Chinese blood-red walls, which had been painted with ten coats of lacquer to give them depth. Other walls were mirrored from floor to ceiling, and at points the room appeared to have no beginning, no end. Jacky thought she saw Marisa Berenson but couldn't tell for sure under the changing lighting as row upon row of applejack red fluorescent flying saucers skimmed across the heads of the dancers. A man in a black leather riding

outfit shook a tambourine over his head, dancing by
himself, his eyes shut and head thrown back in reverie.
Actor Peter Firth, in a tan-colored Brown's sports jacket,
his hair long and curly, danced with a girl who was equally
dazzling and couldn't have been older than nineteen. A
wrinkled old woman, in mirrored sunglasses, was lofted in
the air by a boyfriend at least fifty years younger than she.
Both were wearing white satin gym shorts. The old woman
shouted, "Go for it! Go for it!" as her partner twirled her
in place. Jacky wondered if the woman was going for a
heart attack. Nearby she could see that Gore Vidal and a
handsome friend, both in black tie, were watching the old
woman dance with detached amusement, chattering to
each other now and then. Almost everyone was making a
point of *not* noticing the half-naked woman, her bare
nipples painted like targets, drinking a Tequila Sunrise
from a baby's bottle. Jacky wondered how Stuart Shorter
had let *her* in. The fashion crowd was stationed in the
usual place on the east wall, perched on and around a row
of leather banquettes in front of a two-story veil-thin
waterfall that cascaded into a foaming pool. Stephen
Burrows, the designer, was animatedly chatting with his
date. Next to him Norma Kamali was serenely studying the
room as if she were somewhere else entirely. Jackie Rog-
ers, Madison Avenue designer and former Coco Chanel
model, floated by the banquette, alternately searching for
and avoiding *Le Grand Couturier* Jacques Bellini and his
sometime companion, Sylvia Miles, who had been nomi-
nated for, but had never won, *two* Academy Awards. Tall
and blond Tara Tyson Kulukundis, wife of the son of the
patriarch of Greek shipping magnates, Michael Kulukundis, was curled on the next banquette, her high heels on
the floor in front of her. Off near the entrance Texas art
collector and patron François Demenil, still looking like a
teenager, arrived with a crowd from a private screening of
his million-dollar home movie.

Music filled the air in pulsating waves, as if it were
solid. The electronic violins and shrieking lyrics urged
everyone higher, faster, harder. Enough was never enough.
Excess to excess the crowd kept up with the music, the
volume so loud it could carbonate blood—yet upstairs in
the soundproofed lounge it was quiet enough to hear the
gentle snorting of cocaine.

No one bothered Jacky as she roamed about. There

were undercover bouncers everywhere at The Club, trying to look inconspicuous while all the time hovering protectively over the celebrities. There were very few problems of that sort at The Club anyway. Drunks were a rare occurrence because the crowd used more drugs than alcohol and they were alternately subdued or ecstatic but not the least bit violent. There were some occasional scuffles over flirtatious women, but The Club's atmosphere was too cool and glamorous for real trouble, and the screening system at the door usually weeded out the possible troublemakers. The bouncers, however, made sure that customers were discreet in their drug use and that nobody got carried away good-naturedly and offended anyone. Even the most reserved banker was known to get swept away at the sight of Farah Fawcett jiggling braless on the dance floor. And if some clod as much as asked a celebrity for an autograph at The Club, a bouncer would intercede politely and say, "Please don't do that." Of course, once a bouncer at The Club asks you to do something, you do it. Otherwise, you are calmly but forcibly ejected.

However, if you were a *professional* celebrity hunter, a columnist or photographer, that would be a different story. A select crew of writers and *paparazzi* was not only allowed into The Club free of charge but encouraged to write about what went on inside, thus tantalizing the rest of the world and keeping the lines long outside. Nobody would stop Liz Smith if she were seen asking Diane Von Furstenberg a question. Columnist Jack Martin, whose information on people literally travels around the world in a matter of hours, is allowed to speak to anybody (although he doesn't). While journalists could come and go, the number of photographers in The Club was usually limited: a columnist can sink into a chaise and sit back and observe, but a photographer's strobe lights are harsh reminders of his presence. No celebrity wants to be photographed using drugs or sweaty and disheveled from the dance floor. Therefore, the photographers who were allowed in were a trusted bunch and special favorites of Stuart Shorter. They had agreed beforehand not to photograph a celebrity continuously. They get it over with all at the same time, take two or three minutes of shots and then disappear until the next celebrity arrives. There are no exceptions from the rule. Shorter himself had been known to take a swing at a *paparazzo* who took one more shot after Shorter had ordered no more photos. Usually at The Club you could find Robin Platzer, an array of cameras around her neck like monstrous necklaces, or superstar photographer Ron Galella, looking very prosperous in suit and tie, or Richard Corkery, the New York *News'* ace cameraman.

At the moment, everyone left Jacky alone while she searched for Ellison. As she came to the edge of the imported hardwood dance floor itself, Stuart Shorter appeared from out of the churning dancers like a skier avoiding slalom poles. There must have been more than one of him because Shorter gave the impression of being truly omnipresent: at the front door, introducing people to each other inside, giving out free drinks at the bar. Tall, wiry, nervous, blue eyes and rich blond hair, he looked, as usual, as if he were nauseated but extremely happy about it. He weaved and bobbed in place, wearing a Lacoste T-shirt with the alligator emblem half falling off and tattered Calvin Klein jeans with frayed cuffs and sneakers. There was a sloppy smile on his face, the result of various combinations of Quaaludes, cocaine and loss of muscle coordination. Sylvia DeLaGrecco was at his side and her husband, Toddy, wasn't far behind.

"Jacky Mel-*lone!* Jacky Mel-*lone!*" Sylvia DeLaGrecco shrieked, so Continental and dripping with accents that it made Jacky want to spit. "You look di-vine! Faabulous!" She picked at Jacky's Ellison outfit. Sylvia was wearing a low-cut Calvin Klein that showed a large portion of her breasts, once lifted and now quite firm and full for a fifty-two-year-old woman. Sylvia presented her young husband. "You know my hoosband, Toddy?"

"Yes, of course," Jacky said, taking Toddy in carefully. Well, he certainly was beautiful.

Shorter stood there beaming at Jacky. He still got a thrill from knowing celebrities. Even though he ran the most famous club in the world and it was filled with stars every night, each and every time someone famous came in he was freshly impressed with the wonder of it all. Shorter believed with every ounce of his being the fantasy that was The Club, and it was his energy that helped make it work. He was the little boy forever thrilled with his king-sized electric train set.

Jacky had met him at the start. The Club had been open only a month at the time, and Ellison insisted she come to

see it. He in turn had been recommended by Sylvia
DeLaGrecco. Shorter was a nobody at the time, a *shmen-
drik* who had made some money in the grocery store
business or something equally boring. He seemed like a
good-natured but star-struck man with a Bronx Jewish
accent who was looking for a piece of the New York
action. He was nearly speechless when he was first introduced to Jacky, he was so impressed with her. He gushed
about what a loyal fan he was, to her and her mother, and
brought her a bottle of champagne. As the months went by
and Jacky made more frequent trips from Los Angeles to
New York, she got to know Shorter and took a special
liking to him. Once he got past the fame bit he was
affecting and cute, with a Woody Allen kind of appeal.
Jacky even had a short affair with him, which probably
would have lasted longer if he hadn't tried to convince her
to join one of his weird three-way scenes. He remained a
great friend, a kind of little brother to her who still had
some kind of starry crush.

"Don't say it! Don't say it!" Jacky said, hugging and
kissing him. "I know I haven't spoken to you all month."

"Where were you? I missed you," Shorter cried. "You've
been in New York a month, and the only time I ever see
you is in here when I'm running around like a chicken
without a head. You mean you haven't had time for *one*
dinner? What is it, this new guy?"

Shorter had developed a way of talking to be heard over
the sound of the music. Instead of shouting, which made
him hoarse, he spoke from the back of his throat, using his
nose for amplification. An unpleasant but effective way of
being heard. Indeed, people made fun of the way Shorter
spoke because with the added effect of the drugs and
alcohol he sounded like a phonograph record being played
at irregular speed.

"We're just busy rehearsing," Jacky said.

"We all wonder about your show, darlink. It is divine,
no?" Sylvia DeLaGrecco asked.

"It is wonderful, yes," Jacky told her, smiling stiffly.

"And we all die to meet your handsome director. Why
do you never bring him to The Club?"

So none of you can get your hands on him, Jacky
thought.

"Oh, yeah," Shorter chirped in. "Let's all go visit him
one night. I'll pay for dinner, and then we'll bring him

here." This was usually Shorter's plan for bringing reticent celebrities to The Club; he actually went out and brought them back there himself.

Jacky promised one day they would do exactly that, content with the knowledge that Eddie Bernardo would never come near The Club.

"Champagne?" Shorter offered, motioning toward the bar.

Jacky shook her head.

Shorter leaned close to her and whispered, "Would you like a lude?"

Quaalude was the favorite drug of The Club. The use of cocaine was probably more widespread, but Quaaludes were delicacies. That was because great quantities of cocaine were available if you had the money to buy it, but Quaaludes were a pharmaceutical drug made by Rorer, Incorporated, and very hard to come by. They sold on the black market for $5 or $10 each. It was easy to build a tolerance to them, and habitual users found themselves having to take three and four to feel the effect. The drug wasn't physically addicting, but it was psychologically and physically so pleasant it was very hard to resist. The wonderfully tingling, dreamy effect of the drug matched the light, slippery quality of The Club perfectly. Although it was easy to get sloppy or overaffectionate on them, the right amount of Quaalude was a perfect nightcap for many at The Club.

Jacky almost broke down and took one, but instead, she said to Shorter, "I'm on the wagon. No booze or drugs till the show opens."

"Yeah, well, we've all said that. I'll forgive you if you fall off," Shorter said.

"Come on, now, be constructive," Jacky warned.

"I'll be constructive," Shorter said, his expression turning to one of concern. He looked over his shoulder for a moment to see if anyone else was standing near, and not satisfied with their privacy, he excused them from Sylvia DeLaGrecco and took Jacky by the arm and steered her back into the direction she had just come from. Finally, he found a more secluded spot that seemed to satisfy him next to a tropical palm tree in a ceramic tub.

He was acting so suspicious that Jacky said, "Aren't you afraid there's a microphone in the palm?"

Shorter's eyes searched the tree. "What made you say that? Why'd you say *that?*"

"I was being funny."

"It's not funny. I'm so freaked out, you wouldn't believe it. I feel like there are people looking over my shoulder all the time," Shorter confided in her.

"New York paranoia, Stu. It's only New York paranoia."

"No, this is more serious. Hear me out. You've got to be very careful what you do in The Club because we think the place is crawling with cops of some sort."

"Cops?" Jacky said.

"Cops. Or FBI guys. Or maybe investigators from the State Liquor Authority. Maybe even federal drug guys."

"Narcs? Holy shit!" Jacky said, the empty vial of cocaine burning a hole in her purse. "Will there be a raid?"

Shorter snorted. "Not likely. How can they raid a nightclub that has two or three judges, the President's son and probably all of the mayor's staff in it at the same time? What would they do, arrest everybody? No. David Willick says that as soon as they can pin something on me, they'll come drag me and Dubrow out of bed and arrest us."

David Willick was one of the most powerful criminal attorneys in the East. He had represented in his time more of the most notorious criminals, embezzlers, swindlers and murderers than any other lawyer in history. He had always represented Shorter's silent partner, Sandy Dubrow, and was guardian angel of The Club in all legal matters.

"What a hideous notion. But what would they have on you? What could they arrest you for?"

"Nothing," Shorter said, looking her in the eyes. It was a terrible, guilty look, full of remorse and fear.

She knew he was lying. For the first time she realized that something terribly wrong was going on at The Club. She thought of telling him that it didn't matter to her, that she would protect him if she could, but instead, she asked, "Could they arrest you just for using drugs?"

"Naw, they're into bigger than that," he said, his voice low and worried. "In the meantime, we gotta figure out who the informant is."

"An informant! Who's the informant?"

"That's exactly what we wish we knew. It's gotta be

somebody who's around here all the time. Maybe somebody who works here or is a good friend of mine."

"A good *friend?* How could a good friend be an informant?"

"That's exactly what an informant is. Like a spy. Somebody who pretends to be *for* you while they're out gathering information *about* you. Then they turn it over to the other guys and testify against you. If we could only figure out who it is."

"How creepy. Why do people become informants? Why would anybody do that?"

"For money, usually. David Willick said there are two kinds of criminal informants. One is the professional, somebody who purposely takes a job to find out information and then gets paid for testifying. Sometimes a couple of thousand bucks. But Willick said that most of the people who turn informant do it out of hate. Jealousy. Revenge."

"Who could *that* be?" Jacky asked him, frightened but intrigued.

Shorter laughed, his peculiar staccato bray. "It could be anybody. Do you realize how many people you can offend when you run a discotheque like this? How many people are hateful because sometime they were denied admission in front of their girlfriend or boss? There are people that don't even know me, never saw me in their life, who hate me because I'm the guy who says they're not good enough to be in with the elite. It could be anybody, just anybody. So you be cool. Don't use in front of anybody. And if you see or hear anything weird, tell me."

Jacky promised, but she half wondered if this whole thing wasn't something out of his very paranoid imagination. Although, come to think of it, lots of people did seem to hate Stuie.

"Do you have any leads?" she asked him.

"Yeah, two people," he said, his eyes darting over her shoulder into the crowd.

The doorman and a security guard from the front door found Shorter behind the potted plant. "We need you up front," the doorman said urgently, putting his hand on Shorter's arm.

"Who?" Jacky asked, but all Shorter would do was put his finger up to his mouth in silence as he rushed off to the front door.

She wondered again who the informant might be. She'd love to catch the informant for him.

The best place to look for Ellison was probably the disc jockey's booth. The booth was a prime position to hold at The Club. Only the biggest celebrity of the evening would be invited up there by Shorter, although there were a few special favorites and exceptions to the rule like Jacky and Ellison, who were welcome up there anytime. Andy Warhol was another—he loved to watch from the booth and made an appearance there almost every night. Diana Ross could go up there when she wanted (although she was *always* the biggest celebrity on *any* night, Shorter explained) and play with the lighting controls. Lillian Carter once watched the dancing for an hour from the booth. And one night Mick Jagger accidentally jostled the turntable with his elbow, sending the stylus screeching across the record and causing an uproar in The Club.

If the discotheque was Oz, the booth was the Wizard's hidden controls behind the curtain. In it were two floating Teac 1400 turntables, suspended in custom cabinets of thick mahogany. The featherweight Koss arms and stylus had been fashioned in Germany especially for the Teac turntables. The amplifier banks, some 9,000 watts of usable power, were stacked in vertical modular cabinets at the rear of the booth. The records: singles, albums and twelve inches, were in a revolving bin, each numbered and stored. Even the Stoss headphones were tailor-made with ear cushions that cupped the talented ear of Raymond Iannachi, the Wizard and disc jockey.

Most disc jockeys were Italian or Puerto Rican, although no one could explain exactly why except that perhaps the job was handed down through family members. Raymond Iannachi had indeed got his first job playing a discotheque from his cousin Sal eight years before. Iannachi was a veteran of two or three dozen discotheques over those years, finally working his way up to The Club. He had impeccable, middle-of-the-road disco taste: nothing too wild, nothing too tame. Shorter paid him $1,000 a week, and if Shorter hadn't supervised The Club's record playlist himself, Iannachi could have been making an extra $5,000 a week in bribes from record company promotion men. Music that got played at The Club always sold in record stores. It was known as a breaking club. Tastemakers, magazine editors and critics heard the music at The Club, and there was not a more influential audience assembled in one place.

Iannachi, his head shaking as he cued up a new record on his headphones, was standing next to Ellison. Ellison was gazing off over the dance floor, deep in thought. He didn't even notice Jacky climb up the lucite steps into the booth. He was tall and thin, dressed in black from head to toe, looking like an elegant exclamation point.

"Hi! Remember me?" Jacky shouted to Ellison over the din of the music. Ellison came back to the present, and they both made a pass at the air between them that signified a kiss. The two of them were aware that they were very visible together in the booth. Ellison was a handsome middle-aged man with a square midwestern face and a long patrician nose. His hair was jet black, parted down the middle. He was most of all elegant, reserved. Even the bone structure of his face was somehow aloof. His eyes were a dark, uneven blue, and he was, privately, very proud of them. He had a tiny cleft in his chin and a flashing smile that could range from grandmotherly to imperious in a matter of seconds. He spoke in an accent he once described as "mid-American ennui."

"Pussy, where *were* you?" he asked, shaking his head. "I've been standing around this fucking booth for an hour."

"Oh, honey, I'm sorry. But I got stuck at my place with Eddie. We had this long, important talk tonight. Major changes. Major changes. Look, let's get out of this booth and go someplace to talk," she suggested.

"Wait a minute. Look out there." Ellison gestured toward the dance floor. "Look at Warren Beatty. Do you believe he's forty-two?"

Jacky looked out over the twirling crowd. Warren Beatty, in jeans and white tuxedo shirt, was dancing with a tall, lovely girl with natural blond hair down to her shoulder blades whom Jacky didn't recognize. He moved easily, dancing in a soft fluid motion unlike that of the twitching dancers around him. Liz Taylor, dressed in a smart black dress that managed to hide some of her hips, was standing not far away, clapping hands to the music. She had a big lovely smile. Her husband, John Warner, stood beside her. Jacky thought he was handsomer in person than in his pictures. Liz Taylor's hands and neck sparkled with diamonds, and Jacky couldn't believe they weren't a paste set with the real ones safely tucked away in a vault. But Liz swore privately to her friends that she always wore the real thing, and Jacky just stood there and gawked.

"I don't care what they say," Ellison told Jacky. "She's fat."

"She's still beautiful," Jacky said.

"But she wears dumb hats. I swear once I saw her at a party in a hat with plastic flowers on it."

"You're just jealous because she buys all her clothes from Halston," Jacky said. She had had enough of the star-studded dance floor and Ellison's dishing. She took him by the hand, and they left the booth together, crossing the enormous crowd hand in hand like two little children lost in a dark forest. Finally, they navigated their way to the wide spiral staircase and went up to the lounge.

At the very top of the carpeted steps Jacky and Ellison ran into Polo Prann and Melissa Mayhew. Prann, the international rock star and beloved angel of decadence, had fallen madly in love with naïve, debutante-cum-fashion-mannequin Melissa Mayhew. The two were as unlikely a pair as they were inseparable. Prann was a ten-year-veteran of the rock scene. He was one of the world's few rock stars whose fame transcended their craft. Like Roger Daltrey, Paul McCartney and Mick Jagger, Prann was an international figure. Foremost, he was a dazzling entertainer, an involving and calculated talent with a good business head that had made him into a millionaire many times over.

He had a well-founded reputation for being one of the most debauched, dissolute and divinely bad people in the world. Prann had tried, perhaps quite literally, everything. Sex in pairs, threesomes, orgies, homo and straight. Sadomasochism. Religion. Therapy. Acupuncture. Booze. Pills. Cocaine. And occasionally, still, heroin. Unbelievable at thirty-six he looked young and fresh and had the skin of a baby. With his big brown eyes and rubbery smile he was quite the charmer. People wondered where and when his Portrait of Dorian Gray would turn up.

Melissa Mayhew was a tender little sheep in the den of the big bad wolf. The daughter of a Pulitzer Prize winner for a book on Egyptian history, she had just begun a career in fashion modeling and had become *Elite*'s number one print girl in only three months. Although Melissa wasn't exactly Candide—she was both a gold digger and a starfucker—in comparison to Polo Prann, she was a virgin. It was guessed that either Melissa Mayhew was learning very fast or everyone had misjudged her.

Polo Prann's first wife, Horay, was more his kind. She was a great South American beauty from impoverished royalty. Or so the story went. She was also accused of masquerading as a Brazilian when in fact she was an American Negro. Another, widely believed story was that she was a famed Pan American hooker, the crème de cacao child of a wartime prostitute. As an international hooker she was the favorite trick for a while of Maxie Vogel, the chairman of the board of Universal Records. Vogel swore she had a magic pussy, so well trained it could suck up a cock and spit it out. When Vogel got bored with her, or she proved too hot to handle, Vogel turned her over to Prann. Prann had never met a woman who could handle him so well before. She slapped him around in bed and was the hottest fuck on either side of the equator. But after eight years it was over, and she and Polo hardly spoke to each other anymore.

The trouble was, of course, that Horay was always broke. Prann had long ago cut her off without a penny. Although she could have easily become a model, it was beneath her dignity to work. The only money she had was an allowance Prann gave her for staying with their son, Scorpio Prann. He actually paid Horay $100 an hour for every hour she spent with Scorpio. Most women would have considered it the ultimate insult, but not Horay. She was so irresponsible ("Irre*press*ible," Ellison would say) that spending more than two or three hours a week with the child was an impossibility, no matter how high the price.

Oddly enough, Prann had recently paid Ellison a $12,000 bill that Horay had incurred when they were still together. Ellison thought it was a gentlemanly and responsible gesture and respected Prann for it. Now, though, Horay had literally to beg her dresses from Ellison—who secretly would give them to her anyway; Horay was the best public model for his clothing. She was thin and elegant, and Ellison had no trouble dressing her because she could wear virtually anything and manage to look smashing. She was a big favorite with *Women's Wear*

Daily and one of the most important figures in Ellison's coterie. In her own way, as important as Jacky.

What was so fascinating was that although Polo Prann, Horay and Melissa Mayhew were frequently at The Club at the same time, their paths never crossed. This took extraordinary navigation and forethought by all involved, motivated by the fear that one night Horay would be a little too high or spirited and want a showdown with Melissa—a dim, but frightening possibility.

"Pussy, you look faaabulous. Wonderful," Ellison said to Melissa.

"Hi, how good to see you," Jacky said to Polo Prann.

Prann, in answer, said, "Faaaaabulous . . . Wonderful. Lookin' great."

Ellison shook hands with Prann and said, "Wonderful to see you. You look simply faaabulous."

This nonsense was part of a meaningless chant that people greeted each other with at The Club, unable to communicate on a more meaningful level except to exchange gossip. This appropriate passage conducted, Ellison and Jacky bade them good-night.

"He looks a little green from the drugs, don't you think?" Ellison asked, watching Prann walk off down the steps.

"What drugs make you green?" Jacky wondered, following Ellison into the lounge.

The lounge was a long rectangle, the walls and ceiling painted in a rich bottle green shellac that translated to a warm earth color on the large Art Deco velvet furniture groupings dotted about the room. The fabric was imported from Paris, and the overstuffed arm chairs and settees were interspersed with fig trees nearly twenty feet tall, each lighted with a recessed pastel spot. The room very easily could have been a sultan's sitting room in a Casbah.

There was a general turning of heads as Jacky and Ellison entered the room, like a small breeze through a leafy tree, but no sooner did it happen than the cool occupants of the lounge went about their business.

"We can talk in here," Jacky said to Ellison, leading him into the ladies' room, not giving a second glance to the washroom attendant, a middle-aged woman in a black uniform who was hired to look the other way; the bathrooms of The Club were used least for bodily functions; in the bathrooms, which were virtually coed, anything was expected to happen, from drug deals to blow jobs. Indeed, it didn't seem very odd to anyone when Ellison followed Jacky right into a toilet stall and closed the door behind them. They stood on either side of the bowl, and Ellison rested his shoe on the seat as he poked around in his pants pocket for his vial. He produced an amber-colored glass jar an inch long with a tiny silver spoon attached to the cap by a chain. He scooped up a load of powder and proffered it under Jacky's nose. He did this three more times until she indicated she was satisfied and then proceeded to hit himself up an equal number of times. They spent a few moments sniffling and snorting away tears and runny noses before they straightened their clothing and went out of the stall.

The attendant acted as if she did not see them, but an unsuspecting middle-aged woman in a black beaded gown indignantly rushed out of the bathroom when she saw Ellison. Jacky giggled at the sight.

In the outside powder room they stopped in front of the mirror, side by side, and began to primp. Ellison refolded his turtleneck collar and recombed his hair while Jacky attended to her makeup.

"How about a fitting tomorrow at four-thirty?" Ellison asked her. They had fittings practically every day for the costumes for *The Performance.*

"Four-thirty? How long will it take?"

"Maybe an hour."

"All right."

"And don't be late. Why were you so late tonight?"

"I can't wait to tell you. Eddie and I were having this big powwow. It was ultimatum time."

She flushed at the thought of Eddie's "ultimatum": his cock throbbing in a curving arc, about to enter her.

"Ultimatum about what?" Ellison asked, not really wanting to hear but responding as was expected. Jacky was *always* in the middle of a crisis.

"I have to turn over a new leaf. I promised Eddie, and he's right. I just can't go running myself ragged."

"You don't look ragged," Ellison offered, although she did look a little peaked.

"No, no," Jacky insisted. "Eddie is right. We talked it

all out tonight. No more late hours, no more drugs. No more hanging out *here* until five in the morning."

"It sounds just awful, pussy," Ellison said. "Just what does he want you to be, a *Cosmo* girl or something? Anyway, I don't believe in changing long-term habits when you're under pressure. This isn't the time to become a Girl Scout. This is the time to *relax*."

"I *will* relax. Eddie knows what he's doing."

"Honestly, honey, he's known you only three months."

"But he's intuitive, especially with women. And he loves me, Ellison, that's the truth. This time it's for real."

"Aw, I know, kitten, but I know you, too, and if you're going to get through this opening night, it's best not to try to rearrange your whole life."

"But I *want* to. I want to stop using cocaine. I *want* to be a *big star* again. And I want Eddie, too."

Ellison rolled his eyes. Jacky lighted a Benson and Hedges and laid it in an ashtray below the mirror. "He's moving in with me tomorrow," Jacky added, getting out her mascara.

"Awful," Ellison mumbled.

"Huh?"

"Awful. It's an awful idea, living and working together. It's too close."

"You mean it's OK to fuck just as long as it's not in the same bed you both sleep in?"

"I mean it's an awful idea. The man's some sort of crusader, and anyway, you shouldn't have affairs with your directors. Don't shit where you eat is the plainest way to put it."

Ellison simply could not stomach Eddie Bernardo. He thought he was a creepy little wop and he was having a dreadful effect on Jacky. First there was this ridiculous overblown Broadway show, and now his goody-two-shoes, holier-than-thou attitude. He had quickly learned, dealing with Bernardo over the costumes for the show, that Bernardo was a shallow, old-fashioned Catholic he-man. No more than a hairy chest. The first time they met, at a meeting about the costumes for *The Performance*, Ellison good-naturedly offered Eddie a toot of cocaine, and that was the beginning of the end; as far as Eddie was concerned, Ellison was virtually the worst culprit in Jacky's life. And he certainly had Jacky on a leash, trying to take her away from all her friends. Well, Ellison decided smugly, watching Jacky in the mirror put on too much eyeliner, he always said there was a terrible lesson to be learned from Jacky Mellon, but he could never make up his mind which of the many lessons it could be. Here was another: She was cockled.

Of course, Ellison adored Jacky, and well he should. Not only was she his best pal, his girlfriend, so to speak, but she paid him dearly for his attention—he had costumed her last five movies and was designing all the costumes for *The Performance*—and she was also helpful in his transformation from a merely successful designer into a household word with his own cosmetics line and scent that grossed well into the hundreds of millions a year. It was safe to say that Ellison's clothing on Jacky Mellon's back had done more to popularize Ellison than the clothes did for Jacky's bottom-heavy figure. Ellison couldn't think of enough ways to cover up her long neck and was forever telling her to stand up straight so she wouldn't look so round-shouldered, an aspect of her physique he couldn't possibly hide with his clever designs. And he never understood how anybody who took so much cocaine, so much that he had nicknamed her Shake and Bake last summer because she fluttered so much, could still manage to gain weight.

Yet if Jacky had a problem controlling her addictions, Ellison knew he made her look like a novice. A ten-year cocaine *aficionado*, he loved the glistening white powder. At that point Ellison was up to three grams of coke a day, and his weight had dipped to a gaunt 155 pounds, much too thin for a six-foot-one-inch frame. And he wasn't snorting any cheap street cocaine either. This was medicinal stuff, fresh wrapped in a wrapper from Merck, Incorporated.

Ellison had only one consolation about his habit: He could afford it. Even at a cost of $300 a day his heart would go before his pocketbook. He had more money than he could snort, and money bought a lot of solace. He had already had part of the septum in his long, patrician nose, which had rotted through, replaced with plastic by Barry Meritt, The Club's favorite surgeon who made a specialty of nasal-cocaine problems. Meritt had warned Ellison the rest of his nose would soon disintegrate if he didn't quit cocaine, but Ellison had no intention of stopping, even if it killed him, an outcome that wouldn't surprise Ellison in the least. Life had become too dull, too repetitious to get through the day without it. He had done it all: every last dare, last scene, last rush. He had lived it *all*. At fifty-two (his official age was forty-six) Ellison had hidden behind a lot of screens, as he would say. There were some mornings when he could not bear the thought of another day in the fashion business. A thirty-year veteran of the industry, he was even tired of seeing his own initials, initials that at one point he would have tattooed up and down the arms of his customers to sell a dress. Even the conglomerate that owned him, which six years ago had made him into a multimillionaire, now treated him like so much chattel, much to his daily humiliation. So cocaine was the perfect salve, the perfect soothing of his ego, the way he could meld the day into a white, tolerable snowstorm.

After ten years it was beginning to show. What was once a meticulous career was now getting frayed around the edges. Ellison's last three seasons' collections were far from inspired. New ideas didn't flow so quickly. The drug made him even meaner than usual. Too much of his work was coming from the drawing boards of subdesigners upon whose talents he had begun to depend. And the worst nightmare, his fashion crown, which already rested uneasily on his head, was being strongly contested by a brilliant newcomer: the very young, very handsome and very talented Alvin Duff. Duff had already put Ellison to shame by winning three Coty Awards in one year, and he was outgrossing Ellison by the enormous revenue from blue jeans, which Ellison refused to produce. In an interview with *W*, Duff had the nerve to call Ellison "a relic of the past."

That pig, Ellison thought, remembering it now, anybody who puts his name on a pair of jeans is a pig.

Standing next to him at the mirror, Jacky finished filling him in on her new regimen. She ended triumphantly with "And no more of *this* place," as if they were standing in a cesspool. For a second Ellison wanted to take her by the shoulders and shake her. Jacky was a moron if she didn't realize how important The Club was to her career. It was her biggest publicity outlet and showcase. If Jacky was too naïve to realize that, she was practically dangerous. For Ellison, The Club was virtually a personal publicity mill. If it weren't for The Club, the younger designers would have easily eclipsed him. He made sure that he and Stuart Shorter were the best of friends, although he privately thought Shorter a slob and a bore. At The Club, at least, there was no designer in the world more important than Ellison.

Jacky opened her purse and pointedly threw down her throat a mouthful of vitamin pills, which she downed with Ellison's glass of champagne.

"That makes a lot of sense," he said. "Champagne, cocaine and vitamins. What effect will this new health kick have on our little dinner party tomorrow night?"

Jacky turned to him. "What dinner party?"

Ellison found a strand of imaginary lint to busy himself with on his jacket. "Don't be silly, pussy. I asked you to dinner a week ago. At my place. Eight. Tomorrow."

"Oh, I don't remember any dinner party. I doubt if I can make it, but I'll mention it to Eddie anyway."

"Mention it to Eddie?" Ellison said, the rise in his voice belying his nonchalance. "Pussy, you're the guest of honor."

Jacky was furious. She put her hands on her hips, demanding, "What is this all about? What 'guest of honor'? I never agreed to be guest of honor at a dinner party."

"My God!" Ellison said to his reflection in the mirror. "You'd think the girl were being condemned to an evening of torture. We're talking about a very chic party in your honor. I've only invited eighteen people, so it's not too big."

"Eighteen!"

"And it's very, *very* chic. Andy. Truman. Diana Vreeland. Maybe Liz Smith and Joel Schumacher. And guess who's *dying* to meet you? The Princess Hazanni, the sheikh's sister. And I don't mean Valentino."

"El, you bastard, is this true? Did you really invite all those people and tell them I was going to be there?"

He turned to her, wide-eyed and innocent. "But I asked you, pussy. *Really* I did."

"Well, it's simply out of the question. Call it off."

"Pussy, this is *tomorrow night* we're talking about. You can't embarrass me that way."

"I can so. You can't *use* me that way, as a drawing card for a dinner party without telling me. Eddie *hates* those things. I'll never get him there. Especially after all the promises of a new life-style tonight. And *I* hate those things. I've never had a good time at one of your dinner parties."

"Really, now Jacky!"

"But it's true. Really. I'm not coming. You'll simply have to call it off."

Ellison grunted noncommittally. When pushed into a corner, Jacky could become aggravatingly stubborn, so at the moment the subject was better left alone. However, he would do no such thing as call off the dinner party. It had taken him two months of finagling to get the Princess Hazanni to accept the dinner invitation, and it was only with the lure of Jacky Mellon that he was able to pin her down to a night. Princess Hazanni was the perfect new client for him. She spent a fortune on clothing and was still one of the worst dressed women in the world, like Queen Elizabeth or Liz Taylor. Somehow those poor women never managed to look stylish. Now, if Ellison designed a wardrobe for Princess Hazanni he could turn her whole image around. And she had oil money by the barrelful. The dinner would simply have to occur as planned. Ellison would find a way to make Jacky show up if he had to send a posse to shackle her with handcuffs and chains.

Jacky was startled to hear a deep man's voice from behind her say, "What's the commotion about?"

She spun around and saw Sly Stallone, a sweatband wrapped around his forehead holding up his thick black hair. He was perspiring heavily from dancing, and his shirt was opened, exposing a thickly developed chest. Jacky was galvanized by the sight of him. On his arm, not the least bit disheveled in contrast, was Horay. Jacky felt the hackles rise on her back. Why did Horay always look so damn good? She was wearing a layered white crepe dress that would have looked ridiculous on Jacky.

"Hi, cutie," Jacky said to Sly, fumbling nervously for another cigarette. She introduced Ellison, who had never met Sly before.

"A pleasure, I'm sure," Ellison said.

Jacky frantically searched around in her head for something witty to say, but all she could come up with was a limply coy "Did you know you were in the ladies room?"

Sly looked puzzled at this. He probably didn't realize he

was in the ladies' room, or even care. He looked from Jacky to Ellison to Horay, who couldn't tolerate Jacky's nervous flirtations, particularly with *her* quarry.

"How would *you* know what a lady is, darling?" Horay asked ever so sweetly.

"At least I know a dyke when I see one," Jacky flashed back.

Ellison snapped, "Girls! Girls! Girls! Now behave yourselves!"

He took each of them by the hand and tugged them toward him like two little girls. Jacky was bravely choking back tears of humiliation. How she *hated* Horay!

"Now, now, now. I can't have my friends bickering in front of me. It's not fair."

"Then good night now, my darling," Horay said huskily, kissing Ellison on the cheek. Sly, absolutely stupefied by the proceedings, mumbled good-night and walked Horay off. Jacky could hear Horay saying, "You can't have a catfight with a dog."

"I could kill her! I could absolutely kill her!" Jacky cried to Ellison, stubbing out her cigarette in an ashtray. "I don't see how you can be friendly with that woman and still call yourself *my* friend."

"One thing has nothing to do with the other. We never speak of you."

"But she's such a pig. A lowlife. It reflects *poorly* on *you*," Jacky said, grasping at straws.

"I don't want to hear it, Jacky And don't give me any ultimatums, pussy. You can't afford to lose me with Eddie directing both your show *and* your life. You'll end up losing all your friends this way."

The cocaine and adrenaline surged through Jacky's system in hot rushes. "Lose my friends! People who give *that girl* dresses for *free* are not my friends. People who use my name to throw dinner parties are not my friends. I'd just like to remind you that we're paying you a pretty penny for the costumes for *The Performance*. We didn't get a *friendly* break!" she said, her voice cracking.

Ellison reared back an inch. This rude girl. He was *so* affronted.

Jacky regretted having said it even as it came out of her mouth, but it had been spoken anyway, and she felt obliged to turn on her heel as curtly as she could and stalk out of the ladies' room.

3

Trying to hold back tears, Jacky bit her bottom lip like a pouting child. Her head shook nervously from side to side as she charged down the steps from the lounge. People turned to stare at her, whispering her name, but she was oblivious to anyone else. She was in turmoil. She knew in her heart that she hadn't argued with Ellison about Horay, as much as she hated Horay. Her anger was with Eddie and his plans for her. She didn't want to admit it, but Ellison understood her far better than Eddie did. To go on the wagon completely, plus go on a heavy diet, was simply too much for her when she was in rehearsal. A change in habits under so much stress was all wrong. That was what they had always done to her mother, wasn't it? When Momma wasn't working, they let her drink and pill herself to death. But as soon as she was under real strain and needed the damn drugs, they cut her off. Yet Jacky was also determined not to let Eddie down. He believed in her so much. He had respect for her talent, for her ability as an artist. He had such high hopes and dreams for the show. And wouldn't love conquer all? With him there to lean on. And so what if Eddie was old-fashioned? She liked being treated like a real woman once in a while. So what if Eddie didn't have Ellison's fine taste or sensitivity? Eddie did something Ellison could never do: He fucked her pleasurably and often.

A cool hand gently touching her arm brought her back to The Club. Margaux Hemingway had stopped to say hello and was introducing Jacky to her companion, a young diplomat from Argentina. He was darkly handsome and had a deep cleft in his chin and was dressed in a navy blue dinner jacket with a silk ascot at his neck. Tall and statuesque, Margaux was animated and pleasant as always. She loomed over Jacky's squat frame as Jacky nervously lit another cigarette and grinned up at her, although the music was far too loud to hear what Margaux was saying.

Eventually Margaux and her date excused themselves,

33

and Jacky moved off to stand in the shadows behind a
banquette, where she had a good view of the bar and
dance floor. She wondered how Margaux managed to keep
in such good shape. Youth, she supposed, was a great
advantage. And she stayed thin. It was *so* important to be
thin. Jacky swore she'd never eat another dessert. A
minute in the mouth, a month on the hips; nobody wanted
to look at a fat actress. Her thighs were at least two inches
too big already, giving her body an unfortunate wide area
in the middle. And already the top of her buttocks were
covered with fatty-white striated stretch marks. Her
breasts, once her best asset, had become too full from
birth control pills. And Ellison was forever complaining
about her "love handles." She had been in her costumes
only once, and already she had outgrown them by half a
dress size.

Yet Eddie seemed to like her body, and that was most
important. It was probably because he was Latin, she
decided, remembering that one of her mother's old boyfriends once told her that Latin men preferred full-
bottomed women. The man, a penniless count, would
lovingly smack her mother's ever-widening behind and say,
"How much a man likes a good spread."

Jacky wondered if she had been this fat when she first
met Eddie or if she had gained the weight after she met
him. They first talked on a warm September day, just eight
months before, at a brunch at Ali MacGraw's Tranchas
beach home. Jacky hardly knew Ali at all: they didn't
travel in the same circles, and she had met her only once
when she was still living with Steve McQueen. But on the
one occasion Jacky found her to be an independent,
down-to-earth girl, and Jacky was pleased with the brunch
invitation.

Ali lived in a three-story adobe brick-and-glass beach
house, with one glass wall facing the ocean. The party
crowd was small, chic and famous. Jane Fonda was there
with her husband, Tom Hayden. Zeffirelli spent an hour
talking to a very European-looking couple in the corner.
John Schlesinger and Michael Childers sipped Bloody
Marys with Cloris Leachman.

And there was Eddie Bernardo. He was standing outside
the sliding glass doors on a red brick patio, sulkily talking
to Michael Douglas and his wife. He was deeply tanned,

and he wore a tight Lacoste green shirt, slacks and sandals with white socks.

Jacky asked Jeffrey Steinberg, the screenwriter, who the hot husky Italian was.

"That, my dear, is the *rage* of Hollywood. The man who every young actress wants to be directed by. That is the man who makes ingenues into leading women and women into Academy Award winners. That's the famed Eddie Bernardo."

"I'm pleasantly surprised," Jackie said to Steinberg as she studied Eddie. "From his movies and his reputation I always expected Eddie Bernardo to be an Italian intellectual, you know, the male version of Lina Wertmuller."

"There are no intellectual Italians," Steinberg said, draining his Bloody Mary. Steinberg, a Jew from Brooklyn, had made his fortune in Hollywood writing black movies for what he called the *shvartzer* trade. He watched Jacky stare at Bernardo for a moment. "If you're wondering what I think you're wondering, I'm told he's hung," Steinberg said to her.

"You know I'm not interested in that," Jacky scolded him, but not very convincingly. Indeed, she was into that. She liked big cocks, although she unfortunately hadn't been with many men of exceptional size.

"And he just walked out on Suzanne St. Jacques last month," Steinberg added.

"But I heard they hadn't lived together for a long time," Jacky said.

"It's your move, then, darling. I know the man, want an introduction?"

Jacky nodded, and the two of them went off to Bernardo together.

He was very Europeon, charming, considerate. After an appropriate amount of time Steinberg discreetly left them alone. Jacky was feeling loose and relaxed from her third white wine and didn't feel the least bit clumsy or intimidated with him. They took their Huevos Rancheros out to the beach and ate them together, sitting on red canvas chaises while they talked about Hollywood and the motion-picture business. He had a deep, resonant voice and a charmingly provincial way of putting things. His eyes moved nervously about, so dark and deep and warm. He told her he was a great fan of hers and had been following

her career for years, pleasing and flattering her no end.
Under the warming sun, sand crabs scurrying across the
dunes around them, the Pacific breaking in her ears, Jacky
listened dreamily while Eddie Bernardo spun a glorious
scenario for her future. He saw her as more of a serious
actress, capable of starring in major dramas instead of the
fluffy musicals she had been trapped in. He felt that for a
while she should stop recording albums, which apparently
didn't sell anyway, and limit herself to dramatic parts. His
eyes were moist black onyx stones as he told her he'd love
to direct her in a movie and asked to take her home.

"Home?" Jacky repeated, squinting in the bright sunlight, her heart skipping beats. "Now? The party is hardly
over."

He lowered his head and smiled, sleepy-lidded. "I can
think of a better way to pass the afternoon."

In five minutes she had said good-bye to the other guests
and they left the house together.

Steinberg waved knowingly from the front door.

She was still living in her mother's old house, a modest
three-bedroom California Tudor with a swimming pool
and circular drive on Belagio Road. She made Eddie a
drink in the bar, put Nilsson on the stereo in the den and
excused herself to go up to the bathroom in the master
bedroom. She had taken over the master bedroom when
her mother died but never bothered to have it redecorated.
In the bathroom drawer she found a premixed douche,
which she emptied into a syringe and quickly cleaned
herself with it. Flushing with guilt that she had thus
prepared herself for him, she walked out of the bathroom
to find Eddie Bernardo already in the bedroom, looking at
a picture of her mother on the dresser. Jacky felt a wave
of resentment drown out her excitement; again her mother
was there. She'd have to get rid of that picture.

"She was very beautiful when she was young wasn't
she?" Eddie asked, not taking his eyes away from the
picture.

"Yes, she was," Jacky agreed, "but not so pretty when
she got older and sicker."

"I can imagine," Eddie said sympathetically, putting his
arm around Jacky. It gave her a warm tingle up her spine.
"You know, as beautiful as she was," Eddie went on,
looking at the picture, "I never thought that she was that

good an actress. Commercial, yes. But not in the league with the greats." He paused and looked into Jacky's uplifted eyes. "Like you could be," he added.

Nobody had ever said anything as sweet to her before. Nobody had ever confided in her what she had secretly believed for years, that her mother wasn't all that terrific. Most people were so involved in canonizing her mother that Jacky never heard anything truthful or negative. Eddie had just confirmed her deepest secret.

"Really? Do you really think that? Because I've always thought that and was afraid to tell anybody."

Eddie laughed, and she started to laugh at him, dispelling all the accumulated pain and guilt, and then he began to kiss her laughing mouth, fitting his open mouth over hers, drawing her up into him, sucking at her tongue with a gentle pressure. She trembled as his hands went up the front of her body to her breasts, afraid he would find them too soft or droopy or not to his pleasing. She never even especially liked to have her breasts touched, but they seemed to excite Eddie so much as he squeezed and kneaded them passionately, searching for the tender nipples through her bra and pinching them between his fingers until she moaned. She felt his hard cock pushing against her stomach through his linen pants as he ground into her. He lowered her on her back, pushing her backward onto the bed, still kissing her, his hands roughly moving up and down the sides of her body in tandem, giving her chills as he dug into her flesh through her dress. Slowly he lowered his face to her waist, lifted her skirt and buried his mouth and nose in her panties, licking at the curls of her brown pubic hair sticking outside the elastic band with his tongue. She felt herself filling with a creamy wetness as she held tightly onto the thick black hair of his head, riding his face like that, letting out tiny gasps of excitement, trying not to let him know that she was soon to lose control, not to let him think that he was so easily driving her so crazy, that no other man had gone down on her right away and she loved that, loved what he was doing as he slid down her panties to her thighs and buried his face deep into her crotch, slurping into her opening with his tongue, licking at her clit.

Jacky threw her head back, her mouth wide open, breathing in heavy gasps when a few seconds later she heard him say, "Strawberry."

She wondered what that could mean. Maybe she was hearing things, it sounded so muffled. But no, he had stopped eating her, and when she propped herself up on her elbows and she looked down at him wedged between her legs, he was sniffing at her vagina.

"Strawberries," he said. "You don't smell like a woman. You smell like a fruit salad."

She felt so hurt that tears sprang to her eyes.

"Come with me," he said gently, pulling her up off the bed before she could compose herself enough to say anything and led her to the bathroom, where she wobbled with her panties caught around her knees. He pushed her down into the bathtub, removed her panties and hung her legs up over the side while he turned the tap to lukewarm water. Then he spread her legs and lifted her under the tap so the water gushed into her pussy. The rippling warm water on her clitoris drove her crazy. In a few minutes she couldn't stop herself from wiggling in the tub. She was breathless when Eddie finally climbed in on top of her and tore off her clothes. He stood above her and unzipped his fly. A huge cock, like a rubber hose, lolled out of his pants. He held it in his hand as he looked down at her.

"You want this?" he asked just above a whisper. "You want this?" he asked again louder, tantalizingly waving his cock at her.

"God, yes, I want it," she said breathlessly.

"Then suck it," he ordered her. He lowered himself to her mouth by squatting above her, feeding himself into her until she was beyond choking on it and wanted only to devour him whole. She was exhausted and quivering when he finally rolled her over onto the white rug on the bathroom floor and slowly and intensely fucked her for an hour.

Jacky spent the next three weeks in bed. Eddie was unlike any other man she had ever known—or dreamed she would know. He became her sexual Svengali, a satyr who drew her into the dark pleasures of her hottest fantasies. He moved about her beastlike, his hairy chest thick with muscles, wide shoulders with an animallike ridge of hair across them. Buttocks indented and firm. His thick cock was always hard, his hairy balls hanging lazily between his thighs as he forced her to adore his body. He taught her how to take a cock all the way down her throat without gagging. He taught her how to suck him so well that she could manipulate him to orgasm just by giving him head, finally tasting the mystical sweet, sticky lotion right from the source. He always wanted to be inside her, in some way, some part of her. Her throbbing clitoris ached from his tongue and fingers, from when he was relentlessly there playing with her and when he was not. Eventually he peeled away all the shame she felt for her body, all the inhibition. All that Sunday and following Monday she lay spread-eagled beneath him, begging him on, up into her. The days melded into three weeks of creamy orgasms for her, weeks when she was always so wet and high and dizzy on Eddie that she thought and cared for nothing else.

4

"Are you OK?" somebody asked Jacky gruffly.

Jacky peered forward in the darkness of The Club to see who was speaking to her. Polly Daffney was peering back.

"You were just standing there staring," Polly said, concerned.

Jacky shook her head, trying to figure out an explanation. Polly owned Daffy's, the famed celebrity haunt on East Fifty-third Street. Seat for seat, Daffy's rivaled The Club for its notable customers. But where The Club needed barricades and a retinue of bodyguards to keep out the undesirables, Daffy's needed only Polly Daffney, so awesome the magnitude of her personality that she could turn aside the most persistent gorilla.

It was Polly Daffney's foul mouth and abrasive personality that first drew attention to her restaurant. The theory was: If I've offended you, please tell your friends. She goosed male customers, insulted women with small breasts and in short made such a nuisance of herself that people adored it. Polly was a regular sideshow of sarcasm. As Polly's fame grew, so did the restaurant, so did her figure. Before long, she was thick-loined, rotund; at 245 she looked and moved with the swagger of a heavy-jowled bull.

Norman Mailer loved and worshiped her. He brought Woody Allen, who brought his crowd of reticent New York intellectuals, who brought writers, who brought newscasters, and on it went.

Eventually Polly mellowed and stopped insulting her customers. Unbelievably, she lost 150 pounds and turned out to be not unattractive. She was even sweet and lovable —when she wanted. But she still wasn't anybody to fool with. After all, she was supposed to be outrageous. Her prices were. A bowl of soup could run up to $5—the prices changed from day to day on whim—and there was never a printed menu. Not only were the dishes priced outrageously, the greatest insult of all was that Polly

40

padded the checks. It was well known that she would add an extra bottle or two of wine to a check when the customer was too loaded or polite to notice. Customers were so afraid of her wrath, or being banished from her influential kingdom, they never called her on it.

Only once did someone call Polly on a check, a woman named Ester Fillbrook, and she had the misfortune of doing it in front of a table of regulars. Norman Mailer was sitting off in a corner and didn't hear it, which would have made it worse, but Neal Travis and Woody Allen and socialite D. D. Ryan were sitting not three feet away in any direction when Ester Fillbrook drunkenly reached out to Polly and said, "C'mere, you!"

The restaurant fell quiet. Ester Fillbrook was nobody to fool with either. She owned Face-Ups, the most exclusive makeup and hair rejuvenating emporium in the city. As a testament to herself she had built a multimillion-dollar architectural wonder on Madison and Sixty-ninth. She was a tough, hardworking business lady, but she had the big mouth of a street vendor.

"What's up?" Polly Daffney asked her daringly.

"This check's padded," Ester said loudly, taking a beat to make sure everyone was listening before she added, "There's an extra bottle of wine on here."

Actually, Polly Daffney had added *three* extra bottles, but that wasn't the point here.

"You're a lying cunt," Polly Daffney said matter-of-factly.

There was a sharp intake of breath around the restaurant. Ester pulled her chair back and, still sitting down, threw a glass of red wine into Polly's face.

Polly didn't hesitate for a moment. She pulled back her right fist like a champion prizefighter and slugged the sitting woman square in the face. The smack reverberated through the restaurant as Ester's chair tilted backward and over with her still in it. The waiters and customers restrained the two women from ripping each other to shreds, but the next morning multimillion-dollar lawsuits went flying. The cool-headed lawyers prevailed and begged, "Please, let's be *ladies*," and eventually both women dropped their charges. As a favor to powerful Polly, the columnists kept the incident quiet.

"I'm terrific," Jacky lied to Polly at The Club, trying to look cheerful but succeeding only in making more nervous movements with her head. She dropped ashes over her dress from her cigarette.

"Are you all alone?" Polly asked her.

The truth was that Jacky was all alone at this point and could have used some company, but she said, "No, I'm here with Ellison."

Polly politely inquired why Jacky hadn't been in the restaurant more often, and Jacky begged off by saying she was busy rehearsing.

"Well, come on by after rehearsal, and bring your director with you," Polly suggested. "I met him a few nights ago, and he's terrific."

"Eddie? You met Eddie a few nights ago?"

"Sure. The guy who's directing your show."

"You must be mistaken," Jacky said, the color draining from her face. "What night was this?"

A whole scenario crossed Polly Daffney's mind in a fraction of a second; she knew she had already let some sort of cat out of a bag. Wisely she shrugged away the question.

"Here's Ellison now," Polly announced, grateful for the interruption, looking over Jacky's shoulder. Ellison was gracefully descending the steps with a big celebrity smile on his face. He floated into position next to Jacky as if nothing had happened between them and exchanged greetings with Polly. Jacky was surprised to see him but too preoccupied with pursuing her line of questioning with Polly to acknowledge it. But before she could say another word, Polly chucked her on the arm like a fellow football player and went off into the crowds. Jacky finally turned to look Ellison in the eye.

"Just because I rescued you from Polly Daffney don't think I'm not still angry with you," Ellison said, being nicer to her than she had a right to expect. Jacky melted, grateful to be let off the hook so easy.

"Oh, I'm sorry, darling, but you have no idea how tense I am," she said, inhaling deeply on a cigarette. "My nerves are just *shot*." Her mind wondered back to Eddie. Could it have really been Eddie at Polly's place? She must have been mistaken. Why wouldn't she say whom he was with?

"Want a Quaalude? Or a Valium?" Ellison whispered.

"Don't tempt me when I told you I'm on the wagon," she whined.

"Pussy, I'm not tempting you. You need it. You're

wired, taut like a tightrope on cocaine, which is how I'm excusing that outburst upstairs. Why don't you take something to calm you down?"

Jacky shook her head violently.

"All right. But I have one more point to make before this thing about Horay is put to rest," he said, moving her against the rear wall away from the staring crowd. He brushed the ashes off the front of her dress. The changing light on the dance floor made her face first bright pink and then deep red as she listened.

"I heard that you take my dresses and have them copied in other colors and fabrics by some seamstress in California."

"It's a lie," Jacky interjected, but Ellison knew it was the truth. Sissy Berstein, a good customer of Ellison's and the wife of Columbia Pictures' vice-president Bob Berstein, told Ellison she had discovered Jacky at a Beverly Hills seamstress having one of Ellison's dresses copied—and with a different neckline. Jacky had told the seamstress she hated the original color and synthetic fabric and the collar was "old-fashioned." At first Ellison was livid at the thought of Jacky's ripping him off like that; then he was amused by her miserly childishness.

"No matter, no matter," Ellison said, leaving the impression that it mattered a great deal. As Jacky went on protesting, he stared imperiously at the people watching them. "Let's go find a place to stand away from the tourists."

"The disc jockey's booth?" Jacky suggested.

"No, let's see who's in the Playpen," Ellison said, taking her arm and leading her into the crowd. Above the dance floor a set of twirling glass cubes dropped from the ceiling and began to spin in a bath of laser beams. The pastel-colored sheaths of lights reflected swirling fragments above the dancers. As Jacky and Ellison picked their way through the room, Jacky could hear people saying her name under the din of music.

Unexpectedly the music dropped to half its volume, and the sound of a jet plane shuddered through the massive sound system. All heads in The Club turned to the disc jockey's booth. A disembodied voice rang out through The Club.

"I hope ya havin' a good time," Shorter's Bronx accent sounded. " 'Cause I'm havin' a good time."

Ellison looked at Jacky and snickered. "This is *so* embarrassing, this sincere nightly speech."

"I want to tell you that we've got a beautiful crowd here tonight," Shorter continued. "Ellison, Jacky, Senator Javits, Muriel Cohen, Warren, Liz, and I want to remind you about the next party. . . ."

The speech over, the restless crowd returned to dance, and they moved on. Ellison almost groaned aloud as they ran into Jack Fisher at the edge of the dance floor while Fisher's fat, round face lit up at the fortuitous random meeting.

"Hello, hello, hello!" Fisher said jubilantly. Fisher was a New York legend, a fast-talking con man with all the charm of a door-to-door encyclopedia salesman. He was the oldest, lowest kind of publicity flack. His clientele was mostly rich old ladies who took him out to dinner in exchange for his harmless bits of gossip about the glitterati. He also fed newspaper columnists shreds of information about divorces and lovers' quarrels. Jacky thought he was sad, but she couldn't bear being near him nevertheless. Since The Club had opened, Fisher had added a sideline to his business: celebrity introductions. He was usually with some desperate social-climbing Long Island or Westchester woman who wanted to break into New York society. Most of them were overweight, rich and bored. A few had aspirations of becoming actresses. Rumor was that Fisher was paid an insulting $50 a person for each celebrity to whom he introduced his clients. At least by the way he was beaming it *seemed* he had just made a hundred bucks by running into Jacky and Ellison. His escorts this night were a midwestern couple in the best of polyesters. Jacky figured the man for a plumbing king of some sort. They stepped forward to meet Ellison and Jacky as if they were at a chili-tasting contest. The woman stared unabashedly at Jacky to make sure it was really she, and the husband pumped Ellison's hand till he was exasperated.

Ellison smiled graciously and excused them to set out across the dance floor to the Playpen entrance on the other side. As they walked away, Jacky heard Fisher saying, "They're my dearest friends. Oh, look, there by the bar, Britt Ekland."

To her right Jacky saw Steven Ford, hot and sweaty, his white shirt open two buttons and a black tie hanging untied around his neck. He pounded up and down without even looking at the pretty blond girl on the floor with him, who also had her eyes closed. Two of the official Club *paparazzi* descended on Ford and his date for a moment and then buzzed away. Jacky held tightly to Ellison's hand as they actually entered the fray of the dance floor and fought their way across.

Throughout The Club on the powerful speakers the crystal clear voices of soprano harpies rang through the speaker system, *"Round and Round til the break of day, candles burn, fiddles play. Why not be wild if we feel that way? Reckless and terribly gay . . ."*

Crossing the dance floor, Jacky began to hum the infectious melody out loud. In a clearing of people, under red and yellow melting candy-colored lights, she saw Paramount chief Barry Diller dancing with constant companion, designer Diane Von Furstenberg. Jacky tried to get their attention (Barry was so terribly powerful and influential and perhaps the shrewdest man in the entertainment business, and Diane was one of the most admired women in the world), but the crowd closed around them again, and they vanished.

"Hey, I like this song," Jacky said, beginning to dance.

Ellison smiled at her but stood in place and clapped his hands; he would not be seen dancing on the dance floor of a discotheque, *ever*. He was no go-go girl. And dancing was for commoners.

"Round and Round neath the magic spell, velvet grown, Pink lapel, Life is a colorful carousel, Reckless and terribly gay . . ."

The cocaine jangled through Jacky's nervous system. She felt electric and alive. A casual circle formed around her, watching her spin and laugh. The wild abandon of the discotheque was exhilarating to her. She felt released. For a moment all the attention, all the energy of the discotheque were focused on her. The *paparazzi's* strobe lights captured the moment in a dozen eruptions of white light. Not far away from where she danced Jacky noticed Horay start dancing, waving her arms above her head, like a graceful snake, a cobra shimmying out of its wicker basket. Jacky kept smiling as the *paparazzi's* attention slowly began to shift to Horay, and resolutely Jacky danced harder and more dramatically. Streamers of silver foil began to shower the dancers from the ceiling in glittering shades of red and purple.

Horay dashed over to a dancing, mustachioed man twirling in circles and snatched his bottle of butyl nitrate vapors from his hand. Ellison was not at all surprised at this move; he knew stealing butyl nitrate from another dancer was one of Horay's tricks for attention. At first her surprised victim started after her until he realized it was Horay Prann; then he backed off, smiling into the crowd, thrilled at the encounter. As the crowd opened around her, Horay held the amber bottle under her nose and took a deep breath. Her face flushed as the fumes opened her veins and increased the flow of blood to her brain tenfold. She exhaled deeply and danced toward Jacky and Ellison, bringing the photographers with her. Throwing her head back, she offered the bottle to a bemused Ellison, who shook his head and turned away, afraid the *paparazzi* would photograph them.

Her eyes flashing, Horay defiantly offered the bottle to Jacky. Jacky clearly wanted not to, but she gamely took the bottle from Horay and inhaled deeply. The lights exploded around her. The violins soared as she rocketed wildly, the butyl nitrate opening her veins, loosening her muscles, the blood careening madly through her head.

"I'm ready anytime, if you'll take me, I'm ready to go," the voices sang.

In an instant, like a fragment of a photograph, Jacky spotted a familiar face in the hundreds in the crowd. It was a face that froze her body in a vise of anxiety. Addison Critch was staring down his silver-rimmed spectacles at her. The sight of him managed to bring her crashing down from the lofty heights of butyl nitrate rush. Addison Critch! Standing there, watching her doing a popper on the dance floor! Jesus, what next?

It would be all over the *Post* tomorrow afternoon.

Critch, the most widely read columnist in New York, was as hateful as he was powerful. His specialty was cruelty. He staged the most pointless, elaborate vendettas in his column with dozens of people, some of whom actually insulted him in some small way, others of whom committed crimes of Critch's own devising. He was read by everyone in the media, all of whom were largely fascinated by how pathological and vicious Critch could be. He cut an elegant, if somewhat old-fashioned, figure in his fussy black suit, white shirt and black tie, like a skinny old mortician out on the town.

He was vicious because he was angry. He was angry because he couldn't get along with people and angry because he had spent the last twenty years going to therapists to stop being angry. Addison Critch was such a conundrum, a snake eating its own tail, that it was better only to observe him from afar, perhaps by reading his column or watching him at a party.

Jacky had once foolishly taken him to task. It was two years ago, on a pleasure cruise through New York on the way to Europe with a sound man she was having a fling with, when she read in Critch's column that some stripper had claimed she had had an affair with her mother. Jacky knew that Angela was a lot of different things, and all of them out of the ordinary, but a lesbian wasn't one of them. Two nights later she spotted Critch across the room at Orsini's restaurant. She was a little high on booze and grass, and cut across the room like a bee homing on pollen and told Critch he was "a menopausal old lady."

That was the end of it. After that she was in his column weekly. He seemed to have spies everywhere, and there was no quarter of her life that he would not delve into, no secret too tender or too ghastly for him to write about. It was in Critch's column that it was announced she was hospitalized in Los Angeles for an infection of the vagina caused by an intrauterine coil. It was in Critch's column that her various romances were exploited and defeated. It was in Critch's column that her career was being derided and *The Performance* was being tried before it opened.

Just seeing him in public always set off an eruption of items about her, as if the sight of her incensed him. At first she would glower at him in public, but she quickly learned that paying Critch any mind at all was only pouring oil on the fire. A glower would be exploited into a screaming scene in his next day's column. A glance was good for three days' worth of barbs about her looks, her figure, her career. Critch remembered everything he saw but still used a notebook so people could observe him using his power in action. In a vengeful gesture Critch would whip his note pad out from his jacket pocket as if he were pulling a gun and scribble away in it.

Jacky threw her head back and smiled in another direction as if she hadn't seen him. Through clenched teeth she said to Ellison, "Let's go," grabbed him by the arm and led him away to the Playpen.

Two bouncers standing next to the doorway separated respectfully as they approached. Just as Jacky ducked out of sight behind the rust-colored fire door, she peeked over her shoulder and saw that Addison Critch was carefully noting where she was going.

Where she was going was the inner circle of The Club, a ninth circle, so to speak, filled with the choice delights of heaven and hell that Addison Critch would never be allowed to view as a troublemaking member of the press.

It was invented as the setting for a private party, the first spring of The Club's existence, and its name, the Playpen, was so smugly correct for its purpose the place was an instant hit. It began with Harrington Sainte Juste, the cosmetics king, who wanted to have a "face-lifting party." Most face-lifts were done without fanfare or attention, although certainly at The Club nips and tucks and steroid shots from Dr. Norman Orentreich or various other plastic surgeons were a mark of money and prestige and nothing to be ashamed of. Youth was as valuable a commodity as any at The Club. Almost everyone in The Club's clientele, even Stuart Shorter, even The Club's powerful attorney, David Willick, had had a bob or a lift or eye tightening or made some small effort to improve his or her appearance. But Harrington Sainte Juste, after all, had made his fortune in cosmetics and perfume and was making a big fuss about it. Young was his theme, and he wanted to have a celebration of his rejuvenation.

The party was on a Thursday night when The Club was open to the public, so special arrangements had to be made for the Sainte Juste party. Shorter thought of closing off the upstairs lounge, but it was too small and impractical. So he decided to use the basement. The basement was a veritable cavernous maze of catacombs and cul-de-sacs. The only entrance was through a heavy metal fire door at the west end of the dance floor. Beyond that was a narrow, dimly lighted flight of metal steps two stories down to the bowels of The Club. The walls were raw brick, caked with the grime of a century of New York dirt. Even the spider webs were covered in a fine film of soot. It was dark, a forest of support poles, electrical and plumbing conduits. The passageways ran off like a fun house, the only light from dim yellow bulbs encased in metal mesh shades.

It was a bizarre setting for the Sainte Juste fantasy of

"Second Childhood." A fortune was spent on the decorations to transform it from a dirty brick basement into a giant infant's playpen. There were building blocks the size of the average dining-room table and dolls as big as a grown man. The floor was covered with a quarter of an acre of real turf, and in the largest expanse of space a four-foot-deep wading pool was constructed. Guests at Harrington Sainte Juste's party were able to sip their "milk shakes" aboard a real carousel sprayed in red glitter.

After the party was over, most of the decorations were removed, but the wading pool still remained, as did a sliding pond and some swings. But without the bright lights and party atmosphere it quickly disintegrated back into a dingy dark hole. In a few months it was all but forgotten, and an old mirrored ball was stored down there along with some extra carpeting from the lounges. Later the dirty white banquettes from the main floor were moved to the Playpen, and eventually Stuart Shorter moved in a bed.

In the beginning it was just a hideaway for Shorter to escape to in the middle of a frenzied night, a place where he could sit quietly with friends and snort cocaine. At first he had hidden in the small office on the first floor, but too many people easily found him there, and he eventually retreated to the Playpen. Ironically, this dirty and dank basement became one of the most desired places to be by the *cognoscenti* of New York, a symbol of status. It hardly seemed to matter to anyone in his or her designer gowns and suits that just feet away, underneath the city vaults beneath Fifty-seventh Street, rats as big as dogs scampered about, scavaging for food. Most people were more concerned about the dangers that lurked from the people rats in the Playpen itself.

One Saturday night a crowd of at least a dozen of New York's choicest glitterati were milling around the Playpen self-congratulatingly. The nucleus of the crowd was formed by Shorter, Ellison and interior designer Olga Giacometti. The three of them were perched on the back of an old banquette. Olga was a smart, sharp-looking woman in her middle fifties who had decorated some of the lushest and most expensive apartments and homes on the East Coast. Olga knew what she was doing, too, for she had grown up in castles and villas all over Europe with her stepfather, Prince Bianchi Giacometti. Recently, however, Olga had been drinking a little too much vodka, and the sharpness of her figure and taste had run to her tongue. This particular night Olga, flanked by Shorter and Ellison, was insulting everyone in sight, getting ruder by the minute. D. D. Ryan and Halston had already fled in terror. John Samuels IV took two minutes of abuse but was too polite to say anything back. In twenty minutes Olga had drunkenly cleared the whole basement except for Shorter and Ellison, who sullenly stuck by her side.

"You've got to stop this, Olga," Ellison admonished when the Playpen was empty, "or you won't have a friend left in the world."

"What do you know, you cocksucker? You couldn't design a tepee in the desert," Olga slurred. Ellison knew it was time to leave.

"Are you coming?" he asked Stuart Shorter. Shorter turned to Olga to see what she was going to do.

Abruptly Olga threw a drink in his face and screamed, "Kike!"

Shorter and Ellison left her there. The next afternoon the security men rang Shorter at home; Olga Giacometti had fallen asleep behind the banquette on the dirty basement floor and spent the night in the Playpen of The Club. They found her wandering around the dance floor that morning, crying, hungry and hung-over.

Ellison led the way down a dimly lit metal staircase to a second heavy metal fire door. He pushed the door open and peered inside. The lighting was shadowy, and dozens of passageways led off into the dark. Near the door two very pretty young boys, both in their teens, were smoking a joint. They were shirtless and dressed in the uniform of busboys: green and gold satin shorts. They seemed to look right through Jacky and Ellison as they continued to smoke the marijuana languidly.

With Ellison leading the way, they walked farther on into the Playpen. Up ahead, on a white banquette, Veronica Meadwright, the daughter of the senior senator, sat with two other girls Ellison didn't recognize. Veronica Meadwright was a steady patron at The Club but not the kind of person who was usually allowed into the basement. She had obviously been passed in by the bouncer or by Shorter himself, who was probably repaying or asking for some sort of political favor from her father. Senator Meadwright was a vocal and popular politician in Washington; Veronica was a social-climbing New Yorker and a showoff. Ellison didn't trust her.

Just around the bend they ran into Agee Simpson, searching for her children, who were somewhere in The Club. Agee Simpson's kids, a sixteen-year-old girl and an eighteen-year-old boy, had been around so much and were so terribly sophisticated they were even allowed in the Playpen by Stu Shorter. One night, much to their mother's horror, they set up a counter to sell cocaine the same way suburban kids sell lemonade at roadside stands. (She quickly put them out of business.) Agee was one of the most socially influential women in New York. A former editor of *Woman's Book* magazine, she had retired some twenty years before to marry an international industrialist, Alfred Simpson. Peculiarly Agee had stopped buying new clothes when she met Simpson. Yet, without buying a dress in a decade, she managed to remain imperishably fashionable and in vogue. Her personal style transcended momentary fashion. Her hair was clipped classically short, and she had nature's gift of exquisitely high cheekbones. As a family the Simpsons were rather bohemian, even for the fast-moving New York set. Alfred had recently run off with a twenty-four-year-old actress who was just previously dating his oldest son. Agee was busily competing with Alfred, dating men even younger than her husband's girlfriend (rock stars a specialty). When Agee and Alfred separated, the couple insisted that friends declare whose camp they were in, much to everyone's dismay.

Ellison had sworn allegiance to Agee and even lent her $15,000 to pay for the summer rental on a house in Southampton when Alfred cut off her support funds. But tonight Ellison was determined not to become embroiled in her domestic life and only nodded hello as he and Jacky sauntered by.

On another banquette an unlikely pairing: Ellen Saville, the attractive wife of a U.S. senator, and Stuart Shorter, who were chatting with actress Eloise Clair and her manager of the moment. There was also a tall, lanky man in a black velvet suit and shaggy haircut of a rock star whom Jacky didn't recognize. Eloise Clair was much smaller in person, quiet and very pretty in an unexpectedly sweet and innocent way. Clair and her manager nodded, as did Mrs. Saville and Shorter. It was obvious that Jacky and

Ellison were not at the moment welcome in their circle. Neither of them minded. They wanted to get as far away from the other people as they could and sat on two wooden chairs behind a brick stanchion with large fuse boxes mounted on it.

Ellison took out his vial and held it up to the light, flicking it with his middle finger to knock all the powder to the bottom.

"Going fast," he said to Jacky.

"I have maybe four or five hits left of my own, and that's it for me forever," Jacky repeated solemnly.

Ellison decided against commenting. His own vial was running low, and he could have used a refill. There was always a possibility of scoring here at The Club. Everybody in Shorter's crowd bought from Mr. Roberts, but never at The Club itself, out of respect for Shorter. He didn't mind using drugs at The Club, but selling them there was going too far. Anyway, Mr. Roberts worked days only. Roberts was a thin, perpetually suntanned man in his mid-thirties. He gave the sense of being vaguely dangerous, not because he was tough, but because he appeared high-strung and maniacal, just the type of fellow who turns out to be an ax murderer. Ellison never would have dealt with him if it weren't for Shorter's personal approval as being safe to deal with. It was assumed that Shorter got his kosher certification from his partner, Sandy Dubrow, who supposedly knew about such things, but no one ever asked Shorter point-blank why Roberts was safe to buy cocaine from. He worked by appointment only. A customer would call him, mentioning he would like him to pay a visit, and he would come by the following day with a delivery or the customer could visit Roberts, if the client preferred. Roberts was good for any amount from grams to ounces and had the finest-quality, least-cut cocaine in the city.

There was also an on-the-spot dealer at The Club called Richie Hack, so named because he was a limousine driver who hung around The Club while his car was double-parked outside. Shorter would normally have thrown anyone out of The Club who was there for serious cocaine dealing, but he always left Richie Hack alone. That kind of tacit permission made Hack a good contact to know in case of an emergency—but Hack was considered too

"Yes, I know." Jacky giggled. "A *very* famous dancer."

"Why, thank you," Glesnerovsky said, tilting his head in a little bow.

"I saw you dance last year at Lincoln Center," Jacky told him. She was lying.

"It was my honor to have you come to see me," Glesnerovsky replied. He was too gallant and polite to be true, Jacky thought. Maybe he was gay.

"Want to smoke?" Shorter asked, offering a joint to Glesnerovsky.

"Is it safe here?" Glesnerovsky asked.

"The only thing that isn't safe down here is to perform an abortion because there are too many germs and not enough coat hangers," Shorter said. Glesnerovsky seemed confused.

"You have an odd sense of humor," he commented to Shorter, smiling all the while at Jacky.

She was dying to have him. She felt moist between her legs just standing next to him. She would do anything to impress him. Anything to get him. She thought of talking about her movies, but that was too obvious.

Beads of perspiration appeared on her forehead, and the basement seemed warm and stuffy. Over Shorter's shoulder she saw Horay appear in the doorway.

"Oh, shit," Jacky mumbled.

Horay was alone, and her face actually lit up when she spotted Glesnerovsky.

"You've got to meet Horay," Shorter said to Glesnerovsky, and Jacky thought, Over my dead body, and swooned right into Glesnerovsky's arms. "Oh, my!" Shorter said. Both men grabbed Jacky around her waist and tried to help her stand up straight. Jacky was taking deep, dramatic breaths, her eyes rolling up behind her lids, while across the Playpen Horay stopped dead in her tracks, not believing her eyes.

Ellison, watching from behind the pole, was biting his lip so not to laugh out loud.

"Want to lay down?" Shorter asked, frightened for her.

"Fresh air," Jacky gasped. "The alley."

"This way," Shorter said, motioning them to the far end of the Playpen and opening an exit door. Jacky held tightly onto Glesnerovsky as they stepped outside into a subterranean opening not more than five feet wide between two huge buildings. Hundreds of feet above them a slab of the blue night sky was visible through the canyon opening. Dozens of garbage cans and waste products from The Club were lined up in massive black plastic bags at the far end of the alley, waiting to be elevated into the street the next morning.

Jacky put her hand behind Shorter's neck, pulled him close to her and whispered in his ear, *"Beat it!"*

Shorter pulled back in surprise and rushed away, leaving the door ajar behind him.

"It was just so warm in there," she apologized to Glesnerovsky, leaning against him again.

"You were not dizzy at all, were you?" Glesnerovsky asked.

Jacky smiled meekly. "It's an old trick. Terribly corny. But always effective," she confessed. "My mother did it once in a movie."

"Ah, yes," Glesnerovsky said. "Your mother was an actress also."

How sweet, Jacky thought. He didn't even remember Momma.

She moved up against him, pushing her groin into his crotch. He seemed surprised at first, but he recovered himself quickly enough to take her head in his hands and kiss her lightly on the lips. It was a dreamy, spongy, romantic kiss, but the cocaine surging through her body made him feel electric and hot, not dreamy and romantic. She quickly bored of his lips and began working down, kissing the open spot at the top of his collar and licking at the patch of blond hair crowning his pectorals. She nuzzled against his chest, breathing in deeply. Unexpectedly she lowered herself to her knees. Right to business, she thought. The surprised ballet star was about to lift her up when he realized what she was doing. Surrendering, he rolled his head back dreamily and closed his eyes. Jacky pulled down the metal tab on his fly as he thoughtfully undid his belt buckle for her. She peeled back the sides of his pants, and she could see the baby blue cotton briefs underneath his jeans in the moonlight. She pressed her mouth up against the long bulge in his underwear and breathed warm air on his cock through the material so he could feel the heat of her mouth. She lifted his shirt to expose a magnificently hard and rippled belly. A wispy blond line of pubic hair led down from his navel, disappearing into his shorts. She pulled down the elastic band,

and his cock sprang out. It was uncircumcised; the tip was peeking out of his foreskin like a small, wet, shiny ball. It looked very similar to Eddie's, but not as big. She took it in her hand like a microphone and put her lips to it. Then, breathing in deeply, she took his cock first into her mouth, slurping saliva on it, and then quickly down her throat, shoving it past the glottis. She knew she wouldn't be able to sing at all the next day, but she would rather have been mute than give Glesnerovsky a bad blow job.

Moaning softly, Glesnerovsky took her head in his hands, gently putting one forefinger in each ear, and moved her head up and down on his cock. He crouched a little, and with an admirably fluid motion, he fucked her mouth. Jacky worked hard on him, occasionally letting his stiff cock out of her mouth to catch her breath while she licked hungrily at his balls. In minutes more, when Jacky thought she would finally give up, he heaved a deep, relieved sigh and came long, thick spurts of sweet come in her mouth.

Not a moment later she strutted back into the Playpen and didn't even try to hide the broad smile on her face. She felt ecstatically happy and cheap, and it thrilled her. Glesnerovsky was still in the alley, recovering from what Jacky prided herself had been excellent head. She searched around for Horay with a victorious look on her face, but her rival was gone.

"Thank you for waiting," she said to Ellison, who was leaning against a brick stanchion.

Ellison imperiously pulled an embroidered handkerchief from his back pocket and offered it to Jacky, saying, "Wipe your lips."

Her ecstatic expression turned to horror as she wiped her face. "Do I . . ." she started to ask Ellison, but couldn't bear to complete the thought and shuddered.

Ellison broke into thrilled laughter. "No, you don't," he told her, "but it would serve you right if you did after that cheap trick."

"He's taking me home," Jacky said proudly, as if it proved some point.

The least he could do, Ellison thought. "To bed?" he inquired.

"No, to sleep. He's dropping me off. He's got to get home for an early rehearsal tomorrow."

"And not a bad idea for you either."

"Or for you," Jacky added.

Ellison suddenly felt a bit nervous that the evening was so quickly drawing to a close. We live so close to the bone and so far from satisfaction, he thought.

"You will try with Eddie, pussy, will you? I mean about dinner . . ."

Sometimes he was so cute and adorable he was irresistible. She wrapped her arms around his lanky frame and hugged him tightly. "Yes, I'll do my best with Eddie," she told him. The poor man seemed so brittle in her arms. She looked up into his blue eyes and was about to kiss him tenderly on the lips when he gently pushed her face away with his forefinger.

"No kisses just after you've gone down on Glesnerovsky, thank you, pussy."

Jacky broke away from his embrace. "You are a royal bitch, Ellison."

"I love you, too, pussy. See you tomorrow at eight."

5

As soon as Jacky left him, the basement seemed empty and dingy. Jacky's kookiness was very special, Ellison decided, even if she'd never learn to appreciate it herself. For the rest of his life he would never forget watching her go down on Glesnerovsky from the doorway to the alley. What technique of seduction! That girl was so trashy; that's why all the gay boys loved her. And she was a publicity mill. The best drawing card for a party. Dinner tomorrow night would no doubt be the talk of the town. For ten minutes at least.

Sitting by himself on an old banquette in the basement, he wondered what time it was. The cocaine was making his head buzz with the resonance of a finely tuned drill. Sometimes the rush of the cocaine running inside his ears sounded so loud he was sure people around him could hear it. With that kind of head on he knew he'd never get to sleep if he went home right away. He decided he'd allow himself a half hour more; then he would go home.

The basement door opened, and in came two of the bartenders from upstairs. The bartenders were a select breed at The Club, and a few special favorites were even allowed in the basement. The Club bartenders were some of the most attractive young men from all over the United States. Becoming a bartender there was one of the most sought-after jobs in the city for a young man looking to make his fortune. Not only did Club bartenders make $300 or $400 a night, but they were also exposed to the most glamorous—and influential—people in the world. The possibility of breaking into modeling or acting always seemed imminent.

Somehow, though, none of the bartenders had broken into *anything*.

One of the boys in the basement was named Billy Crabtree, a college dropout from someplace in Tennessee. The other was an aspiring actor of twenty-six, Jake Dillerman. Ellison had seduced both of them on various occasions, after elaborately planned evenings of dinner, cocaine and Quaaludes. The boy from Tennesse, tall, angular and dark, had been very good in bed and was probably a better actor than the aspiring actor himself, whom Ellison found to be totally unresponsive sexually. In the final analysis Ellison always got the feeling that most boys were turned off to him in bed; he was convinced they were with him only because he was rich and famous and had good drugs. Ellison despised people who went with him for those reasons but nevertheless used exactly all those tools to seduce people. It was yet another conundrum in a self-defeating plot. It gave Ellison built-in contempt for anybody who chose to be with him.

No matter, he thought, watching the bartenders snort cocaine, sex was sex. A physical and psychological necessity. No need for love.

Although there was always that one moment in bed when for a second, just that second, he could convince himself that this time it was for real.

That was exactly what Jacky had said to him earlier, Ellison remembered now. Such a fool, that child. So naïve. Doesn't she know that people who are famous but unattractive never have it *for real*? There are only stars and starfuckers. And people in between who lie to themselves. Once he had actually told a young boy, "You may be beautiful, but I have forty million dollars." He laughed aloud now in the basement at the thought of it, that he could have been so desperate as to bring himself to say anything so ludicrous to someone.

There was, of course, Raul Hooding—and probably always would be—but you could hardly call their relationship loving at this point. They had met ten years before, when Raul was a young, handsome Puerto Rican window washer at Saks Fifth Avenue, whom Ellison managed to transform into a well-known fashion illustrator of Venezuelan extraction. Wild, sexy and fun-loving, Raul and Ellison had three blissful years together before familiarity snuffed the flame of passion, and they settled into a marriage of sorts. Perhaps they would still be together these years later if Raul's pranks hadn't become so impossible.

In the beginning Raul's pranks were like the annoying tricks of some adolescent practical joker, and they were easy to overlook, but as the incidents became more embarrassing and more obnoxious, it became clearer that Raul had a problem and couldn't stop himself. His sense of humor was bizarre, and some people even found his escapades quite humorous and inventive. In his own right he became a kind of court jester of Ellison's kingdom, albeit a deep embarrassment to Ellison, to whom he belonged.

The stories about the pranks were legion in New York society.

There was the time Raul decorated the windows of Ellison's Fifth Avenue retail store with toilet seats painted in Day-Glo pink, on which Raul displayed Ellison's swimsuit line. There was the night Raul arrived at the opening of an Ellison retrospective at the Met dressed only in a black bandolier across his chest and a black leather studded jockstrap. (He was arrested by New York's Finest for indecent exposure, and it cost Ellison $5,000 bail to get him out.) And the time Raul and Ellison had a lovers' spat and he burned Ellison's entire wardrobe in the bathtub, coating the house in a layer of soot and fetching every fire engine on the Upper East Side. Or the time he disrupted the finale of the Coty Awards by running across the stage in diapers. . . .

On and on it went for years, Ellison never knowing what to expect next. The incident that really ended it all happened on an American Airlines 747 flight to Houston, Texas. Ellison was on his way for a debut of a cocktail-dress line he had designed exclusively for Neiman-Marcus. On the plane with him were nine young models from Ford, a makeup artist, a hairstylist, a dress stylist, a reporter and photographer from *Women's Wear* and a boring, stuffy account executive from Simon Morrow. And there was Raul, who had sweet-talked Ellison into taking him to Texas, from where they would go on to Puerto Vallarta. Raul insisted on bringing his portable cassette player with him to play on the beach at Vallarta. It was an oversized machine with huge speakers they called a portable jukebox in the New York ghettos, where they were carried on every block, blasting disco music at earsplitting decibels. When Raul boarded the plane, he was politely asked by the stewardess to keep it off, especially during the takeoff, and landing, when a radio could interfere with the crucial transmissions between the pilot and the tower. Raul seemed agreeable, but as soon as the plane leveled out at

32,000 feet, he went into the bathroom, got high on a joint, came back to his first-class seat, turned up the portable jukebox as high as it would go and began dancing down the aisles with it on his shoulder.

The reporter from *Women's Wear,* a prim, fashionable young woman in her early thirties, whose reportage of the fashion business was filled with more jealous venom for the models, designers and their boyfriends than it was with information, was obviously shocked at Raul's performance and quickly began to make notes in her book. The account executive from Simon Morrow also watched carefully as Raul danced back to the coach section, where he tried to provoke the models to mutiny and help him take over the first-class compartment, where there was a lobster smorgasbord. The stewardesses were at their wit's end, trying to get him to turn off the "jukebox" and get back into his seat, but the more the proper, blond midwestern stewardesses insisted, the more the stubbon, wild and spiteful Raul danced and whooped. Eventually the captain himself was summoned from the cockpit with a final warning that Raul would forcibly ejected from the plane if he didn't turn off his "jukebox" and sit down.

Raul spit on his uniform.

Ellison was mortified! The plane was diverted to Chicago O'Hare, where it was boarded by federal agents and Raul was arrested, handcuffed and carried, screaming, off the plane. He cried, "Ellison! Save me! Save me!" but Ellison just sat in his seat with his head down, mumbling, "Who is that awful man? I never saw him before in my life . . . I don't know who he is. . . ."

So, enough was enough. Two years ago Raul was moved out of the town house and into his own loft in Soho and given a handsome allowance to live on for a thirty-eight-year-old man. The locks to Ellison's town house were changed, but somehow Raul always managed to get in, and he was always lurking around at The Club or at Ellison's office, still getting into trouble. Ellison actually had a very tender place in his heart for this zany, incorrigible man. He surmised that somehow Raul would always be there, and when they were old men together, Raul would still be throwing pies at him.

In the interim, however, there had to be fresh faces! New and exciting fantasy and romance. Desire was what kept Ellison young and alive. The pursuit of sex was the only real intrigue left in his life. Like an old eagle, always on the hunt. Who was next? he wondered. What about the bartender, the hunky one in the center carousel? He was *terrific*. Ellison had seen him do something that won Ellison's heart forever. While all the other bartenders pranced about and seemed eager to please, this one remained aloof but polite. One night Stuart Shorter told the bartender to bring a bottle of Moët et Chandon to the banquette of Princess Elise Volbrook and her guests. The bartender brought the champagne over, circulated glasses and was treated as if he didn't exist. When it came time for him to open the bottle, he made sure everyone on the banquette got a spritz of champagne from the exploding bottle. Then he calmly poured drinks for the drenched patrons and toasted the princess.

Now that boy had spirit. And he was just about ripe for picking. Ellison had been working on him for more than a month already: compliments, big tips, name-dropping, the works. Oh, Shorter had warned him a dozen times that the kid was straight, but he didn't really believe that. *Everybody* was available for a price or the right combination of power and drugs.

He strolled to the basement door and climbed the steps with a straight spine. On the dance floor the crowd was just beginning to thin. Most of the tourists were gone; only the hard-core crowd remained, waiting for their various drugs to wear off, waiting to get laid.

From where he stood on the dance floor, Ellison could see the bartender behind the center carousel bar. The boy was a stunning centerpiece for The Club. He had frothy chestnut hair capped with shades of amber, large, sad brown eyes and lashes so long and light they seemed spun of ostrich feathers. He was shirtless, 155 pounds of rippling muscles and gleaming with sweat. He snapped open a bottle of Perrier and poured it into a crystal fluted glass.

Ellison strolled to the banquette nearest the bar and stood there in the anonymity of the shadows. The Club was filled with the syncopated beat of a tomtom and a chorus of black voices calling, *"Full moon and empty arms. . . ."* Off to his right Ellison saw Addison Critch chatting animatedly with Senator Meadwright's daughter, Veronica. *That* meant trouble. Veronica Meadwright had taken special note of Jacky's trip to the alley with Glesnerovsky. Critch caught Ellison's eye and gave him a knowing nod, too knowing for Ellison's liking; nonetheless, Ellison nodded back at him politely and moved away. As he got closer to the center carousel, he could hear the people crowding the bar, calling out to the bartender to get his attention before the bar closed for the night. The customers shouted drink orders at him all at once, while the boy stood calmly in the middle of it, continuing to pour drinks at his own speed. Ellison noticed that he had no particular system for serving customers; he served first whom he felt like serving. He ran the bar very much the way Shorter ran the front door. When a customer would come to the end of his rope, the bartender would give a characteristic shrug, and his droopy eyelids and long lashes would shut for a lazy second of disgust. Yes, Ellison decided, the boy did have all sorts of potential.

Standing not a few feet away, lost in her own world, was Grace Dunn. Ellison was not surprised to find her there; recently she had become a very good customer at The Club. He immediately recognized she was in an Alvin Duff dress of black linen, artfully cut low and full-bodied. Dunn had a great figure to dress, and he wished he were her designer; who wouldn't want to dress a famous woman who was tall and thin and stood like a lovely orchid on a stalk? Ellison dressed all the dumpy ones, all the problem cases. Duff had glamor girls. He strolled closer, nonchalantly peering at her to see her hands better; people always mentioned her hands in interviews, how beautiful and graceful they were, with delicately boned fingers. Her hair, a natural tawny blond, was pulled back from her face and turned out loose under her jaw. It was held in place by a buckle of jade and emeralds which glittered ever so slightly as she moved her head. The crisp blue color of her eyes danced with the twinkling lights. Yes, she was a handsome woman for forty-nine, Ellison thought. He wished he knew her secret. It just wasn't lack of lines or wrinkles; it was her bearing, her attitude, the ability to be youthful and yet not lose the dignity of her age.

And now to have returned to Broadway after so long and become the most beloved star of the theater was quite an achievement. Certainly the best show on Broadway this year had been hers. Ellison had gone opening night. Hal Prince and Stephen Sondheim had never worked better for anyone, not even Angela Landsbury. Instant culture in the making, her show was the hottest, hardest ticket in Broad-

way history. Every night of the week people were paying
scalpers $250 a seat to see her before she left the show. He
also knew that her name was *verboten* around Jacky
Mellon. Jacky lived under the cloud of Dunn's success.
Dunn was the front-runner for a Tony award, and Jacky's
name would never be as important as Grace's on Broadway, and Jacky didn't think the Great White Way was big
enough for the two of them.

Ellison wondered whom she was with. It didn't seem
like anybody. She was strange, coming to The Club so
often recently and never with anyone. She had been linked
romantically with many prominent men, including Henry
Kissinger and Burt Reynolds. But lately there had been no
mention of her personal life anywhere.

Ellison turned to the bar and made his way up to the
bartender, who ignored the other customers and turned to
him immediately. What would convince this boy to spend
a night with him? What was the bartender's price?

"How are you doing tonight?" Ellison asked him.

"Fine, Mr. Ellison, how are you?"

"Why don't you call me just Ellison or El, won't
you?"

The boy smiled agreeably.

"What's your name?"

"Bobby. Bobby Cassidy. The usual?" he asked. Ellison
always ordered Black Label with soda, and his drinks were
always on the house.

"No, just a Perrier right now." He watched Bobby bend
over the barrel of ice water and fish out a chilled Perrier
for him. The band of his jockey shorts rode up out of his
jeans, and the muscles in his back fanned out into his
shoulders in a meaty V shape. "Do you ever feel self-
conscious behind the bar?" Ellison asked him.

"How do you mean?" Bobby asked, pouring the Perrier
into a glass.

"People stare at you all the time, stripped to the
waist. . . ."

Bobby laughed out loud. "I guess it's pretty low," he
admitted good-naturedly. Ellison was very impressed with
his honesty. "I took the job because I needed it," he went
on. "I never thought I'd be here long."

"Hmmmmmm," Ellison murmured. "What sort of job
would you prefer?"

The bartender shrugged. "I'm not sure. When I came to

New York a few months ago I figured there were so many things I'd like to do that one of them would just pop up in front of me and find me. I guess things don't happen like that in New York."

"No, I guess not," Ellison said. My God, how naïve. But salvageable. "I don't suppose you'd like a job in the fashion business?"

"Are you kidding? I'd love to be in the fashion business," Bobby said, pouring a drink for another customer.

"Well, you can have a job with me."

Bobby smiled knowingly. He wasn't *that* naïve. "As what?"

"My assistant," Ellison said tonelessly.

"*Sure,*" Bobby said.

"No, I mean it," Ellison insisted. "I'll give you a chance to prove yourself with no strings attached. To show you I mean business, there'll be no pay."

"No pay?" Bobby asked, bewildered, blinking his big cow eyes.

"No pay. That way I'm not buying you and you're not using me. If you're any good and you turn out to be an asset, I'll give you a fine salary and a lot of responsibility."

"Why me suddenly?" Bobby asked.

"The truth is, because you're attractive and bright. I'd be lying if I said any different."

"What would I do?"

"Everything. Anything. Can you sketch? Design? Do you have any fashion sense."

"*Sure.*"

"Then what can we lose? A month trial period. Start tomorrow. You can still work here at night at The Club if you want."

"Work *two* jobs? Work here until four-thirty in the morning and then go into work for you?"

"I do it!" Ellison snapped. "*I'm* here, aren't I? I'll be in at *nine*. Can you be in by *ten*?"

Bobby didn't hesitate another second. "Absolutely!" He reached over the bar and excitedly shook Ellison's hand. "If Shorter doesn't mind. . . ."

"He won't mind. It's all fixed," Ellison said smugly; he always got his way with Shorter. "See you tomorrow, then." He sauntered off, smiling.

Well, Ellison thought, that was easier than he had expected. He glanced at his watch. Time for him to get a move on. Reluctantly he fished a Quaalude from his jacket pocket and swallowed it with his Perrier. Then he made one last, lingering pass through The Club. It was starting to fade now, the glamorous call girl transformed into a dozing, honky-tonk tart.

On one banquette a distinguished white-haired man in a satin-lapeled tuxedo was napping while his wife tried to fasten the broken buckle of her silver pump.

On the dance floor, near exhaustion, two pretty lesbian girls, one brunette, one with long blond hair down her back, were spinning in circles, not wanting to end their magical night of glamor. Truman Capote, who often was there until the doors closed, was still dancing near the waterfall against the far wall.

A man in black tie with a blowup doll under his arm searched for a lost date.

In the upstairs lounge Lucia, a famous transvestite model, was talking to herself in the mirror while putting on lipstick.

In the balcony the seats were dotted with necking couples. Aloysius Pontaff, the top black male model in America, was kneeling between the legs of a beautiful white woman, her white matte jersey dress pulled up over her belly. Ellison politely turned away.

To his left three boys lazily passed a joint of Angel Dust and stared foggily at the last moments of splashing lights.

Another couple leaned against one of the exit doors and kissed hungrily.

From somewhere between the rows of seats Ellison heard the sound of a sharp slap and then a moan of ecstasy.

He sighed again. Snort and suck. Snort and suck. Sometime The Club was so boring.

He went through the swinging front doors on West Fifty-seventh Street and squinted in the harsh bright lights of The Club's marquee. He was not surprised to find that a few bouncers were still guarding the entrance; although The Club was officially closed, there were a few desperate stragglers who had never made it inside who were still waiting, hoping to catch sight of celebrities on their way out. There was a young black couple, tightly holding each other's hands. A few ugly, very drunken college boys in rumpled suits. A couple dressed in some sort of radish costume. Ellison wondered who they were, these desperate

people who allowed themselves to be humiliated and dis-
criminated against because of the way they dressed or
looked. To be sure, he didn't want any of those people
socializing with *him*, but nevertheless why they came to be
humiliated was beyond his comprehension. Luckily none
of them seemed to recognize him as he turned his jacket
collar up to the chill spring morning air and ventured
beyond the ropes.

His limousine driver sprang from the car when he saw
him, but he waved him away. He was too high and speedy
to sit quietly in the back of the car. The walk home would
do him good and get the Quaaludes working. So he strode
up Fifty-seventh Street by himself, a tall and lonely figure,
stalking off into the east, where the skyscrapers gave a
reflected hint of the deep rosy dawn billowing up beyond
the horizon.

6

The State Liquor Authority Alcoholic Beverage and Control Law specifically cites in Section 106, Subdivision 5, "No alcoholic beverages should be sold, offered for sale or given away upon any premises licensed to sell alcoholic beverages at retail on premises for consumption during the following hours: (A) Sunday, 4 A.M. ante meridian to 12 noon ante meridian or any other day 4 ante meridian to 8 ante meridian."

But that didn't mean that a bar had to close its doors during off hours. As far as the board was concerned, a club could stay open twenty-four hours a day as long as it didn't serve booze during those hours. Studio 54, for instance, often stayed open for hours after the bars closed. A club owner, however, would have to be crazy to stay open without selling booze.

Stuart Shorter was crazy.

At The Club people got high on drugs, not booze, and although The Club did a phenomenal liquor business during legal hours, Shorter saw no need to shut the whole place down when it was really cooking at 4:00 A.M. just because the bar had to close. The dance floor was often still crowded hours after the bar had shut, and nobody even noticed. Often people would just be arriving at The Club at 4:00 A.M. from other nightclubs that had just closed. Therefore, The Club had no set closing time. Occasionally, on the night of a major party, like Halloween or New Year's, when patrons paid up to $250 a ticket to get in, The Club would stay open until the following morning, when a champagne breakfast of eggs Benedict and French toast would be served. On most nights, particularly Sunday or midweek nights, The Club would close when Stuart Shorter felt he had had enough. That meant one of two things: Either Shorter had found a way to get laid and wanted to go home or he had passed out from Quaaludes. Shorter's passing out from Quaaludes

69

was far from an unusual occurrence; recently it began to happen more than he got laid. His employees secretly joked about dosing his drinks with them so he would pass out early and they could go home. The only problem with the scheme was that Shorter had built up such a tremendous resistance to the drug it took highly lethal doses just to get him sleepy.

This particular Sunday night the fifty-three employees of The Club were lucky. Of its own accord the discotheque had emptied out enough at 4:30 A.M. to order it closed with Shorter still up on his feet, but tipsy. At his command Ray Iannachi played one last record, a slow, dreamy version of "Good Night Ladies," while the security guards shooed the last half dozen people off the dance floor. The strobe lights blinked to a slow stammer and then not at all. The massive waterfall, a veil of shimmering water, seemed to disappear into thin air. The last note of music played, and there was suddenly eerie silence accompanied by an uneasy feeling, like the moment before an earthquake, when everything gets deathly still. Lethargically a janitor in overalls lowered a glaring 500-watt clear work light from above the dance floor. Suddenly The Club looked gawdy and shabby, like a painted whore fallen asleep in her pimp's Cadillac. Under the steady white work light it was easy to see the cigarette burns in the furniture and carpeting, and the dance floor looked scuffed and dirty. The smell of smoke and stale alcohol and spent dreams permeated the air. Four teenaged busboys, sleepy-eyed and stoned, loped about, clearing up the last remnants of used glasses and dirty ashtrays.

Bobby Cassidy was finishing up his nightly cleanup ritual. First he emptied his "speed rack" with the name-brand bottles into a carton marked FULL. Then he emptied the rack of cheap "well" brands, which the bartenders served when a name brand wasn't called out by a customer upon ordering. Then he packed the array of name liquors and fancy bottles that were displayed in the middle of the bar into a third carton. Later he would put the full and half-full bottles in the liquor storage room. His final chore was to carry all the empty bottles downstairs to the basement, where they were counted at the end of an evening to make sure that bottles weren't being stolen. An exact count wasn't possible; many bottles broke during the course of a busy night. But there was still an acceptable limit before pilferage was suspected.

Earlier in the evening The Club's bar manager, a husky, handsome man named Keith Brown, and two security guards collected the last of the receipts from the cash registers. Through the night Brown and the security guards periodically emptied the six cash registers in The Club so they wouldn't literally get overstuffed. The money was then brought to an office somewhere in the basement and locked in a safe until it was deposited at the bank the next morning. On a busy weekend night the center carousel bar would gross $17,000 to $20,000. Bobby figured the other bars grossed $2,000 or so less. With approximately 2,000 admissions at $15 apiece, there was maybe $75,000 or $85,000 in cash floating around The Club at the end of a night.

Keith Brown also collected the tip money from each bar at the end of the night. This money was then pooled and counted in front of another bartender in the kitchen. The glass washers in the kitchen, who worked for minimum wage, got fifteen percent off the top of the bartenders' take, and the nine bartenders split the rest. On this particular night the bartenders made $170 each—not a bad salary for five hours' work.

No matter to Bobby, he thought, hefting a carton of empties up on the bar. There was no salary in the world that would make staying behind the bar worthwhile. There was no price anybody could pay him to go on being treated like a piece of meat in a cage every night, all those people screaming at him, treating him like a servant. It wasn't too long ago that he had been one of those people, on the other side of the bar. And now with Ellison's offer he had found a way to get back there. To become a player again.

He went to the other side of the carousel and continued collecting empties, wondering how much of a toll New York had taken on him in the months he'd been there. Did he look five years older already? Certainly this was the most unhealthy existence you could lead anywhere in the world. Or was all the aging inside, all emotional?

"Hey, hey, hot stuff!" Tinder Kaufman called him, coming up to the bar. "Don't forget to drain the work sinks tonight, Bobby, baby!" Tinder grinned brightly at him. Tinder was Bobby's closest friend in New York. He was also The Club's best-known bartender, famous for his twirling and dancing as he poured drinks, always in a good mood, never keeping still for a moment. There were times when Tinder put on such a show he had a crowd watching him. Shorter loved Tinder and encouraged the other bartenders to follow suit, but Tinder was the original. Inimitable.

Bobby couldn't figure out how Tinder kept going every night, five or six nights a week; Tinder was always looped. His finely shaped, muscular body was pumped full of booze and drugs each night. Even Bobby, who was a teetotaler, took a few shots to steady his nerves at The Club because if you weren't sedated in some way, you would have a nervous breakdown behind the bar with the bass drum relentlessly beating in your ears, and the customers screaming orders at you. But Tinder knew no limits. The night before, a busy Saturday, Bobby watched Tinder consume two bottles of Amaretto, one Quaalude and a gram of cocaine. Bobby thought it was a miracle that Tinder was even walking, let alone whirling and dancing behind the bar.

"How ya doing?" Tinder asked.

"Just great. I think I might have found a way out of here," Bobby said happily.

"What's that, the Midnight Express."

"I got a good job offer tonight."

"Here? From one of the customers?"

"Yep. Ellison asked me to be his assistant!"

"Ho, ho, ho!" Tinder cried. "You better come prelubricated!"

"Fuck you, Tinder," Bobby said. "Ellison seems like a perfectly nice guy."

"He only wants to screw your ass."

"I don't believe you," Bobby said.

"Then you're a fool. You'll be back behind the bar as soon as you say no to him."

Poor Tinder, Bobby thought. It was impossbile to escape unmauled in New York; it was just a question of how badly you let the city damage you before you began to fight back.

"When are you quitting here?" Tinder asked.

"I'm not. I'm gonna do both."

"You're nuts," Tender said, helping him hoist a heavy carton of empties up on the bar. "We are all believers in the myth, Bobby, boy, I suppose. We just refuse to acknowledge the fact that a pretty face and attractive body are the major motivations behind anyone's interest in us. To admit it would be a denial of your own talent, and you believe you're talented, don't you?"

"Of course." Bobby shrugged, although he wasn't sure at what. Tinder and he each carried a carton of bottles across the dance floor toward the Playpen door.

Bobby had heard this litany from Tinder Kaufman before. Tinder had espoused a whole philosophy about The Club one night over juicy rare hamburgers at P.J. Clarke's. He had been noncommunicative during most of the meal when suddenly a blond girl Bobby recognized from The Club was seated on the other side of the room with a tall, good-looking man who could have been her father. Tinder became very interested in the girl.

"You know her?" Bobby finally asked.

"Sure I know her. She's an orgy girl. By day she works as a salesgirl at Fiorucci, and at night she fucks in groups with her girlfriend. You'd recognize the girlfriend; she's in The Club all the time."

"How do you know that?" Bobby asked, peering closely at the girl. She seemed like a perfectly respectable girl from where he sat. She wasn't the most beautiful girl he had seen in the world, but she wasn't cheap-looking or a slut as far as he could tell. In fact, in her high-buttoned blouse and tan skirt she could have been an English public school teacher.

"I fucked her," Tinder said, waiting to see Bobby's reaction. When there was none, he went on. "Along with about three other guys. And I don't even know how many other chicks were there. Maybe half a dozen."

Bobby, who thought he had either done everything in Miami or heard the rest since coming to work at The Club, flushed with the thought of it. Orgies. He secretly hoped that such things were actually occurring other than in the pages of dirty novels, but he didn't expect it was happening under his nose at The Club.

"How did you get involved in something like that?" Bobby asked. "I mean, were you invited?"

"Invited? I was auditioning for a trip to Barbados. And a thousand-dollar cash bonus. Shorter's always auditioning in the Playpen. Once Shorter held auditions for a trip to Barbados for the longest shooter. He wanted to take two

couples away with him, and one of the prerequisites was
that the guy could shoot across the room."

Bobby, who had lost his appetite, put down his sandwich and looked Tinder hard in the eye. "I don't believe
you."

"It's a true story. I was there for the auditions in the
basement of The Club. Shorter laid on a mattress while
the guy—"

"Stop it, Tinder, you're full of shit."

"You're still a child, Bobby. When people make a lot of
money—I mean, a lot of money—they can indulge themselves in any kind of fantasy, and don't think they don't.
Don't you have some secret, dirty little scene you'd like to
act out sometime if you could afford it?"

Bobby shook his head. "None of my sexual fantasies
have anything to do with money."

"That's only because you're still young and good-looking. The people at The Club use money and power to get
what they want. Money is the best aphrodisiac for them.
You know what Stu Shorter once told me? The first week
of The Club, when they first started to make a lot of
money, he brought home the weekend receipts in a shopping bag. There must have been fifty grand in cash. And
when he got home, he turned on all the lights in the living
room, spread all that green money on the living-room floor
and jerked off on it."

"That's ridiculous."

"*That's* the essence of The Club. In practice money is
power. People buy you, and then they jerk off on you and
pass you on."

"Is that what happened to you?" Bobby asked. "Did you
get passed around?"

"The bartenders have a joke. We always say that we
don't get passed around; it's the customers who get passed
around from bartender to bartender."

"Then why are you so bitter? Why do you feel used?"

"I *wanted* it. I'll admit it. I thought sleeping with
everyone made me ... hot ... desirable. I *was* hot and
desirable. So everybody got what they wanted. I got to
meet famous people; they got my dick. There is, however,
something loathsome about fucking for a good time, more
loathsome than hooking for money, because pretending is
really the lowest. But I thought, because for five minutes
these people treated me like an equal, that I was one of

them. I was living in their penthouses and limousines, listening to their secrets, using their drugs. So I let them fuck me to stay around."

The two boys silently finished cleaning up the bar. Bobby's elation at getting the new job had disappeared, and he felt tired and glum. He wondered if Tinder was right, if he was letting himself in for more than he could handle with Ellison. Bobby glanced at Tinder on the other side of the bar, his hands trembling as he dried off glasses. Somehow he couldn't summon up any pity for him.

Yet he wouldn't cast the first stone either.

In the last six months Bobby's life had been as bizarre as any of the stories Tinder told. And who knew where it would all lead to? Probably he would end up jaded and alone like Tinder.

In Miami, where Bobby grew up, he was jaded only by the ladies wearing too many diamonds or too many minks on the hot summer nights. He was spoiled only by the fresh salt air, the palm trees and the constant tropical sun. His father, Benjamin Cassidy, was the majority stockholder and proprietor of the swank beachfront Coronet Hotel, where Bobby grew up in a penthouse apartment with his younger brother, Sam. Being the older son of a hotel scion had its advantages; he went to the best schools, orthodontist, and never needed money. He spent his adolescence swimming and practicing gymnastics on the beach and had ripened into an impressive young man.

In his teen years Bobby's interest was limited to one subject: sex. He was the anathema of every mother of a virgin teenage girl on Miami Beach. And when he was through fucking the daughters, the mothers were next. It was just that it was so damn easy for him; tan and muscular, he was the perfect fantasy for the hordes of lonely female tourists searching for vacation romance. And the hotel was a gold mine of horny women. Every winter the clothing moguls and fashion kings from up North came down to the hotel like pashas traveling through the desert. They brought wives, children, teenage daughters, maids and grandmothers. They rented Cadillacs and sailboats and spent money as if they had manufactured it at home instead of earned it.

Bobby's sexual activities were a cause of great scandal at the hotel among the employees, particularly during the slow seasons, when Bobby didn't draw any class barriers against bedding chambermaids in the empty guest bed-rooms. And it was much to his parents' consternation that Bobby was carrying on with both daughters *and* mothers, mothers who were very much married to the men who paid the hotel bills. His parents' greatest fear became a nightmare when one of the season's most esteemed guests stumbled upon Bobby mounting his wife in the poolside storage room where the volleyball equipment was kept. Bobby, twenty years old, with his father's determined encouragement, packed his luggage and his life savings of $2,000 and went to New York.

The plane landed at Kennedy Airport in a torrential summer rainstorm. Bobby took a taxi directly to the Plaza Hotel and found a dry booth in the lobby of the hotel and phoned a woman he had met on the beach in Miami who had promised him a place to stay if he ever came to New York. But he quickly found out that women receptive to the charms of young lifeguards in Florida are rather reluctant and nervous around their Wall Street husbands in New York City. As a result, he checked into a cheap hotel in midtown and began to call guests who had stayed at his father's hotel over the years to ask for a job. Most politely said to call back in a month.

By then it was October, Indian summer had vanished and the chill of winter settled in to stay. Bobby, who had never been out of a warm climate, felt as if the siege of the Ice Age had begun. He hated the thought of a jobless winter in New York.

In desperation, he signed up at an employment agency. But without any special skills there were very few jobs available except as a dishwasher or waiter. The very best the employment company had to offer him was a job as an apartment sitter and dog walker. Bobby, who had never even petted a dog in his life, claimed he had had work experience in a kennel in Miami, forged a letter of rec-ommendation and was sent out on the job interview.

The next morning at nine o'clock he arrived promptly for an interview with a Mrs. Elizabeth David at 1050 Fifth Avenue, although until he arrived at the building and saw the apartment, the address hardly impressed him. Mrs. David, an attractive woman in her early forties, took one look at his shoulders under his lime green T-shirt and the deep V at his crotch in his jeans and invited him in. During a short tour of her twelve-room apartment she

explained that her husband was an international industrialist who spent three months a year in Paris; she would be
joining him there the next day. The dog, a prizewinning
Irish setter, belonged to her sixteen-year-old son, who was
away at boarding school. Bobby would have to feed and
walk the dog, water some plants and do some minor
painting. The tour ended in the master bedroom where
Bobby spent an hour in the king-sized bed fucking Mrs.
David.

When it was over, she sat in front of her dresser in a silk
brocade bathrobe and combed her hair. Bobby, naked, his
legs spread on the bed, lay back watching her.

"Have you ever slept with an older woman before?" she
asked him, straightfacedly concerned.

"Of course," Bobby said. "When you're my age, the
majority of the women *are* older."

"But certainly there are enough girls your own age."

Bobby smiled. "There aren't enough women of any
age," he told her.

He got the job, and he never even had to show her his
letter of recommendation.

The arrangement was perfect. The freezer and refrigerator were stocked with food, the phone was free and the
apartment was exquisite. He didn't even mind taking care
of the dog, who indolently slept behind one of the sofas
most of the day. He ran with Brandy through the park
every morning, eventually outrunning the dog, who tired
after two miles. He spent his day fiddling around the
apartment or going to the Sixty-third Street Y to work out.
He dutifully fixed broken lamps, painted the terrace and
watered the apartment's many plants. Most nights he spent
at home reading selections from the Davids' vast library.

Each morning he sorted the mail, throwing aside the
brochures and advertisements that the Davids seemed to
get by the hundreds. He was most curious about the party
invitations, which came every day. He could tell they
were party invitations because they were clearly in en-
graved envelopes, usually hand-addressed. He wondered
why the Davids got so many of them and what the parties
were like. Then one day an invitation came that Bobby
couldn't resist opening. It was a small Mylar-covered box
with something loose jiggling inside. The address was
beautifully hand-calligraphed, and the return address was

to a place called The Club. It was too bulky to forward to Paris and too pretty to throw away. Finally, after it had sat on the desk in the den for three days, Bobby ripped off the Mylar wrapping and opened the box.

Inside were two oversized pair of dice. They were loaded or weighted to one side, because no matter how many times Bobby tossed them they always came up to the sides with the lettering THE CLUB, and on the reverse side a message: "Try your luck. Gambler's Party, Nov. 20."

7

What in hell was so important about getting into a discotheque Bobby couldn't figure out for the life of him. At least 150 people in evening clothes and highly stylized disco drag were clamoring for a position up against the barricades under the silver and red marquee of The Club. As Bobby sauntered down Fifty-seventh Street, casually dressed in a blue leather baseball jacket and bright yellow T-shirt he wondered just what was going on inside that was so terrific. Just by looking at the mob from a distance he decided that he didn't even want to try his luck getting inside, but he was nevertheless determined to get up to the front of the ropes and have a look for himself.

He dived into the mob where the crowd looked the thinnest. The people around him were pushing so hard that at times it was difficult to keep his balance, and it took some minutes of determined elbowing to make his way to the inner ring of people. Behind him a woman kept crying, "Giorgio! Giorgio!" A very harried bald man in a conservative banker's suit waved a $100 bill over his head. The other side of the ropes was even more surreal. It was an empty quadrant that was a no-man's-territory. Five manly but goofy-looking men were self-consciously horsing around with each other as if they were in a locker room, slugging shoulders and patting asses. There was also a concerned, effete-looking blond man in a finely tailored suit. He wore orange-tinted glasses, and his eyes restlessly scanned the crowd as if he were looking for a familiar face. Right behind him was a tall, intense man whom everybody seemed to be screaming at. This man had the ability to look right through everybody, as if there weren't a mob there at all but a serene and empty landscape. Slowly the man turned his head and stopped at Bobby's eyes. They locked gazes for a moment; then he pointed Bobby out to the man in the orange glasses and said, "Him."

Two bouncers moved toward Bobby's position at the

rope. For a moment he was terrified; he was about to step back into the crowd when one of the bouncers unclasped the velvet barricade and held back the crowd behind him. Suddenly he was standing in the relatively empty space behind the ropes. He turned to the man who had let him in but couldn't figure out what to say.

"What are you waiting for?" Stu Shorter asked him. "Go on in."

Bobby obediently walked through the swinging doors, and he was in The Club.

It took him at least half an hour to get adjusted. At first he just marched in circles and stared. He had never seen as many attractive people in his life in one spot. There was a party going on, a charity gambling function for the American Institute of Cancer Research. The walls were lined with sparkling wheels of fortune. There was a "Guess Your Weight" booth for $100. A group of girls right out of the skin magazine center folds manned the blackjack tables, dealing out cards with slick professionalism. The clothing and the surroundings were so beautiful and glamorous that it was hard to believe this kind of party—better than any New Year's or Carnival—was going on every single night in this place. *That's* why people fought to get in the door. It felt so good, so warm and happy just to be there. The beautiful girls swung by him by the dozens, each with an aura of availability. He checked his baseball jacket and swam out into the crowd.

When in doubt, Bobby's motto went, always pick up the best-looking girl in sight. He started a conversation in the lounge with a lovely blond girl who was waiting for her friend to come out of the ladies' room. Her name was Noonie Brooks, a name exotic and wonderful to Bobby. She said she was twenty years old and had just completed a national modeling campaign of TV and print ads for Fabergé. Bobby had no idea that this meant Noonie Brooks was earning more than $150,000 a year. It wouldn't have made any difference to either of them if he did. For her part Noonie Brooks was fascinated by Bobby's confidence and naïveté as he was by her beauty. She had a long, thin nose and flashing oval eyes. And if Bobby thought she was beautiful in person, he should have seen her photographs. There was no such thing as a bad angle for Noonie Brooks, or a bad moment on film. She had

but it probably wasn't even four months. Well, that wasn't too bad, four months at hard labor behind the bar. He had found his own apartment, cleaned up his act. And he was having the best affair of his life.

"If you don't take chances, you won't get anywhere," Bobby told Tinder solemnly. Tinder laughed at him.

"I'd rather be behind the bar. It's safer back there. It's safer than working for Ellison."

"Lay off, Tinder. Help me carry these bottles downstairs to the alley, huh?"

Tinder picked up the second carton and followed Bobby across the dance floor to the basement steps. They were wet and slick with drippings from the garbage cans, and the two men picked their way down the steps uncertainly with the clumsy cartons. At the bottom of the steps Bobby hesitated while he tried to remember which way to go. He didn't come down to the basement often, and it was dark and confusing. In the distance he could hear the clinking of empties being counted, but the sound reverberated through the brick labyrinth, and it was impossible to tell which direction it was coming from. Tinder stepped in front of him and said, "This way," leading Bobby off in the direction he was certain was wrong.

About 100 feet farther down the dim passageway he saw a light ahead of him. As they came closer to it, Tinder slowed down his speed and walked quietly and light-footed. Bobby instinctively followed behind him, stopping just over his shoulder in the shadows. Almost directly ahead was an open door and a brightly lighted office. There was one flourescent fixture, several metal folding chairs and a large desk. In front of the rear wall there was a massive safe with the name Mosler across it.

Sandy Dubrow was seated behind the desk, counting money aloud, while his wife, Ella, stood at the other side of the desk and waited. A third person, a mean bald-headed man with a bull-like stare, his hands folded across his chest, watched Dubrow carefully. There were stacks of bills in bright-colored little bands all across the top of the desk, the bills fanning out in fluffy piles at the end. Bobby would have whistled aloud at the sight of so much money, but Tinder put his finger to his lips to signal silence, and the two stood in the shadow a moment longer, Bobby feeling scared and nervous.

Dubrow turned to his wife and said, "Here's ten thousand," and to the other man, "Here's your two." They both took large packets of bills and pocketed them.

Suddenly Bobby felt the unsteady pressure of cold, clammy human hands on his bare shoulder. He swung around in the dark to see Shorter, bleary-eyed and lurching drunk.

"Whattaya doing here?" Shorter demanded of Bobby. At the sound of Shorter's voice Dubrow jumped to his feet in the office, and his wife slammed the door. In another moment the office door opened again, and Dubrow marched out, furious.

"What are you two doing here?" he demanded of the bartenders.

"We were looking for the alley," Tinder said, "and we got lost."

Dubrow looked at them suspiciously. "What's your name?" he asked Tinder, who had started to tell him when Shorter suddenly lurched forward and vomited a little on the front of his Lacoste shirt.

Dubrow said, "Oh, shit," and held Shorter upright. "Goddamn him! Get him upstairs!"

Tinder and Bobby put down their cartons and wrapped Shorter's limp arms over their shoulders. They managed to half carry, half drag him down the hallway and up the slippery steps.

"Over here," Tinder said, motioning to a banquette off the dance floor, where they laid Shorter out on his back.

"What do we do now?" Bobby asked.

"Just leave him here, I guess. They'll take him home. He sure is heavy for a skinny guy," Tinder said, grinning. "Dead weight."

"Yeah, dead weight," Bobby repeated, rolling the phrase over and over again through his mind. "What do you think Dubrow was so upset about downstairs?"

Tinder smiled smugly. "There was a lot of money on that desk," he said. "I guess people don't like to be watched counting their money. Did you see Ella Dubrow stick ten grand in her purse?"

Bobby preferred not to answer, and Tinder put a friendly arm over Bobby's shoulder. "What say we get a late-night cheeseburger?" he asked.

"No, thanks, I'm bushed," Bobby begged off. "I'll see you tomorrow."

Tinder smiled understandingly and wandered off into The Club. Just then Sandy and Ella Dubrow came up out of the basement steps with the bull-like man. The man and Ella left The Club while Sandy Dubrow stayed behind to attend to Shorter, who was moaning quietly on the banquette. Tinder Kaufman stepped out of the shadow and followed Ella Dubrow and the man out the door.

Bobby went to the employees' locker room, put on his shirt and jacket, then strode through the empty club. Shorter was already gone from the banquette.

Outside a light, milky blue haze lighted the city. The early-morning streets were hushed and deserted. It was Bobby's favorite time in New York, a peaceful, soothing moment, just him and the cold glass and steel canyons. Up and down Fifty-seventh Street the streetlamps shut off in flickers, one by one, to the East River, as the dawn increased in brightness. Across the wide street one last, lonely sleek black limousine, dark and silent, waited quietly for something. From the corner of his eye he saw the rear window of the limousine receded into the chassis and a woman's arm extend from the dark interior, beckoning to him.

She waited for me, that crazy lady. She waited.

Even as Bobby vaulted across the street the engine of the car started, the lights went on and the rear door was flung open from the inside. Bobby climbed through the portal and slammed the heavy door behind him. As the car pulled away from the curb, he settled on top of the woman who waited there for him, passionately kissing her on the mouth.

"You shouldn't have waited. You promised me," he said to her between kisses, running his hands up the sides of her legs. The driver made a left turn up Sixth Avenue, and in another moment the car was swallowed up by the park.

"I didn't want to go back to the apartment alone," she whispered as the car swept silently up the drive. "I can't face it anymore at night without you."

Encased in Bobby Cassidy's muscular embrace, Grace Dunn was hardly aware of where she was at all as her limousine rushed her home through the early-morning mist. Just being with him numbed her into ecstasy. She was shamelessly galvanized by him, by everything about him, the way he looked, the way he smiled, the way he put things and the way he made love to her. She was distracted by the thought of him when she was apart from him and giddy in his presence, as head over heels in love with him as a schoolgirl with a first crush.

Just a few months ago no one could have convinced her life could have developed into this second-rate melodrama, that she'd be waiting outside a nightclub into the early hours of the morning in the back seat of a car so she could neck with a veritable child on the way home, trembling with anticipation of what lay ahead.

The first time she laid eyes on him he was behind the bar, stripped to the waist, rippling, like a beautiful bronzed stallion, glumly pouring drinks for the guests of a charity function. While the other bartenders whirled and danced around the bars, he stood still, moving gracefully and with a conservation of energy. She was particularly bored that night; her date was an aging stockbroker with gout, and she fell into a minor depression. At least that was the excuse she gave herself when she gave into temptation and did something she hadn't done since she was a young girl: flirt. She smiled at the bartender, asked his name and tipped him well for the drink.

After that, he pursued her.

First a note at the theater, well composed, intelligent and respectful, complimenting her on her evening's performance, which he had made sure to see.

Then flowers to her apartment, with his phone number included on the note.

Out of control with the memory of him behind the bar, she called to thank him and made a date for tea the next day at the theater between the matinee and evening performance. He was so charming, so alive, so interested in life that she asked him to stay, and he was waiting for her in her dressing room when she finished the evening's performance.

Later that night, for the first time in nearly thirty years, she had sex with a man other than her late husband, and the next morning again wasn't soon enough.

He pushed her down across the seat of the limousine now, out of the vision of the rearview mirror. Grace worried what the driver would think, and she felt so self-conscious that she forgot about Bobby for a moment until he began to lick the inside of her thigh just above her knee, the soft scrapy feeling of his beard tingling through her nylon, and she could think of nothing else. He pressed his head against her inner thigh, inhaling deeply, intoxicated by her musk. Grace, a little frightened she would lose control, tried to push his shoulders away from her but too late as he moved closer, kissing, licking, eating through her pantyhose until she could only throw her head back on the leather seat and try not to scream.

8

At exactly ten o'clock the following morning Randy Potter was sitting in the back seat of his limousine amid a sea of rare orchids in clay pots like an emperor among his subjects. On his right, an *Andropopius orchidaceae,* one of the world's rarest and loveliest flowers, its gray and orange raceme dotted with moist blue pollen, bobbed and swayed from a thin, noble stalk as the car crept down Fifth Avenue, Around his feet were three pots of *Hydropolinate,* orange and green and junglelike, springing into a series of delicate blooms at the top, keeping him company. On the front seat with the driver, a handsome young man dressed in blue jeans and suede sports jacket, sat three pots of common *Leopardis* orchids like poor cousins. And the prize of the day, a rare yellow and hot pink South American *Maosipollitinae,* sat on the back seat against Randy, like a lover. He sighed. If only orchids were fragrant; it was their only deficit. The pungent aroma of his driver's marijuana cigarette drifted to him from the front seat.

Randy squinted through the tinted windows of the car. Outside, a fine but persistent drizzle shrouded the city, capping the skyscrapers down Fifth Avenue in a foamy white mist. The rain had caused the traffic to a crawl along the crowded thoroughfare as pedestrians darted in and out of taxis, avoiding the giant puddles of water from the backed-up sewers. Randy sighed impatiently as the car inched along. He had ten deliveries to make before lunchtime. At least he had the *Post* to keep him busy. He opened that morning's edition and lit his own joint. Randy loved the *Post.* It was the perfect way to start off the day, always amusing and informative. The serious news items took only a minute or so to read, and where other newspapers ran stories about world affairs and national crises, the *Post* ran stories about freak accidents or miracle drug cures, sex assaults and UFO sightings. And the *Post* had "Page Six." "Page Six" was a daily feature, a page filled with some of the most important gossip in the world, if there's any such thing as important gossip. There was, however, gossip of merit. Watergate, after all, had started as gossip. And "Page Six" was a mother lode of items of political and publishing note, often with serious implications or ramifications. Careers were launched, maimed and ended, mistresses uncovered, lawsuits announced or threatened, feuds inflamed, deals consummated. The gossip page was dotted with items of fluffery and villainy, and it was a gossip's delight. And although nobody ever actually quoted the *Post*'s "Page Six," every magazine editor, TV commentator and media personality had read it with religious conviction by lunchtime. For Randy it was a necessity. In his business gossip was just as important as orchids.

Randy Potter was the most sought-after—and expensive—florist in Manhattan. He dealt exclusively in orchids. His "less is more" philosophy was that the bloom of one lovely, expensive orchid was more tasteful and impressive than a gross of cut flowers. His prices started at $150 for a single bloom and often went as high as $750 or $1,000 for a rare spray. Sometimes he would have an orchid so very rare that he would only "rent" it to a client for a week and then whisk it back to his greenhouse for rest and recuperation and breeding. At the greenhouse the parent orchids, or "studs," were often worth as much as $100,000. Randy's business was so unique and successful it was conducted only by word of mouth. He had no retail shop, and his phone number was unlisted. He saw his exclusive clientele as people who could both appreciate and afford his orchids, and that took Randy into the bedrooms and back rooms of some of the most famous homes and offices in Manhattan, an often incestuous route. Randy saw his customers in the same light he saw his orchids. Delicate, neurotic, sensitive, complicated blooms that mated best at full moon or high tide. And Randy wasn't just another tradesman to these people; he was a personality in his own right. In his profession he was the perfect conduit for gossip that would make "Page Six" pale in comparison and often Randy's clients were paying as much for the rarefied information he brought with the orchids as they were for the plant.

Randy opened to "Page Six." On the page opposite were a photo gossip page and a column by Jack Martin, which was more internationally flavored. Randy first went through all the names in large type in Jack Martin's column; then he checked the photo captions that ran alongside it.

One of them read, "HORAY PRANN HELPS JACKY MELLON HIGHER."

There was a picture taken at The Club the night before. You could see a little bit of Ellison's smile in the corner of the photo if you knew Ellison's smile. But most of it was a photo of Horay holding her fist up to Jacky Mellon's mouth. At first it looked as if Horay were threatening her, but on closer examination you could see a small bottle in Horay's hand. Butyl nitrate. Randy read the caption again and then the body copy: "Last night at The Club Polo Prann's estranged wife, Horay, helps actress Jacky Mellon to new heights with a bottle of butyl nitrate. That's the stuff the disco darlings use for an instant high on the dance floor. It's legal, folks, and sold in stores as novelty 'room odorizer.' (See *Addison Critch* for full story, page 44.)"

Randy laughed aloud. Will they never learn? He turned quickly to Addison Critch's column to see what the Master of Evil had to say about it. He inhaled deeply on his joint and began reading.

CRITICISMS
by *Addison Critch*

Last night I spent my obligatory one night a week in that bastion of heaven and hell The Club. Once again it was a fascinating sojourn into the realm of the rich and famous. Some highlights included **Cheryl Tiegs,** who lost an earring on the dance floor and had twenty men climbing around on their hands and knees, looking for it, **Veronica Meadwright,** the senator's daughter, smoking pot in the lounge, and model **Soigne Calvarez.** Calvarez (you pronounce his first name *Swan-yay*) is the black model you know from the distinctive TV commercial for chic colognes. Although Soigne earns upwards of $75,000 a year modeling, it seems he's been making a little extra income at The Club. Often unescorted ladies of great importance come to The Club and would like to dance. While there are many dime-a-dance ladies available, good male disco partners are hard to find. According to Calvarez, Club owner **Stu Shorter** has been offering him $200 a dance to inveigle important women out on the dance floor for photographers—all in the name of more publicity for The Club. Calvarez, who was photographed only last week dancing with **Jacky Mellon,** tells how he did it. "I stood in front of her that night and tried to tantalize her. Shorter had introduced us, but she was shy about dancing with me. I just stood there and shook my ass at her until she followed me onto the dance floor." Really, now!

And while we're on Jacky Mellon, she was anything but partnerless last night at The Club. First she was squired by fashion *mayven* **Ellison,** who took her down to the private domain of The Club called the Playpen. Not a half hour later Jacky was seen leaving The Club with ballet star **Glesnerovsky,** who was first-timing it at the famed night boîte. Word from my spy at *The Performance,* Mellon's Broadway spectacular with a budget over $2 million, is that there's lots of trouble with the show. Mellon just isn't plugging away, and there's more trouble with her director-*con-in-namorato,* **Eddie Bernardo.** Maybe it's just a case of The Girl Can't Help It?

Meanwhile, New York State Assemblyman **David Essex** insists he will run for reelection, despite his recent scrape with *scandal* in the demimonde of sado-masochistic prostitution. Essex was officially. . . .

Randy's driver pulled up to the curb at 800 Fifth Avenue, one of the most expensive buildings in the whole city, the New York dwelling place of Rita Lachman, Dolly Parton and Jack Martin. Randy let himself out of the back door, choosing an *Aphrodite rimestadiana* to take with him. He stood on the sidewalk in the rain for a moment, lifting the orchid heavenward and letting it drink up some of the wet. Randy also turned his head upward into the refreshing rain, gratefully breathing in the clean smell that washed over the city. Up and down Fifth Avenue the manhole covers smoked like steaming teapots, puffy gray clouds of steam dramatically soaring into the spring rain. It looked as if the city were cooking and bubbling beneath the surface of the streets. Refreshed, Randy walked into the building.

"I'm here for Mr. Duff," Randy told one of the doormen in a braided blue uniform. The man stared uncomprehendingly at Randy's wet shirt and the single orchid in the clay pot. Randy lifted it forward and said, "It's four hundred dollars."

The doorman seemed unimpressed. "Is this a delivery?" he asked stiffly, prepared to send Randy around the corner to the delivery entrance. Randy raised his eyebrows in surprise, practically every doorman of any prominent dwelling in New York knew Randy by sight. And nobody made Randy deliver rare orchids through the service entrance. Randy Potter was at least as important and celebrated in New York as the clients he brought his flowers to.

"This is the best delivery you're going to see all day," Randy said breezily to the doorman, walking by him to the concierge's desk.

"That's all right, Joseph," the man behind the desk cried to the doorman, who was rushing after Randy to throw him out. "I know this gentleman."

Defeated, the doorman sulked back to his post.

Moments later the elevator whisked Randy upstairs to Alvin Duff's tenth-floor apartment. A small Chinese man in a white jacket opened the mirrored door to the apartment and bowed perfunctorily to Randy, who nodded back and sauntered in, chewing on an imaginary piece of gum.

"Hiya, Chan," he said, "is your boss around?"

"Mr. Duff is dressing," the houseboy, whose name was Michael, told Randy coldly. He thought it was very rude to be called Chan. "I'll take that." He reached out for the orchid.

"Unh-unh, Chan," Randy said, moving the orchid out of Michael's reach, "I get to deliver my own goods." Randy moved through the white hallway into the spacious, partially decorated apartment that Duff had lived in for only six weeks. He followed the sound of Duff's voice past the empty rectangular living room with a commanding view of Central Park into the dining room, where he found Duff at a makeshift breakfast table with his ten-year-old daughter, Janey, and a tall, distinguished European man whom Randy recognized as Rudolfo Sloane, the man who had designed the lounges at The Club. A portable TV set tuned to the *Phil Donahue Show* stood on two packing cartons.

"But you promised we'd be able to go to *Disneyland*,"

Janey was complaining to her father, who was sectioning a grapefruit for her.

Duff smiled patiently at the little girl. "Disneyworld in Florida is just as good as Disneyland, and it's only half as far—"

"But you said Disney*land.* . . ."

"Hello, Randy," Duff said, looking up. "What a lovely orchid."

"It's very rare," Randy assured him. He touched the little girl's blond hair. "Hello, Janey."

Janey grimaced and pulled her head away.

"Do you know Rudolfo Sloane? This is Randy Potter. Sit and have some breakfast, Randy," Duff said encouragingly.

"Well, just a little." Randy pulled a folding chair over to the table while a maid came out of the kitchen with a cup of coffee for him.

"So Rudolfo, when do you think the living-room furniture will be finished?" Duff asked, chewing his toast. "The den is too small to live in." Randy listened quietly as Duff tried to manipulate Sloane into promising him an earlier delivery date for his furniture. Randy marveled at Duff's technique. In another month Duff would turn thirty-eight, but no one would have guessed it by looking at him; he had the muscle tone and skin of a healthy-looking teenager, his nose and cheekbones still speckled with adolescent freckles. This youthful appearance had been achieved at enormous expense by having $55,000 worth of tiny silicone shots injected strategically into his face since he was thirty years old—a narcissistically young age to start—by the notorous Park Avenue plastic surgeon William Lankstein, who was allegedly responsible for just as many cases of skin cancer as bobbed noses. But narcissism was much of what Duff was all about. His youthful build, his good looks and self-presence made him a cutting, romantic figure, an image that brought him more success and fans than his good taste in fashion.

Certainly his ex-wife Sheila was not one of his fans, as Randy Potter well knew. Randy had brought orchids to Sheila and Alvin at Duff's apartment when they were still married, and there were frequent mornings when Duff was using every four-letter word in the book and smacking Sheila around. The divorce had been bloody—Duff made good use of the publicity—and the custody fight for Janey had been bloodier. Sheila Duff, as far as Randy knew, was a destroyed woman and an all-out drunk at this point.

"I always thought it was sheer madness for a clothing designer to hire another designer to decorate his apartment for him," Duff told Sloane pointedly. "But I've just never been able to pull an apartment together, believe it or not. It has something to do with the geometry of furniture. I guess it's a question of sources and not talent, wouldn't you think?"

Randy and Sloane nodded politely.

"I want tap shoes," Janey said.

"Off to school," Duff told the little girl.

"Can I have tap shoes?"

"Of course. Ask Mrs. Mulcahey. Now give me a kiss and run along."

Janey did as she was told and left the room.

"Oh, look," Duff said, gesturing toward the TV set, "there's Sue Langeway, on the *Donahue Show*. She's a client of mine."

Langeway was one of the most mysterious, if not the most talented, actresses in Hollywood. She was blond, thin and aloof, with that same kind of icy appeal that Lauren Bacall had. Langeway also remained a woman of great charisma for the public, managing the unmanageable by keeping her marriage to rock drummer Dick Cooper under wraps for five years. She made only one movie a year, for which she commanded a cool $2 million. Donahue had just asked her how it felt to be the highest-paid actress in Hollywood.

She inhaled slowly on her cigarette. "I never think about the money aspect," she said languidly. "I only do the films because acting is my life."

Randy and Duff laughed heartily.

"She forgot to say that working as a waitress at Howard Johnson would hardly pay for her twelve-hundred-dollar-a-week cocaine habit," Duff said. "She's already had part of her nose replaced. Her plastic surgeon told me; I dress his wife. She had a hole the size of a dime. She's been told ten times that if she doesn't stop with the coke, they'll have to restructure her whole nose. How's she going to explain *that*?"

The two men chortled.

"You know what I heard?" Duff went on. "I heard that

she and her husband were guests at Richard Cobb's house in St. Thomas last winter, and she holed up in the guest bedroom for fifteen days straight without ever once peeking out the bedroom door. There wasn't a gram of coke in St. Thomas, and she's a total sugar addict without it to kill her appetite. She gained twenty pounds in one week, they say, and she was too ashamed to get into a bathing suit or even show her face. They had to take her off the island in a helicopter so none of the other guests would see her. And when they sent the maid in to clean up her room, they found hundreds of Yoo-Hoo chocolate drink bottles and empty bags of potato chips and cupcakes stuffed under the bed. Just think, a woman that beautiful is such a secret slob."

"Excuse me, Mr. Duff," Michael said from the doorway, "but these papers just came for you. And Mr. Lynley is on the phone."

Duff looked at his watch and took the papers from Michael. "Would you make sure Janey get off to school in five minutes, Michael?"

Michael bowed and left the room. Duff went to the phone sitting on the windowsill while he opened the manila envelope Michael had just handed him. "Lynley? It's Duff. What's up? Yes, they just came. I can sign them and bring them into my office in an hour or I can send them straight to you by messenger. Which is better?" He listened for a moment and hung up.

Janey came into the room before he could say anything. "I don't *want* to go to school. I don't feel well. . . ."

Duff laid the papers on the table and went to Janey and hugged her. "What if Daddy gets you off to school?" Duff asked. Janey sniffed and nodded yes.

"I'll be right back," Duff said.

Rudolfo stood. "I must go. Let's speak by phone."

"All right, I'll take you to the door. Randy, can you wait and I'll talk to you about flowers for the showroom this month?"

"I can wait," Randy said, and then he was left alone in the room. His eyes strayed right to the papers on the table, open flat, as easy to read as the newspaper. At first glance he could see they were legal contracts made up by Paul, Weiss, Rifkind, Wharton & Garrison, one of the city's prestigious law firms.

Phil Donahue was introducing a housewife who had written a best-selling vegetarian cookbook as Randy leaned over the papers. From what he could make out from the first page, it was an agreement between Duff's company and another company—he turned to page two—Simon Morrow.

Simon Morrow, Simon Morrow. That name was so familiar to him.

Randy turned another page. It declared that Duff would license a line for them. Denims. Overalls. Children's denim. All jeans and denims.

A licensing agreement.

Randy turned another page. It was filled with figures and a plan for payments and disbursements and percentages. The figures were all in the millions, one figure at $50 million.

Oh, shit. It finally dawned on him. Simon Morrow was the conglomerate that owned Ellison!

"Mr. Potter! Please!" Michael yelled from the doorway. Randy jumped two feet off the chair and slapped the contracts shut. "Those are Mr. Duff's private papers!"

"I . . . didn't realize . . ." Randy said, more annoyed that it was Michael who caught him than he was embarrassed. "They were just lying on the table. . . ."

Michael scooped up the contracts and walked off with them. In another moment Duff appeared in the doorway, full of scorn and disgust.

"My dear Mr. Potter, how long have we known each other?" Duff began. Randy opened his mouth to answer, but Duff quickly said, "And how many customers have I recommended to you?" Randy contemplated this in his head. Duff had actually recommended two customers, both of whom had dropped Randy after six months because they couldn't afford him. "Now, Randy," Duff reprimanded, "I'm not very happy with you reading my papers. . . ."

"Did Michael say I was *reading* your papers?" Randy pretended to be affronted.

Duff wasn't fooled. "Those papers were confidential," he said. "How far did you get?"

"I'm sure I don't know what you're talking about," Randy insisted. Duff just glared at him. "Now, if you'd like to discuss the flowers for the showroom. . . ."

"No, Randy, I think we'll hold off all discussion on the

showroom. Those papers, I repeat, were confidential, and I'd like to see how confidential they are kept."

Downstairs in the lobby Randy pulled a $10 bill from a roll in his pocket and handed it to the doorman who had given him trouble earlier. The doorman looked at the bill in amazement and murmured a thank-you to Randy as he strode out of the building into the rain.

Sinking into the back of his car, he cursed Duff aloud. If there was any surefire way to irk Randy, it was to be treated like a tradesman. Screw Duff. Duff wasn't such a big-deal client. He had clients as big, and bigger, and nobody was going to push him around or blackmail him for a showroom. Anyway, Duff's licensing his jeans to Ellison's company was information worth more than a client like Duff. Randy buried Duff forever in his book.

"Where next?" he asked his driver, who consulted an appointment list in the front seat.

"You have a choice. We're just about as close to Diane Von Furstenberg as we are to the Gavins."

Randy mulled this over for a moment. Diane Von Furstenberg wasn't yet one of his customers, but he would love to have her and wanted to deliver a complimentary orchid, especially since she not only had a large apartment but a sprawling seventeen-room showroom, a testament to Von Furstenberg's marketability and business acumen. The estranged wife of dashing, dark and handsome Prince Egon Von Furstenberg, heir to the Fiat fortune, Diane was having a flagrantly open and passionate romance with Paramount Pictures chairman Barry Diller. Hence she had social clout, business clout, brains and beauty. She was exciting and unpredictable and was a great client for Randy.

But Von Furstenberg was strictly business; she was above gossiping with her tradesmen. The Gavins had more allure for Randy at the moment because he was carrying a choice piece of information and going to the Gavins was like going to market with it. By generic profession, the Gavins were publicists, but in fact they were also a covered bazaar of power and influence in New York that would make the deals in smoke-filled back rooms seem like child's play.

A publicist is an image maker, a manipulator of the facts, a pigment to color truths, an engineer who can make

mountains out of molehills and vice versa, an interpreter
who can construct tragedy as triumph. Each publicist
approaches this endeavor in an extremely personal man-
ner, and a client must choose a publicist with the same
care which a young woman chooses her first gynecolo-
gist.

The kinds of publicists vary, and there are sharp divi-
sions. There are music publicists, Broadway, literary, movie, unit and personality publicists. Some publicists publicized themselves, although allegedly a good publicist never
finds his way into print himself. The best known is
probably Bobby Zarem, a lovable and socially prestigious
publicist in New York, who is like a nervous character out
of *Gatsby*. On the other hand, Roger and Cowan and
Solters and Roskin are big agencies, capable of grabbing
international media space for their clients. For Broadway
openings crusty pros like Betty Lee Hunt and Maria Pucci
can't be topped. But the Gavins, the Gavins were the
monarchs of the publicity business in New York because
they combined all the elements of the others and wielded
not just space and publicity but power.

The Gavins believed in power. Crafty, aggressive and
smart, the Gavins were a well-matched pair. They had
been married thirty years and went into business the day
they took their nuptial vows, when Elliot talked the minis-
ter out of a fee in exchange for free advertising in a local
paper. Their personalities played against each other like a
well-rehearsed play. Mary Gavin's sweet-mannered, nurse-
like, motherly understanding as she wrapped you around
her little finger, her sharp eyes and adept probing were
distracting counterpoint to Elliot Gavin's mumbling, old-
softy ploy, masking his subliminal plotting and manipula-
tions.

Over the years the Gavins had arranged publicity for a
multitude of New York events. They supervised the birth
of Broadway shows and movie premieres, the openings
and anniversaries of nightclubs, restaurants, concert halls
and banks. They arranged major celebrations for giant
conglomerates, museums, book publishings and Gracie
Mansion functions. On an individual basis they touted and
publicized actors, directors, record company executives,
designers, singers, politicians and trial lawyers. They gave
birthday parties for poodles starring in movies and wrote
press releases about clients' divorces and hysterectomies.

Over the years the media and power elite had crisscrossed in so many ways that the Gavins quite literally knew more people in the power structure of New York than, say, any of the last three mayors.

Since the Gavins were not Randy's clients but were capable of getting him many jobs, his deliveries to them were gratis, a typical barter with the Gavins. He picked out one of the inexpensive leopard orchids from the front seat to bring to Mary Gavin. When Randy arrived at the Gavins' East Side town house, the rain was worse then ever. He found her in her office on the first floor rear of the town house. It was one of Randy's favorite offices in the city. It looked like the living room of a country farmhouse. It was a large, comfortable room with a pale blue Austrian rug and big oak furniture.

Mary was alone in her office, sipping a cup of coffee, smiling and peering up at Randy from behind her silver-framed spectacles. She looked like a country schoolmarm, a brown cardigan thrown over her shoulders, a pleated beige shirtwaist dress. Randy always thought she was a pleasant, gracious woman to spend time with.

"My, what a lovely orchid, Randy! Is that for me?"

She got up from behind the desk and took the orchid from him. For Mary, Randy was an interesting source of information, but highly unreliable. Randy was in all the right places at all the right times, but he heard so many things incorrectly, or jumped to conclusions from small pieces of an event half understood, that Mary Gavin found she had repeatedly to check his information to get a correct story. But it was enough that Randy could smell smoke because Mary could always discover the fire. And his orchids were lovely and free. Almost free. "Isn't this a pretty orchid?" she said, fussing over it. "Aren't you thoughtful."

"Yes it's very rare," he lied. "A very extraordinary orchid."

Mary poured him a cup of coffee and asked him to have a seat at the large round oak table near the rain-streaked window. Each morning the Gavins had breakfast at this table with their staff. The Gavins had seven publicists working for them, each with his own desk and four phone lines. Every morning over croissants and coffee the Gavin "family" exchanged stories, information, salable gossip items, ticket sales and reviews as if they were in preparation for a combat mission. By ten-thirty the staff was already at their desks, manning the phone lines.

From his office adjoining Mary's, Elliot Gavin stepped into the room. Elliot was a portly, energetic man with smiling eyes and a shrewd business mind. While Mary was more gentle and enticing, Elliot could be a cunning aggressor in a business situation. His clients got space preference and positive exposure from journalists; otherwise, the journalists went on his shit list. And that wasn't a good place to be. A blacklisted journalist suddenly faced a dearth of precious information, tickets, press screenings, parties and promotional records. Elliot was capable of more whitemail (arm twisting that verged on the immoral) than anyone in the business.

"Look at what Randy brought us," Mary said sweetly.

Elliot looked over at the orchid but didn't seem impressed. He wondered what Randy wanted. He showed Mary a letter, raised his eyes significantly at her and asked, "Did you invite Dick Cavett? Because I didn't invite Dick Cavett, and I'll be damned if there's room for him."

Mary shrugged. "Then screw 'em. Remember when he turned us down on booking the guy from Atlantic Records?"

"True, true," Elliot said, "But who's gonna tell him?"

"I'll send a letter," Mary said calmly.

"A *letter?* The party's *tomorrow.*"

"I'll call then, Elliot."

"All right," Elliot muttered, still absorbed in his problem as he left the room.

"Now, what brings you by to cheer us up on this dreary, rainy day?" Mary ventured.

"I've made a delivery to Alvin Duff today," Randy began.

"Oh? And what is so noteworthy about that? Hasn't he been your client all along?"

"Yes, but today, while I was there, he received something that might interest you."

For a moment Mary hated Randy. It took him forever to get to the point.

"Oh, hello, Randy." R. Howard Kirby sneered from the doorway. "I didn't know you were here. How's things in the florist trade?"

Randy had long ago decided that R. Howard Kirby was

one of the nastiest and lowest people on earth. The Gavins kept Kirby on staff to handle the really dirty gossip, the kind of chitchat that was an important part of their business but too low for them to handle personally. Kirby was an affected young man from a well-to-do Shaker Heights family who didn't have any particular talent except that he could afford the right clothes and the right restaurants and went to the right parties, where he never seemed to have much fun. For a long time Kirby had lived on the fringe, but when he joined the Gavins, he became a virtual pit of ugly information, yet somehow finally a cog in the wheel of the shakers and makers.

"What is it, Howard?" Mary asked testily.

"Edgar's just called and said come in any time for a free dinner for getting them mentioned in *The Times,* Mary," Kirby said.

Mary nodded and smiled, filing it away. She held thousands of pieces of IOUs and favors in her head. She had so many offers for free trips and meals that she could have traveled and eaten for free for the next ten years. The way it just worked was typical; Edgar was Edgar Hodgkiss, who owned a midtown theatrical steak restaurant that depended heavily on tourist trade and needed constant mention in the columns. When Mary set up an interview the other day for one of her budding actresses, she had the reporter meet the girl at Hodgkiss Restaurant, which was then mentioned in the column. The restaurant in return offered Mary a free meal.

"And do you want to talk to Liz Smith? She's holding on line two."

"No, tell her I'll call her later. Say I'm having lunch with Neal Travis and I'll have something for her after that."

R. Howard Kirby nodded and scooted away.

"Well, Randy, what were you saying?" Mary poured herself another cup of coffee. She turned her back to Randy and stirred slowly as she looked out at the garden behind the house in the rain.

"Do you remember who you were going to introduce me to?" Randy asked. "Vivica Goldstein."

Mary turned to face him. Vivica Goldstein was one of the most successfully trendy decorators in New York. She was the wife of Murray Goldstein, the executive president of Universal Records. Goldstein was always busy with corporate forays to exotic brothels and managing the company's soccer team. So Vivica did what the wives of all bored executives did: She started her own business. One started limousine services, one an excellent bakery on Madison Avenue to satisfy her sweet cravings, one opened a cooking school and Vivica decorated the apartments of *nouveau riche* New Yorkers for small fortunes.

And as far as Randy knew, she didn't work with a florist. Yet.

"I know Vivica Goldstein well," Mary said. It was time-consuming to banter with this boy.

"I'd love to meet her. Professionally, of course."

"Perhaps." Mary sniffed.

Randy felt he'd better offer his goods right away. "So at Alvin Duff's house this morning for breakfast—"

"Breakfast? I thought you made a delivery?" Mary said dubiously.

"Well, yes, but I was invited to stay for breakfast—"

Kirby stuck his head in the door again. "Do you care that Norma Kramer's husband was busted for cocaine possession at the airport in Italy this morning?" he asked happily.

"No," Mary sang back, "and neither does Norma Kramer."

The intercom buzzed, and it was Elliot. "James Reilly was fired from the *Daily News* this morning," he intoned.

"Praise be the gods," Mary said. "I've been begging his editor to get rid of him for months." Then to Randy: "So, the meek *do* inherit," she said heartily. "Now, breakfast at Duff's. . . ."

"His daughter was there. Obnoxious. Spoiled. Belongs with her mother. And Rudolfo Sloane, the decorator, was there. Duff told him he had to be crazy to let—"

"Randy," Mary interrupted gently, "you wanted to meet Vivica Goldstein?"

Randy swallowed. "Simon Morrow, the conglomerate that owns Ellison, is licensing jeans from Alvin Duff."

"Alvin Duff? How do you know? He could be lying or putting you on."

"He didn't tell me. I saw the papers in his den. I got to read four or five pages before his Chink servant stopped me."

"But why? Why would Simon Morrow do that?" she wondered, buzzing Elliot to come into her office. Perhaps Duff had won a couple of Coty Awards, but he had no public credibility. He was only a *pisher* compared to some of the major companies that clothed half the Western world. Compared to the greats like Halston, Anne Klein, Calvin Klein and Ellison, Alvin Duff was practically a nobody. According to *Women's Wear,* for instance, Geoffrey Beene did a combined $50 million a year gross in ready-to-wear clothing, fragrances and other licensed products. Bill Blass grossed approximately $85 million, in furs, robes, tennis clothes, patterns for *Vogue,* fragrances by Revlon and the design of an automobile by Lincoln Mercury. Diane Von Furstenberg grossed $18 million in cosmetics and fragrances alone. Her licensed products raked in $55 million on the wholesale level, including dresses and sportswear, rainwear, jewelery, furs, luggage and even home furnishings. Halston made a piddling $50 million a year wholesale in comparison, while Calvin Klein was reportedly topping the $200 million mark, with more than $100 million in jeans.

"How do you know this?" Elliot demanded of Randy when he came into the office.

Randy couldn't imagine why they were making such a big deal. What was so important? He knew it was good gossip but—

"What did the papers say exactly?" Elliot probed.

"How much?" Mary asked.

"Just jeans?" Elliot wanted to know.

"Call Megan at Simon Morrow's and nonchalantly find out when Ellison's contract runs out with them," Mary suggested.

A few minutes later Elliot put down the phone. "Eighteen months," he said, smiling. "Ellison's contract with Simon Morrow is up in eighteen months, and they haven't made a move to renew it."

"But why?" Randy asked, confused.

"Because," Mary said slowly, as it dawned on her, "Ellison refuses to manufacture jeans. He must be cutting Simon Morrow out of millions of dollars' worth of jean sales."

"*Hundreds* of millions," Elliot said zestfully. "Now, the question we will put on the lips of everyone in America is:

Will Simon Morrow drop Ellison's contract and license exclusively through Alvin Duff? Is this the beginning of the end? Is Ellison through?"

The three looked at each other.

"Excuse me," Randy said, "but I have lots of other deliveries to make."

9

Grace Dunn's housekeeper had been tiptoeing around the apartment all morning with the kind of determined silence that is louder than a brass band. Grace, who was a light sleeper, despite the fact that she hadn't closed her eyes until after six that morning, heard Lenora arrive at eight and quietly begin her chores in the apartment. Lenora, a middle-aged Norwegian woman who had worked for Grace for fourteen years, no longer woke her with breakfast; several months before, she had stumbled in with breakfast and the morning paper and got the surprise of her life. Grace, fast asleep, was entwined alongside Bobby Cassidy's naked body. Since that day Lenora not only didn't come into the bedroom until after he had left the house but showed her tacit disapproval of the affair by coming in a half hour earlier than usual every day and sneaking around the apartment in a subdued fury, as if there were a terminally ill person in Grace's bedroom. To complicate matters, Bobby insisted on making love in the morning, a new experience for Grace and one she found a delightful way to start the day, but not with Lenora outside her door. This Monday morning was Lenora's shopping day, and if Grace waited in bed long enough, Lenora would eventually leave the house. Then she could have her moments with Bobby without worrying whether the sounds of her sex life were mortifying Lenora in the living room.

She pressed up against him; a big overgrown boy, vulnerable and childish-looking. His mouth was open a little, showing large white teeth and the touch of a pink tongue. One arm lay outside the covers, his bicep funneling into a long, thick forearm, his large, masculine hand at rest on his own thigh. She leaned into him, breathing in the smell of his body under the down cover. Slowly she moved her right hand between her legs and touched herself, sending ripples of electric waves up her belly.

Why in forty-nine years had she never felt like this before, as she did lying in bed next to this child? Was it simply because the sexual thrill was so illicit? Had she secretly become the infamous dirty old lady, the society woman who keeps up a straight front but goes down on bartenders in the back of limousines? Or was this perfectly reasonable, that a sophisticated woman could be charmed by the attentions of a precocious, sexy young boy? And at what cost?

How much she was prepared to give up for the affair was another question entirely, one that worried her increasingly. The dangers of this relationship were enormous, but she could not bring herself to end it. Perhaps she had gone truly mad. The disapproval of her housekeeper would seem like an Easter pageant compared to the sneers and jokes that would come from the public. If the press found out, they would have a field day with it, she was sure. A twenty-three-year age difference! They would eat it up. She had nightmares of how would they find out. She pictured some lowlife peeping Tom photographer who made his living from the trials and tribulations of celebrities, catching them leaving an out-of-the-way restaurant together. One picture could ruin her. Just one. And what would happen to her career? She could just wind up doing Tennessee Williams Off-Broadway. She was a self-made woman who had struggled hard for her career and her marriage, and she was determined not to throw it all away for erotic love.

Born and reared in New York's Hell's Kitchen, she worked her way out west as a waitress when she was sixteen: a golden-haired, blue-eyed beauty. By her twenty-eighth birthday she had become one of Hollywood's most celebrated young actresses. She was still considered a budding star when she shocked Hollywood and captured the heart of America, giving it all up to marry Elvin Rosenthal, who sat on the board of five of *Fortune*'s top twenty companies. Not since Grace Kelly had showbiz been so stunned. Against all odds—the movie star and the business mogul—the marriage was an unmitigated success. Grace stopped acting but appeared at hundreds of charity functions, chaired balls and gave exquisite parties for Elvin's business associates. Neither frivolous nor stupid, she was the perfect wife for him.

And he the perfect husband to her. He gave her a life of security, away from the frivolity and fickleness of Hollywood. He was a fine man, dedicated, faithful. And if she had sacrificed her career, she knew that Elvin sacrificed even greater for her.

Elvin Rosenthal was the eldest of five brothers. The Rosenthal family, which owned businesses all over the world, was comprised of forty-six members. Each brother had three or more children and grandchildren growing up and eagerly waiting to take over the reins of the family business.

Except for Elvin and Grace, who could have no children. When the doctor discovered it was Grace's problem and a hysterectomy soon followed, Elvin was supportive and cheerful. The following year, 1960, they adopted two children, Paul, a Chinese boy, and Eloisa, nine, an adorable Mexican child. Grace would always remember the year because it was exactly one decade and one month later that she lost both of them in a private plane crash on their way from school to meet her and Elvin in Lake Tahoe. Elvin never recovered from the shock. He himself died of a heart attack a year later. He left Grace a very wealthy, very lonely woman.

Grace returned to her career, shattered, and threw herself into her work.

And now this, this delightful boy sleeping next to her. In the end, she knew Bobby would have to go. Her own sense of propriety told her so. And the more she hung on, the worse it would be.

The front door slammed. Lenora had left.

He stuck another strawberry into his mouth and bit it off just below the stem. He was sitting up in bed next to her, naked under the blue satin sheet. Strawberries and fresh sour cream were his favorite breakfast, and Grace had asked Lenora to stock the kitchen with them at all times. A dollop of cream fell on the right side of his chest an inch above his nipple, and he left it there, waiting for Grace to wipe it off with a long finger and pop it into her mouth.

"When you were in The Club last night, did you hear the song 'Forbidden Kinds of Love'?"

"I'm not sure. How did it go?"

He began to hum it, off tune, then stopped and smiled. "Do you ever listen to the words of the songs?"

"Not really," she admitted, wanting to wipe off the cream, but holding herself back.

"I suppose you think I'm silly to like disco music," he said.

"Not at all."

"Do you think I should move to California? It's a lot safer to ride a motorcycle on the streets of California than it is here."

"I don't really know."

"I think I need a haircut. What do you think?"

Grace smiled again. There were some moments of an affair with a youngster that weren't all cream.

"C'mon, eat up," she told him. "Maybe you can beat it out of here before Lenora gets back with the groceries."

"How come?"

"She always shops on Monday."

"No, I mean how come I have to beat it for the maid?"

Grace felt puzzled for a minute. "Well, you know, so she can get in here to clean up."

Bobby looked into his sour cream again. "You know what I think? I think you're still ashamed about being seen with me."

"Ashamed?" Grace said. "It's not shame; it's a question of propriety. I wouldn't want my housekeeper to see me in bed with *any* man." That was true enough.

"I mean, who cares what anybody says as long as we get off on each other?"

Grace cringed a little inside. "I do . . . *get off* . . . with you, Bobby, but this relationship is very complicated for me."

"For both of us." He put the sour cream on the night table and leaned across the bed to take her hands. "I have great news. Maybe now you won't be so ashamed to be with me—"

"Bobby," she protested, "I'm not ashamed—"

"Shhh, listen a minute. I have a new job. I've gone legit. Ellison asked me to become his assistant last night. There's no pay at first, but I can still keep working at The Club for a little while and—"

Grace's somberness silenced Bobby.

"What's the matter? Aren't you happy? I thought you wanted me to get out of the discotheque and work toward something. This is exactly the kind of break I've been looking for."

She studied her folded hands for a moment and said, "Look, Bobby, I don't want to hurt your feelings, but I don't think it's a good job for you."

"Why not?"

"Because it's just too fishy. Why would one of the most famous designers in the world—who could have anybody as his assistant—ask an inexperienced bartender at a discotheque?"

Now Bobby *was* hurt, and it showed clearly on his face. "Maybe he thinks I'm bright. Maybe he thinks I have promise."

Grace tried to be soothing. "I wouldn't blame him. If he only got to know you, I'm sure he would think you're bright and have promise. Both are true. But I'm sure Ellison has no conception of that—or any interest in that either."

Bobby thought of Tinder Kaufman taunting him: "To admit they're after your ass is a denial of your own talent. And you think you're talented, don't you?"

"I think you're wrong," Bobby said stubbornly, "and anyway, I'm not about to *not* take the job."

"When were you supposed to start?"

"Today. In an hour."

"Today?" Grace was incredulous. She was surprised Ellison hadn't wanted him to go straight home with him. "Call him and say you're not coming in."

"I will not."

"Bobby, this is impossible. Two jobs?" He nodded. "I can't have you working for Ellison."

"What do you mean, you can't have me? It has nothing to do with you."

"It has very much to do with me. Do you know how embarrassing this could be if he found out you and I—" She couldn't word it. "That man is an infamous gossip. It would be all over New York that I was going out with a youngster."

"He wouldn't know."

"He would know. He would find out."

Bobby nodded as if he had just understood some great

mystery. He got out of bed and pulled on his jeans. "So that's it. It doesn't matter what I do for a living, does it? No matter what I do, to you I'm a youngster."

"That's not so."

"No, it is. At first you said we had to be secretive because of your career and because I was a bartender and how would that look, but it doesn't look bad if I work for a fashion designer, and now that's not good enough either."

"Bobby," she pleaded, growing more frustrated by the second with his naïveté, "it's just not *any* fashion designer. It's *Ellison*. He's a famous, bitchy, dangerous man. He's a notorious homosexual. The people who like him like him because he's so outrageous. It's not my style. And I wish it weren't your style either." She went to him and took his shoulders. His dark eyes were glistening black and cold. "As a friend, I implore you. It's not a good job. Don't insist on it."

"What do you want?" Bobby asked quietly and evenly. "Do you want to keep me? Keep me like a stud in a barn?"

Grace released his arms. "That's rude."

"It's no more rude than telling me who I can work for."

"And what if he finds out about *us*, what if—"

"Stop it!" Bobby shouted, putting on his shirt. "I'll do what I damn please! If it embarrasses you so fucking much to be seen with me, *don't see me!*"

She turned and walked to the dresser.

"Then maybe we shouldn't . . ." she began with her back toward him, her voice drifting off hesitantly.

"Shouldn't what?" Bobby challenged.

"Maybe we shouldn't see each other for a while," Grace said somberly.

"That's just fine with me," Bobby answered, pulling on his socks.

There was a long, tense silence in the room while Bobby finished getting dressed, taking a long time to tie his shoelaces. When it was apparent he was about to leave, Grace got up from her dressing chair and went to him. She tried to pull him to her, but he pulled away and kept his body stiff.

"Please, Bobby, reconsider," she implored softly.

"What am I to you, Grace? Muscles? Do you know how

humiliating it is to be just a body and not a person? Am I just a young boy you're screwing because you can't get it from guys your own age? Am I?"

That stung her as hard as if he had slapped her, and she felt a hot rush in her cheeks. She thought for a brief second of slapping him, but dramatics weren't her style. Anyway, she believed she had it coming, as if it were punishment for making herself vulnerable to someone so young in the first place.

"Yes, Bobby, I'm bored with men my own age. I'm bored with men who talk only of golf and baseball and smoke smelly cigars and try to put their hands on your knee in the back seats of taxis. Yes, I like your muscles. A lot. But I am not being serviced. I respond also to your heart and to your potential...." She tightened her robe and walked back to her dressing table. "So neither of us is at fault... nobody is used. But I have to admit that perhaps I've made a mistake. I find that I'm not up to the role I thought I could fill, in your life and in mine. If this relationship causes me public embarrassment... well, I really do not... need or love you enough to give myself over to you to the detriment of my career."

"So," Bobby said, nodding his head.

"I am the one who will suffer, Bobby. I will miss you more than you will miss me."

"Fat chance," he said, glaring at her.

"Did you understand anything I just said?" she cried. How she didn't want him to go!

"I understood it only all too well," Bobby said sadly. He turned and walked out the door.

Grace waited a moment, then decided to go after him. She rushed into the living room, but he was already out the front door. She could catch him waiting for the elevator in the hallway, but no sooner did she hear the sound of the elevator door opening and fling open her apartment door than she found Lenora standing before her.

"Mrs. Dunn! Am I glad to see you awake!"

Grace stopped in her tracks as the elevator doors closed with a final clank behind Bobby.

10

Jacky Mellon sat in a red velvet seat in the tenth row of the orchestra of the Janoff Theater, determined to take a short nap behind her big sunglasses, oblivious to the activity around her. A Broadway theatre in the throes of rehearsals for an opening is at once seedy and spectacular. Dirty, drafty, dramatic, the bare stage becoming the nucleus for one of the most intense collaborative experiences in the twentieth-century arts. The mounting of a live work on Broadway entails such tremendous technical, creative and social achievements it is often more complicated than the production of a major Hollywood movie, and the stage of the Janoff Theater on West Forty-sixth Street was frenzied with activity. Dozens of stagehands rolled scenery flats across the back of the stage on truck-sized dollies while a team of carpenters busily constructed a Mylar ramp that led into the orchestra. The lighting men were hanging and refocusing lights on thirty-foot ladders sprouting up around the stage. The entire chorus, nearly forty of them, were sprawled to one side of the stage and listening as Eddie Bernardo argued with the show's choreographer about a dance number.

She wrapped her gray cashmere shawl tighter around herself, shivering a little, wondering why it was impossible to get warm that morning. She wore a red satin turban to hide her unwashed hair and big black sunglasses, half the size of her face, with matching red frames to hide her bloodshot eyes. Aside from her being cold, exhausted and grumpy, her throat was so bruised it was impossible for her to sing. Glesnerovsky didn't get her home until after four in the morning, when they first sat in her car for another hour and talked. She thought he was sweet and intelligent, and she hoped that maybe she'd see him around sometime again. By the time she got upstairs and took off her makeup and took a sleeping pill it was nearly six in the morning, and she had had just three hours of sleep before rehearsals. It took her so long to get started that she had arrived an hour and forty minutes late at the theater and was too exhausted to rehearse and begged off with a headache in front of the whole cast. Jacky really wanted to go home and get back in bed, but Eddie grudgingly made her sit in the audience and watch.

"Coffee wagon!" a woman's froggy voice called behind Jacky.

Jacky looked up. Another pair of oversized sunglasses was looking down at her.

"I figured you'd need some picker-upper this morning, kitten," Alice La France said to her.

Her husband, Ken La France, was peering over her shoulder. "Screw the coffee," he said. "What you probably need is a little bit of the hair of the dog that bit you."

"Oh, God, the sanity boat has arrived," Jacky cried. "Thank goodness!"

Ken and Alice sat down on the aisle in the row ahead of her and began to pass out espresso laced with rum, cheese danish from Dumas and Empirin Compound. The La Frances were producers of *The Performance* and old buddies of Jacky's from her early days in New York. They were an adorable team who looked more like twins than husband and wife. They both were petite, nervous and full of verve. Alice had an inimitable froggy voice which rang out like a bullhorn and false eyelashes so thick she could hardly see through them. Ken was pixieish, cute, shrewd, and a real killer in business. A Jewish lawyer from Long Island, he had made millions in real estate under his real name, Ken Lefkowitz. On his forty-second birthday he changed his name to La France, moved to Manhattan, smoked pot and decided to become a Broadway producer.

The La Frances' first show was *Arthur,* a small, not-very-inventive off-Broadway musical about hot rods, teen-age love and the fifties. Fortunately the show was staged well, the props were flashy enough and the La Frances pushy enough to convince the Janoffs to let them bring their little show to Broadway.

The Janoffs, who justifiably had no respect for the La Frances' ability, insisted on 5 percent of the total profits of the show beyond the theater's net. *Arthur,* of course, is still running on Broadway. It has been transformed into a successful book, movie, illustrated novel, television series, cartoon and marketing device which have netted the La

Frances more than $150 million in nine years. The Janoffs made $7 million for nothing but a nod. Thus indebted to Ken and Alice, the Janoffs were allowing them the use of their flagship theater to produce *The Performance*.

Up on the stage the dance captains were demonstrating a step for the rest of the chorus and Eddie.

"Did our modern-day Michelangelo figure out how to get the disco dancers moving yet?" Alice asked.

"I guess not..." Jacky murmured, watching Eric Chomsky try to deal with Eddie. Chomsky was a small man with short cropped black hair and an agile body. By reputation, at least, he was considered the best choreographer in the theater. Alice and Ken insisted they were lucky to get him to work on the project with them. Eddie had precious little knowledge about the theater, and Chomsky was a noted director-choreographer on the Great White Way. He had skyrocketed to prominence five years before with his show *Dazzlin'*, an innovative and visionary musical that won both the Pulitzer and Tony prizes and inspired the rest of Broadway into a Renaissance around it. Chomsky was summarily rushed out to Hollywood with a carte blanche from every studio and independent producer in L.A. He took with him one of the girls from the *Dazzlin'* chorus, Merry Cooper. They were married in Las Vegas the day before Chomsky started to shoot his first feature film, *Heart and Mind*.

Seven months later the film was four months over schedule and $3 million over budget and Merry Cooper had flown back to New York to rejoin her lesbian lover. Chomsky had his film taken away from him and returned to New York in great disgrace amid rumors he would suffer a nervous breakdown. Jacky remembered passing through New York at the time, and Chomsky's nervous breakdown was a favorite cocktail topic. But Broadway is the last bastion of romantic fantasy and theater is fantasy and Chomsky had given them *Dazzlin'*. The theatrical community rallied loyally to his side and there were scores of plays for him to direct and eager backers and producers for any stage project he wanted to do.

What Chomsky wanted to do was a musical adaptation of an obscure poem by Robert W. Service called "The Cremation of Sam McGee," titled *Cremation*. The best that could be said about *Cremation* was that it came in on budget and Chomsky wasn't replaced, although the leading lady was—twice. It was a disaster that lasted seven days. Chomsky, it seemed, had staged the one show of his life. But there was still one aspect of his talent that was impeccable: dance.

When Ken and Alice came up with the large amounts of money Chomsky demanded to ease his ego about being relegated back to a choreographer, and Jacky herself called to ask him to do it, Chomsky relented and agreed— if his name was half as big as Jacky's on the credits. With a box.

It hadn't taken an hour into the first day of rehearsals before it became obvious that Eddie had absolutely no concept of how to use the proscenium stage. He saw it all as a large box, like a long shot in a movie. Chomsky worked hard to keep his mouth shut for as long as he could bear it and then gently offered Eddie some suggestions about the use of the stage in the theater. Eddie did not take to advice from his choreographer, particularly any offered in earshot of the cast, and it was only a matter of days before Eddie took to reminding Chomsky that his one outing on the motion-picture screen was an unreleased disaster. Soon each man declared a private war on the other, and it sometimes seemed that the battle of the two egos mattered more to them than the show itself.

It was always something, but the problem of the moment was that Eddie wanted the chorus to look as if they were dancing at a party in assorted styles and composures while Chomsky insisted that each couple be choreographed into a stylized version of the same dance.

"If they dance separately, it looks uncontrolled. We *control* the stage, not let dancers loose on it," Chomsky explained slowly to Eddie at the side of the stage.

"There is naturalism in theater, as there is in films," Eddie reminded Chomsky.

"No!" Chomsky shouted, pacing across the stage. "This is not a documentary film. If I'm not going to choreograph *all* the dancing, I want my name off the project."

"Off the project!" Eddie gasped.

"Or say exactly in the program which segments of the show I'm responsible for and which segments you're responsible for."

"You're a child!" Eddie shouted across the stage.

"*You're* a child!"

"Oh, God," Alice said, "Kenny, *do* something."

"Gentlemen!" Ken called meekly from the orchestra. The entire cast and crew turned to look at him, and Alice huddled near Jacky in the orchestra, the three of them in sunglasses. Chomsky and Eddie expectantly stood where they were, staring him down, daring him to interfere. Ken swallowed loudly and said, "Good morning," before he sat back down, defeated. Chomsky and Eddie triumphantly returned to arguing.

"Eddie must stop being so stubborn," Alice said.

"It's not Eddie; it's this disco music that's causing all the trouble," Jacky said protectively. *The Performance* was one of the first traditional Broadway shows to incorporate disco music as a serious part of the score. When Jacky first heard the idea, she was strongly against it. It was too trendy, too fashionable in the wrong kind of way. She spent two weeks trying to track down whose brilliant idea it was in the first place, and she thought she had it pinned on Alice, who was as trendy as anybody, but Chomsky came forward and told her the brutal truth.

A third of the show was being backed by Universal Records, almost $400,000 worth. This was not an unusual setup for a Broadway show, which was commonly financed by corporate entertainment companies in return for movie rights or cast album rights. In this case, Universal Records had also guaranteed an additional $275,000 budget to record the cast album—an unprecedented amount, but an easy investment to make back if the show was a hit. In return for this support, Universal got a small say; Jacky Mellon's records hadn't sold for a long time. Her last hit was from *Lateral Horizons*. The times had changed. Jacky was slowing down. In order for Universal to support the show in good faith, there had to be disco music with a composer of its choosing.

Jacky had no choice, and anyway, there *did* seem to her to be an appropriate place in the book for it. The show traced three generations of women, all of whom Jacky played. The grandmother is a Viennese opera singer at the turn of the century; her daughter becomes an American singing star with a big band and the grandchild is a Vegas chorus girl. The chorus girl finally gets her big break to star in a show, and the action reaches a climax when the girl gets to give one unbelievable, shattering performance and prove to herself forever that she is as good as her mother and grandmother were. The climactic Vegas scene was the perfect place for disco music.

After all, disco was selling records, and why shouldn't *she* sell a few records for once? And as long as it wasn't billed as a "disco musical," what could be so bad? She insisted there be a sufficient number of old-fashioned ballads and traditional Broadway production numbers. Rob Steiner, who had written "Love in My Life" for her, was hired to do the traditional part of the score. Steiner was considered one of the great show composers—of the fifties and sixties. When he wrote "Love in My Life," it was just the kind of schmaltzy, middle-of-the-road song that was still selling big on the radio—and already five years behind the times. Nowadays Steiner was an anachronism; he was still excellent at writing special material, but his concept of show music was strictly two decades old. Worse, the four ballads he allegedly wrote for *The Performance* had been retrieved from his trunk; he had written them many years before for a French parlor comedy that he had discarded. Jacky thought the songs sounded oddly baroque and wondered why; some of the lyrics about gazebos and quails didn't seem to fit into the book of *The Performance,* and it didn't help that Eddie was a foreigner and his ear for English idiom wasn't very good.

Universal hired Ralph Fabruzzi to write the disco music specially for her. Fabruzzi was a short, fat, jowly greaser from New Jersey, who thought he was Tchaikovsky because he churned out disco hits the way McDonald's sold hamburgers. In the record business he was known as Disco Doc because he had made millions revitalizing the careers of sagging singers with surefire, yet mediocre disco hits. Of course, Jacky didn't think he was going to do that for her; he was just a good songwriter. At the moment he sat at a piano on the stage, waiting for Eddie and Chomsky to get down to business. Eddie gave Fabruzzi the signal to begin playing, and he tinkled out a pretty little disco tune on the piano to accompany Eddie as he began to demonstrate the way he wanted the dancers to dance.

Jacky thought she heard the chorus giggling as Eddie boogied across the stage.

"Well, no wonder he doesn't want to go to The Club; he doesn't know how to dance," she told the La Frances mirthfully. "At least there's one thing I can teach him."

"I bet there are a few," Ken said. "Don't underrate yourself." He smiled at Alice.

"Tell her," Alice prodded.

"No, it's too premature," Ken said firmly.

"Tell me what! Oh, you've got to tell me, now!" Jacky begged, playfully tugging on Ken's lapels.

"Now, it's not definite," Alice warned her, her thick eyelashes beating excitedly against her cheeks, "so don't get carried away but I think we've made a deal to televise your opening-night party!"

Jacky let go of Ken's lapels and sank back into her seat. She didn't know what she felt about that except scared. "Do you really think that's such a good idea?" she asked. "I mean, what if the show is a flop?"

"Nonsense!" the La Frances scolded.

"The show is already a smash," Ken explained. "After all, we've already sold out through the summer. If you'd guarantee us more than four months, we could sell out longer. . . ."

"But *TV* . . ." Jacky moaned.

"Just listen to the idea, it's faaaabulous. A Jacky Mellon TV special called *The Performance: An Opening*. Network, NBC. Klieg lights, cameras, screaming fans, the works. We'll get a name talk-show host to emcee it, and we'll have dozens of celebrity interviews. It's the best publicity in the world for all of us. It'll be bigger than the *Grease* or *Saturday Night Fever* parties, which were only syndicated."

"I don't know. . . . What did Eddie say?"

"Eddie? Eddie has no authority in this area, kitten. It's *you* that matters."

"Listen, we tape the opening arrivals in front of the theater and broadcast *live* from The Club. We're trying to get Lorne Michaels to produce it for us."

"Who's he?"

"The guy who does *Saturday Night Live*."

"Big deal."

"And maybe a live fashion show of all the Ellison costumes in the show. Sounds hot?"

"Too hot."

"Not to worry, kitten, everything is wonderful."

"We're off to the meeting. Anything else we can do before we go?"

"No, just call later." Jacky made them promise as they went up the aisle. Trying not to worry, she leaned back into the seat and tucked a scuffed Capezio dance shoe into the opening between the seats in front of her, searching the stage for her "carrot." Her carrot was a young man sitting on a folding chair on the stage near the fire door. His legs were spread in front of him, causing the terry material of his orange pants to bag largely between his legs. He was young, handsome, with high cheekbones and limpid green eyes. Her mother had told her about carrots backstage in a dressing room in Australia. Jacky was only a teenager at the time and was exhausted being *shlepped* around from city to city, country to country. She wondered aloud how her mother managed to keep up the pace, let alone the interest.

"It gets very boring," Angela admitted, her head shaking nervously. "You know how I do it? I suppose you're old enough. You know how I sing the same songs every night? Break down at the same moment at the same time each show? I always make sure there's somebody around the show that I want to sleep with. Sometimes it's the dresser or one of the stage hands or even a chorus boy. Sometimes he's just an extra. Whoever the guy is, I'm kind of sweet on him, you know? I use him to get to work every day, like a carrot to get the donkey to move. When I need to feel emotion for an actor who smells of garlic in a love scene, I think about the carrot. The carrot gets me through a lot of shit, honey. But I never, never sleep with the guy until the show closes or the movie finishes shooting. Because then he would lose his whole allure, and you can't eat your carrot and have it, too."

Jacky spotted her carrot for *The Performance* during the first open call for auditions. He was in the crowd of dancers at the rehearsal studios, dressed in a red sweat shirt three sizes too small for him and a pair of tight jeans. She picked him out at thirty paces the minute she laid eyes on him. He was tall and had the perfect dancer's body, the kind of man that she always fantasized about fucking but the type that was never attracted to her. She took Chomsky aside during auditions and asked him to hire the boy in the red sweat shirt.

"But he can't dance," Chomsky whispered.

"For me, he's Baryshnikov," Jacky said. Chomsky wisely hired the boy.

Once rehearsals got under way Jacky found she had very little need of a carrot. Although the boy was fun to look at and fantasize about when she got bored, the daily drama of the production and her love for Eddie were enough to keep her interested in coming to the theater. And as far as being sexually satisfied, Eddie made her perfectly happy. There were, of course, those diversions, like the night before with Glesnerovsky, but for one more hour in bed with Eddie all the carrots and ballet dancers in the world could go to hell. The texture of Eddie's muscular body floated across her mind. She was able to close her eyes and smell and taste him across the theater, the electricity of it giving her that unbearable churning feeling in her groin.

There was nobody in the world for her like Eddie. Never before and never again would there be. Eddie made her feel complete, like a woman for the first time. She had never even known she had feminine wiles until she fell in love with Eddie. She had never thought about settling down and having a family until Eddie. But now she wanted a child, his child, and for the first time in many years the thought of giving up her career for something entered her mind.

Eddie was the first real man she had known in her life, and it had been a long time in coming. She had grown up an awkward and innocent little girl whose only impression of men was from her mother's impressive retinue of boyfriends and husbands. She had no memory of her own father, a would-be actor who had married Angela just before the Second World War and walked out on her when Jacky was less than a year old. He was killed later that year in a boating accident on the Gulf Coast. His parents were long dead, and the only thing Jacky ever knew about him was that he was from Milwaukee and that he had a good sense of humor and her mother was in love with him for a time. He was an enigma to her, the missing man in her life and a dark gap in her childhood. As far as father figures went she best remembered her mother's third husband, Jerry Plotkin, a rich, sweet Jewish TV producer, who stayed with them the longest of any of her mother's men—five years. There was a long succession of "uncles" with heavy colognes, and there were "steadies" and eventually two-week "visitors" and finally one-nighters. Most of them were broke; all of them were on the make.

There was only one constant in Jacky's young life, but that constant seemed as unshakable and steady as anything in the world to her: Angela. The men came and went, the scenery changed, they were poor and rich alternately, but Angela was always at her side, always there for her. Perhaps, Jacky would realize in later years, Angela was there too much, for at her mother's side she was also in her shadow, and Angela was a complex woman, an ill-equipped soldier in a war of her own devising. Warm and fun-loving, with an indomitable spirit and a destructive streak just as wide, she knew what was good for everybody else in the world except herself. Her career rose and fell according to her emotional state, which in turn depended on alcohol and drugs, but not her advice and wisdom, which she dispensed with regularity to every lost soul and groupie who came to adore her around the world.

Like Jacky, she was generous to a fault. When Angela had money, it belonged to all the people around her, too. When Angela could afford it, no expense was spared. Jacky was chauffeured in limousines, dressed in the best clothes and attended elite private schools. When times were especially good, shortly after Angela had made her spectacular "comeback" and won her unexpected third Academy Award, Jacky went on tour with her mother around the world with a private tutor and a retinue of servants.

In later and darker years, however, when Angela was unhirable and in debt, she and Jacky were attended to only by Suie Foster. Suie was a fussy, portly, no-nonsense black woman from Atlanta, Georgia, with a bottomless heart and the congeniality of a mess sergeant. Suie was a cornucopia of home remedies and homilies, a walking volume of the poor man's Mark Twain, straight from central casting—quite literally. Suie had applied for extra work at the MGM lot and was offered a job as Mellon's dresser. Suie was already in her late thirties, widowed and childless. From that first day working for Angela, Suie never left her side. Suie moved in with her, dressed her, cleaned the house, cooked and kept Angela together when she fell to pieces. Champagne or beer, salaried or not, Suie was there. When the men were gone, the booze dried up and the last pill popped, Suie was a trusted member of the family.

In bad times Suie became the last bastion of defense against all comers: truant officers, bill collectors, angry producers and their lawyers. Suie was also an important prop of prosperity the years they lived one step ahead of the bill collectors. Frequently they would live in splendid hotel suites, and Suie became an important part of the getaway team, smuggling clothing past unsuspecting desk clerks when they ran out on bills. It was also Suie who got Angela out of jail at the Beverly Hills sheriff's office for drunken driving and Suie who led the search for Angela after she had been missing for three days and Suie who discovered her downed out on Seconals in a little white house on Norma Drive in West Hollywood, listening to her own records over and over again with an alcoholic interior decorator dying of TB. And it was Suie who dressed Angela in the mornings and who made sure she passed out in the bed at night and didn't drown in the toilet bowl.

Once, when Angela was arrested by a California state trooper for possession of narcotics, the judge released her on bail in Suie's custody, but only if Angela agreed to consult a court-appointed psychiatrist for six months. Angela hated psychiatrists and scoffed at the idea. She was devastated when her lawyer told her she would have to comply or go to jail. Every week after, Suie would drive Angela to the psychiatrist's office in downtown Los Angeles with Jacky in the back seat, and the three of them would make up preposterous stories for her mother to tell the doctor.

At twenty, Jacky was still a virgin. She had dated only a handful of insipid young men from the neighborhood in Beverly Hills who were mostly curious about her famous mother. None of them had as much as put his hand on her breast. As far as Jacky knew, she was doomed to be an old maid, the perennial virgin daughter of Angela Mellon.

Naturally, it was her mother who introduced her to Maxwell Pudding. Angela probably would have married Maxwell herself if she weren't already married at the time. Angela adored and worshiped Maxwell and always considered him her own special discovery.

Angela met him in London, literally outside the stage door of the Palace Theater, where she was doing one of her farewell tours that seemed never to end. Maxwell was

standing in the alley of the theater when she arrived for
her matinee performance one Saturday, a bouquet of
garden flowers picked from his own English garden and an
English sheepdog, Toto, on a leash.

On Angela's leash was her fourth and final husband,
Alexander Garguilo. Garguilo was a fading Italian beauty
of forty-seven, a onetime internationally esteemed ladies'
hustler and high-class gigolo from Rome. Garguilo, with
his small, finely manicured mustache and highly styled
European-cut suits, was totally dedicated to Angela—and
dependent upon her. He was not very happy when Maxwell Pudding alighted on her at the stage door and gently
tried to discourage an introduction from taking place, but
something about the clear blue of Maxwell's eyes and his
wicked, wise smile drew Angela to him, and she insisted he
come into the theater with them.

In her dressing room she and Maxwell talked for hours.
They chatted about music, hairstyles and where to go on
the Riviera. Maxwell even entertained for her. He played a
very pleasant folkrock guitar and sang funny, cynical
songs about life and love that charmed Angela. Much to
Garguilo's consternation and jealous confusion Angela
had Maxwell to dinner three times that week in her suite
at the Savoy Hotel, and he became a backstage fixture, a
relaxing talisman against her stagefright.

The following month Angela was home in Los Angeles,
and she could not bear to be away from him. She borrowed an advance from an agent against a book of
memoirs that she was always intending to write and sent
Maxwell Pudding his first-class plane fare and even fare
for Toto. The boy and his dog arrived a week later in a
great flurry of excitement at Angela's house. Jacky was
there waiting.

She was sitting on the edge of a chair, pigeon-toed, an
awkward, uncomfortable girl with no comprehension of
feminine mystique. Maxwell, with his wise blue eyes and
beautiful lilting English accent, seemed a worldly and
knowledgeable older man to her. Angela encouraged the
relationship from the start. They took drives to the beach
for Malibu sunsets and drank too much wine at Musso &
Frank, and soon Angela arranged for them to borrow her
agent's house in Emerald Bay on a cliff overlooking the
ocean. The first morning they arrived, a fire crackling in
the fireplace, the glass patio windows coated with a thick

white smog that enveloped the house and beach, they made love on the living room floor and Jacky lost her virginity. The sex was tender and cautious and sweet, the embarrassed fumblings of two children discovering the delights of their own bodies.

When they announced their engagement two weeks later, Angela was ecsatic, as was Alexander Garguilo, who had disposed of not only Maxwell and his damn dog but Jacky to boot! Angela wanted Jacky's wedding to be the event of the year in Hollywood. *"Tout le monde"* was the way she insisted it be at the outdoor affair to be held in the backyard of the Bel-Air house. She insisted there be a dance floor suspended over the swimming pool, a small society orchestra, French service Boeuf au Jus, orchids from Hawaii and every film star in town.

The only problem was that Angela was again practically broke. She sent a sorrowful Alexander Garguilo to see her third husband, Jerry Plotkin, who was still producing TV sitcoms. Plotkin, who had nothing but disgust for Garguilo, who sat supplicatingly in his office, out of pity for Jacky wrote a check for $20,000 and paid for most of Jacky's wedding.

The bride and bridegroom wore white with yellow daisies in their hair, and John Phillips sang "California Dreaming" at the ceremony. Angela got drunk and fell off the raised dance floor and broke her ankle, an event that rated equal space in the newspapers with Jacky's marriage itself.

The newlyweds went off for a honeymoon to England, where Maxwell frequently left Jacky alone in their hotel suite while he went off to play with his old cronies. But once back in the United States, in New York, with Jacky Mellon as his wife, Maxwell Pudding became a minor celebrity himself and very attentive to his new wife. The two of them very suddenly found themselves in the New York social whirl, a kind of glittering tornado in which they were spun around from party to discotheque to party. Jacky and Maxwell became New York's *adorable au pair.* All New York wanted to meet Jacky to peer curiously at Angela Mellon's daughter to see if she had any of her mother's symptoms. Although nobody at *Women's Wear* thought the young couple had any taste in clothing, they latched onto them and photographed them everywhere. Maxwell accepted a few jobs playing society parties at Le

Club and Arthur, and it wasn't too long before he was offered a recording contract with Warner Brothers Records. The young marrieds jauntily moved back to Los Angeles and into a small apartment in Brentwood while Maxwell went into the studios to record his first album, *All the Right Moments*.

Jacky, bored, lay in the sun at her mother's house, eating Goldenberg's Peanut Chews, having erotic fantasies about men other than Maxwell. Maxwell had been kind and attentive enough since their London honeymoon, but he had stopped making love to her shortly after their move to New York, a fact that she objected to in spirit but not in deed. Maxwell had turned out to be a boring, repetitive lover who had no creativity in bed. Perhaps that was why Jacky was not at all surprised when Maxwell brought home a very handsome blond drummer from the studio one night and went out drinking with him, not to return until the next morning. He told Jacky he had passed out in the back seat of the car in a restaurant parking lot, but Jacky knew better. She wasn't her mother's daughter for nothing. In yet another week Maxwell and the blond drummer were out two or three nights a week, and Jacky complained.

"You'd like him, too, if you only got to know him," Maxwell told her wistfully. But that wasn't what Jacky wanted from her life. She moved back with her mother and Garguilo and filed for divorce.

"So be an actress, like your momma," her mother's agent, Betsey Flint, said to her one hot Sunday in the backyard of the Bel-Air house. Betsey was in her late fifties, a patient, practical woman who had taken over her mother's failing career five years before. Under the circumstances, she had done a miraculously good job.

"An actress? Me? Look at me," Jacky protested. She was greased with suntan oil and sweating. She had gained ten pounds since she left Maxwell.

"Don't be ridiculous. You're a fine-looking girl, and you could have a career. Your momma said that when you were a little girl, that's all you ever talked about doing."

"At the time I wanted to be like Momma," Jacky said, her eyes closed.

"And you sing. You sing wonderfully. And you probably act just as good as your momma. Acting is an in-

herited talent. Why don't you let me get you a part in
something to keep you busy?"

Jacky didn't expect the part in something to be the
leading role in a low-budget film about a doomed college
love affair, *The Keening Winds*. With her mother's proud
encouragement Jacky screen-tested and won the part. The
thought of being a real actress galvanized her as nothing
had before. She dieted, exercised, and studied dance and
acting. She immediately forgot about Maxwell and lost
herself in the film.

The script was a tender little love story about a not-
very-bright midwestern girl on a special state grant at a
big-city university. At the university's business school she
meets and falls in love with a handsome metropolitan boy
whose father is a millionaire industrialist. Although the
handsome young male lead who starred opposite her was
never heard from again, the film made Jacky into an
overnight star. Jacky's part was a gem, the kind actresses
wait years for, and she played it to the hilt, with perfect
nuance and pathos. Her average looks were so endearing
on the screen the audiences practically leaped out of their
seats to hug her. And Jacky's eight-minute monologue at
the movie's denouement remains a classic of modern
cinema. In a static camera shot Jacky sits at a bare wooden
table in the pantry of the boy's parents' mansion and tells
them not only that their son has just been killed in a car
accident but that she is carrying his child.

Hollywood and the nation rallied to Jacky as the under-
dog of the year. Not since Dustin Hoffman in *The Gradu-
ate* did a *shlep* have so much public appeal. What had first
sounded like a scheme to cash in on her famous mother
turned out to be the potential talent find of the decade. But
even more surprised than the public, critics and columnists
was Jacky herself.

The four months that followed the release of *The
Keening Winds* was the best time Jacky ever had with her
mother. Jacky's sudden success—and income—delighted
Angela so much it seemed to take a load of responsibility
away from her. Jacky was suddenly bankable, and just for
guaranteeing a production company a movie sometime in
the next two years, she was offered a million-dollar contract. Angela blossomed. She cut down on her alcohol
until she was at least a presentable drunk and kicked
barbiturates. There was talk of her going back to work,

doing a small part in a good movie. Jacky and Angela often spent the days in Laguna together with Garguilo and Maxwell Pudding or had brunches poolside at the Bel-Air house with Suie clucking happily around them. For a short time, Jacky felt like an adult with a family of sorts.

They were on their way to a dress fitting in Angela's station wagon, Suie in the back seat, when Angela first complained of a harsh burning feeling in her stomach. Later that day Suie tried to cure the pain with some home remedy of starches and corn syrups, but the pain kept up for a few days and eventually was accompanied by a strange sinking sensation that made Angela sick to her stomach all the time. Finally, Angela checked herself into Cedars of Sinai for what was expected to be some old drug-abuse related problem, like liver damage. She wasn't in the hospital eight hours when they discovered her white blood count soaring. Two days later her diagnosis became final: leukemic carcinogenai of white blood cells. They gave her six months to live, maybe longer with the proper radiation cobalt drinks they could give her at Memorial Hospital in New York. The next day Angela flew there, where she checked into the Regency Hotel, a grief-stricken Alexander by her side.

The next night, at two in the morning, the phone woke Jacky, the shrill ringing like an arrow in her chest. She was alert by the time the receiver was at her ear. Her mother's slim voice crackled like a metallic thread over the long-distance line.

"Hello, Jacky?"

"What's the matter, Momma?" Jacky asked.

"It's five o'clock in the morning here, and I miss you," Angela said quietly.

"Is Alexander with you?"

"He's here. He's asleep in the other room, poor dear. He's exhausted."

"Why aren't you in bed, Momma?" Jacky asked, lighting a cigarette from the bed table without turning on a lamp. The pool glittered in the moonlight below her bedroom window.

"I had that drink today, Jacky, that cobalt glue. It was horrible. I can't take it."

"But it can help you, Momma. You have to drink it."

Angela was quiet for a moment. Then she said, "I love you, princess," and hung up.

Suie knocked on her door four hours later. It was dawn and smoggy out. "Miss Betsey's here to see you," Suie called.

That was odd, Jacky thought, Betsey here so early. She quickly wrapped a robe around herself and bounded down into the kitchen. Suie was making a pot of coffee, and Betsey was standing at the counter. Jacky gave her a perfunctory kiss on the cheek.

"What's wrong?" she asked. Betsey motioned for her to sit on a stool and took her hands at the counter. "It's Mother, isn't it?"

Betsey nodded somberly. "Momma saved herself and the rest of us a lot of pain this morning," she explained. "It's just like her to have yet another twist ending. Alexander found her in the hotel bedroom when he woke up. She took an overdose of Tuinals—finished the whole bottle of them. He called an ambulance, and they tried to pump her stomach, but this time her heart just gave out before they could bring her to. She was dead on arrival at the hospital."

They flew Angela's body back to Los Angeles, where Jacky hoped to have a quiet funeral for her, but she soon realized it was not her decision. Angela Mellon belonged to her public as much as she did to Jacky and her funeral would be for them also. There were news crews at the airport to photograph the coffin's being unloaded from the plane, and reporters and cameramen from all over the world descended on the funeral parlor the next day. The cortege route to Forest Lawn was lined with thousands of fans. All day long the radio played nothing but Angela Mellon tunes. And at the grave site Maxwell Pudding sat in a metal folding chair and sobbed and wailed while Jacky quietly listened to them eulogize her momma for the first of many times.

Not two hours after the services Jacky was back in the Bel-Air house with Betsey Flint, Suie, Alexander Garguilo, playing the suffering widower, Maxwell Pudding and three estate lawyers. They sat around the dining-room table, and Suie served coffee while the lawyers read her mother's will and explained the situation Angela had left Jacky in. The house was heavily mortgaged and two months behind in payments. The bank was about to take it back, but it would have to hurry to beat the federal government to it;

Angela was $55,000 in arrears in taxes—and that had nothing to do with the penalties. More statistics: Angela Mellon owed bills at every florist, drugstore and Liquor Locker in Los Angeles. She owed one Beverly Hills hairdresser $8,000 alone. Even the living-room furniture, it turned out, was rented and about to be repossessed for nonpayment. Naturally there was no life insurance; Angela's drug problems had long ago made her uninsurable.

Alexander Garguilo was inconsolable. The realization that he was broke and out in the cold was almost too much for the little man. He got the chills and almost passed out, and Suie laid him out on the sofa in the living room and gave him some of her special tea.

Jacky had two choices. She could let it all take its course—the house repossessed, the furniture repossessed, her mother's reputation wrecked all over Hollywood—or she could pay all the bills and wipe herself out.

She was alive. She could start over. Angela was dead, and the least she could do for her was to clear her name. By the time Jacky was finished paying off creditors and signing notes, she was virtually broke.

But she was freed. Free not to repeat her mother's mistakes and free from being Angela Mellon's daughter. Or so she thought.

She began to look for a niche she was comfortable in, but she couldn't seem to find her right style. She felt ill at ease no matter what she was wearing or how her hair was cut and combed. She went through a series of life-styles like disguises. She tried being a Santa Monica hippie for a while, but she loved junk food too much to eat macrobiotics, and smoking pot made her nervous. She experimented with the Beverly Hills natural look, but she wasn't gaunt and blond and tan and didn't play tennis or surf or even like Bob Evans; Jacky was medium short and dark and needed exercise, and she got very nervous around famous people like Bob Evans, and she still got stomach cramps. She had dozens of movie offers and read hundreds of scripts but was too frightened to choose one.

Finally, Betsey Flint recommended she see a Hollywood doctor named Dean Purdy. Purdy was a trendy analyst who was having a great deal of success with actors, rock stars and various studio executives. It was said that Purdy ran his own psychiatric studio, redoing personalities and sagging careers the way plastic surgeons reconstructed

faces. Purdy was more of a groupie than an analyst and
often moved in with clients for a close-up look at their
glamorous lives. Jacky fortunately was spared this because
Purdy was too involved with a big-bosomed country western singer who was busy shooting heroin. But after two
dozen sessions at $150 each Purdy's advice to Jacky was
that she go out and *buy* a new image, just hire the very
best advisers in the business to transform herself into
whatever it was she wanted to be.

So she hired the very best. Way Bandy studied her face
for an hour before he decided on her new makeup. It
made her large eyes even larger and emphasized her
pouting lower lip. He spent another two days teaching
Jacky how to put it on, how to tweeze her eyebrows and
how to bring up her cheekbones. Kenneth flew to Beverly
Hills with an array of wigs for Jacky to choose a new
hairdo for her difficult melon-shaped head. Kenneth
straightened her hair into a chin-length bob with fluffy
forehead bangs. Her nose was tipped by Dr. Ralph Gold-
stone, a Century City cosmetic surgeon who performed the
operation so she would photograph better without notice-
ably changing her face. At long last the homely young
ingenue was slowly turning into a glamorous leading lady.

At this point Jacky's search finally ended for the right
property to follow *The Keening Winds*. It had been under
their noses for a long time: a musical version of *Lateral
Horizons*, the George Cukor picture of 1932 that had
catapulted Cary Grant and Carole Lombard to superstar-
dom. Bob Evans had bought the property years before but
never considered doing it as a musical until Peter Allen
and Carol Bayer Sager suggested two songs for it. When
Jacky agreed she would be interested in doing it, Evans
had them write ten more. After much negotiations, it was
decided that the new script would be hand-tailored for
Jacky by Sterling Silliphant. Paddy Chayevsky graciously
agreed to do rewrites. Dustin Hoffman and Jon Voight,
who had worked so brilliantly together in *Midnight Cowboy*, were her costars. At the last minute Arthur Penn
had a change in schedules and was available to direct.

Jacky played a poor Latvian cleaning girl, who through
fate, fun and fortune is hurtled to international stardom as
a funny-faced Parisian model and eventually marries a
prince. They shot all over Europe, and from the moment
they turned on the cameras it was magic.

Lateral Horizons turned out to be the top grossing film of the previous five years. The title song was the number one hit in thirty-six countries. The movie sound track was the largest-selling in the history of Columbia Records. Even Jacky's costuming started a trend, a very Eastern European peasant style popular for a few seasons, called the Horizon style.

Newsweek did a cover story on her, and after that winning an Academy Award nomination for "Best Actress" was easy. At the time of the award votings she was enormously popular in Hollywood and everyone expected her to win. Even Jacky herself was surprised when she lost the Oscar to Audrey Hepburn. But you couldn't take it away from Jacky. She had exploded on the screen as the biggest female star of the year. And she got rich. Money seemed to flow to her, from the film, from the record, from everywhere. She was suddenly richer than her mother had ever dreamed of becoming. And popular! Everybody wanted to meet her, get to know her, brush up against her at parties. Every producer in town wanted her to star in his next picture. Jacky Mellon had come of age.

Now she needed a man.

She spent the next few years in search of one, but the supply was scarce. Jacky didn't want a movie star; she wanted a Beverly Hills dentist who would insist she give up her career in five years and have kids. It was hokey and old-fashioned, but she hadn't been fooled by her mother's glamorous and empty life. Yet it wasn't so easy. Jacky had no social life in the ordinary sense, no way to meet regular people. Her world had always been the show business world, and although she knew it was no place to look for a husband, she was drawn further and further into it. Somewhere along the line she fell in with a fast crowd, a trendy Hollywood bunch, and the dream of a house and picket fence faded behind her. Her new crowd didn't give her much time to think. They were a show business group of people in their twenties with many things in common: top box-office draw, new money in their pockets and a yen to drive their foreign cars too fast. She had few close friends; nobody seemed to stay in one place too long. Along the way she met Beatty, Nicholson and Polanski, but they had no interest in her. She hit Puerto Vallarta, Southampton and Aspen, where she learned to make a good café Jèrôme, yet she never once fell in love.

"Go back to work, Jacky," Betsey Flint told her. "You can't be on a full-time search to get hitched. It's not normal. Anyway, you know it's true that you find somebody when you're not looking. And what about your career? It's time to make another movie and show them you can do it again!"

Nobody expected *Presidential Cabinet* to be as good as *Lateral Horizons*, or even half as good, but for it to turn out to be one of the biggest bombs in movie history was a great scandal. A mediocre slapstick comedy that cost the studio $17 million before advertising, it starred Jacky in the implausible role of the First Lady, garnered 100 percent bad reviews and fell dead at the box office its first week. Out of pity for its stars the studio withdrew it from distribution in theaters and sold it to cable TV and a network for a special.

Jacky nervously laughed off the failure and started smoking a pack more cigarettes a day.

She started eating and drinking more, too, and her girlish figure was soon coated with a layer of pudge. More frequently than not she got tipped on grass and booze, and one night, driving down from a party in Benedict Canyon, she wrapped her red Porsche around a tree and broke her collarbone. Betsey Flint, visiting her in the hospital the next day, was not pleased.

"You know what this is? Deteriorating symptoms of Angela Mellon disease . . ." she told Jacky.

"All this is a simple car accident, Betsey. Don't blow it up. You know how I hate people who predict doom."

"Honey, I know the symptoms, and you're on your way. Something is eating at you."

"I'm lonely."

"We're all lonely. Look, why don't you try a change of pace, get away from the old crowd?"

"And go where?"

"Paris. For six months. Or London."

"Paris and London? My God, who would I know there?"

"That's exactly the point. Nobody."

"It's too far."

"Live in New York then. It's only four hours away."

So Jacky moved to New York. She hadn't been to New York in years, not since she had been there with Maxwell. She intended to be anonymous, to get lost in the great crush of humanity she had always heard about. But New York had not yet tasted Jacky Mellon, movie star, and it afforded her anything but anonymity. Chubby, neurotic, slightly demented Jacky was a delicious drink for the sharp and thirsty tastebuds of New Yorkers. From the moment she moved into a leased apartment on Park and Seventy-fourth Street she was swamped with invitations to parties, art openings, lunches and fashion shows, and Jacky just couldn't say no.

She had been in New York three nights when she met Ellison. He spotted her at a Lowell Nesbitt opening at the Andrew Crispo Gallery, standing in the corner, pressed against the wall by photographers and curious fans. Dressed in black pants and white blouse, she looked the Poor Little Matchgirl, intimidated by everything around her. Her mouth hung open, and her head swung nervously from side to side. She was like a helpless baby chick, and his heart went out to her like a mother hen. He swooped down on her, rescued her from the crush of people and took her off into the gallery's private office, where it was quiet. Strangely powerful, hypnotic and witty, he had her giggling in a matter of minutes, but she was with him for an hour before it dawned on her exactly who he was. He had a stunningly satirical sense of humor and seemed to know about everything and everybody in New York. Soon he was suggesting a whole new look for her, and he insisted they both go to his showroom that very moment so she could try on some of his newest creations. He took her out to his waiting limousine, and she realized she had left two people behind at the gallery.

"I can't leave. I have two friends waiting for me upstairs," Jacky said.

"Darling, you're a star," he said, shaking his head increduously. "All New York is waiting in line for you. Two more won't make any difference."

And she was his forever.

Manhattan, as Ellison unfolded it before her, was a glittering, elegant kingdom, like stepping inside the diorama of a crystalline Easter egg. It was a far cry from the party scene she had known with Maxwell Pudding. New York was electric, exhilarating and exhausting. And no matter how many tinsel Hollywood premieres Jacky had been to with her mother, not one of them had the glamor, drama or do-or-die tension of a Broadway opening night.

In California money was used to be ostentatious; the rich in New York used money to achieve a quiet kind of elegance. Although the women were modernly beautiful in California, in New York they had classic style and timeless grace. At Ellison's side she dined with senators and prime ministers. She chatted with princesses and countesses and diplomats. She met men who ran countries and controlled empires. She felt the pulse of the world rushing around her, and the movie-light glow of her native Los Angeles began to seem pale and dim.

But she had to return there to make movies, and return she did to make two more movies in a row. They were surefire, couldn't-miss hits, bolstered by top-name directors and costars, but Jacky just couldn't draw the crowds to the movie theaters. And both parts were similar, too similar, to *Lateral Horizons*. It soon became clear that Jacky wasn't able to do more than that one role singing the same kinds of heart-wrenching, I'll-Face-the-World-Alone-To-morrow songs that had started her off. Between the movies and the men the years drifted by, and Jacky, without even noticing it, was gently touched by the deft hand of failure. She never even noticed how far downhill her career had gone until it was too late; she seemed to always be in the papers and she never needed money; the casinos were happy to pay her $250,000 a week to headline in Las Vegas whenever she wanted.

And in between, in New York and L.A., there was distraction. A kind of madness. A frenzied carousel.

And one day she woke up and she was thirty-two years old and she was alone and empty. And then she met Eddie Bernardo.

11

"Would you like a *Post?*" a voice asked Jacky.

Jacky thought for a moment she might have dozed off, she was so far away. She looked up from her seat in the theater, and Nancy Beale, Eddie's secretary, was smiling down at her with her perfect pearly white teeth. Nancy spent her day trailing after Eddie at a respectful distance, tending to the details of his life and the show. Nancy was so solicitous of him that sometimes Jacky was a little annoyed with the girl. It wasn't jealousy she felt exactly, just a sense of mistrust, as if the girl were Eve Harrington in *All About Eve.* Now Nancy stood in the aisle, holding a copy of the *Post* in front of her.

"Yes, of course, thank you," Jacky said, sitting up. She swallowed hard, her mouth dry and cottony, and leafed through the paper, turning to "Page Six" and the columns. The first thing that hit her eye was a headline: DISCO SCANDAL. She started to read the story only to find it was about a discotheque in Washington involving foreign diplomats. Thank God nobody she knew. She was looking at the opposite page to read the names in heavy type in Jack Martin's column when her eyes passed an oddly familiar scene. There was a small moment in time when all the world paused while it dawned on Jacky exactly what the scene was. The caption under the picture seemed to ring out in the theater: HORAY PRANN HELPS JACKY MELON HIGHER!

A hot flush rushed through her body, overwhelming her so she couldn't stop herself from exhaling loudly, as if she had been punched in the stomach.

There was a photograph of her and Horay on the dance floor at The Club.

"Is anything the matter?" Nancy Beale asked Jacky, who looked up from her seat to find the secretary staring at the newspaper page over her shoulder. Jacky slammed the paper shut and sad bolt upright.

"Not a thing," Jacky said, her head snapping nervously to the side.

Nancy Beale knelt in the aisle next to her till their eyes were level. "If there's anything I can do, you tell me," she said.

Jacky wondered if Nancy had already read the column. Yes, there was one thing she could do, help keep the paper away from Eddie!

"There's nothing you can do," Jacky told her coldly. She didn't like this woman *one bit*. If she would only stop being so unctiously solicitous and get the hell away from her, she'd be able to open up the paper again and read the goddamned thing. But before Jacky could shoo the girl away, the activity onstage came to a halt. Eddie was calling for a lunch break, and the indolent cast burst into activity. As they scurried off, Eddie athletically jumped off the stage into the orchestra and strode up the aisle with his assistant director, Mickey Cowell, trailing behind. Cowell was a purebred flunky and yes-man, carrying a clean white shirt for Eddie, who was drenched in perspiration. Eddie unbuttoned his shirt and pulled it away from his ribs as he came up the aisle. He leaned over Jacky's seat to kiss her, and his familiar sweaty musk filled her nostrils and made her loins throb. She opened her mouth to kiss him deeply, but the kiss he gave her was a perfunctory public kiss.

"I'm starving," Jacky said, standing up, hiding the *Post* with her pocketbook. "I made lunch reservations for us at Quo Vadis. Just the two of us." And everybody else she knew in New York.

"Ah, my sweet," Eddie said, "lunch is only an hour and a half long, and I have so many things to do." He took off his shirt to reveal his thickly muscled chest. A cord of thick black hair ran from his solar plexus to his navel, disappearing into his pants. Jacky sucked her breath in quietly.

"I guess I have to eat alone," she said, hoping to make him feel guilty.

"Why don't you come with me?" Eddie suggested. "I have a meeting with the accountants in ten minutes, but then I'm going to jog. Why don't we jog together? It's better to jog than eat, no? What do you need lunch for?"

The thought of jogging when Jacky was so sleepy and chilled irked her. Where did Eddie get this impossible energy from? "Jog in the rain?" she asked sweetly.

"Of course. Runners in the rain." He took her hand and walked up the aisle. She tucked the *Post* tightly under her arm. "Jacky, my darling, you're going to be the prettiest, skinniest star on Broadway. That's what I want for you. Do you think?" Eddie always asked, "Do you think?" when he wanted to be reassured.

Jacky looked up into his eyes. They were moist and hopeful, like a child's. "Yes, of course," she said. She would jog to please Eddie. She would do anything to please Eddie. Her life hadn't begun until she had met him.

"All right, then," she said, so happy for a moment that she choked on her words and tears welled in her eyes. "You meet with your accountants and meet me in front of the Olympic Tower in half an hour. OK? I'm going to put on some jogging clothes."

Eddie pecked her on the forehead as if she were a good little girl.

"Give me the *Post* to read in the car," he asked as they walked through the theater lobby, with Mickey Cowell and Nancy Beale trailing behind them.

"*No*," Jacky said adamantly, then softening: "I'm not through."

"I'll get you another," Nancy Beale offered, flashing a victorious smile at Jacky.

That bitch, Jacky thought. She knows. What a cunt. I'll get her.

Jacky stood by helplessly as Eddie hailed her a taxi to go home and change, while Nancy went off diligently to find Eddie another copy of the *Post*.

She had sublet an apartment on the twenty-ninth floor of the Olympic Tower building on Fifth Avenue and Fifty-second Street. Mary Gavin got the apartment for her as a favor from a Texas oil millionaire who kept the place as a New York pied-à-terre. It was the perfect location for her: central, chic and safe. Aristotle Onassis had built the sleek black glass monolith that rose majestically above the Gothic spires of St. Patrick's Cathedral. Even with the rain, with her view of the city below masked in a light blue mist, the scene from her window was awe-inspiring. Low clouds of fog clung to the spires of the cathedral below, swirling in the spring wind.

The bed was covered in a sable throw and littered with

different outfits. As Jacky stood in front of the full-length mirrors that lined the folding closet doors, she knew she looked stunning. She was wearing a one-piece red terry-cloth jump suit with beige leather piping down each arm and leg. The piping was set off by the deep rich beige of her running shoes, and for that touch of the outrageous Jacky had put on a matching chocolate brown cap, with just enough of a rounded peak to keep the rain out of her eyes. She added a wisp of blush to her cheeks to look warm and glowing in the damp cold.

Downstairs in the lobby she waited just inside the glass doors for Eddie to pick her up. She looked out at the puddles in the street. The rain had let up a little, but it was still not ideal weather for jogging, and she was tired and cranky. For a moment she was tempted to rush back upstairs to the bedroom drawer where she hid her vial of cocaine. But it was better that she save it for later. There were only two, maybe three snorts left in the bottle, and that would be the end of it until *The Performance* opened. She should at least save some until before dinner at Ellison's, when she would really need the energy. Actually, if she could always hold off using it until after dark, there was no need for her to stop altogether. Using a little coke at night, she reasoned, wasn't any worse than having a few cocktails every evening. Hell, she was kidding herself; if she had the coke, she did it all day, any hour, anytime. Resolutely, when she finished off the little left upstairs, that was it. Definitely.

Eddie's limousine pulled up outside the building, the pellets of rain beading off the shiny black surface. The rear door flung open, and Eddie got out. He had already changed into a royal blue running outfit and sneakers.

Jacky froze in terror; there was a copy of the *Post* in his hand. This was the showdown. She tried to compose herself with something funny and loving to deflect his torrent of angry accusations when he suddenly opened the paper and held it above his head as he dashed through the rain and into the lobby. Jacky held her breath until he spoke.

"Let's go," he said curtly. She had no idea what mood he was in. There was no message from the expression on his face.

She looked down at the wet *Post* in his hand as the doorman held the door open for them.

"Did you read that?" she asked. He held it above them as they dashed into the car.

"No. I haven't had time," Eddie said.

Gratefully Jacky climbed into the car after him and nonchalantly took the paper away from him and tossed it into the street before closing the car door. As the limousine pulled away from the curb the paper sank into the gutter and was drenched with the cold spring rain.

The car crawled up Sixth Avenue to Central Park. Across the wide streets, flooded with the rain, a bobbing sea of umbrellas scurried wildly across the street, pedestrians unsuccessfully trying to avoid the tidal wave of water splashed by passing taxis. The traffic broke at Fifty-seventh Street, and the limousine surged into the park drive, winding away from midtown into a country setting. Central Park was at an odd moment in its spring transformation. The trees, still wiry, uncovered branches, were just lightly budded with the promise of green summer. The park looked clear and fresh. It was deserted of people except for the silent stream of traffic, a path of headlights cutting through the wet mist as they sailed around the drive.

Jacky held Eddie's hand in the back seat of the car and looked silently out the window, counting her blessings, content just to be there with someone she finally, truly, loved. Along the Seventy-second Street transverse the driver pulled into a temporary parking space and left the engine running.

"Ready?" Eddie asked her. Jacky nodded, feeling as if she were about to jump out of a plane with no parachute. "Then let's go!" Eddie shouted, bolting from the purring car into the pouring rain. Jacky tumbled out after him into the wet. The pellets were chilly and cutting, but after she had run a few hundred yards, she hardly felt it at all for the pain in her legs and aching in her chest. She ran as fast as possible, and Eddie slowed up alongside her. All she could hear was the squoosh, squoosh of their sneakers in the rain. Unexpectedly a car swerved around the corner, piled deep into a mammouth puddle and showered them in a wave of dirty rainwater.

"Yuuuch!" Jacky yelled, wiping the water out of her eyes. "I'll get polio."

"Keep running, keep running," Eddie encouraged, trotting back for her and taking her under his arm.

"Can we talk during this?" Jacky asked him, gasping for breath.

"Talk while jogging?" Eddie asked, "Sure, if you can talk, talk."

"I can't even breathe," Jacky admitted. They jogged another hundred paces, and Jacky stopped to double over.

Eddie jogged back to her, yelling, "Breathe! *Stugotz!* Breathe through your mouth, not your nose!"

She managed another ten feet before she thought her lungs would collapse. For a moment she even contemplated sitting down in a puddle on the path just until she regained her composure. Eddie finally realized it was hopeless, and he stopped jogging and walked back to where she was leaning over, hands on her knees, trying to breathe.

"No more, no more," she finally managed to gasp, clutching at him for support.

Eddie smiled and hugged her to him tightly. "All right. No more torture."

He walked her up the path to a little mound of earth behind the benches. The skyline of Central Park West was dotted with the warm yellow lights of the sprawling apartment buildings. The towers and penthouses looked like medieval castle turrets looming over the trees of the park. Jacky felt euphoric, light-headed from the running, clear for a moment. New York swirled around her and at once came to an abrupt crystalline halt. Eddie pulled her roughly to him and kissed her fiercely on the lips, clutching her body to his. They stood there for a long time, oblivious to the curious people peering at them from passing cars or the cold rain soaking into their clothing as his kisses took away what little breath she had left.

"Can we talk during this?" Jacky asked him, gasping for

12

Bobby Cassidy glanced down at his Rolex Oyster watch. He could hardly believe it; it was two-thirty in the afternoon already, and it seemed like only ten minutes in the most fascinating and arduous day of his life. He had just finished a delicious lunch of watercress salad and cucumber soup with Ellison and his staff in Ellison's private offices. A maid in a black uniform and white apron was clearing dishes to a silver cart. Ellison sat silently at the head of the table, rolling what appeared to be tons of thousands of dollars' worth of precious stones around in his hand.

"They help me digest my food," he explained.

Bobby didn't know what to expect next. Ellison was the most extraordinary man he had ever met. He had arrived at Ellison's Seventh Avenue office promptly at ten. On the thirty-seventh floor he stepped out in an ocean of rust brown carpeting monogrammed with a giant gold *E* every square foot, the walls floor-to-ceiling glass, overlooking the southern part of Manhattan, the World Trade Center's twin peaks looming up above everything else in the distance. The receptionist took his name, and he was asked to take a seat on the reception-room sofa. A long time seemed to go by while he leafed through an old copy of *Women's Wear Daily*. Suddenly the inner office doors burst open, and he was set upon by a brusque woman in her mid-forties, her blond hair pinned businesslike on top of her head, a pencil stuck behind her left ear.

"Are you here for El?" she asked him. Bobby nodded. She looked him up and down. "Then you must be breakfast."

She turned and walked back through the doors, and Bobby, a little confused and a lot put off, followed her, wondering how he was supposed to take the breakfast remark. For the moment he shrugged it away and cooperatively followed the woman into the main design room. The room was a field of frenzied activity. To one side a flock of tall, exotic models were making quick changes of outfits behind a makeshift dressing curtain while salesmen from fabric houses hawked their goods to Ellison's textile buyers. The walls were covered with corkboards pinned with hand-colored sketches of fabric patterns stuck to swatches of matching fabrics. Large bolts of material were strewn about the room. A vast cutting table as big as four Ping-Pong tables stood in the middle of the room, littered with tissue-paper designs. A photographer and reporter from *Women's Wear Daily* chain-smoked cigarettes and drank black coffee while a rack of clothing to be photographed for the next day's edition was pressed.

"Ellison said you'd be coming this morning, but I didn't think you'd be so punctual," the woman leading Bobby told him over her shoulder. "Most of them aren't."

That was enough. Bobby tapped her on the shoulder and stopped dead in his tracks. The woman turned and put her hands on her hips defiantly. "Are you trying to give me the impression that this job won't last?" Bobby said loudly to be heard over the din. He hadn't meant to ask quite so loudly because several people stopped what they were doing and waited for the woman's answer.

She studied him hard for a moment and said, "Smart boy. You might just make it till lunchtime."

"I might have you for dinner," Bobby said. Satisfied, the room went back to its business.

"Are we going to be friends?" she asked. "Because if not, you're in deep water, I promise you."

Bobby held his hand out to her. "I need to know your name if I'm to be your friend."

The lady shook his hand and introduced herself as Pat Kelly. Pat was Ellison's crackerjack, no-nonsense first assistant. Along with a man named Larry Gatsby, she ran Ellison's daily business life. Years ago, when she was younger, she had once been an Ellison runway model, making $50,000 a year. But she fell in love with a fashion photographer, got married and foolishly left the profession to rear a child before the marriage crumbled eight years later, leaving Pat twenty-five pounds heavier with a child in tow. When Pat tried to go back to work modeling, no one would have her, and Ellison, who liked her balls and style, offered her a job as his assistant.

Pat led Bobby into a small office where Larry Gatsby was typing a memo to the sheet division. He was in his mid-thirties, had a devilish twinkle in his eye and large, round glasses. To Bobby's amazement, he and Pat were wearing the exact same outfit: black pants with a red ribbing down the outer leg and a black top with red stitching across the yoke and buttonholes. It was like some sort of Ellison uniform. He wondered if he'd be expected to wear one, too. He wouldn't. He just wouldn't.

"Is this breakfast?" Larry asked.

"Watch it, Larry," Pat chimed. "This kid may be in the major leagues."

"I assume that means he has an IQ over that of a rock," Larry asked.

"You assume correctly," Bobby said, introducing himself. Larry took his hand, shook it like a gentleman.

"May I inquire how you met Ellison?" he asked.

"I was a bartender at The Club."

"Typical," Pat said.

"Not so typical," Larry said, studying Bobby carefully. "You're straight, aren't you?"

"Yes, I am."

"Really?" Pat asked incredulously. Bobby nodded.

"Well, it's my guess that either you'll be queer at four o'clock or we'll be having you for tea."

Finally, he was taken into Ellison's private office. He was overwhelmed with how big it was, nearly the size of a tennis court. It was carpeted in the same color beige as the reception area except without Ellison's baroque initial woven into it. The far side of the office looked like a plush living room, with two sofas, and a dining-room table. Midway, in front of an arched window, was Ellison's travertine marble desk. There were orchids in clay pots everywhere, and the room was filled with a distinctive, light perfume. A distant stereo was playing soft disco music. The maid was just clearing Ellison's morning tea from his desk.

Ellison was unaware of Bobby's presence. Dressed in an outfit identical to Pat's and Larry's, except somehow more elegant, he was deeply contemplating his office model, Mallorey. In all his years in the fashion business he had never found a model so perfectly *average* as Mallorey. Mallorey was five feet ten inches tall, weighed 120 pounds and had the perfect woman's body. Not oversized, not too small, just average. She couldn't have been sculpted any better as a mannequin for mass design purposes.

Beyond that, however, Mallorey would never make it as a model. She had a large, sloping, beaklike nose, and her right eye was slightly walled. She wore heavy layers of pancake makeup to hide her bad complexion, which seemed to get worse toward the end of the day.

"Turn," he ordered her. "Now walk." He studied the way the fabric of her dress hung. She was modeling a one-shouldered chiffon evening gown in three different shades of pink. The chiffon wasn't layering properly, and it irked him. He needed the dress to ship to a show in Paris only two days away, and the seamstress had resewn it four times already. Mallorey turned again for him and almost fell out of the high-heeled shoes she was wearing. A stylist in the dressing room had given her a pair hastily dyed to match the chiffon that was two sizes too big for her.

"You're so clumsy," Ellison said to Mallorey, who was tilting like a ship in a storm, although she plainly couldn't help herself.

"I'm sorry," Mallorey said.

"She's always apologizing," Ellison complained to Pat and Larry. "If she could only do it right instead of apologizing." He pulled on the chiffon. "Well, tell the seamstress to sew in some support in the middle layers or something. There's got to be a way to make this chiffon hang correctly."

At this moment Ellison seemed to recognize Bobby. "Good morning," he said to him expectantly.

"Good morning," Bobby said, smiling warmly at Ellison despite himself. Pat and Larry watched with interest. "Everyone here seems to think I'm some kind of food," Bobby said.

Pat blushed. She would *bury* this kid if he didn't watch it.

"Vipers," Ellison mumbled, glaring at them. "Well then, put yourself to use, and nobody will take a bite out of you. However, if you make it through the day, don't come back tomorrow wearing *those*." Ellison was pointing down at Bobby's black moccasins. "They're only fit for a Puerto Rican."

Bobby spent the next hour lugging huge bolts of fabric in and out of the storage room so Ellison could match a piece of red flannel fabric for a woman's suit. He unfurled each roll on the floor in front of Ellison, who stared at it for a while before he shook his head and asked for another.

The brunt of the work seemed to fall on Pat, who spent the morning making appointments and rearranging business meetings to fit in with Ellison's constantly changing schedule while all the while she made sure the work of the day happened around him, marching people in and out to see him, shooing him off the phone when he was on too long, making sure a certain number of projects crossed his desk. On the other hand, Larry seemed to be responsible only for socializing with clients and relaying general phone gossip back to Ellison. The major topic of the morning was a customer named Joyce Banks. From what Bobby could make out, Joyce Banks was a brassy, buxom, Off-Off Broadway actress whose milieu was really burlesque, unbeknown to her oil-rich Arab husband, named Syaid Tanzid. Joyce Banks had landed him, according to Larry, by fucking him from Paris to Rio and back again. Now she was using his money to buy herself a legitimate acting career and a place in New York society with lavish parties in her Park Avenue duplex. When no one paid attention to her, she threatened to have her husband finance a Broadway show so she could star in it.

"The trouble is, even though she's a fake, you can't ignore her. She's just too rich. Do you know that last week she bought five of the same dress?"

"I know. *Five* of them," Larry said. "Would you believe it? Two of them in the *same* color. Now what is she going to do with two of them in the same color? Maybe she'll use one to hang over the portrait she had commissioned of herself. Have you ever seen it? It's embarrassing. It hangs over her bed, and it's as big as a sailboat."

"What she doesn't know," Ellison said gleefully, "is that we've sold a dozen of that dress already. It'll be all over town this summer. People will be sick of it in the Hamptons, and Betty Nigelson was already photographed in one for *Interview* magazine. Joyce Banks will spit."

By the time Pat announced lunch Bobby was exhausted from the pace. Ellison had already seen three customers, had a fight over the phone with Diana Ross, spent fifteen minutes with (and didn't bother to introduce Bobby to) Carol Channing, who picked out a new dress, fawned for half an hour over Eartha Kitt (whom Bobby did get to meet because Pat Kelly tried to introduce him and then forgot his name) and fired the tailor for ruining a $6,000 sequined gown that he had custom-made for Raquel Welch.

"Do you realize I fed fourteen gypsy families having all those sequins sewn on that dress?" he screamed at the guilty tailor.

Pat Kelly shunted everything and everyone out of the office while a maid wheeled in a serving cart and served lunch around the glass table. During the lunch Ellison finally sat back and relaxed.

"What are we going to do with Mallorey?" he asked. Mallorey had been banished to the design room to eat her lunch. "She's so dumb."

"You're so mean to her," Larry chortled.

"She needs to get laid, that's all. A good *shtup* will fix her up," Pat said.

"You fuck her," Ellison told Larry.

"Let *him* fuck her," Larry said, gesturing at Bobby with his fork.

"I'm probably the only one who can," Bobby interjected, and they all laughed.

During dessert of strawberry sherbet Ellison went to his desk drawer and brought a small green felt bag to the table. He dipped into it and fished out a magnificent pair of jade, diamond and opal earrings. He held them up in the light and let them glitter. Bobby had never seen stones shine so brightly or cut so gracefully. "These are over two hundred years old," Ellison said proudly, passing them to Bobby. "I love pretty glass." He overturned the bag in his palm, and four large stones plunked out, one uncut and unpolished and one roughly cut. The two others were perfect diamonds, neither of them under ten karats. Ellison rolled them around in his fingers and sighed deeply. Bobby watched the muscles in his face relax and thought it must be like going into an alpha state for Ellison.

The phone rang loudly on Ellison's desk. He shot it a stare so icy that Bobby thought it would stop ringing and fall off the desk.

"Don't they know its lunchtime at the switchboard?" Ellison demanded of Pat, who got up to answer the phone.

"No calls until three," she said sharply into the receiver. She listened for a moment and then put the call on hold.

"Guess what, El? It's an emergency from your favorite customer."

Ellison looked meaningfully at Larry and walked slowly to the phone. Dramatically he pressed the button to connect himself.

"Hello, darling!" he said, his joviality brittle and forced. "But I *will* see you, at dinner tonight!"

He listened tentatively. "I'm very happy for you. I told you that last night." Pause. "But what has that got to do with me?"

At this point Ellison's face so darkened with anger that Bobby hoped he never got off the phone. He turned his back to the rest of the room and snarled, "I cannot be subjected to this kind of terrorism day and night! One moment you're giving it all up; the next minute you blackmail me and involve me! If you insist upon this, I shall not forgive you!"

He tapped his foot impatiently on the carpeting, listening quietly. Pat smiled knowingly at Larry. Finally, Ellison slammed down the phone without another word. He turned to face the rest of the room and shrugged helplessly.

"That bitch," he said, "she's got me."

Five minutes later Bobby was downstairs in the middle of rainy Seventh Avenue, trying to hail a cab for Ellison. Since this was his sole responsibility of the day aside from carrying bolts of fabric, he pursued it with great enthusiasm, narrowly getting hit by a city bus. Much to his chagrin, Ellison finally got a taxi simply by waiting for someone to get out of one in front of his office building. Defeated and wet, Bobby piled into the back of the cab with him.

"Well," Ellison said, shaking off his umbrella into a puddle in the corner of the cab. "How do you like your day so far?"

"It's fine," Bobby assured him, trying to muster some enthusiasm. "Not what I'd expected but fascinating."

"What did you expect? You must not think that every day is like today," Ellison warned. "Today's been especially crazy. Also, spring is a very busy time of the year in the design business."

Ellison stared out the rain-streaked window for a moment. "What are your hobbies? You know, what do you do at night?"

My hobbies, Bobby thought, smelling the beginning of a personal pitch, are very different from what I do at night. "Who, me?" he asked innocently. "Well, you know, I work at The Club three or four nights a week. . . ."

"But do you date?" Ellison asked him.

"Of course I date," Bobby said.

"Who?" Ellison asked.

None of your business, Bobby thought. "Noonie Brooks," he said, pulling a name out of the past.

"*Her*?" Ellison grimaced bitterly.

Bobby nodded uncertainly.

"Oh, my," Ellison said disapprovingly. "She modeled for me once, Noonie Brooks." He sniffed. "She has a terrible scalp condition," he confided, "and that junk food habit is the ultimate in disgusting personal traits. But I suppose you know all this if you've slept with her."

Bobby looked out the opposite window, ignoring the implication politely. "What was that you said?" Ellison prodded Bobby, when it was obvious he had said nothing at all.

"That's right . . ." Bobby said placatingly. The taxi glided to a stop in front of a white apartment building on East Seventy-second Street off Fifth.

Ellison turned to Bobby and said, "You wait here." He started to leave the cab and then said, "No, on second thought, you come with me," and he paid the driver.

Everything that happened in the next half hour Bobby found most peculiar. Ellison told the doorman that he was Mr. Brown to see Apartment 12C. The doorman rang, announced Mr. Brown and allowed Ellison and Bobby up.

The man who answered the door to Apartment 12C was very suntanned, very nattily dressed. His hands and wrists were full of bracelets and rings. Ellison treated this man very respectfully and introduced him to Bobby as Mr. Roberts.

Mr. Roberts was quite peculiar on several counts, Bobby thought. His suntan looked artificial, as did his mustache, which was long and pencil-thin. He had the distinct carriage and voice pattern of someone from the lower classes who was trying to elevate himself. Since the apartment building was just another one of those white, bathroom-tile boxes that showed no particular taste or distinction, Bobby was surprised to see the walls of the apartment covered in expensive modern art. Mr. Roberts immediately led Ellison past the hallway to the dining area, where there was no furniture but a beautiful sky and clouds covering the entire wall.

"It's a Georgia O'Keeffe," Mr. Roberts told Ellison proudly. "It just came this week."

"Wonderful. Faaabulous," Ellison raved, but Bobby could tell that Ellison wasn't at all impressed and wanted to move on. Mr. Roberts led them into the living room, where they sat on an overstuffed sofa around a large square coffee table with a wooden sculpture on it.

"Would your friend like to see the rest of the art while we talk?" Mr. Roberts asked Ellison pleasantly about Bobby.

"If you would prefer, but I can vouch for him. He's my assistant," Ellison assured Mr. Roberts.

Mr. Roberts shrugged. Ellison stuck his hand into his jacket pocket and came up with a stack of money wrapped in a red paper band.

"Three thousand dollars?" Mr. Roberts confirmed, taking the money and throwing it into a wicker basket under the coffee table as if it were nothing. Ellison nodded, stood and the three men shook hands while Mr. Roberts ushered them to the door. They were out in the hallway before Bobby knew it.

It wasn't until they were in the elevator going downstairs that Bobby realized Ellison was wearing a Gucci binocular case with a tan shoulder strap. Bobby had just seen the case on the coffee table upstairs. When Ellison noticed him staring at it curiously, he smiled and looked straight ahead.

The next stop was only minutes away: the Olympic Tower. Again Ellison asked for an apartment number, but this time he gave no name at all. The doorman rang up, said, "There's a gentleman here for you," and sent them up. The elevator man let them off on a high floor, and Ellison rang the doorbell, which sounded softly inside. They waited a long time until the door opened a crack, an eye blinked at them and then the door swung open wide.

Jacky Mellon motioned them inside.

"I love you for this," she said, closing the door and throwing her arms around Ellison's neck. She stood on her toes to kiss him. Then she warily turned toward Bobby. "Who's this?" she demanded.

Ellison introduced Bobby as his new personal assistant. Bobby and Jacky were smiling at each other as this phrase was spoken, and Bobby was certain he detected a flicker of some emotion cross Jacky's face that he didn't like.

"Drink?" Jacky asked them. "I'm on wine spritzers."

Ellison shook his finger at her and sat down on the sectional sofa in the living room. "It's got a nice view," Jacky said, waving toward the floor-to-ceiling glass wall overlooking Fifth Avenue. "Eddie is moving in here late this afternoon."

"Good luck," Ellison said, suddenly very schoolmarm-ish. "What if he finds *this*?" He put the binocular case on the table.

"He won't. Dear Ellison, I would never have asked you to do this, but I'm simply too exhausted to move. I couldn't rehearse at *all* this morning because of last night" —she raised her eyebrows meaningfully at Ellison—"then Eddie made me jog with him in the park this afternoon, and I'd never make it through the party tonight. So it's for our *mutual* good...."

"This is a far cry from the pitch you were giving everybody last night, Miss Mellon," Ellison reminded her.

Jacky looked down at the floor guiltily, her mouth open a little. She looked very sweet and vulnerable, and Bobby had the impulse to hug her.

"Now, I want your *solemn promise* that you will be at my dinner party tonight—with Eddie Bernardo," Ellison suddenly announced.

Jacky pursed her lips.

"Promise aloud," Ellison ordered, "or I'll take the binocular case back with me."

"Ellison!"

"Promise!"

"I promise," Jacky said.

Ellison handed her the binocular case, and she fumbled with the catch until it sprang open. She tossed the contents out on the coffee table, and two large plastic bags of white powder plopped out like dice from a tumbler.

"Each one is half an ounce," Ellison explained. "One for you, one for me."

"How much do I owe you?" Jacky asked, going for her checkbook.

"Two thousand for your half," Ellison said, smiling slyly at Bobby.

Without flinching, Jacky wrote out the check and handed it to Ellison. He put the check in his sports jacket pocket along with one of the plastic bags.

Now Jacky turned to Bobby, who up until this point could have been invisible. "You look familiar. What was your name again?"

"Bobby Cassidy. I might look familiar because I often wait on you at The Club. I'm a bartender."

"Oh, of course. I didn't recognize you with your shirt on." She giggled.

"We must go," Ellison interrupted curtly. "Bobby will be at dinner tonight, and you can get to know him better then."

Bobby's head swiveled to Ellison; dinner was news to him. In the back of his mind he was hoping to get in touch with Grace, apologize to her and have dinner with her. Clearly Ellison was taking too much for granted. He thought of stopping him right then in front of Jacky Mellon and correcting him but thought better of it.

"I went through physical torture to get Eddie to say he would come to dinner with me," Jacky impressed on Ellison on the way to the door. "I hope you appreciate it."

"You got what you wanted, didn't you?" Ellison said, gesturing to the plastic bag on the coffee table. "Don't ask me to do this again. Remember, pussy, I'm a couturier, not a drug pusher."

"All right, all right. I'm sorry. What time then?" Jacky asked petulantly.

"Eight. Sharp. Don't make an entrance; you're the guest of honor."

They kissed each other on the cheek, and Jacky shut the door behind them. Standing alone in the tiny landing waiting for the elevator, Ellison looked at Bobby, and his eyes twinkled.

"You understand you must never repeat what just happened, under any circumstances," Ellison warned him.

He hoped the boy was impressed. It wasn't every day you got to meet Jacky Mellon that way.

In the taxi on the way back to Ellison's offices Bobby told him he was unavailable for dinner that night.

"I will not hear about it. You have to be there as part of the job because tonight's dinner is work, not socializing," Ellison said haughtily. "It's a *business* dinner."

Bobby said nothing.

"What is it, do you have some sort of date?" Ellison asked him in the same badgering tone he used to Mallorey. "Because if you're seeing somebody, or you're in love, you should tell me *right now* because working for me, the hours are long and hard. You won't have much time for a lover if you want to continue in this job."

So that was it, Bobby realized. Just for the hell of it, he felt like telling him he was involved with someone, but why lose Grace Dunn and a new job in the same day? You get what you deserve, Bobby told himself; everybody had warned him. Bobby just shook his head and said quietly, "All right. I'll rearrange my plans and be there."

The taxi stopped with a jerk in front of Ellison's office building, and Bobby reluctantly got out of the cab behind him. They arrived at the revolving doors of the building just in time to find Randy Potter rushing up with a leopard orchid in his hand.

THE CLUB

will not hear about it. You have to be there as part of

13

Jodi Becker stirred in bed next to Stuart Shorter, wrapping her warm smooth leg over his thigh, unaware of what bed she was in, what thigh, what time of the night or day it was. She slept soundly and content, like a girl satisfied with herself, a dreamless sleep of Quaaludes and champagne. Next to her Shorter's eyelids fluttered into two sleepy slits. The only sound in the room was the patter of raindrops on the concrete terrace and the distant rumbling of city traffic. Slowly he remembered where and who he was. Simultaneously he became aware of a dull aching spot between his eyes and a hot, cottony taste on his tongue. He turned his head slowly toward the terrace windows; they were dark and streaked with rain. He tried to lift himself gently out from under Jodi, but she was too settled into the crook of his body for him to extricate himself without waking her, and surrendering, he temporarily dozed off to sleep.

Ten years ago, if Stuart Shorter had brought home a girl like Jodi, his mother would have called her a whore and thrown them out of the house. But Shorter's mother was long dead, and so were her morals. In the 1980s a whole new set of standards were in effect. Jodie Becker had gone with almost everyone of any importance at The Club, and that was her attraction. Twenty-three-years old, a Vassar dropout and daughter of a Connecticut banker, she was a professional fuck machine, a pretty, well-built young girl with hard 34C tits and a tight, well-oiled pussy that she offered to the rich and influential in the balcony of The Club or in orgies in the back seats of limousines roving through the park or to impotent bank executives, who had to strap on rubber splints to fuck her. In the pecking order of The Club, her attractiveness and availability were as highly valued traits as the skill of the prominent physician or the esteemed politician on the dance floor next to her. In the world of The Club, Jodi Becker was no slut. Jodi Becker was a prize and a highly desired commodity.

Shorter had seen hundreds of girls like Jodi pass through The Club. Just when it seemed there were no new faces, a whole fresh crop of girls would turn up, younger and more beautiful than the week before. There had always been girls like them, at every nightclub from El Morocco to Regine's. These girls were one of the precious elements that made a nightclub glamorous and popular, just as much a part of the night life as the music and lights or the dancing bartenders.

There was no pot of gold at the end of the rainbow for these girls in the traditional sense. They didn't want to marry rich older men or swindle fortunes. The most they ever wanted was a chance to eat at the best restaurants or wear expensive clothes. They offered themselves primarily to live in a social set that was written and talked about around the globe. Most of them desired only glamor. Glamor was their sustenance. They ate it for breakfast, lunch and dinner.

Shorter pushed Jodi's leg off his and swung over the side of the bed, trying to steady himself on the floor. His bed was only two mattresses and a box spring laid out on the floor in the middle of a flokati rug. His clothing and Jodi's from the night before lay in piles on the floor; there were no dressers, no other furniture. He had lived in the apartment for a year, but his life changed too fast for him ever to decorate. He was always on the verge of moving to a bigger, more expensive apartment. He could have hired a decorator to fix it up, but he figured he had no idea what his own place should look like until he understood himself a little better.

He slowly got to his feet, shivering at the touch of the cold hardwood floor, and sleepily hunted around the bedroom for his robe. When he realized the search was futile in the jumble of clothes, he took a chenille spread from the floor and wrapped it around himself, stumbling down the hallway toward the kitchen with his teeth chattering, rubbing his arms to try to keep warm. He shielded his eyes against the harsh white light inside the refrigerator to find it empty of Coca-Cola, save for a half dead can. He swore aloud and went to the pantry, where he found himself a warm six-pack of cola. Then he rummaged through a carton filled with different kinds of potato chips, fished out a garlic- and onion-flavored pack, and clutching his breakfast to his chest, he went into the living room.

Asleep on the sofa, naked, was Jodi's boyfriend, Alexander. The sofa was the only piece of furniture in the room aside from a large glass coffee table cluttered with ashtrays, candles and enough drug paraphernalia and leftover joint roaches to equip a head shop. Shorter cleared himself a space on the corner for his potato chips and sat down on the floor Indian-style, pulling the blanket underneath him. He broke into his bag of potato chips and studied Alexander, who didn't seem to mind the chill morning air at all. He liked Alexander. He wasn't a bad-looking kid, and he sure had fucked the hell out of Jodi the night before.

Before The Club, Shorter's sex life was limited to a handful of unsuccessful experiences with not very attractive partners. And even when he was able to get someone home with him, he usually found himself hopelessly impotent, never able to fullfill his own sexual need—whatever it was going to turn out to be. Until he stumbled upon the scene with couples, Shorter was mystified by his sexual drive, about what he wanted from whom.

He was born in the Bronx, New York, where he grew up in a three-room apartment behind his father's grocery store on Tremont Avenue. He was a classic momma's boy—a skinny, constipated child, who clung to his mother's side behind the counter of the store every day after school. His mother's sudden death from cancer when he was twelve years old was a shock he never recovered from. He withdrew into himself completely and into his late teens returned home every day directly from school, where he spoke to no one, and worked with his father in the store. By the time he was admitted to City College at eighteen, he was a tall, string bean of a guy with a receding hairline who looked thirty-eight years old and had never dated a girl.

Still a virgin at twenty-one, he tried sex with men, both other City College students who cruised him in the locker room after a gym class. Shorter sodomized one and was sodomized by the other. Neither experience repulsed him in the least, but he felt no excitement from them either. In lieu of a social life he threw himself into his schoolwork. Six months before graduation his father died of a stroke behind the counter in the store while arguing with the eggman, and Shorter dropped out of school to take over the grocery store himself.

The grocery store was a trap. Bored, his unused and

undirected sexual energy burning him up, Shorter soon bought a bankrupt *bodega* fifteen blocks south and ran both stores to keep himself more occupied. He quickly found that by selling rejected foods, damaged cans and day-old bread to the unsuspecting Spanish customers, he could increase his profits by a third; what they wouldn't buy in the white neighborhoods, he could still sell for a profit to the Puerto Ricans. In the next two years he bought four more failing or bankrupt *bodegas* to add to his collection and even helped put a few more out of business with stiff competition. Eventually he opened a supermarket in Spanish Harlem and bought a freezer truck so he could transport cheap pork products over the state line from New Jersey against federal regulations.

His little grocery kingdom might have gone on forever if it weren't for Sandy Dubrow, who gave him horizons farther than the next poor Spanish grocery store owner. Shorter had met Dubrow in an accounting class at City College and kept in touch over the years through an occasional game of poker. Dubrow, a handsome, well-dressed man, had a sly, sarcastic sense of humor that Shorter responded to. His father, Barney Dubrow, was reputedly one of the biggest Jewish gangsters in New York, an allegation that Sandy often laughed off without qualifying. No one will know for sure; Barney Dubrow disappeared one day on his way home from his Madison Avenue office, and nobody ever filed a missing person's complaint.

It was Dubrow who wanted to get into the restaurant and nightclub business and thought that Shorter's knowledge of food buying would help. Shorter was at first disbelieving when Dubrow asked him to go into business with him, then dubious. Shorter was an introverted man with few social graces. The thought of dealing with the public scared him. But Dubrow convinced him that *he* could stay behind the scenes if he wanted and that the nightclub business was two times as much fun as running grocery stores.

Their first venture was a smartly decorated neighborhood discotheque and restaurant on Long Island called Lillyland. Lillyland was almost too chic for the locals, and it never really took off or made a lot of money, but they managed to milk it enough for a few years while Shorter learned the ropes of the business. Then the pair sold the club and moved to downtown Manhattan, where they opened a disco called Palm Courts. Palm Courts was a unique club, the forerunner of the exotic modern discotheques to come five years later. It was tucked away behind a factory building on a deserted downtown street, and the allure of the forbidden and furtive brought thousands of people from all over to the unmarked black doors. The club's interior was Shorter's fluorescent fantasy of rocket ships and planets, and it became the setting for the birth of a new element of New York society: the seventies' glitterati. The *nouveau riche, nouvelle vague,* the hookers and hawkers and the hustlers of the city descended on the place. And instead of hiding in the office, Shorter manned the door, and a new world opened to him, an unveiling of a place where perhaps one day he could fit in.

He didn't. The people came and went, as did the years. He tired of trying to score all the time; he dreaded his failure with women each night. It wasn't until The Club that it all changed.

The space for The Club already existed, and it was only luck that they stumbled upon it. It was initially started by Merryweather Gold, the great-grandson of studio head Hiram Gold. Merryweather dabbled in extravagant restaurants and amusement parks. It was Gold who had the vision to transform the old department store into a disco, but zoning problems and other red tape held up the project so long he quickly became bored with the idea, and the gutted space on Fifty-seventh Street was up for grabs. A few department stores put in bids with the landlord, but with a little pushing from Sandy Dubrow's connections the zoning was changed to house a discotheque, and he and Shorter moved in. Dubrow, well aware he was about to enter the major leagues finally, unleashed a torrent of money on the place.

The Club and its success didn't change Dubrow much, but Shorter's whole life seemed to swivel around, to Dubrow's great displeasure. Every night at The Club was electric for him, a new discovery. All the pretty and rich people wanted to know him and give him gifts of clothing and money and drugs, some of which he took. At The Club suddenly everybody wanted to touch and kiss him and tell him how good he looked. He snorted coke and took ludes and became the darling of society.

And for the first time in his life he felt like a man.

Still, he could not come.

He tried everything, or at least he thought he had until one night, when The Club was just celebrating its first anniversary. There was a girl, a twenty-one-year-old model whom Shorter had dated a few times and tried, unsuccessfully, to fuck. That night she was with a young photographer of twenty-five who was making a name for himself photographing women in lingerie against a backdrop of garbage cans and tenements. They stayed at The Club dancing until it closed, when Shorter invited them to his apartment with him for a champagne and cocaine breakfast, Shorter's equivalent of asking someone to come to see his etchings. When they arrived in his bare living room, he turned on the lights and stereo and went to the bathroom to urinate. By the time he got back to the living room he found them in the middle of the bare floor, the girl's legs up in the air, she being fucked by the boy with his pants still on, his cock jutting out of his open fly.

The sight of it galvanized Shorter more than ever before. He stumbled toward them, tingling and woozy from the pill, unsure he was really seeing this most deliciously incredible sight. The large cock was red and gleaming with pussy juices as it plunged in and out of the hair-covered opening between her legs. Shorter dropped to his knees on the carpeting next to them, leaned forward in a trance and licked both their organs together in one stroke and came in his pants.

Finally, he had found the magic combination! One of each!

The ménage was the birth of his sex life, as if someone had given him a new and magical toy that he could never operate before. He wasn't straight; he wasn't gay. He wasn't anything. He hardly ever got involved himself. He just watched. He had invented his own specialized perversion, a mixture of everything rolled into one. Of course, finding couples to fuck for him was difficult to arrange on a regular basis at first, but as soon as word got out that spectator sports were Shorter's scene, young couples arrived to present themselves to him by the dozens.

This was not to say, however, that Shorter had found peace and sexual fulfillment. He was, ultimately, an observer and not a participant. His sexual thrill and orgasm were dependent on the other participants' satisfaction. But it was something, and that, and The Club, had finally made him happy.

Shorter's life-style and behavior had attracted much comment and criticism, all of which he was able to shrug off except the disdain he felt from Sandy Dubrow. Over the years the two men had grown in completely opposite directions. Dubrow was strictly a businessman. He was indifferent to celebrities and hated the snobby fashion crowd that Shorter seemed to adore so much. He disapproved strongly of drugs, and when Shorter's sexual life was divulged to him, it disgusted him. Dubrow had long ago married a sweet little Jewish girl he had met in Miami, bought a house in Westchester with a swimming pool and was happily bringing up three-year-old twins. His world revolved around his wife and children; The Club only made him money.

Sitting on the living-room floor, Shorter thought about the informant, and a curl of anxiety wrapped around his colon.

Who could it be? Who was the turncoat? Who hated him that much? David Willick had warned him, "You can't make yourself famous by treating people like garbage and get away with it. The informant is only the tip of the iceberg. Sometime, without even realizing it, you insulted some faceless guy who was a judge or a mafioso or a narc. Say, the son of an IRS investigator from Washington, D.C., who got turned away and complained to his right-wing Bircher father that you didn't want his Baptist wingtips in The Club, and Daddy put the heat on you."

At least Shorter had Willick on his side. Willick had one of the finest, shrewdest legal minds in the business, and he was none too concerned with the innocence or moral quality of his clients. The law was an instrument that Willick played brilliantly to his own devise. And he was paid better than any lawyer in history for it. Shorter and Dubrow alone paid him a $10,000-a-month retainer to protect them from the continuous barrage of lawsuits that harassed them. The Club was an easy target for lawsuits, some crank, some justified. There was a million-dollar suit by an Off-Broadway actress who was turned down at the ropes and tried to crawl under them. She was kicked in the face by a bouncer, who claimed he didn't see her. And a $5 million suit by the parents of a boy who died from a concussion he suffered falling down the flight of steps from the lounge, or the less spectacular suits like companies that had parties at The Club and hadn't had their guests admitted because they weren't dressed well enough.

The phone started to ring, waking the boy on the sofa, but Shorter let it ring until the service picked it up. It began to ring again right away, as if somebody had demanded to ring through, but Shorter had no interest in talking on the phone yet, not until he finished another cola or two and digested his potato chips. He watched as Alexander's eyelids fluttered open and the boy's brown eyes focused well enough to know where he was and that Shorter was sitting there watching him. Then he asked, "Do you think you could get it up to fuck her again before you go?" and the boy managed a weak smile in reply.

Later that day, at his customary hour of five o'clock, Shorter got out of a taxi at Fifty-seventh and Sixth and walked down the block toward The Club, stopping along the way in a candy store to fill his pockets with marzipan, which he munched on till dinner to give him energy. He glanced at himself in the store windows as he strolled by, dressed in a fresh green Lacoste shirt and laundered jeans. When he arrived at the marquee of The Club, he was surprised to find the front door ajar, unlocked and no security guard in sight. Even during the day, when The Club was closed to the public, there were always a few security people lurking about. Shorter couldn't believe that The Club had been left unattended in broad daylight. Certainly Sandy Dubrow was inside, and there was some explanation.

Shorter hurried into the dark, cool Club, searching for some sign of life. But The Club was still and deserted.

He walked further to the dance floor. Even the work lights were shut, and The Club was eerie and forbidding.

There was a noise behind him in the shadows. "Sandy?" he called, frightened now. Slowly, almost imperceptibly, a tall man in a dark suit emerged from the shadows but did not answer.

"Who are you?" Shorter shouted, backing away.

Two other men followed out of the shadows and approached him. "Stay where you are!" Shorter warned as they came close to him, and he had turned to run for the door when suddenly from everywhere there were men in

suits darting out of the dark into the light, descending on
Shorter all at once. Shorter stumbled backward, tripped on
the carpeting and fell to the rug. Two of the men reached
him at that moment, grabbed him under the arms and
hoisted him to his feet.

"Don't hurt me!" he screamed, searching around him in
amazement; there must have been thirty men there, all
dressed in suits and ties.

"Are you Stuart Shorter?" one of the men demanded.

"Who—who are you?" Shorter asked.

The man reached into his jacket pocket and withdrew
not the gun that Shorter was expecting but a folded piece
of paper. "This is a warrant for your arrest. My name is
Agent Grey, and I'm a representative of the Federal
Bureau of Investigation."

"Arrest for what?" Shorter said, an ugly backtaste of
onion and garlic chips on his tongue.

"That's getting more complicated by the moment. This
warrant is for income tax evasion. And I have another
warrant to seize your books. But I'm afraid there's a third
charge now. Would you come with me, please?"

Shorter hardly had a choice since the two men at his
side held his arms closely to him and practically carried
him across the dark dance floor to the doorway to the
basement. When they reached the door, Agent Grey called
for the lights, and suddenly The Club was flooded. Shorter
was again astonished at the great number of agents, all
almost carbon copies of each other.

"Where does this door lead to?" Grey asked him.

"The basement," Shorter said.

"Is there an office in the basement?"

"No," Shorter said.

The agent nodded as if he were satisfied. "Would you
follow, please?" he asked.

Again they walked Shorter down the steps and through
the labyrinth. In a scenario right out of his worst nightmares the agents walked him directly to the secret office as
if they had had a map.

The lights were on inside, and there were five agents
standing around. Sandy Dubrow was sitting behind the
desk, his head in hands, his hands handcuffed together. He
looked up at Shorter as he was ushered into the room.
"You prick," he said to him, "you drug addict little prick!"

Shorter shook his head in disbelief that Sandy was

saying this to him in front of the FBI. "Sandy, what's the matter? What's happening?"

"I'll explain, Mr. Shorter," Agent Grey interceded. "We first came here under a directive to seize your records and arrest you for questioning. But when we came down here to get the records, we found this."

The agent held up a thick envelope. Shorter recognized it at once. It was his stash of cocaine that he left in the safe at The Club. Worse, he had purchased some of it for his friends, and if he remembered correctly, he had written their initials and the amounts he had laid out for them on the inside flap of the envelope.

He wanted to throw up.

"You know whose fault this is, don't you?" Dubrow demanded, clanking his handcuffed wrists together. "It's your fucking big mouth, full of Quaaludes all the time, that caused this!"

"Calm down, Sandy," Shorter begged. "David Willick will get us out of this."

"I'm afraid the charges are more complicated now," Agent Grey explained. Shorter turned to see if there was as much of a smirk on his face as there was in his voice. "But as you said," Grey continued, producing a pair of handcuffs from his back pocket and slapping them on Shorter, "David Willick is on your side."

Sandy Dubrow stood behind the desk and spit at Shorter.

14

Late that afternoon it was still raining as Jacky left from the rehearsal at the Janoff Theater to get the apartment in order for Eddie to move in before Ellison's dinner party. There really wasn't much to do except make some room for him in the closet and empty one of the dressers for his socks and underwear. As Jacky knew well from living with him in Los Angeles, Eddie took up little space and made few demands. As a special touch she thought about buying some caviar and pâté to stick in the refrigerator for a late-night snack. After all, Eddie was being so wonderful to her. After their jog in the rain they had gone home and showered together. It had been only twenty minutes, but it had been bliss. And he had even agreed to go to Ellison's party with her tonight.

She searched about for a taxi, but it was impossible in the rain in the theater district, so she pulled her raincoat up around her neck and marched through the puddles east on Forty-sixth Street. She was about to turn the corner up Fifth Avenue when Jacky spotted a familiar figure hurrying along the opposite side of the street. It was Alexander Garguilo, and he was just coming out of a record shop, dressed only in a blue blazer with frayed cuffs, the collar pulled up around his neck against the rain. He was an odd-looking character rushing along in the rain, forever the manicured, foppy, if somewhat frayed Italian lover. The poor man was hurrying toward Fifth Avenue almost as if he were frightened, dodging his way in and out of umbrellas and people. Jacky rushed along the opposite side of the street from him, waiting for a break in the traffic so she could go across the street and say hello. She was almost at the corner before the light turned red, and she darted between a bus and a Porsche, calling, "Alexander! Alexander!"

Alexander stuck his head between his shoulders and quickened his pace.

Jacky frowned and wondered why. Why should Alex avoid her?

Stubbornly she rushed down the block after him, shouting, "Alex! Alex!" but this only made him start to run up Fifth Avenue, frustrating Jacky so that she took off after him full trot down the street and nabbed him at the next corner by the shoulder. He swung around to face her with such terrified force that he nearly knocked her over.

"Oh, Jesus!" Alex screamed in relief. "It's you!"

"Alex, you're petrified! What's the matter?"

He looked down the block behind her apprehensively. "Please, let's go away from here. I need a drink."

"Of course," Jacky said, frightened a little for him. They rushed out into the street together and commandeered a taxi from in front of Air India. Jacky instinctively told the driver to take them to the Plaza Hotel. Alex sank into the dirty cab seat and opened his worn jacket. Underneath, stuck into his belt, were three packages of cassette tapes.

"What's that?" Jacky asked curiously. She thought immediately of hand grenades or plastic bombs or shoplifting from a store.

Alex shook his head sadly as he removed the packages and stuck them into the shopping bag he was carrying. "I will tell you once we have something to drink," he promised.

A few minutes later they were in the Oak Room, where they were escorted into a private booth in the corner. Alex was ashen white and silent the whole time. Only when a waiter served him a double cognac did the color come back to his face, and he spoke.

"Are you all right, my darling?" he asked Jacky.

"Me? Oh, yes, I'm fine, just fine. But what about you?"

Alex examined Jacky's face very carefully, searching over each minute part of it, making comparisons in his mind. "You look more like her every day," Alex told her.

From anyone else this would have irked her; from Alex she found it sweet.

"She was very beautiful," he told her.

Jacky wondered for a moment if Alex really had loved her momma. He had always been good and attentive to Angela, but Jacky could never figure out if Alex had really cared for her. It pleased Jacky to hear him compliment Angela that way so many years later.

"Why did you run when I called you on the street, Alex? I saw you rush out of the record store, and when I called your name, you ran."

Alex polished off his drink. "I have a terrible confession to make," he said mournfully. "I am a petty thief so I can live."

"What?" she whispered.

"It's true. I shoplift to eat. Clothing, silver, most often records and cassette tapes because they're so easy to resell and impossible to trace. When you called my name, I had just . . . taken some tapes, and when I heard my name called out, in my paranoia, I started to run. . . ." Alex stared dolefully into his lap.

"But why?"

"Simply because I'm broke. I have no job, no trade. Angela left me nothing. What was I to do?"

"For so many years?"

"There was another woman at first. She was a wealthy woman I met through an introduction in New York. She was nothing like your momma, a society lady who didn't go out much and never got her name in the papers. It was boring, but she was very rich. It lasted two years until her sons threw me out. And then there was a much older woman in Queens, another widow, but she died in less than a year. In the last few months I've had . . . nothing. . . ."

"But to steal . . ." Jacky began.

Alexander straightened his spine and narrowed his eyes. "I would rather . . . die . . . than take a job as a waiter. I would prefer to steal. . . ."

Jacky was devastated. She never heard anything as sordid or pitiful in her life. No wonder Alex had loved her mother; compared with old Jewish ladies in Queens, her mother had been quite some prize. She had never thought about Alexander's life after her mother before this moment. What else was he going to do? Something. Anything but steal. Poor, poor momma. It turned out that Alexander was just a hustler through and through. She was sure all those other women had been just as convinced as her momma that he loved them. And this was how hustlers ended up.

She didn't want to sit in the booth with him one second

longer. "Alex, you must stop shoplifting right now," she implored him. She opened her pocketbook and found her checkbook. Alexander watched with interest as she took out a pen and wrote him a check for $1,000. She handed it to him, and he gave her a wan smile.

"This is very generous of you," he said, leaning forward to kiss her on the cheek. He smelled of sweet cologne and sour sweat.

Jacky quickly leaned away. "I have to go, now. I'm late. . . ."

"Yes, of course," he said, as if he understood that she wanted to run away from him.

"Good-bye, Alex. Take care now," she said.

"Jacky?" he called to her.

She turned to look at him. He looked small and lost in the big booth, like a little boy.

"I'm . . . so . . . embarrassed . . ." he stammered.

"No, don't apologize . . ."

"No, you don't understand. I have no money to pay for our drinks here. I appreciate your check, but I need some cash, too."

She bit her bottom lip as she reopened her purse, fished out a $20 bill, handed it to Alex and left the Oak Room without looking at him again. No matter, the sight of him at that table with his shopping bag full of stolen tapes was a vision she was sure was emblazoned in her memory forever.

15

In the closest he had ever come to a wild rage, Ellison stormed from his office building into the pouring rain.

"Shit!" he cried aloud, pushing aside the limousine driver, who tried to shield him from the rain with a huge black umbrella. He got to the car and opened the door himself before the driver could get to it, threw himself in the back of the car and slammed the door behind him. In the few moments he was alone in the car before the driver could rush around to the driver's seat, Ellison exploded into a string of four-letter words.

First, he would have the florist tarred and feathered. He had already called David Willick to take care of *that,* and he was sure Willick would show no mercy in the gossiping florist's business affairs. Next, he would take care of Alvin Duff. The name made his blood run cold. That cheap *jeans maker.* Pandering to the lowest common denominator of American mentality. That—that—*trend follower!* Who cared how much money there was to be made from blue jeans? It was tacky and a sellout. There was nothing more to it. Ellison was a *couturier!* Duff was a common tailor, a Jew from Brooklyn who pretended he was straight because he had a kid but who was just as big a fairy as everybody else. That *vonce,* that. . . .

He groaned loudly in frustration as the car took off down Seventh Avenue. He reached into his jacket pocket for his vial and looked at his watch. His dinner party guests would be arriving in only half an hour, and he wasn't even dressed yet. Fortunately the sheikh's sister would probably be late. And at least the food would be ready. Fabulous Foods had been there since noon. Fabulous Foods catered most of the important events in the city. A catering service run by two brothers, the Cohens. The senior Cohens had been prewar refugees in Paris, where both the brothers were five-star cooks. They had moved to Manhattan for the Kennedys. They owned a stately East Side carriage house in Manhattan with one of the largest and best-equipped kitchens in the world. They stocked only the best china, silver, flatware and crystal for rent. Their waiters and bartenders were culled from the ranks of unemployed models and actors and tutored in the art of serving the rich and demanding. Fabulous Foods would do dinners as small as four ($250 per person, which included the servants, but not the bartender) or a party like tonight's, which was running Ellison $14,000. Curiously, the lavish and exotic dishes Fabulous Foods prepared weren't especially delicious—although they tasted *very* good—but the presentation was first-rate. Each dish *looked* incredible, and it was obvious that infinitesimal detail was given, down to the way the color of the food matched the color of the pattern on the plates or the way the thinly curled slices of truffles were placed as a garnish. At least Ellison wouldn't have to worry about the food; it always matched the *haute couture* of his guests.

The limousine turned up Madison Avenue into the fabulous Sixties and supersonic Seventies, a twenty-block stretch of retail stores rivaled only by Rodeo Drive or Faubourg. St.-Honoré. The names of the stores glittered as the car went swiftly up the avenue; Emanuel Ungaro; Christian Aujard's gold-encrusted men's store; the fabulous live blooms of Rennie's florist; Tony's Flowers, just a block or so away; Halston; Le Relais Restaurant, which is heaven on Saturday afternoons when the front is opened onto the street; Norma Kamali's fascinating women's wear; Lady Madonna, where pregnant mothers are chic, too; and Kron chocolates, where they hand-dip fruit practically by the moment and you can order an entire life-sized leg of chocolate.

Ellison saw nothing, not the shops on the street or the people. He wondered only if Simon Morrow would drop him. And if it was true that they were buying Duff's jeans, could they intend to represent both designers? He just couldn't have it. It was too compromising. The conglomerate wasn't big enough for both of them. Another designer, maybe, somebody like Vera who did cute little scarves and bed sheets, but not a prime competitor like Duff. He would have to leave the conglomerate, and leaving Simon Morrow was no simple matter. It would start talk in the business that would do irreparable damage to his prestige and business. There had to be a sensible way out of this, some sort of compromise. If he could only communicate with Simon Morrow, but he was never able to have even a simple conversation with the man. He had signed with his conglomerate purely out of greed and confidence in Marrow's track record of turning American businesses into international phenomena. But at the quick of it all Morrow was the antithesis of Ellison and everything that Ellison stood for. Morrow was always in a three-piece business suit, cordovan loafers and full of Princeton '39 heartiness. He actually once told Ellison a *war* story. Ellison couldn't fathom how a man who had managed to build such a successful empire had no imagination or sense of humor. Morrow should have owned a conglomerate of steel mills or electronics corporations, not a prime grouping of fashion and beauty businesses that depended on emotion, style, imagination and personal nerve.

How could anyone dare insist that Ellison, America's only true courturier, manufacture blue jeans!

And what did that all boil down to in the back of his car stuck in traffic on Madison Avenue to the rock of the fashion business? Beans. Because he had had his time in the limelight, and now they wanted somebody else, somebody new, somebody younger who made blue jeans. Was he old? In some ways, he supposed, he felt very, very old.

Stanley Henry Ellison was born in Havingham, Illinois, the change-of-life child of an alcoholic high school teacher and his Methodist wife. His childhood was marked by harrowing and chronic bouts of bronchial asthma, which miraculously disappeared when his mother died when he was ten. But the asthma was soon replaced by deep guilt: guilt about his mother's death and guilt about his recurring homosexual desires.

In Havingham, a small industrial city of 11,000, there wasn't anybody vaguely like Stanley Ellison for him to compare notes with. At the age of eighteen, lost for a solution to the problems of his life, he married the daughter of a next-door neighbor for want of anything better to do, a young girl of seventeen named Beverly Pulansky. The young couple settled in the Havingham Garden Apartments, only five blocks from the house he grew up in. The marriage lasted for a miserable but miraculously long eight years before Beverly had a nervous breakdown and was committed to a state sanitarium by her family. Stanley Ellison summarily left for New York without a forwarding address and got a job on Seventh Avenue as an assistant to a women's sportswear designer he had met in a Times Square bar. He spent two years carrying fabric bolts and going to the deli for black coffees.

But he flourished in New York. The environment suited his temperament and personality. He was anonymous for the first time. In a city of so many people, so many different people, he could be ... himself. He learned how to dress with some flair. He realized he had taste. Using wile, some tricks, good sense and a fair share of talent (and not hesitating to fuck anything in pants that would further his career), Ellison went from assistant designer to a fashion coordinator and designer and finally to manufacturing his own dress line for Bonwit Teller, where he shortened his name to just Ellison. From there he went to his own company of better dresses, and within fifteen years, with luck, good timing and a flair for public relations, Ellison had built his line into one of the most successful in New York.

But he was hardly the pasha of the fashion empire he was to shortly become.

Not until the story of his marriage managed to become newspaper headlines. The only child of that marriage, a marriage that Ellison had effectively eradicated from his memory fifteen years before, was by then a grown man of twenty-four. The man had been kidnapped in his hometown of Chicago, and Ellison was being asked for $250,000 ransom money.

It was a most embarrassing problem to Ellison in many ways. First, being disclosed as a closet heterosexual was most inopportune; he had several male lovers in New York, and his homosexuality was enhancing to his business image. Secondly, and more important to him, the son was simply hideous: a fat, pimply telephone repairman, whom Ellison hadn't seen in two decades but who bore a mortifying resemblance to his father. The picture of his son in the New York newspapers so humiliated him that Ellison actually fainted in his office when he saw it. And last and most important, who had $250,000 for that beast?

Ellison immediately refused to pay the ransom. At an impromptu press conference in the street in front of 1407 Broadway he told reporters, "What, a quarter of a million dollars for *that* pig?" and the kidnappers cut off one of the son's fingers and mailed it to Ellison's showroom. When

Ellison was asked for further comment from the media, he said, "At least they could have sent a finger with his school ring," a joke that did not go well with the kidnappers. Fortunately for his nine-fingered son, the FBI traced the kidnappers through the postmark and wrapping sent along with the finger and apprehended them before Ellison could incense them any further.

But that was far from the end of it. Ellison's cold, monstrous attitude about the incident brought him unprecedented publicity. And there was nothing that the fashion industry and *Women's Wear Daily* liked better than a good Queen Bitch. The media continued to dog his every move and quote his better barbs long after the kidnapping was over. For a time he was as popular as Jackie Kennedy with the *paparazzi*. And with New York society he was a *cause célèbre*, a man who thumbed his nose at the terrorists of the rich and remained an individual instead of a hypocrite. Diana Vanderbilt herself crowned him "The Prince of Bitch." Jackie Kennedy, before she married Ari, was his dearest friend and best customer. Elizabeth Taylor worshiped the ground he walked on. His career soared year after year; his line enlarged by quantum leaps. Soon came cosmetics, perfume, a licensing deal and finally, five years before, a $40 million conglomerate buyout. By then he had become a legend. With the addition of Jacky Mellon as a sort of mascot to his flock, he was the single biggest designer on the face of the earth.

Ellison's limousine turned down a street off Fifth Avenue and pulled up in front of his town house. A gleaming, opaque glass structure, it looked impenetrable from the street; it was a monument to his achievements.

The architectural plans for the house had taken half a dozen prominent architects a year to design, with Ellison himself supervising the final draft. The first construction crew he contracted with informed him that his complicated architectural ideas were impossible to execute safely, and Ellison fired them and hired another, more expensive company that specialized in skyscraper construction. By the time those contractors had erected the basic shell of the building Ellison had spent more than $1.8 million and hadn't even started decorating yet.

Producing his own key, he vaulted into the rain from his car and went inside.

His Arab houseboy, Abdullah, took his wet jacket from him. Abdullah was the illegitimate son of an oil-rich Kuwaiti family, who were probably richer than Ellison, but Abdullah had insulted his father and been banished from the family. He had been Ellison's excellent servant since they had met at the Kuwaiti Hilton Hotel five years before, when Abdullah was living as a homosexual prostitute.

Ellison jaunted up the four wide steps that led up to the main living level of the house, and for a moment he wished he lived in a small, warm one-room apartment with an old comforter on the sofa and a TV in the corner instead of the vast white townhouse. There were no warm corners, no places to hide away and soothe a tattered ego, only a luxurious expanse of white Ellison Megafur that at the moment seemed as cold as plastic. In the living room two bartenders polished Steuben crystal behind a mirrored bar. White-jacketed waiters from Fabulous Foods were making last-minute preparations, lighting hundreds of delicate little Rigeaux candles on the tables and shelves, which scented the room in a fabulously light, sweet smell. The room was filled with orchids tied to bamboo shoots, and the distant sound of sweet disco music filtered out of stereo speakers hidden about the town house.

"Is the food ready yet?" Ellison asked Abdullah. Abdullah nodded as Ellison turned into the kitchen. There were three chefs in white aprons and tall hats roasting two giant legs of lamb. Lined up on the butcher-block counter were molds of mint Jell-O and individual watercress and tomato salads. A dessert chef was working at the industrial-sized stove, dipping pieces of freshly cut strawberries, oranges and apples into two huge copper pots of melted Swiss chocolate.

Satisfied, Ellison turned up into the dining room. The table was breathtaking, aglow with candles, five streams of orchids and flowers draped around the table that Randy Potter had arranged for him. It looked perfect. Satisfied there, he left the dining room and checked the den to make sure everything was just so.

Sitting on the white Megafur sofa were what appeared to be four men from a construction crew, dressed in muddy overalls and worker's boots. Raul, kneeling by a coffee table, was spreading lines of cocaine on the glass top. The four men and Raul were contentedly drunk and at home in the surroundings. They didn't even notice Ellison standing there with his arms across his chest until he screamed, "Raul!" All heads in the room turned toward him. The dessert chef stuck his head out of the kitchen. Abdullah appeared in the doorway. The men in the construction crew didn't look amused.

"Who *are* these people?" Ellison cried. "Are you out of your *mind?* I'm having a dinner party here any second."

The four construction workers turned warily to Raul for some explanation.

"They make the hole!" Raul said defiantly, as if Ellison should have known.

Ellison's eyes widened. "What hole?" he asked quietly, afraid to hear the answer.

Raul looked innocently affronted. "The swimming hole. You do not remember you promised me you would do the swimming pool instead of the house in the Pines?"

Ellison's mind reeled. One night, to shut Raul up, when they were stoned on drugs at The Club, Ellison sarcastically said that instead of paying the $15,000 rental on a summer house for Raul on Fire Island, he would build him a swimming pool in the backyard of the house. It was drug talk that no madman would take seriously. But Raul was exactly that madman.

"Pool?" Ellison growled. "Pool! Get these lowlife trash off my white furniture and out of my house! Nobody is building any swimming pool!"

One of the construction workers got to his feet threateningly. "Who are you calling a lowlife, you old faggot asshole?"

Another roared, "Who is this guy? Who is this fucking faggot?"

Ellison didn't flinch. *"This is my house,"* he said imperiously, his steely voice rising above all else until all activity in the house stopped dead and there was listening silence everywhere. *"I want you four the fuck out!"*

Tamed, one of the men said, "Come on, let's go get our equipment and get the fuck out of here."

"What equipment?" Ellison asked.

Everyone turned toward the backyard.

Terrified of what he would see, Ellison walked stiffly to the glass rear wall of the room and looked out. The property was lighted by spotlights and surrounded by monolithic apartment buildings made of white tile. There was a fifteen-foot oak fence lit with pastel spotlights surrounding the garden, but where the formal topiary had been only that morning stood a large digging machine and a gaping hole big enough for a swimming pool.

The sound of the front doorbell rang through the house and seemed to restore everyone back to life. Abdullah rushed to answer it, and the waiters and bartenders took their places.

Ellison started screeching at Raul, "You Puerto Rican moron! This is the end. Look at my backyard! I've had it. You're through. Get these men out of here! Get out of here with them! Get out of my sight! I don't want to see you at this dinner party! I don't want to ever see your face again!"

The construction workers looked at each other in disbelief as Raul blew a kiss at Ellison.

From out of the shocked silence that followed came a sweet, squeaky little voice saying, "My, my, my." Ellison spun around to find Truman Capote and Andy Warhol standing in the entrance of the room. Warhol was dressed casually but elegantly in jeans and a suede sports jacket, his white hair like an angel's halo. He was with his frequent companion, Catherine Guinness, and journalist Bob Collacello. Capote was alone.

"Truman! Andy!" Ellison said, flushing with embarrassment.

Capote eyed the construction workers and asked, "Is this the entertainment?"

"Introduce us," Warhol suggested. "Who are they? Is this your new spring line?" Catherine Guinness laughed at his silliness.

"These people are leaving! Now!" Ellison ordered, pointing his finger at the door. The men grumbled as they left, walking around Warhol and Capote like suspicious bears.

"Now really, who were they?" Catherine Guinness demanded.

Raul pushed by Ellison and rushed up to Warhol. "Oh, Andy I am so happy you are here," he said. Warhol liked Raul's zaniness, and Raul knew in Warhol he had a willing fan. "El is just so mean about the new pool."

"What new pool?" Andy asked. Andy always spoke quietly and managed to sound amazed at everything, even if you just told him what time it was.

"I have a pool put in the garden," Raul explained, as if it were quite a natural thing. He pointed to the back window. Everyone crowded along the window and stared out at the muddy hole.

"How fabulous," Warhol said. "I love the idea of a pool. Good for you, El."

"Yes, what a terrific idea," Truman echoed. "You beat the summer heat and avoid the tacky people at the Hamptons."

"Well, yes," Ellison said, flustered at their enthusiasm, "I thought it was . . ." Quickly, before anybody else could go on further, he said, "Let's have champagne!" He herded his guests away to the bar.

Without Ellison's even noticing it, the party began to happen around him. He was aware of the distant ring of the front door and that Diana Vreeland had appeared at the door by the bedroom staircase, where she was chatting pleasantly with Francesco Scavullo. Mrs. Vreeland was the headmistress of American fashion. A onetime editor of *Harper's Bazaar,* at nearly eighty years of age Mrs. Vreeland remains the Empress of Fashion, making and breaking designers with the wave of a hand. She is best known for her pervasive cool and sense of grace. There is a probably apocryphal story about her at the opening of one of her annual fashion retrospectives in the Metropolitan Museum, a black-tie event that is certainly one of the social highlights of Manhattan night life each year. Out of the crowd a young man in a well-cut suit approached Mrs. Vreeland. He told her, quite loudly, that he wanted to perform various kinds of sex acts on her right there on the museum floor. Those who heard in the crowd gasped aloud and a deathly silence followed.

Mrs. Vreeland stared icily at the young man and demanded, "Would you now?"

Cowed, the man backed off into the crowd.

Scavullo is known as the Rembrandt of photographers. His striking photographs set the style for the seventies, immortalizing a feeling about a time more elusive than most. Always dressed in black, he's a diminutive, warm midwestern man and a popular guest. He took Ellison by the arm and said, "I just heard all about your pool, and I can't wait to take a dip this summer."

Ellison smiled. "Oh, it's not to swim in, Frank. I'm gonna cover the top and lock Raul in it."

Warhol, standing nearby, shook his head and said, "My, my."

Ellison spotted Simon Morrow across the room with his back toward him, and felt his pulse quicken. For a short time he had managed to put Alvin Duff and his jeans out of his mind. Now he was confronted with the nemesis of the conglomerate in his own living room. Bearding the lion in his own den. Ellison would know Simon Morrow's bald pate and bull-like stance anywhere, a most ungraceful individual. True to form he was wearing a factory-cut suit and cordovan loafers. Ellison refrained from cringing and had started to make his way over to him when Morrow turned slightly and Ellison for the first time recognized his date.

It was Grace Dunn.

He had just seen her the night before at The Club and was wishing he could find a way to speak to her. Now here she was in his living room. Well, that was a coup! Warhol and Capote were staples at all the better parties, but Grace Dunn was a rarefied commodity. The princess would have to be most impressed. The only possible problem was that Jacky was going to be easily outclassed by Grace Dunn's presence. And she would be *furious!* She'd never believe that he didn't know Grace Dunn was coming with Morrow.

Oh, but she was a magnificent woman. Standing in his living room, she was even more beautiful than at The Club the night before. She was wearing a low-cut simple black sheath with a single strand of pearls. How could this woman not have a lover?

He rushed to her side. "I'm enchanted that Simon brought you," he told her.

"It's a great pleasure to meet you, too," Grace said.

"Your show is marvelous. Just marvelous," Ellison told her. A maid came by with a tray of hors d'oeuvres, which Ellison sniffed at and passed along.

"I've always thought you'd be one of the most exciting women in the world to dress," he said.

Grace tried to stop his flattery, but Ellison had uncorked the load. "No, really now, what more could a fashion designer want? Tall, thin, graceful. *Anybody's* clothes could look terrific on you."

Maybe that was *too* close to the point, Ellison thought.

"I just made something that would look fabulous on

you. It's perfect for your height and coloring. It's rust. Do you like rust? Well, then why don't I show it to you? Could you stop by the showroom sometime on Thursday and let me give it to you as a gift? I'd just love to see it on you, even once."

Grace turned to Morrow for some kind of protection from the predatory spiel, but even Morrow seemed helpless to deflect Ellison's unmitigated sales pitch.

"I'm busy Thursday," Grace said diplomatically, "but maybe some other day. Why don't I call?"

Ellison was about to insist they make a tentative appointment on the spot, about to throw in some conversation about some of the famous women he dressed when he found Abdullah at his side, looking worried.

"What is it?" Ellison asked, excusing himself from Simon Morrow and Grace Dunn.

"There's a young woman at the door who insists she's a friend of yours," Abdullah whispered, "but she isn't dressed, and she doesn't seem to know anything about the party."

"What's her name?"

"Marjorie something," Abdullah said, distressed. "I'm sorry but I couldn't tell—"

Oh, my God, Ellison thought, not *her*.

Marjorie Valasquez was the estranged wife of the president of Venezuela, who once saw herself as a kind of modern-day, jet-setting Eva Perón. Except that all she had in common with Perón was her lust for power, and since she couldn't get any herself, she seemed to be after power-by-insemination. In other words, this beautiful wife of a great political figure had become a common groupie. She had given up Venezuela and politics to run around with rock stars. And when the rock stars had run out, she turned to athletes and then finally to almost anybody who was interested. She was presently pursuing a career as a photographer but hadn't sold—or even developed—one picture as far as anybody was aware. She was always at The Club and had a high profile with the media because she was such an easy target and a good font of gossip. She idolized Ellison and wanted desperately to be in with his entourage, but he was afraid to be seen socializing with her. Not only did she have a bad reputation for using drugs, poorly, but everybody he knew detested the girl. They were actually a little afraid of her because Margie had proved recently that she had a very big, very lethal mouth.

"Marjorie, darling," Ellison said, mustering a smile for her. "What are you doing here?" She was dressed in jeans, cowboy boots and a work shirt. Next to her was a young man, about twenty-one, in the tightest pants Ellison had seen since Sylvia DeLaGrecco's husband, Toddy, at The Club last night. In fact, Ellison was sure he had also seen this boy at The Club last night.

"This is my friend, Freddy," Margie said. "He works as a busboy at The Club. We met last night."

"How nice for you," Ellison said with a frozen smile on his face.

"We were just out taking pictures of each other and we saw all the limousines outside and I thought I'd ring the bell and see what was happening."

"Ah, yes, I see," Ellison said, wondering what to do. "Well, as it happens, I'm having a very elegant dinner party and I'd invite you, but you're not dressed."

"Oh, that's all right. I don't mind. I won't feel out of place. Will you, Freddy?" she asked the busboy, who shook his head no.

"I fit wherever the vibes are good," the boy confided in Ellison.

Ellison wondered how he was going to get rid of these two when from behind him he heard Raul loudly proclaim, "Everyone! Look who is here! It is the *faaaaaabulous* Margie Valasquez!"

Margie screamed adoringly, "My Raul, darling!" and rushed into the house past Ellison. Helplessly Ellison turned to see them embracing in the living room like two children. Raul was dressed in a blue floor-length terry bathrobe.

"Ellison, you naughty liar, I thought you said everyone was dressed," Margie said, pulling at Raul's bathrobe.

"Everybody *is* dressed!" Ellison said with a forced smile. He would not lose his temper in front of guests. "Raul! Why are you in that bathrobe?"

Raul sprang to the top of a nearby chair. "I am going to have a drink in the hole for my new pool," he announced to the guests. Mrs. Vreeland listened politely, wondering what in heaven he was talking about. "I invite all of you to join me for champagne in the pool!"

Ellison smiled cheerfully while he thought of all the ways he would kill Raul. Raul turned to him defiantly, untied the belt of his bathrobe and let it fall off his shoulders to the floor. Everyone in the room let out a communal gasp. Raul was wearing a one-piece woman's swimsuit. He had filled the breasts of the Spandex suit with rolled socks. In the rear of the room Truman Capote's shrill laughter led the group in cheers and guffaws.

Raul marched off to the backyard, leading the party guests behind him while Ellison sat down on the steps to the living room, defeated but amused.

"Aren't you coming?" Margie Valasquez asked him excitedly.

"No, darling. But you run on ahead."

"Ready?" Jacky called into the bedroom. When she got no answer, she stuck her head in the bedroom door. To her great dismay, Eddie was in the same position she had left him in twenty minutes before, sitting on the bed in his jockey underwear drinking a can of beer. The hockey game was on TV, and Eddie was transfixed.

"Oh, darling, we're so late. *Please* get dressed," she begged, handing him his pants and shirt.

"Must I wear a tie?" Eddie asked, not looking up from the TV.

"I've gone through this a dozen times with you today. New York is just not California. In California you could get away with anything and not look like a slob. Actually, a lot of people in California really were slobs; you just didn't notice. But in New York you just cannot go to Ellison's black-tie dinner party in a sports jacket and not look inappropriately dressed." She had compromised when Eddie refused to wear a tuxedo; she compromised with a black suit; she was lucky to get him to agree to go altogether, but she put her foot down at no tie. She had already had to change her outfit three times to dress down to what Eddie would be wearing, and the great irony of it was that what she had decided to wear wasn't even an Ellison. It had been an exhausting day, keeping up with him so he wouldn't get near a copy of the *Post*.

"All right, all right," Eddie said, finally standing up. He went to his suitcase and picked out a tie. The suitcases had arrived late that afternoon, and the second they came through the door Jacky began to regret insisting that he move in with her. She suddenly had a very married, very trapped feeling. Frightening, but secure. Trying not to be too much of a wife, she hurried him along and managed to get him out by the elevator in another fifteen minutes.

"I hate this," Eddie said, tearing at his tie.

"I know, darling, but there are some people in New York that are important to impress."

"We need only to do a good show, Jacky, not to impress anyone. No?"

"No. We need to impress the critics. And we need to have friends." She kissed him lightly on the lips before he could answer.

Outside on the street the rain had stopped, and New York smelled washed and fresh. The chauffeur, a tall man in silver-tinted glasses, opened the car door for him. Jacky bent over to get in first.

Lying on the back seat was a copy of the *Post*.

"Who left that there?" Jacky asked. Eddie shrugged his shoulders and settled back in the seat.

"Good," he said. "I never got to read it."

"What address, ma'am?" the driver asked. Jacky paid no attention.

"Who left that paper here?" Jacky asked again.

The driver turned around to look at Eddie opening the *Post*. "I'm sorry, I don't know. It was tucked into the back seat when I picked up the car."

Bewildered, Jacky gave the driver Ellison's address and leaned back against Eddie, crushing the paper.

"Don't read now," she suggested coyly.

"Why not?" Eddie demanded, turning on the reading light behind him.

"Talk to me."

"Now? Let me read until we get there, please. We have all night for talk." He reopened the paper and began to leaf through it. "Anything about the show in the gossips?" The "gossips" was what he called the columns.

"Please, Eddie," Jacky said, squirming against him and kissing him, ripping the paper under her weight.

Eddie pushed her off him forcefully and shouted, "What is it you don't want me to read?"

"Nothing," Jacky said quickly, guilt all over her face. "Nothing," she said again more quietly.

Eddie testily reopened the paper. Almost immediately his eyes fell on what must have been Jacky's photograph because he held the page up to his nose, and his mouth fell open.

"Where was this taken?" Eddie asked, baffled, not understanding the headline.

"A few weeks ago, at The Club, when we first got to New York," Jacky said. "I don't know why they finally used it. I guess there was nothing more important for them to run."

Eddie wasn't listening; he was reading the caption underneath the photo, his lips moving as he translated each word into Italian in his head.

"Last night," he repeated aloud from the article. "This say 'last night.' Did you go *last night?* After I went *home?*"

Jacky sank into the farthest corner of the limousine, defeated.

"For a little while," she said in a small voice.

"Last *night?*" Eddie repeated, stunned that she had lied to him so forthrightly. "You said you were going right to sleep. You mean you got *up* and *dressed* after we made love and went *out?* You *still* needed to get out to that *disco?*"

"Please don't be angry, Eddie. I had already promised Ellison that I would meet him there. I had forgotten and then—"

"But you promised *me!*" Eddie exploded, his Sicilian lava boiling over and pouring out. He threw the *Post* at her and hit her in the arm. She recoiled like a cat. "Do you know why you were so fucking exhausted today in rehearsal?" he shouted. "Why you couldn't move all day and sat in the orchestra and slept?"

The driver looked in the rearview mirror.

"I did not sleep," Jacky said timidly.

"Slept! Yes, you did! And you lied! You lied to me and went out last night!"

"You're not my husband!" Jacky said, finally managing to raise her voice. "And even if you were my husband, that wouldn't give you the right to tell me when to go out!"

"Thank God I'm not your husband! I'm even worse! I'm your director! And as long as you're in my show, you'll listen to *me*. Otherwise, you can just get out, Jacky!"

"*Your* show?" she sputtered. "You dumb Italian lout! *Your* show! Without me to raise the money you couldn't direct a puppet show in New York!"

She felt instant regret as the car came to a jerky halt in front of Ellison's house.

"I'm not going in," Jacky said flatly. "Driver, take me home!"

"Oh, yes, you are!" Eddie said, grabbing her arm roughly. "You dragged me away from the hockey game for this, and we're going in!"

He leaned across her, threw open the car door and pushed her out into the street.

She turned to him and hissed, "If you embarrass me in front of my friends, you're going to regret this as long as you live."

"Champagne! More champagne!" Raul called from the ladder in the dirt pit in Ellison's backyard. For the last ten minutes he had been futilely trying to convince Mrs. Vreeland to climb down the ladder into the pit with him. Warhol was gamely climbing around the dirt and shovels to take pictures of Raul dancing about the hole and pouring Dom Pérignon over his head. Just inside the doorway to the house Grace Dunn and Simon Morrow watched Raul carry on. Ellison wondered if he should try to excuse Raul's behavior to them but thought better of it; best to just pretend it wasn't happening at all or at least it was nothing to be embarrassed about. After all, Capote and Catherine Guinness seemed to be enjoying themselves, and Janet Villella was calling encouragement to Raul as he persistently ordered Abdullah and the other servants to bring him more champagne to pour into the hole. He and Margie Valasquez began to wrestle in the muddy pit while the busboy from The Club sat on the mound of dirt, rolling a joint.

Ellison felt a wet drop on his forehead. "It's starting to rain again," he called to his guests, grateful there was a reason to call an end to the outdoor activities.

Mrs. Vreeland and Capote started to make their way back into the house before they got drenched.

Inside the living room there was a frozen tableau. Jacky Mellon and Eddie Bernardo were standing at opposite ends of the living room, glowering at each other. Grace Dunn and Simon Morrow were uncomfortably chatting in low tones in front of the fireplace. As the rain came down heavy outside, all the guests burst into the room behind Ellison.

"The lovebirds!" Ellison cried out, and Jacky looked as if she were about to break into tears. "How long have you two been here?"

Jacky stared at the carpet and shook her head. Slowly, the room seemed to move back into gear. Scavullo started talking amiably to Grace Dunn, and the doorbell rang again. Ellison crossed the room to Jacky and kissed her on the cheek. Then he extended his hand to Eddie, which Eddie shook heartily.

"We've just had the most terrible fight," Jacky whispered to Ellison. "I don't think I can bear to stay here with him."

Ellison whispered back, "If you try to leave this party, I'll have your hands cut off. Now come upstairs with me, and I'll fix you up. Diane! Catherine! Do you know Eddie Bernardo?"

He and Jacky slipped out of the living room and went upstairs.

"He pushed me! He actually pushed me out of the car! And he *threw* the newspaper at me. The nerve of him!"

"What was it all about?" Ellison asked, handing over his vial.

"Didn't you see the *Post* today?"

"Did I see the *Post*?" Ellison asked facetiously. He turned on the tap in the marble sink, wet his fingertips and dripped water into his nostrils to cleanse his nose of caked cocaine. "Fifteen people pointed it out to me. That was my glorious face in the upper right-hand corner."

"Can I sue them for that? I mean, that photograph could have ended my relationship with Eddie. Did you see what that son of a bitch Addison Critch wrote about me?"

"Yes. And you can't sue."

"Why not? How can people get away with saying such vicious things?"

"First, in order to sue, you have to prove that whatever was said is untrue. Then you have to prove that it's not only untrue but hurtful to you in some way, to your life or your career. And then you have to prove that it was written with malicious intent. You *were* at The Club, a public place. You *did* do a popper. And you *did* leave with Glesnerovsky. And as far as Addison Critch's malicious intent—well, that's the only thing we're sure about. What did Eddie have to say when he read it?"

"*Say?* He didn't say; he screamed. And he only got as far as the photograph. He threw the paper at me and pushed me out of the car."

"Poor pussy," Ellison said, putting his arm around her. She shook her head nervously from side to side. "Did you see Margie Valasquez downstairs?" he asked. "Do you believe she had the nerve to just ring the bell and invite herself in off the street without an invitation?"

"*No.* Is *she* here? Where was she?"

"Out in the backyard cavorting in a mud hole with Raul, wouldn't you know? She came with some hot bus-boy from The Club."

"You're kidding?" Jacky said, a little jealous. "Well, she just better keep her greasy little hands off Eddie."

"I thought Eddie just pushed you and threw the paper at you and that the *Post* probably ended your affair with him."

Jacky sniffed. "If he didn't love me, he wouldn't care enough to scream and push me." She searched her purse for her makeup.

"I can't keep up with you," he sighed.

"And who invited Grace Dunn?" Jacky demanded. "She makes me so nervous. She acts so superior and well bred all the time."

"Don't be intimidated by well-bred people, pussy. She came with Simon Morrow. It was a shock to me. Don't worry, though, darling, you're still the guest of honor. This is very much your affair. Now let's get downstairs and get dinner started. The princess will be here any minute."

Suddenly there was a loud pounding on the bathroom door. Ellison put his vial away and called, "One moment! Who is it?"

"It's me, Margie. And Freddy. Let us in. We want to take a shower."

Ellison rolled his eyes in exasperation.

"My God, that girl is such a slob," Jacky whispered. "Who keeps her around? I mean, who is she that she thinks she belongs with all of us?"

Ellison muttered, "So capricious and vengeful, this girl,

it's best not to offend her. She'll tell the press anything for publicity."

He opened the door wide and tried to smile. Both Margie and her boyfriend were dripping mud on the Megafur carpeting.

"Darling!" Ellison choked, his voice rising to mask hysteria. "Do I walk through your house caked in mud? Get into that shower before I spank you!"

Margie giggled and pecked him on the cheek petulantly, brushing mud onto his dinner jacket. He jumped back in horror and raced out of the bathroom as the busboy began to remove his pants. Jacky stayed to glare at the couple for a moment, and Margie playfully opened her shirt and popped a tit at Jacky, who harrumphed and followed Ellison out of the room.

Bobby Cassidy's American-line Yves Saint Laurent sports jacket that he wore all day in the office was as formally dressed as he could get for Ellison's dinner party. As he left work, he borrowed $100 from Pat, who was determined to see Bobby get a new pair of shoes to replace the ones that Ellison hated so much. But even with his new Bally loafers he hardly looked dressed enough for the formal setting in Ellison's town house. He was dazzled with all the space and luxury in the heart of Manhattan and truly impressed when he first arrived and heard the guests talking about a swimming pool Ellison was building in his backyard.

He searched the room for someone to talk to but didn't see one person he would have felt comfortable starting a conversation with, so he got himself four fingers of Stolichnaya from the bar and sat on a white chair near the fireplace and nervously buttoned and unbuttoned his jacket. On a wall near him was a David Hockney painting of boys in a blue swimming pool, and he stared at that for a while, waiting for Ellison to appear.

Suddenly he jumped to his feet. Grace Dunn had just appeared in the doorway. And she was smiling and chatting with an old, bald guy with a big belly!

Bobby felt a wave of anger and jealousy. That old, fat man with beautiful Grace! They stepped into the room and went to Mrs. Vreeland, who was standing with Capote and Warhol on the far side of the sofa. Grace's back remained toward him practically the whole time, and there was nothing he could think of to do except stand where he was and breathe deeply, trying to compose himself. Eventually he sank back into the chair and sat there waiting for her to spot him, his heart pounding deeply against his chest, not understanding what he was feeling except for overwhelming, possessive anger. He *loved* Grace, it dawned on him. Why would he feel this way otherwise? But how could she go out with an old guy like that? It was so depressing. He felt he would do anything to get her away from him, and he even fantasized leaping from the chair, punching the old man out and running off into the night with Grace.

Instead, he just sat there and felt bad.

The attention of the room suddenly became focused on the doorway at the top of the stairs, where Princess Hazanni had just arrived. She was a petite, attractive Arab woman in a trim gray suit, not dressy enough for the party, but expensive-looking and proper. Ellison swept into the room right behind, on cue, grasped each of her hands and kissed them with a bow. As he bent over, his eyes roved over her opal and diamond rings; by Ellison's quick appraisal at least twenty-five karats on her right hand alone. Jacky was right behind him, and he glowingly introduced her to the princess, who appeared truly charmed to meet the American star. Jacky was, as usual, endearingly nervous and shy. The princess introduced Ellison and Jacky to her country's ambassador to the United Nations, Jacques Alluahtan, who said flowery things with a beautiful English accent. Behind him was a swarthy, very serious-looking bodyguard who hovered protectively through the night.

Ellison put Jacky on one arm and the princess on the other and swept them around the room, making introductions as he went, bantering, signaling for a fresh tray of hors d'oeuvres and champagne, dropping his legendary stinging little barbs about the room. As Jacky made the rounds with him, she was again in awe of his social grace and power. This was Ellison at his peak; for the first time all day he was in complete control. He stopped occasionally to chat with guests as their social status dictated. Andy Warhol and Truman Capote were given a few deferential moments for small talk with the princess; other guests were given shorter social shrift. Eventually Ellison brought the women to the fireplace, where Bobby was standing with his back half turned toward Grace, who still had not looked in his direction.

"And here," Ellison announced to the princess proudly, "is my personal assistant, Bobby Cassidy. He's an invaluable aid." Ellison smiled proprietarily at Bobby, who in turn blushed bright red as he bowed and kissed the princess's hand. The princess said something polite and soft that Bobby didn't quite hear. He was about to ask her to repeat herself when he saw Grace turn and start toward them. Ellison called to her, "You must meet the princess. Princess Hazanni, this is one of the great ladies of the stage, Grace Dunn."

The hackles stood up on the back of Jacky's neck.

"Ah, yes, I am a fan," the princess said, smiling.

"And this is my personal assistant, Bobby Cassidy."

The two of them stood frozen until Grace said, "How do you do?"

When Bobby shook her hand, it was as cold as ice.

At dinner, Jacky Mellon sat next to Barry Meritt. Meritt was Ellison's physician. If anyone could deal with Jacky during dinner it would be Dr. Barry. He was handsome, appealing, reassuring, evangelical. His patients were rich and spoiled. He had amazing capabilities with people. He was a man blessed with a talent to heal. But Meritt was also a man of human fault. He loved cocaine. Merck cocaine. He loved beautiful women. He loved valuable art and furniture and cars. He was indulgent. In short, he was just like the clientele that was drawn to him, magnetically, because Dr. Barry would understand. Best of all, you could tell Dr. Barry *anything*. He had heard it all and seen it all. The bottom line was his office. He had seen Ellison's hemorrhoids and Polo Prann's appendix scar. He gave Horay the shot of penicillin when she got the clap and talked to Greta Garbo when she was in bed with the flu. And Dr. Barry had a range of information no other doctor in the city had, like prescribing a great deal of vitamin C for patients who did poppers or knowing when a patient was nauseated because his drugs had been cut with belladonna instead of milk sugar.

Ellison sat next to the Princess, who was an excellent conversationalist and seemed to have seen every important play in London and New York in the past year and was reading, of all things, Anaïs Nin. She was pleasant and

convivial, and she dwarfed the small, catty New Yorkers
at the table around her. For one moment Ellison stopped
wishing he dressed her and was just pleased that she had
agreed to dinner at his home.

At the far end of the table Portia Witticker, Ellison's
favorite black model, was convulsing the people around
her with the elaborate tale of how she and Ellison had
convinced everyone she was an African tribeswoman while
she had been born and reared above a hock shop in
Harlem. Portia also managed to raise a few eyebrows
when she disclosed that the Ellison original gown she was
wearing that evening belonged to the company and she
was being paid $200 to attend dinner.

This irked Bobby, who wasn't making $200 all week.
And he should have been paid to attend. The dinner party
was one of the most painful events he had ever attended,
particularly with Grace sitting midway down the table, just
a few feet from him. She seemed to be having no problem
at all chatting and eating while Bobby was choking on
every bite.

Raul had cleaned himself up and dressed in a black suit.
He situated himself with Marjorie Valasquez at the far end
of the table between Mrs. Vreeland and Scavullo and was
blowing kisses and winking at Ellison at the head of the
table, who ignored him completely. Ellison's biggest chore
at dinner was to keep smiling through the performance
Marjorie Valasquez and the busboy were putting on at the
end of the table. First, when they walked into the dining
room, the busboy made a hearty, loud hello to Bobby, his
fellow worker at The Club, much to Ellison's consternation and Bobby's great embarrassment. He couldn't even
bring himself to look at Grace for five minutes after the
incident. Then the busboy and Margie insisted on sharing
one chair, sitting "one cheek on, one off" as Marjorie put
it, and picking at Ellison's Fabulous Foods dinner with
their fingers.

The servants had just wheeled in a large silver-covered
carving tray with the lamb when the sound of the doorbell
began to ring insistently over the soothing music. In
another moment Stuart Shorter arrived in the dining room
with Horay holding his hand. He looked shocked to see
the room crowded with people.

All the men at the table stood up, and an instant chorus
of names went up around the table.

"Stuart!" Jacky cried, relieved somehow to have another friend there.

"Horay! Stuart!" Ellison said, embarrassed he hadn't invited either of them. He glanced quickly at Jacky to see how she reacted to Horay.

"Darling!" Horay cried to Ellison.

"Andy!" Shorter called.

"Truman!"

"Darling! You look faaabulous!"

"Wonderful. . . ."

"Do you know. . . ."

"Faaabulous!"

"Eddie!" Horay cried.

Jacky's blood froze in her veins.

"Horay, my darling! What a good surprise," Eddie said, kissing her on the cheek.

"You know each other?" Jacky asked involuntarily from the other side of the table.

Eddie looked into her eyes and saw a well of insecurity and selfishness, and at the moment he despised her.

"For years," Eddie said triumphantly.

"Sit down, please!" Ellison asked Shorter.

"Dr. Barry!" Horay screamed.

"Marjorie!" Shorter cried.

"Faaabulous. . . ."

"I want a picture! I want a picture!" Marjorie ran off to get her camera.

"From where do you know each other?" Jacky asked tonelessly.

"Grace Dunn . . . and this is Her Royal Highness Princess Hazanni . . . and of course, you know Frank for years. . . ."

"From Europe. . . ."

"From Cannes . . . ."

"I didn't know there was a formal dinner here," Shorter said to everybody, "or I wouldn't have come over."

"Nonsense, nonsense," Ellison said, "I'm glad you did. We'll get more chairs."

"We must get together," Horay said to Eddie.

Jacky thought she was going to faint. It was very hard for her to take deep breaths.

"I suppose you'll hear it on the news tonight," Shorter announced. "I was arrested today."

"Arrested!"

The princess regarded Shorter warily.

"I suppose you're going to read about it in the papers tomorrow. So I might as well be the one to tell you. David Willick just got me out of jail."

Everyone at the table spoke at once. Marjorie Valasquez ran up to Shorter and took his picture. In the confusion Grace took a peek at Bobby; he hadn't taken his eyes off her all night.

"Arrested for what?" the princess asked.

"How long have you been in New York?" Horay asked Eddie.

"You won't believe it," Shorter said.

"I'm directing Jacky in her show. You know Jacky, don't you?"

"At first it was just income tax evasion, but then they found drugs when they came to seize the records."

"Income tax!"

"Twenty-two counts. Conspiracy, too."

"It's *you* that's directing her!" Horay cried. "Oh, *no!*"

Jacky's stomach tumbled. She stood at her seat and mumbled, "Excuse me," but she spoke so quietly that only Dr. Barry saw her lips move before she fell forward on the table and passed out.

16

EQUITY NOTICE:

DUE TO THE ILLNESS OF MS. MELLON, REHEARSALS
FOR THE PERFORMANCE WILL RESUME THE MORNING
OF THE 29TH, 10 A.M., THE JANOFF THEATER.

MITCHELL-MOREFIELD, FOR THE PRODUCERS,
KEN AND ALICE LA FRANCE

CRITICISMS
by Addison Critch

*It's My Party and I'll Cry If I Want to Depart-
ment:* Some girls just can't help themselves, no matter
how posh the surroundings. I guess your upbringin'
just shows through. The scene of the crime was an
elite dinner party last night thrown by fashion pasha
Ellison in his white Megafurred East Side town house.
Guest of honor was Ellison's darling and best pal,
Jacky Mellon, in town with live-in director **Eddie
Bernardo,** to open in the much talked-about *The
Performance* on Broadway. Jacky was feted by celebs
like **Andy Warhol, Janet Villella, Truman Capote,
Grace Dunn, Scavullo, Marjorie Valasquez,** society's
private healer, **Dr. Barry Merritt,** and **Horay Prann,**
the beautiful, outspoken and unpredictable wife of
rock star **Polo Prann.** Dinner, provided by Fabulous
Foods, was going just fine as the guests munched on
roast lamb when it was revealed to all that Eddie
Bernardo and Horay Prann were "dear old friends"
according to one source, much to Jacky's chagrin,
who was so disturbed at Horay's flirting that she
allegedly threw herself on the dinner table in a fit,
thus disrupting and ending her own party. At the
Janoff Theater, where *The Performance* is expected
to open a week from Thursday, rehearsals have been

suspended for three days because of Jacky's "illness." Eddie Bernardo has reportedly flown off to Los Angeles for some rest and recreation. Stay tuned for the latest in the continuing soap opera saga. . . .

"Open up, Jacky!" Alice called sweetly.

The door to Jacky Mellon's apartment swung open a few inches but was held firmly in place by the chain lock. Jacky sat in a chair in the living room not ten feet away, dressed in a long flannel nightgown, watching in silence as the door banged open and closed. Her eyes were puffy and red from crying, and she had taken so much Valium she felt disassociated from everything happening around her. The phone had been ringing for some seventeen hours straight without her answering it, ever since Eddie, in a rage, had packed and moved his suitcases out of her apartment, after only six hours of living with her. In a last-ditch effort to get him to stay, Jacky had flushed all the cocaine that she had just bought from Ellison right down the toilet bowl.

"Jacky! Please open up, kitten!"

Outside the door in the tiny landing hallway Ken and Alice La France looked at each other and shook their heads in frustration. They had been outside the door half an hour, and still not a sound from Jacky except distant sighs. Behind them stood the building manager, a fat, balding man in a blue polyester suit, who had used the passkey on the lock.

"If you would only just leave us alone for a few moments, I'm sure we could coax her to open the door," Ken pleaded with the man, who was named Foley.

"Sorry," Foley said stubbornly, rocking nervously on his heels. "I can't open up a door with a passkey and leave people alone unless I get confirmation from the tenant. If you want to get in there, I'll call the police and have them break in."

"No, no. No police," Alice said, forcing a smile. "It's not that serious yet. And we're in the papers enough." She turned to the door and stuck her nose in the crack.

"Jacky! This is Alice. Open the door for me, sweetheart!"

"Go away!" Jacky yelled.

"There! She's conscious at least!" Ken said gratefully. "At least she didn't overdose on something."

"Jacky, darling," Alice called, "we're *so* worried. Why don't you open up?"

"Go away!" Jacky screamed and pouted.

"Think of something," Alice whispered to Ken.

Ken shrugged. "How the hell do you bribe a thirty-two-year-old baby when all she thinks about is sex and drugs?"

Alice contemplated this for a second. "I guess with sex and drugs," she whispered. She stuck her face through the crack in the door and whispered loudly, "Jacky, come closer. There's a security guard with me, and I have to give you something." Alice shuffled around in her purse and found her amber bottle, clasping it discreetly in her fist. She stuck her hand through the crack and cried, "Nose candy!" and tossed the bottle into the room where it fell in the middle of the living-room floor. Jacky's eyes widened when she saw it. Slowly she got down from the chair and crawled across the living-room floor on all fours toward it, sniffling as she went. She sat down cross-legged near the bottle, opened it and did several noisy snorts which the La Frances could hear in the hallway. Jacky remained on the floor for a while, blinking her brown eyes as her bloodstream incorporated the narcotic. The La Frances waited patiently until finally, a few minutes later, Jacky managed to get to her feet and unchain the door for them.

The La Frances burst into the apartment, slamming the door on the building manager behind them without even a thanks.

"Darling, this is impossible!" Alice began, taking Jacky into her arms and hugging her. "We were so frightened when you didn't answer the phone. If you need us, then you must talk to us, not close yourself off from the people who truly love you."

"Why didn't you come to rehearsal?" Ken demanded. Alice tried to shush him, but he wanted to know.

"Because," Jacky said, "I knew Eddie wouldn't be there," and she started to cry again. Alice held her more tightly and looked at Ken guiltily.

"Well, to be truthful," she said, taking a deep breath, "Eddie wasn't there today. He had to go to Los Angeles early this morning, but he'll be back tomorrow."

Jacky started to bawl loudly in Alice's arms. "No he *didn't!* He left me! He hates me! He packed all his luggage and moved out before I even got home. He even took the *vitamins.* He's never coming back. I ruined it! I ruined it!"

Alice rocked her back and forth in her arms. "Oh, darling, I heard all about the party last night, and you didn't sound that bad. Things like that happen all the time. I've passed out a dozen times at embarrassing moments, ask Ken. . . ."

"Eddie said he never wanted to see me again. He said I *threw* myself on the table. . . ."

"He'll be back, sweetie, I promise. He just went to L.A. to sign some papers, and he'll be right back. We suspended rehearsals for three days so you could get a good rest."

"I bet he's with Horay."

"You must not think that, Jacky," Alice counseled.

"He's allowed to be with who he pleases," Ken added. "What's most important now is the show, Jacky. You have to think about the professional reputations of everyone involved."

"Ken, you are fucking heartless," Alice said, shielding Jacky's ears.

"Don't coddle her. She's not an egg."

"How did you know about the fight?" Jacky suddenly asked. "Is it all over New York?"

Ken took a deep breath and broke the news: "It's Critch's lead item."

"Oh, God." Jacky sighed. She got up from Alice's arms and walked dramatically across the room to the windows overlooking the spires of St. Patrick's. Ken rolled his eyes, half expecting her to throw herself through the glass.

"He'll never come back, will he?" she asked wistfully.

Alice came up behind her and held her shoulders lovingly. "It's a bit much for any man, to throw yourself on a table in front of a dinner party. But just give him a little time, and he'll cool down. Ken and I will work on him, won't we, Ken?"

"Will you?" Jacky asked, brightening, turning to Ken.

"You're damn right we will," he assured her, putting his arm around her. "He has a contract and a show to direct."

Jacky wiped the tears from her eyes. "You mean it? You'll get him back?"

"Guaranteed," Ken said, "if he doesn't want a multimillion-dollar breach-of-contract suit."

Jacky kissed Alice on both cheeks. "I love you!" she squealed.

"We love you, too."

"Feel better?"

"Terrific. Now I want you to do me a favor."

"What's that?"

"I want the phone number of a member of the chorus."

17

She told him that she wanted a workout partner, that because rehearsals were called off, she was afraid she was going to get stiff and needed some stretching exercises. "No," she told him, "I'm not sick at all. That stuff in the paper was just an excuse because Eddie Bernardo had to go off to L.A. to sign some papers." He got the idea right away, and he was delighted to help.

His name was Rusty Curtis, a perfect name for a carrot, a name that she could forget in an hour. It was the kind of pretty sobriquet all chorus boys with long blond hair, blue eyes and dancer's buns should have, she thought. Ken and Alice knew immediately which one she wanted from her description; he was the one who couldn't dance.

She felt so secure—the star and the chorus boy—that she dressed only once, in black pants and a black pullover top. She washed and dried her hair for him, dancing around the bedroom and listening to the radio like a teenager. She had asked him to arrive at eight o'clock, and the doorman buzzed her promptly at that time.

She went to the door, opened it and then decided it was more effective if she wasn't standing there when the elevator door opened. Then she opened the door again, and before she could second-guess herself, the elevator door did open, and he was there before her, her heart fluttering in her chest like a little girl's.

Most of all, Rusty Curtis seemed so *big*. As he stood there in the doorway, she realized that she hadn't been closer than ten feet to him since she first saw him. Up close he was tremendous; impressively, gloriously big.

"Hi, there," she said, about to dig her toes into the carpeting.

"Hi. Nice to meet you," he said in a pleasant deep voice. His eyes were an aqueous blue.

"I suppose you were shocked when I called?"

"I was," he agreed shyly.

"Well, I was lonely and I needed to stretch." She led

him into the living room, trying to figure out the meaning of her own words. What she was saying was: *I was lonely and needed to fuck.* "I suppose since you're a dancer, if you miss a day or two it doesn't matter, but for me this is a training period. It's important I keep limber every day."

He nodded silently.

"You're so big," she told him.

"Six-three," he admitted. "It's an advantage for a dancer."

"Would you like a drink?"

"Before stretching?" He was surprised.

That was a little stupid, she supposed, but she needed one anyway. "I always just loosen up a bit," she explained, "just a small one. Why don't you join me?"

He hesitated for a moment and then gave in. "All right, I suppose a small one wouldn't be too bad."

Without asking what he wanted to drink, Jacky poured the best 150 proof vodka she could find on ice in a glass and handed it to him. She filled the tumbler with cognac for herself and slugged back a big gulp.

"So, you're a terrific dancer," she said when she had recovered her voice.

"Have you seen me dance?" he wondered. There really hadn't been a lot of dancing at the rehearsals. Jacky decided another topic was in order.

"What do you think of Chomsky?" she asked.

"He doesn't like your boyfriend very much, does he?" Rusty's face collapsed in embarrassment. "Gee, I'm sorry, I guess that was out of line. . . ."

"Don't be silly. Everybody knows he's my boyfriend. He's in L.A. right now."

"You told me."

There was a stretch of uncomfortable silence. Jacky realized she was perspiring. Seduction was never this difficult. Why couldn't she think of anything to say? Why didn't *he* say anything? She excused herself and went into the bathroom for a lude. She hated to do it this way, but it was obviously the only thing that would loosen her up. She held the large white pill under her tongue, went back into the living room and washed it down with more cognac. Rusty had already finished his vodka, and Jacky went quickly to get a refill for him.

"Where are you from?" she asked, handing him his drink.

"Santa Barbara, California. But mostly I grew up in L.A."

"L.A.! Really? Somehow I expected you to be from around here."

"That's funny. Most people know right away I'm from the Coast."

"That's funny," Jacky repeated. There was a clumsy pause. "Where did you live in L.A.?"

"Beverly Hills."

"Me too."

"I think . . . I think my mother worked with your mother . . ." Rusty stammered bashfully.

"Really?" Jacky said, only mildly interested. "How's that?"

Broadway Melody, I think it was."

That was curious. *Broadway Melody* had been one of Angela's best musicals and had won her her first Oscar. The kid's mother must have been a chorus girl, too. "Oh, yeah? Was your mother in show business?" Jacky took a swig of her cognac.

"My mother was Helen Lawson."

Jacky nearly dropped her glass. The cognac stuck in the back of her throat, and she coughed a little as she gasped, *"Really?"* Helen Lawson was a major musical comedy star five years older than her mother would have been and at least as popular, save for Angela's cult following. In fact, just the last year Helen Lawson had recorded a highly successful disco album of her show tunes. She was a brassy, tough lady whom Angela had never been especially fond of.

"Why is that so unbelievable?" he asked.

"Because nobody ever mentioned it at the theater."

"Nobody knows. I guess I'd prefer to keep it a secret. I mean, I wouldn't deny it, but it just doesn't come up in conversation when you're in the chorus."

"But your name—"

"It's my professional name. My real name is Russell Lawson."

"Why didn't you tell anybody your mother was Helen Lawson when you were auditioning?"

Rusty was amazed. "Why? Why should I mention it?"

Jacky thought about it for a moment. It certainly wouldn't have helped get him the job if he had mentioned it because he couldn't dance anyway. And she supposed that for some people, mentioning you have a famous parent is like name-dropping. Only Jacky's mother was so famous she had very little choice.

"I guess I never thought about it that way before," she told him.

"That's visibility for you. It's a curse, don't you think?"

"How do you mean?"

"Did you ever wonder if you could have made it on your own, without having show business connections."

"I did make it on my own," Jacky said, slightly peeved.

"But you must have had an agent or known a movie producer or something, didn't you? I mean, I think you're a terrific talent and all that, but growing up in your household must have been a help."

"Or a hindrance."

"I suppose that, too."

They fell silent again.

"Then I suppose you knew Fred Astaire?" Jacky asked.

"He was my godfather," Rusty said, unimpressed. He took another sip of his drink and then got his dance shoes from his dance bag and put them on. He pulled off his sweater to reveal a tight white T-shirt.

She went off into the bedroom for a moment and got the entire bottle of Quaaludes, which she shook under his nose and giggled. She spilled the bottle of thick white pills out on the lush carpeting and examined them.

"Are you going to take one?" he asked.

"I already did."

"Why?"

"I was nervous," she admitted.

"Well, don't be nervous," he said warmly. He swallowed one of the pills with his vodka. They sat in silence for a long time, a comfortable, understanding silence. Jacky liked the fact that she felt comfortable with him without having to try to be entertaining or funny. He finally spoke.

"The thing is . . . is after this happens . . . well, I know this sounds silly, but after we do whatever we're gonna do, are you ever going to see me again?"

Jacky blushed and repressed an embarrassed smile. "What do you mean, 'do whatever we're gonna do'?"

"You didn't invite me here and give me vodka and Quaaludes to stretch with you. . . ."

"I didn't?" Jacky said, breaking into a smile.

"No. And I'm glad." He lifted her head up to his and kissed her lightly on the lips.

"I can't believe this is happening," she said blissfully, kissing him harder. Immediately she reached down for the lump in his pants that she had watched for so many days from the orchestra of the Janoff. She grabbed the shaft firmly in her right hand.

Her fingers didn't close.

She reached around to feel it better; maybe she had grabbed his pants, too. But when she looked down at the protrusion in his pants, she realized it was as thick as a can of soda.

She grinned from ear to ear, and he grinned back at her, proud of his size and her obvious delight with it. He gently pushed her back on the carpeting. She kissed his face all over, kissed the green eyes that were so pretty from all the way across the rehearsal room, ran her hands up and down the muscles of his back as she sucked on his tongue. Abruptly he rolled off her and pulled his T-shirt over his head. His nipples were brown and hard, encircled by patches of dark blond hair. His pectoral muscles were chiseled from dancing and stretching and she reached out to touch them, pulling on the nipples like a child at its mother's breast. Soon he stood above her and lowered his exercise pants, revealing an engorged dance strap, conically enlarged by his stiff cock underneath. His hands moved to pull the strap down, but she brushed them away and buried her face in the fabric, reveling in his smell and the feel of his thighs on her cheeks as she pressed her face up against his rock-hard prick. He pushed her shoulders back down and lay lengthwise next to her, pulling her panties down with one stroke. He rubbed the flat of his palm against her pussy, softly at first, then wobbling his huge hand harder and harder across the mouth of her opening. He spread her legs wide, like a doctor doing an internal examination, and gently opened the lips of the vagina, orchidlike, moist and oozing. She closed her eyes blissfully as the warmth of his mouth filled her. She started to come, again and again as he licked hard against her vagina, moving his head up and down as if he were lapping up a delicacy, his nose and chin wet and slick with her.

"Do you want a popper?" he asked her, leaning over to his dance bag. He retrieved a small yellow tube covered with plastic mesh and a pump jar of hand lotion. He sat

back and pulled his cock out of his dance strap. Jacky
stared at it, fascinated; it was a beautiful cock, if there
could be such a thing, like the cock of a giant statue,
pulsing with his heartbeat. He moved her on her back and
got into position over her. His cock was very red now,
almost purple, as he directed it to her pussy. As he entered
her she felt a bolt of electrical current pass right through
her. She felt so tight around him, relieved of some terrible
anxiety that was constantly with her until now. All she
wanted was for him to shove it into her, and she started
begging him, "Shove it. Shove it into me! Shove it!" And
he started slamming into her, swaying from side to side,
jamming it into the outer walls of her vagina full force,
occasionally meeting her thrusts so hard that she felt sharp
pain in her bowels but never stopped egging him on. Beads
of sweat from his face and forehead sprinkled her breasts.
She raised her head and looked down to where they were
joined, entranced by the sight of his cock wet and slick
plunging in and out of her.

"Come inside me," she begged him, feeling the peaks
rising toward another overwhelming orgasm.

"Not this way," he said huskily. "From behind."

He turned her over on her stomach and crouched
behind her. He managed to penetrate her vagina with his
penis, but he quickly withdrew and whispered, "Up the
ass."

"You can't. . ." Jacky began to protest, but he snapped
something in his hand and shoved it under her nose. She
gasped at the sweet, erotic smell of the amyl nitrate and
involuntarily her muscles loosened, and it was difficult for
her to stay up on all fours. Already he was prying into her
rectum with his fingers, wet with the jucies from her pussy.
She groaned loudly as he worked a second finger into her
and then finally, slowly, inserted the head of his cock. She
screamed once in pain, and he gave her the popper to
smell again so he could work his way deeper into her until
she felt pressure in her stomach and lungs and wetness
seemed just to seep out of her, washing over her thighs.
Dazed, she cried out with each of his thrusts, wondering
when it would end, when he would come, her face crushed
against the carpeting, distantly aware of the sweet poppers
and the tingling of the Quaalude and the boy's grunting,
louder and harder with each thrust, until he slammed into
her with one final juice-giving punch and she collapsed

underneath him into unconsciousness as he filled her and
filled her.

She awoke the next morning, aching from head to toe,
lying on the floor next to him, uncovered and chilled. She
tried to sit up, but her head hurt so much and was so
heavy she thought it was bolted in place to the floor. She
tried to lie there for a while with her eyes closed, but the
overwhelming urge to vomit forced her into a sitting
position. Not unlike a child learning to walk, she lifted
herself to her feet on the arm of a nearby chair, looked
down and let out a little scream of horror. "Annnnhh!"

There was a pool of dried blood on the rug. She bent
forward and examined herself; she had hemorrhaged during the night.

Frightened now, she tried to wake Rusty. The boy
groaned softly and rolled over in a deep sleep. On the table
near him was her bottle of Quaaludes, opened on its side,
the thick pills spilling out onto the table.

Slowly she limped into the bathroom and started to
whimper once she glimpsed herself in the mirror. There
was a large black and blue mark on her right thigh the size
of an apple. Her eyes looked blackened, and her face was
so yellow she could have had hepatitis. Her dark hair stuck
in sweaty patches to her neck and head. Weeping softly,
she ran a lukewarm tub and washed away the blood. She
tried to settle back into the water, but the nausea forced
her up again to the toilet to throw up. When she was
finished, she finally felt a little better, as if she had purged
her system of the poisons. Dizzy, her vision blurred with
tears, she stumbled back into the living room and found
her Quaalude bottle, split one in half and swallowed it to
get to sleep. Back in the bedroom she climbed into her
unslept bed and pulled the covers up over her shoulders.
Her mother stood in the doorway, fixing her earrings, just
watching her. Jacky raised herself on one elbow in bed and
called, "Momma?" but the vision turned and walked away
and disappeared.

Whom could she call for help, with Helen Lawson's
naked son asleep on the floor outside? Not Ellison. Not
Ken and Alice. Whom could she turn to at a moment like
this? Dr. Barry? She reached for the bedside phone and
punched in information, got Dr. Barry's number and

called it, but she hung up when a service operator answered.

Why had Eddie left her? Would she ever have a relationship with a man or would she chase them all away? She rolled on her side and cried bitterly into her pillow. What had she accomplished at age thirty-two? Whom had she become? If she had any guts at all, she would kill herself and not wait another twenty years to do it the way her momma did until she was sick and dying of cancer. Why should she go on, a public whipping post, a laughingstock, alone, abandoned, forever relegated to some chorus boy or hustler who really didn't care a fig about her?

The ringing of the telephone was like a knife in her brain.

She reached out for it apprehensively and held it to her ear without speaking.

"Jacky?" Eddie's voice asked hesitantly. Her breath caught in her chest.

"Yes?" she said softly, her voice cracking as if she were laughing or crying.

"Are you awake? It's ten o'clock," Eddie said to her.

"Yes, I'm awake," she said, trying to open her eyes.

"Jacky, this cannot go on. We have meant too much to each other to be ruined so easily. There is too much at stake for both of us." He paused while Jacky wondered if she wasn't hallucinating again. She looked at the doorway for her mother, but it was empty.

"Me, too, Eddie. I'm sorry. I'm so sorry." Now she broke into muffled little sobs.

"I'll come right over, we'll talk," Eddie said.

"Where are you?" Jacky gasped. "I thought you were in Los Angeles. . . ."

"A story we made up for the papers. I'm in my hotel. . . ."

"Oh, God. I need time to clean up, to dress. . . ."

"Two hours then? At noon?"

Jacky's head was swimming. She wouldn't be ready to see anybody for two days, let alone two hours.

"Please, let me meet you somewhere for lunch, say, at one-thirty?" Jacky begged.

"All right, one-thirty, then. Say, at the Russian Tea Room? I'll see you then, darling. And don't worry. Together we can work it out."

She hung up the phone and thought: Now I've done it! How was she going to make it to the Russian Tea Room by one-thirty? Even now the fresh dose of Quaaludes was making her woozy. She laid her head back and tried not to fall asleep. Where could she get some cocaine to stay awake? Whom could she call?

Suddenly the doorman's buzzer rang. From her bed Jacky yelled, "Go away!" but the buzzer relentlessly rang through the apartment. Eventually Jacky managed to stagger to her feet and walked slowly to the house phone in the kitchen.

"What is it?" she shouted into the receiver.

"I'm sorry to disturb you, Miss Mellon, but there's a woman here who claims to know you," a metallic voice pleaded.

"No visitors! No more calls! Don't ring up here, you hear?"

But the voice that answered wasn't that of the doorman. It was a voice from long ago in her past.

"Miss Jacky? You let me up! Suie is here!"

She knew the phrase and thought: Now I've done it

18

"Oh, my God! Look at you! Just look at you!"

Suie rushed into the apartment, her fox-collared tweed coat flying out behind her, the color draining from her face with each step. She helped Jacky down on an overstuffed armchair and surveyed the room in horror. Furniture was overturned, and clothes were strewn about the room as if there had been a wild orgy. When Suie's eyes came to the naked giant on the floor, she reared back. Jacky watched her in fascination. Suie had one of the most expressive faces she had ever seen. Her face was animated, like a Disney figure, able to change size and shape and expression in seconds. Jacky watched it go from anger to pity to worry to sorrow.

"Oh, Suie," Jacky sobbed, still sitting, leaning forward to hug the woman around her waist. "It's been awful, awful."

Suie patted Jacky on the head consolingly but purposely did not take her in her arms. Instead, she pointed to the sleeping figure and asked, "Who is that man?"

Jacky thought of telling her exactly, but instead, she said, "I hardly remember. Some boy from the chorus."

Suie put her pocketbook on a table and took off her coat. "Oh, my, Miss Jacky," she said softly. "Did you go and sleep with your carrot?"

Jacky didn't know what to do: laugh, cry or jump up and kiss the woman. She felt overwhelming relief that Suie understood; with Suie there were no apologies, no explanations necessary.

"Oh, Suie," Jacky sobbed, "what am I gonna do? What am I gonna do?"

Suie sighed. "First, you're gonna cut the dramatics 'cause that never got us anywhere. Then you're gonna help me get this boy outah heah."

Suie went to the boy and shook him gently, then violently. "Hey, you, get up!" she commanded, but the boy only rolled over.

"Which way is the kitchen?" she demanded from Jacky, who pointed feebly to the way. In a few moments Suie had returned with a cooking pot of cold water. Holding it high above the sleeping young man, she poured it over him from head to toe, first in a thin stream and then in a waterfall over his stomach and groin.

Jacky's eyes widened as the boy began gasping with his eyes closed, "Ohh! Ohh! Ohh!"

"Maybe he'll get a heart attack, doing that," Jacky cautioned Suie. Poor Rusty!

"Heart attack, my ass! I know how to get a junkie up in the morning!" And with that Suie kicked him in the behind.

"Owww!" Rusty cried, rubbing his behind. He blinked disbelievingly at the sight of the black woman towering over him.

"Who are *you?*" he asked hoarsely.

"I'm gonna be your ruination if you don't have your trousers on in five seconds and get your ass out this door!" Suie thundered.

Jacky stopped crying now and was more composed in front of the conscious young man. He turned to her for some sort of support, but Jacky couldn't meet his eyes. She gave him her camera left profile, her eyes cold and distant. He resignedly got to his feet and looked about for his pants. Suie, despite herself, took a quick glance at him before turning away and rolling her eyes at Jacky, standing between them, shielding him from view. "Goodbye," he said forlornly when he was dressed and had gathered his belongings into his dance bag.

Suie glared at him.

"Good-bye," Jacky answered, despite herself. He was OK, poor guy. She wondered what would happen to him now as he went out the door. She looked up at Suie, who didn't look very sympathetic.

"Suie, I'm in so much trouble. I need you so much," Jacky said, pulling Suie to her and hugging her around the waist.

"And a good thing for you, too. I was in Philadelphia, seein' my sister Bess, when I read in the Philly papers that you're in New York, readyin' a show. I thought I might come by and see you, child. It's been five years since I was with you, and I raised you like my own daughter."

"How'd you find me?" Jacky asked, looking up at her

and sniffling, trying to keep her eyes open. Suie wiped away a tear from each eye and bent over to kiss her forehead. The touch of Suie's cool lips seemed to lull the pain in her head away.

"It wasn't hard to find you," Suie explained quietly. "It's in all the papers where you're living."

But Suie meant something else, Jacky knew. She meant that it was in all the papers *how* Jacky was living. Jacky dozed a bit.

"Are you on drugs?" Suie suddenly asked, taking Jacky's chin into her palm. Jacky shook her head no, but Suie held it firmly in place, stopping her from lying. "I can tell, darling. I wasn't with your momma for all those years for nothing. Don't bullshit me."

"I'm not on drugs," Jacky said. "I mean I *did* take two sleeping pills a half hour ago. I'm exhausted and I—"

"Never understood," Suie interrupted, "why exhausted people need to take pills to make them more exhausted. If you was so exhausted in the first place...."

"Suie, please, you've got to help pull me together. I have to be at lunch in two hours at the Russian Tea Room."

"I'll call and cancel."

"No, you can't. It's Eddie, my director. We had a big fight, and he's willing to make up. I've got to meet him and talk to him. My whole life is riding on it, Suie."

Suie put her hands on her hips and shook her head disdainfully. "My, my. Just like your momma. No better, no worse. Every minute a drama. Every second another crisis, the end of the world. Why we ever let you become a performer like your momma, I don't know. Betsey Flint should've been shot before they gave you the chance to follow in your momma's footsteps. What would've happened if you were a nice little housewife in North Dakota? Would you have had this many problems?"

"Probably. Why not?" Jacky asked sleepily, the Quaaludes coming for her now.

"Because I figure you got it too good to be having this many problems. I figure that any little girl born to a famous momma who became a big star herself would clean up her act. So why you bein' so trashy?"

"I'm not trashy, Suie. The world is trashy." And Jacky's head lolled forward, asleep.

"Not my world, Miss Jacky. Not my world." Suie sighed. She went to Jacky and kissed her on the forehead.

Then she tried to lift the sleeping girl off the ottoman, but Jacky was too heavy to raise. "All right," Suie mumbled, rolling up her dress sleeves and grabbing the ottoman by the sides. With Jacky still asleep on it, she dragged the heavy piece of furniture across the living room carpet and into the bedroom.

Suie knew exactly what to do; she had been through it many times before with Angela. She ran a lukewarm tub and stripped her clothes down to her half slip and bra. Then she lifted Jacky off the chair and carried her a few feet to the tub, where she gently settled her into the water. The warm bath revived Jacky enough for Suie to give her a cool shower, and walk her around the bedroom for an hour, pouring coffee into her until the girl had to urinate every four minutes. Then back into a cool shower again. Suie didn't even let her towel off but led her back into the bedroom, shivering, and made her walk around until she was dry.

One hour and forty minutes later Suie stepped back to appraise her work proudly. She was still an expert at revitalization. With her makeup on, Jacky looked reasonably presentable. Perhaps she didn't look as if she had been on a Barbados vacation or anything, but she didn't look so bad.

Jacky had to agree. She was dressed in a white collarless peasant shirt, embroidered white on white silk, underneath an open vest, like a fitted shawl, beaded with pale iridescent sequins, and black linen pants.

"How can I thank you for this, Suie?" she asked.

Suie shook her head. "I don't know, Miss Jacky. I don't mind helping you out in a pinch, but I don't like it that the first time I see you in five years, I fall back in the same role, just like I did all those years before with your momma. Here's me doing what I was doin' and you doin' what your momma was doin'. I don't like it at all. I think I should pack up and go away right now, Miss Jacky."

Jacky's eyes filled with tears, which in another moment brimmed over onto her cheeks. She threw her arms around Suie and buried her face in Suie's huge breasts. "Dear God, Suie, I love you. I love you so, Suie. You're all I have left. Please don't leave me, Suie. Stay for a while. Until the show opens . . . see me through. It'll change. I promise it's not ever like this. This was special . . . Eddie walked out on me. . . ."

"All right, all right, now," Suie said, lifting Jacky's chin. "You'll muss your makeup, and we'll have to start all over again. I'm not goin' anywhere. Not at least till you get back from lunch. So hurry up, now, don't be late."

"Where are you going to be while I'm gone?" Jacky asked suspiciously.

"I'm not goin' anywhere. I'm gonna get me a beer from the refrigerator, take off my shoes and watch TV in your bed. So you shoo off now."

Jacky kissed her and squeezed her one more time and then made off to the door. Suie followed her across the living room.

"Now don't fight, but don't take no guff," Suie advised at the door. "Remember, a man is like a good shoe. Until he's broken in, don't put your foot in it!"

19

The cabdriver was a New York wise-ass kid.

He wore mirrored sunglasses and had his hair pomaded back and parted in the middle. He was wearing a blue turtleneck sweater and jeans, and on the front seat a portable cassette player was blasting the Jefferson Airplane *Volunteers* album.

"Could you turn that down?" Jacky asked him when she first got into his cab.

"The Russian Tea Room, huh? Is that on Fifty-seventh?" he asked.

"If you'd turn down your music, you'd be able to hear your customers," Jacky told him.

"I got Michael Franks," he offered, snapping off the Jefferson Airplane and then replacing it with the hazy warbling of a man's voice. He looked at Jacky in the rearview mirror but didn't seem to recognize her.

"So what do they got there, Russian food at the Russian Tea Room?" he asked her.

"I really don't want to talk," Jacky said sullenly. The pain in her temples was beginning again and she wanted to sit calmly and quietly.

"Ex*cuse* me!" the driver said, smiling at her in the rearview mirror. Now he took a closer look at her, keeping his eyes on her in the mirror until he stopped the cab at the corner of Sixth Avenue. There he turned around in his seat, stuck his face through the Plexiglas division, gave her the once-over and asked the question she had expected all along, "You're what's her name, right?"

Jacky nodded. "Angela Mellon's daughter," she said ironically.

"What do you know! My lucky day! I'm a performer, too!"

"The light just changed," Jacky ordered, gesturing for him to drive on. "I'm late for an appointment."

"OK, OK," he said, stepping on the gas. "I'll get you

there lickety-split. It's just that I happen to be a performer, too. . . ."

"Please, I do not want to talk. If you insist on talking, I'll get out."

"OK, OK," he said, shutting up for the moment while he studied her in the rearview mirror. After a brief pause he said, "You're prettier than your mother."

"I said, *no talk!*" Jacky cried.

"OK! OK!"

They were caught again at a light on Fifty-sixth Street, where he rifled through his cigarette pack and lit a joint. He inhaled on it deeply at the red light, smirking at Jacky in the back seat. She sneered back at him, dying to get out of the cab.

"Here," he said through his nose, holding the grass in his lungs. "Have a hit."

"No, thank you," she said tonelessly. She should report this driver. But they were all stoned, anyway, these wise-ass kids.

The light changed, and they drove on. "You opening a Broadway show?" he said. "I've seen the posters up all over the city. Very snazzy. You, too. You're a very talented lady, and I'm honored you're in my cab."

"Thank you," Jacky said grudgingly. As they came down the block to the Russian Tea Room, he offered her the joint again. She stared at it hesitantly this time. The grass would lull her headache and relax her. Finally she took it from him and greedily took five quick, deep hits from it until the cab stopped across the street from the Tea Room.

"I just wanted to see you loosen up," the driver told her from behind his mirrored glasses. She left him a $5 tip and slammed the door behind her. She took a deep breath as she looked at the Russian Tea Room. Slowly she picked her way across traffic on Fifty-seventh Street.

Jacky went through the brass revolving doors of the restaurant and skirted the large queue of people waiting for tables. The dining room was virtually humming with excitement. The restaurant is one of the prettiest in New York with its large red leather booths, deep green walls and impressive collection of paintings. There are brass samovars everywhere, and the chandeliers are forever festooned with tinsel garlands and red Christmas tree balls.

The restaurant was opened in 1927 by a Pole who had served with the white Russians, and the ambiance and menu have been carefully preserved. Richard Burton eats karsy shashlik at the Russian Tea Room and Rudolph Nureyev, who has a favorite booth on the west wall, eats sirloin steak very rare when he eats lunch at all. When Barbara Walters lunches with the Israeli ambassador, both of them eat cold borscht with giant globs of creamy white sour cream. Helen Gurley Brown occasionally stops in for lunch but does not eat. And from November to April, when they live in Manhattan, the Salvador Dalis always brunch at the Tea Room on Sundays.

Jacky tried to hold her head straight ahead as she was led through the green arch into the main dining room, but she could not miss spotting Woody Allen out of the corner of her eye lunching with his best pal Tony Roberts and *Saturday Night Live* producer Jean Doumanian, sitting in the hallowed booth in which impresario Sol Hurok had eaten lunch every day. It was the prime booth of the restaurant, and it irked Jacky that she was to be seated in the second-best booth, where Eddie was already waiting, staring somberly into a martini. As she came up to the table, their eyes met. He edged his way out to greet her and kissed her softly on the cheek expressionlessly. Jacky could practically feel a chill of excitement rush through the Tea Room as he did this.

"Eddie, I missed you so," she said, sinking into the banquette.

"I know, I know, darling. Sit and talk. Let's have a long talk. . . ."

"Why are you so pale?" she asked him, reaching out to touch his cheek. He hadn't shaved in two days. He gently took her hand from his face and held it lightly down on the table. He smiled weakly at her but did not answer. "I'm so nervous," she said. "Everyone said you had gone to Los Angeles. . . ."

There was a clumsy pause while Eddie looked into his drink. "No. I'm here."

"I can't calm down," Jacky confessed, fishing for a cigarette in her pocketbook. She flinched a little at a sharp pain in her temples.

"Have a drink," Eddie suggested.

The very thought of a drink made her stomach churn, and now she wished she hadn't taken the tokes off the joint in the taxi. From the corner of her eye she could see Woody Allen shoveling spoonfuls of dark ruby borscht into his mouth, and she felt a little dizzy. A misty spray of perspiration broke out on her forehead. "No booze for me," Jacky told Eddie.

"No, have a drink, it will calm you," Eddie assured her. He waved to a waiter and ordered two martinis. Then he took her hands in his to stop her from rummaging through her purse and held them in his. "Darling, we must stop fighting. There is only one thing that is important to us, and that is the show."

"I agree, Eddie," Jacky said, so relieved to hear him say anything remotely reassuring. "It was foolish for me to be jealous just because you knew Horay. I mean, she was never a girlfriend, was she?"

Eddie rolled his eyes and shook his head. "It has nothing to do with Horay, Jacky. It has to do with the show, with our careers."

"I think we're important, too," Jacky countered.

"We're important as individuals, but not as a couple."

Jacky was appalled. "But we *are* a couple Eddie, and that's become part of the show."

"Then that is also what's wrong with the show. We must not be a couple any longer."

"But *why?*"

"Because we cannot mix our professional and social lives. It just doesn't seem to be working out for us. As professionals we may share the same creative vision, but not as a couple. It's sad, but that's it."

"That's not it. It means more to me than that, Eddie. It's not so simple. I *love* you. I want the relationship more than the show. I can always do a show. You and I are special."

"I want the show more," Eddie said flatly.

"But we can have both," Jacky was arguing weakly when the waiter interrupted her with the drinks. She leaned back and paused while he served them. Actress Goldie Yardes waved, but Jacky ignored her, rubbing gently at her temples to make the pain go away. Without thinking, she took a sip from the martini and felt the smooth iced Stolichnaya vodka flood into her empty stomach. The light in the Tea Room dimmed a little, and everything had a misty white halo around it.

"I don't believe we can have both," Eddie said when the waiter was gone.

"Then you never should have started on that basis," she snapped. Her body was in revolt. There was nothing that didn't hurt at the moment: her head, her stomach, even her rectum from the night before. She took another sip of the vodka, praying it would calm her.

"It's not too late to change now," Eddie said, his annoyance growing. "We have other people than just ourselves to consider. There's the La Frances and the Gavins and Chomsky and the whole chorus. There are technicians and the Janoffs, who have put their faith in you by giving us their theater. And there is the entire New York creative community peering over our shoulders. Look at them," Eddie said gesturing out at the room. Goldie Yardes waved. "The gossips, the gossips wait to ruin our lives! Now, is this not enough at stake to be selfless about our relationship?"

"But how would that change anything with the show? So what if we stopped sleeping with each other? How would that improve the show?" She noticed Woody Allen staring at her, and she lowered her eyes. She took Eddie's hand from the table and held it in hers again. Quietly she said, "Eddie, I don't understand what's wrong. I know at times I'm unreasonable and overly sensitive . . . maybe I'm even a little crazy . . . but I only want to love somebody, to give myself to him, to his support, to his future. But I just can't seem to make it work. I guess I'm really insecure right now, but I'm thirty-two years old and I want a man. I want a family and a home life. I want that with you. You must not reject me out of hand like this, Eddie, because of the incident at Ellison's house, because I don't deserve that kind of treatment. It's not fair." Her eyes brimmed with tears. "Eddie, if you loved me three days ago, you must still love me today. . . ."

Eddie looked down into his drink. "I do love you, Jacky. But I love myself more. We will continue to know each other as professionals. Until the show opens, our relationship is strictly business, and I expect you to work your ass off."

"And after the show is over, after that, do we go back?"

"Back?" Eddie said.

"Back to being a couple."

"Have you no pride?"

"Pride!" Jacky said, straightening her spine and flattening the creases in her blouse with her hands. "How do you expect me to act during rehearsals, with everybody knowing you left me? I just couldn't face everybody."

"You have to."

"Eddie, I love you."

"If you can't work with me, replace me. Get another director."

"No. Never. I could never face my friends."

"Too bad. It would be more deadly for me to stay."

Jacky looked toward the front of the dining room, where a tall, very sinister-looking man was watching her. At the moment their eyes met she felt her heart freeze over as if she had just been given a shot of chilled novocaine.

It was Addison Critch, who smiled at her, stealthily, serenely.

Jacky tried to smile back, but her jaw was locked in place. From the corner of her mouth she managed to whisper to Eddie, "There's Addison Critch!"

Eddie turned to look as Critch started down the aisle toward them. Jacky's heart beat wildly against her chest, and waves of pain beat at her temples.

"How do you do?" Critch asked, nodding at them. "I'm Addison Critch."

"Yes, we know," Eddie said gruffly.

"Forgive me for intruding, but I'm surprised to see the two of you here. I understood you were ill and you were in Los Angeles. . . ."

"Well, yes," Jacky said, fighting a wave of nausea, "I'm really not well . . . ."

"Mr. Critch," Eddie intervened, "if you could just leave us alone. . . ."

"One question," Critch insisted.

"No questions!" Jacky shouted, losing her temper, passing on into some uncontrollable netherland of anger. "Get away from our table!"

The whole restaurant was staring at her. Eddie tried to quiet her. "Don't cause a scene," he begged.

"Cause a scene! This asshole prick is ruining my life! Get away from us! Leave us alone!"

Critch stepped back a few feet in horror.

Goldie Yardes got to her feet so she could see better and gawked at them.

Eddie shoved the table away from himself and got up from the leather banquette.

"Please, Eddie! Wait, don't go!" Jacky called to him, but Eddie was marching up the aisle out of the restaurant. She jumped up from the table and ran after him, rushing by Addison Critch without another glance. She caught up with him at the bar and grabbed him by the shoulder. "Please, Eddie, don't go!"

He turned sharply, "Stop it! I can't take it anymore, Jacky!"

She was sobbing uncontrollably, her mascara running down her cheeks. Eddie felt no strength left, and his will caved in. He took her protectively in his arms, shielding her from the staring people in the restaurant, and huddled her outside into the street.

"Give me one more night, Eddie," she sobbed into his jacket as he flagged a taxi. "Give me one more night."

In her apartment Suie helped undress her and put her to bed. Then Eddie handed the old woman a $100 bill and told her to come back in three hours.

Eddie went back to the bedroom, where Jacky was half asleep, her breathing finally peaceful and steady.

"Eddie?" she called feebly. "Are you still here?"

"Yes," he said, "I'm here." He sat beside her on the bed and started to kiss her lips, but she started to cry again, and she couldn't seem to kiss him back.

"Please, stop," she begged him. "If it's over, then leave me, don't make me, Eddie . . . I can't help myself with you . . . please go," she sobbed. "If it's over, it's over . . ."

And then he made love to her. One last time.

FIVE
DAYS LATER

had the whole time and there was

20

The first sunny, pleasant days of spring had arrived in New York. The populace was shedding its warmer clothes, the trees were beginning to bud and the romantic were falling in love. The city was clear, crisp, cheery. A strong yellow sun bathed the gray buildings, and Ellison's office was lit with bright, relentless light. He sat with the sun behind his right shoulder, behind a drawing board with a felt marker in his hand. Slowly he drew the shape of a female form, using inverted triangles and long, straight lines for legs. Bobby stood beside him, curious that this great master of design did not know how to draw a figure. In fact, during the week that Bobby had spent working for Ellison, he realized that Ellison had no idea how to do many of the things that Bobby thought he'd have to know to be a designer; he couldn't draw, couldn't drape, couldn't sew a stitch. But he had the best imagination and verbal descriptive powers of clothing, and tailors and illustrators were able to interpret his every whim and nuance.

The sketch on the board was the last of Jacky Mellon's costumes for *The Performance*. He was sketching it himself because he wasn't sure anymore what he wanted for the final scene and couldn't be bothered explaining it. Worse, this was the third variation on the costumes he was designing for the show. Jacky herself hated the first set; she said they made her look too fat. She was right, but that wasn't Ellison's fault. Eddie hated the second set; he said they gave her no freedom of movement onstage—not that she needed to move, the way Chomsky and Eddie were feuding about what should be choreographed and what should not. The third set was supposed to satisfy all involved, including Jacky's cellulite; not too tight—Jacky might gain another five pounds after opening night—and not too loose because Ellison didn't want to make it look as if he were hiding her. And the real pressure: Ken and Alice La France had finalized plans to televise the opening-night party, and there was to be a fashion show of all the costumes for the show.

Ellison shuddered at the thought. It was only three days away, and he was still designing new costumes. The show had taken up so much of his time that it wouldn't be worth it if they paid him three times the money they already thought was exorbitant. If it hadn't been for Jacky, he would have quit the show long ago.

And the day of the opening Ellison would get final word from Simon Morrow on the future of their business relationship.

"There, what do you think?" he asked. It was an idea for an outfit for Jacky to wear to the party. At first she was going to wear the same outfit she wore in the disco climax of the show, but it was too revealing for the party, and once the fashion show at the party was formalized, they decided on another change of clothes entirely.

"I can't figure it out from what you've drawn," Bobby admitted hesitantly. Over the last week Bobby found that honesty was the best policy with Ellison. If you yessed him, he would eat you alive. Often there was nothing you could do to stop the man from devouring you. He was impatient, mean and selfish, and the only way Pat and Larry seemed to survive was by being direct and honest. Bobby didn't believe he had much longer to go at Ellison's anyway. Ellison was just waiting for a reason to fire him. As soon as it became clear that Bobby would not be spending any nights as Ellison's houseguest, Ellison's attitude toward him took a decidedly icy turn. In fact, he was positive that if Ellison weren't so incredibly busy and pressed, he would have been fired days ago. He was glad the designer hadn't given him the pink slip, if only because he couldn't bear to face the I-told-you-sos.

"Oh, God, I hired a blind man for an assistant. I swear you and Mallorey should have children. All right, listen. It's black charmeuse made out of the most fantastic tissue silk. The blouse is low-cut and gauzy, silk also, and this neckline isn't as much ruffled as it is gathered, by the way it's been cut. See? Over this she'll wear a giant, floating chiffon robe that's been hand-painted in army camouflage khaki green. She'll float in it. Kind of swirl around the dance floor in it. Nobody'll ever know she's knock-kneed. Go order the fabric."

Bobby went out to the design room with the sketch and went to hunt up the fabric. Mallorey was sitting outside, forlornly eating a hard-boiled egg.

"Want one?" she asked Bobby, the yolk crumbling onto her chin.

"No, thanks, Mallorey, but I will take a Yoo-Hoo if you have an extra."

Mallorey handed him a Yoo-Hoo, and he shook it. "Sit down, take a load off your feet," she told him.

"I can't right now. El has me on a hunt for black charmeuse."

"Two minutes?" Mallorey begged. "It's important."

Bobby sat on the edge of the desk and swigged his Yoo-Hoo, disgusted with her subservience. Everybody jumped at Ellison's bark. Mallorey took another bite of egg and looked at him carefully. "Why do you work here?" she asked.

"Why do you ask?"

"Just tell me. It's important to me."

"Because it's a good job. It might lead to something better. It's fantastic experience."

"But he doesn't pay you anything. I heard gossip."

"It's no secret. We said we'd try it out. I still work at The Club. If it works out, I'll go on salary."

"When?"

Bobby flushed. "This Friday," he lied.

"Now ask me," Mallorey prodded, finishing her egg and wiping her chin with a napkin.

"Ask you what?"

"Why I work here."

Bobby sighed. "OK. Why do you work here?"

"He pays me, right? He pays me a lot, too. Well, it's just not for me, but I've got kids to support. . . ."

"Really? I didn't know you were married."

"Was. He was killed in Vietnam. Didn't matter much except that I had the twins. . . ."

"Twins, no less," Bobby said, finishing the Yoo-Hoo. "I really have got to find the charmeuse."

"But wait a minute. You're missing the most important part."

"OK, I'm waiting."

"I love to model. More than anything, since I was a little girl, I loved to dress up in beautiful clothes and walk around. If I wasn't a model here, I'd be a shoplifter somewhere because I just love clothes. God, dressing up to me is like sex. And then to have people see you in it!"

"But you don't, Mallorey," Bobby said. "Only Ellison sees you in it. Is that enough?"

Mallorey frowned. "I suppose not. But it's not any different from working for no pay."

Touché, Bobby thought. Mallorey wasn't so dumb after all. He felt sorrier for her than ever.

"You know what, Mallorey? We've both got to do something about it. *Today*."

But he would never get the chance.

Bobby got no lunch break again that day. He hadn't been invited to lunch since that first day but was called into Ellison's office just as he was about to run down to a delicatessen and get a roast beef sandwich to munch in the dressing room.

"We're being bushwhacked," Ellison told him, clearing off his desk. "Jacky Mellon was just let out of rehearsal for an hour by her Italian keeper, and she's on her way over here."

"For what?" Bobby asked.

"For what? To make trouble. To terrorize our lives. What else have you seen Jacky Mellon do in the past week?"

Pat came into the room. "She's in the reception room in a holding pattern," she announced.

"How is she?"

"If she doesn't take another pill or snort another speck, she could come down by next Tuesday."

With that, Jacky burst in the door.

"You've been crying!" Ellison wailed sympathetically, rushing across the room to her with his arms outstretched.

"I'm all right," she said bravely, with everyone in the room staring at her. She was wearing an outfit from the second act of the show, a checkered pattern with looping cape sleeves and chain belts. Ellison waved away the other people in the room. Bobby, who was the last one out, quietly closed the door behind him.

"What's the matter, pussy?" Ellison asked when they were alone.

"My head ... my head is splitting open, and he doesn't

believe me . . . Eddie thinks I'm faking, and it's like two little demons pounding at my temples. . . ."

"Demons? Oh, darling!" He took her in his arms and led her to the sofa. "It's all right, pussy," he reassured her. "El is here." They dropped on the sofa in each other's arms. "Why do you think you have these terrible headaches just a few days before opening? Do you think it could be psychological?"

"Why is it that every time something is wrong with me people automatically think it's because I'm nuts or high on something?"

Ellison decided it was best not to answer.

"Eddie doesn't believe me. I *must not make* him more angry. What can I do?"

"Poor pussy," he said.

"Did I tell you what happened on the plane coming here with Eddie?" she asked.

Ellison shook his head. "Have some brandy, OK?"

Jacky nodded and followed him over to the bar. "Well, there we were, Eddie and I, sitting in first class, eating cold roast beef with horseradish sauce, when they make an announcement that we were going to fly at a lower altitude because the plane seemed to be losing pressure. Can you imagine? Nothing to get excited about, just a little loss of pressure. Well, you know my ears?" She cupped an ear in each hand for Ellison. "Well, my ears are supersensitive. A plane flight for my ears is sheer trauma. I hear Streisand has the same problem. So the plane dropped about ten thousand feet, and my ears would not pop, would not budge. The pressure in them was so intense I thought I was going to faint. Naturally they made an announcement for a doctor on board the plane, and from second class— *steerage* class actually—came this little doctor from San Fernando Valley, with a bow tie and crew cut."

"Oh, my God! Did you let him touch you?"

"Darling, in a plane with no pressure you'd let a veterinarian help you if he could. Anyway, this little man digs around in his attaché case and comes up with—a stick of gum!"

"Gum?"

"Gum. He told me to chew it, that it would break the pressure, but I tell you the pain was so intense I couldn't even chew. So then he told me to sing.

"He said, 'Sing, Jacky! Sing! Singing will help release the pressure!' "

"You sang?"

"Yep. I sang 'Love in My Life' six times from Chicago to New York."

Ellison doubled up with laughter at the thought of it. "Sing, Jacky, sing!" Ellison hooted, but his joy soon shifted as Jacky, at first surprised, had begun to laugh herself at how funny she must have looked when a claw of pain seized her. She held her temples with her fingertips and then began pounding at them as she broke into a fresh torrent of tears.

"My God," Ellison said, "stop pounding at yourself!"

"The pain is *horrible!*" Jacky cried out. "And no one believes me!"

"I believe you, I believe you," Ellison said, already on his way to the phone. If she was faking, she deserved to be locked up. If not, she needed a doctor. Better see Dr. Barry either way.

Like any perfect stage set, Dr. Barry Meritt's Park Avenue offices had the perfect atmosphere for the rich city doctor. All was serene with the appropriate judgment that pervaded all the good doctor's decisions, down to his taste in interior designers and modern art. The room was large and airy, overlooking Park Avenue, with two well-dressed and healthy female patients in the waiting room reading *Vogue*. Even his receptionist, Annie, could have been a runway mannequin, and his nurse, Eleanor, was motherly, spotless, scrubbed and pink, a woman who always vanished and reappeared at all the right moments.

"Demon headaches," is what Ellison told Annie when she asked what was wrong with Jacky. Jacky was huddled in his arms like a sick refugee being towed across the East River from Ellis Island.

"It's not funny," she managed to say, and stuck out her bottom lip.

"It's really not," he assured the receptionist. "I think we should see Dr. Barry right away."

The receptionist went to find Dr. Barry, who returned immediately. He was wearing a navy blue Yves Saint Laurent suit under a white lab jacket. He tugged nervously at his right ear at the sight of Jacky and ushered them into his examination room. "Go into the dressing room and get into a white gown for me like a good girl, would you, Jacky?"

Jacky went off into the dressing room with Eleanor to help her.

"What seems to be the matter with her, El?"

"Headaches. Terrible, demon headaches. And a bad time with Eddie, I think most of all."

Jacky came out of the dressing room, and Dr. Barry had her sit on the examination table. "Maybe you should wait outside, El," he said.

"No, that's all right," Jacky interrupted. "He's dressed me a hundred times; he can see me in a white robe."

Dr. Barry shrugged. "What seems to be the trouble?"

"Headaches and pain. Horrible, searing pain in my temples and head. Every day now."

"Temples? Temple headaches are very rare, indeed," Dr. Barry said, lightly touching her temples. "Are they accompanied by nausea?" Jacky shook her head. "Do they come on slowly, or are there any warning symptoms? How long have they been happening?" He shone a light into her eyes, pulled down the lower lids. He looked up her nose, in her ears, listened to her heart and took her blood pressure.

Finally, he took his pocket flashlight and shone it in her mouth. He was looking down her throat when a very surprised expression crossed his face. "Wider!" he said, shining the flashlight up and down. He nodded at Eleanor over his shoulder, and she immediately left the room.

"Been doing a lot of coke lately, Jacky?" Dr. Barry asked even-toned and nonchalantly.

Jacky flushed ever so slightly and nodded.

"Grinding your teeth a lot?" he asked, going to the sink and washing his hands.

"I have no idea. Maybe."

"When was the last time you saw a dentist?" he asked, fetching a towel from a white cabinet.

Jacky looked up at the ceiling and started computing. After a second Dr. Barry was astonished to realize she was counting years, not months. He stopped drying his hands and watched her. After the longest time she said, "As far as I can remember, I haven't been to the dentist since the insurance papers were signed for *Lateral Horizons*."

Dr. Barry's eyebrows rose. "Well, my dear I hate to tell you this, but your teeth were cracked and rotted." Dr. Barry glanced at Ellison, who was quite embarrassed for her.

"It can't be so," Jacky whispered in shock, slowly climbing down from the examination table.

"Look for yourself in the mirror." He handed her a pocket flashlight.

She walked to the mirror above the sink. Her white robe was slit up the back and tied in two bows, exposing her chunky thighs and white panties, as she stood at the mirror and examined her teeth. Ellison had never seen her look or act more like her mother at any moment.

She shone the flashlight in her mouth and gasped.

"I can see it! I can actually see it!" she cried.

"It's my guess that the cracks are recent, say, since you've been getting the headaches. But the grinding must have been going on a long time. From typical side effects of speed and coke. To draw an analogy, it's like the San Andreas fault finally shifting."

"My God! What do I do? My opening night is in three days!"

"You get yourself a dentist right away. This afternoon."

"I don't *have* one."

"Use mine," Dr. Barry said. "I'll make an appointment for you. And you arrange to have him do as many teeth as he can at one time."

"Omigod. But I *can't*. I have no time. I have rehearsals. I'm opening."

"Calm down, pussy, calm down," Ellison coached. "You'll have it done *after* the opening."

"Just a little work now to hold you together," Dr. Barry said.

"Oh, God," Jacky said, slumping into a nearby chair. "What next? What next?"

"It's all repairable; let's be grateful for *that*. Now cheer up, I have something for you."

Dr. Barry gave Jacky his famous vitamin B_{12} shot, which perked her up immediately, two dozen Darvon tablets and the phone number of his dentist. His nurse took a blood sample before they left.

Later, in the taxi, Jacky broke her stunned silence.

"Fractured teeth. Who would believe it?"

"Not *I*," Ellison agreed. "It's a good thing I was there with you because I'd *never* have believed it if you told me. I must say, pussy, *trés trashy* to have fractured teeth."

"No worse than having a plastic septumology." Jacky sniffed.

Ellison was affronted, but amused, and he looked down his aristocratic nose at her all the way to the theater.

"This is the ultimate!" Ellison gushed to Pat and Larry when he hit the office. He took off his sports jacket and tossed it on the sofa. "You must hear this latest adventure of Our Miss Mellon and never breathe a living word of this or we'll all be dead in the morning! It's unbelievable!"

"What was it? What was wrong with her?" Larry begged.

Ellison looked around the room. "Where's Bobby? I want him to hear this."

Larry and Pat gave each other a long, meaningful stare. "We have a little story for you," Larry said smugly.

"Go ahead," Ellison said warily. Larry was so happy the boy could've fallen out of a window.

"No, no, you can get the story from the horse's mouth. He's due back here any minute. He just called to let us know."

"From where? Where did he go?"

"He didn't go anywhere. He was *taken*," Larry said, sitting on the sofa and crossing his legs.

"By federal agents," Pat added.

"What?" Ellison whispered.

"*Arrested*," Larry said.

"No, not arrested," Pat said. Larry was an impossible embroiderer. "Subpoenaed."

"By whom?"

"The Internal Revenue Service."

"For *taxes?*"

"Not his own taxes." Pat and Larry looked at each other, building the suspense.

"Whose?"

"Are you ready for this?"

"Stuart Shorter's taxes!"

"Shorter! What does he know about Shorter?"

"He was called as a witness!"

"He's the informant?"

"I suppose."

"It would seem that way." Larry hummed, polishing his nails with his breath.

Ellison blanched. "I must get rid of him! Right away. I should call my lawyer and find out if I'm in any sort of danger. My God, he knows all sorts of things. . . ." He was halfway across the room to the phone on his desk when he spun around and looked at his assistants smiling smugly on the sofa. "You're not putting me on, are you?" he asked suspiciously. "Because if this is a joke—"

"No joke," Larry said, holding up scout's honor.

"No joke," Pat said crossing her heart.

"This is no joke," Ellison agreed, and went for his vial.

The IRS agents, with their flat-planed, one-dimensional Irish faces and traditional three-piece suits, couldn't have been more politely officious in bringing Bobby downtown.

"You understand you're not under arrest," one of them who identified himself as Kevin Morrisey repeated to him as he was led to a gray Dodge sedan waiting at the curb in front of Ellison's office building. "You're only being subpoenaed for information."

"I'd like to see a lawyer anyway," Bobby requested.

The two other agents in the car glanced at each other and Morrisey.

"You're in no trouble," Morrisey said. "You're just being asked to cooperate with law officials in the pursuit of justice."

If anything, Bobby was impressed with Morrisey's sincerity as he said the words. These guys really believed in what they were doing, and the seriousness of his situation had just begun to dawn on him.

They brought him to a modern conference room in the IRS divisional headquarters in downtown Manhattan, and at his insistence they agreed to get a public defender to consult with him on his rights. He was ushered downstairs two flights to a bare office, where he waited alone for two hours, tapping the eraser of a pencil on a green desk blotter, squinting at the dust that floated in a shaft of bright spring sunlight.

The lawyer who finally showed up couldn't have been more than a few years older than Bobby, fresh out of law school. His name was Steven Horowitz; he wore small wireless glasses and spoke with a halting, if learned, insistence.

"These are the federal boys, the big guys," Horowitz told him, as if he should be grateful or impressed. "You should cooperate with them to the fullest if you know what's good for you."

"Good for me? I didn't do anything. . . ."

"Then you're lucky," Horowitz told him, "because once the feds get on your ass, your life is over."

"But I didn't do anything that should get me into any trouble. I *pay* my income tax. . . ."

"Then just tell the truth," Horowitz advised. "If you're not accused of any crime, just don't incriminate yourself in one. Listen, did you see anything illegal and fail to report it? Is that it? I mean, did you witness a federal offense and withhold the information from the authorities?"

"No," Bobby said with certainty.

"Then you should tell them whatever they want to know."

"And what about the other people? Am I offered any protection against the people I testify against?"

Horowitz shook his head. "That I can't advise you about."

They came for him half an hour later and took him back up to the conference room where a stenographer with a brassy blond wig took down his testimony on a machine. Bobby was miserable in the dusty, stuffy room, and as the three agents grilled him, he felt pools of perspiration dripping down his sides, sticking his shirt to his ribs. In answer to their questions he told them about coming to New York and getting the job at The Club. At no time did he mention Ellison, nor was he asked. Instead, the rest of the questions were about the scene in the basement office of The Club that Bobby stumbled upon with Tinder Kaufman.

"Is Tinder Kaufman the informant?" Bobby asked again and again, but they refused to answer him. Even as Bobby retold the story in careful detail, he couldn't figure out exactly what he had seen that might have been illegal. Sure, the man that Dubrow gave all the money to looked like a mobster, but for all Bobby knew he could have been a bank president. When Bobby finished his testimony, which took three hours to give and was at least 100 pages long, the agent named Morrisey went to a file cabinet in the corner and with great ceremony took five eight-by-ten photographs out of a manila envelope. One by one he showed them to Bobby.

The first was Stuart Shorter, a publicity shot that Bobby had seen dozens of times in the newspapers. He told them so.

The second man was a middle-aged, rather distinguished man that Bobby had never seen before.

"Isn't it possible you saw him around The Club?" another agent named Grey prodded him.

"It's altogether possible," Bobby said, quickly adding, "But I don't remember."

"Is it possible that you served him at the bar?" the agent insisted.

"It's possible, but I don't remember if I did," Bobby insisted.

The next picture was of Sandy Dubrow. The next of his wife, Ella.

"Is this the same woman you saw in the basement office of The Club?" Morrisey asked sternly. The stenographer's machine click-clacked away. The keys came to a pause for his answer.

"Yes, I've seen her in The Club."

"And is this the woman you observed taking a packet of money in the small office in the basement of The Club?" he insisted.

Bobby wondered what they would do to him for this. He looked off at Steve Horowitz in his three-piece suit, lazily cleaning his nails at the other end of the conference table. Then he simply told the truth.

"Yes, that's correct. She was the lady who took the money in The Club."

The next picture Bobby was afraid even to look at; he knew it was of the bull-like man who was in the office with the Dubrows.

"Is this the man in The Club's basement office who also received a packet of money?" Morrisey asked, a triumphant gleam in his eye.

For a moment Bobby wondered why he hated Morrisey so much when he was supposed to be the good guy. He stared at the photograph for a long time, as if to make sure it was the same guy, when Bobby knew it right away. He'd never forget the fluorescent lighting in that office and the three of them with the big safe behind them and all the packets of money on the desk, the scene etched on his mind, the way the bull-like man looked at him indelible. At that moment Bobby knew that this was the man who would break his kneecaps for testifying if anybody would.

"Yes," Bobby said evenly, walking into the valley of death, "that's the man."

Pat almost choked on the sugar dust of her last ladyfinger when she broke into laughter over Ellison's recounting of Jacky Mellon's airplane trip to New York. Larry Gatsby kept on repeating, "She *sang* all the way to New York? Only she would have the guts. . . ."

Pat caught her breath long enough to answer the intercom on Ellison's desk. "He's here," she announced excitedly.

Immediately there was a knock on the office door, to which Ellison answered, "Come in."

Bobby Cassidy walked into the room. He looked stunning in a black Ellison jacket, but he was obviously shaken by his experience. He was halfway across the room when Ellison said, "You're fired." It stopped him in his path like a bullet.

Instead of dropping, he said, "For what?"

"Where are you coming from?"

"I was subpoenaed to testify at Stuart Shorter's trial."

"Why you?"

"I'm not sure. I think they've subpoenaed lots of people," Bobby lied.

"Who else?"

"I don't know."

"Why you?"

Again. "They think I saw something suspicious while I was at The Club one night." Bobby looked slowly from Pat to Larry to Ellison. "You all think I'm the informant, don't you? Well, they don't subpoena informants. I was subpoenaed because the informant named me as a collaborative witness. . . ."

"What did you see?" Ellison asked him.

"I'm afraid I can't discuss that. There's a grand jury investigation, and I'm not—"

"You're fired," Ellison said flatly. "Leave now."

"But you've got to be reasonable. I didn't do anything. . . ."

"Don't talk to me in that tone of voice," Ellison warned

icily. "I have one good piece of advice for you. Don't
testify against any of my friends if you know what's good
for you."

Bobby shook his head in disgust and laughed at the
man.

"Get out!" Ellison demanded.

Bobby went to the door and turned. "Ellison?" he
called.

Ellison glared imperiously at him across the room.
"Yes?"

"You suck."

21

She had told the doorman that absolutely no one was expected and not to ring up, but she had told him that so many times before and he had not paid any attention that she wasn't surprised the buzzer was ringing in the kitchen. She tried to ignore it, but after two or three minutes of nonstop short rings she lost her temper and flew to the kitchen.

"What is it?" she asked.

"A Mr. Garguilo."

Jacky cringed. "Say I'm not here."

"But he knows you're here, Miss Mellon. He claims you're expecting him."

Jacky wondered what to do. She couldn't send poor Alexander away if he knew she was in. She guessed she was stuck. Wonder what he wanted. A handout no doubt. "All right," she sighed to the doorman, "let him up."

A moment later he was ringing the doorbell to the apartment. She found him in the hallway wearing the same frayed sports jacket and pants that she had last seen him in. His shirt, at least, looked new and clean, and she hoped he hadn't shoplifted it. He was also carrying an old piece of luggage.

"Alex, come in," she said, her head swimming with questions and apprehension.

"You must forgive me for dropping in on you like this, but it suddenly became necessary for me to see you," he said apologetically.

"I understand. It's just that this is my naptime. I'm in rehearsal, you know, and I really can't—"

"Yes, well, that is important," Alexander interrupted.

"What's wrong?"

He looked about the room, apprehensively. "Please, Jacky, could I have a short drink?"

"Yes, of course," Jacky said, walking to the built-in bar and fetching a crystal canister of Rémy Martin and two

233

glasses. Alexander sat uncomfortably at the edge of the sofa, and Jacky poured them drinks. When he picked his up, she saw his hand was shaking, and he drained the cognac as if it were whiskey. Immediately he poured himself another.

"You'll have to excuse this excess, but you see, I have just been arrested," he said, exhaling loudly. "It was very upsetting. Not a pleasant experience, to be arrested in New York City. The police in this city have no respect for breeding, you can well imagine. They were animals."

"I'm so sorry, Alex," she said softly. "What were you arrested for?"

"Shoplifting. I was caught pilfering a camera in one of those Arab bazaars on Fifth Avenue."

She was filled with pity for him, but she was just as disgusted.

"But why the suitcase? Are you leaving town?"

Alexander took a healthy sip of cognac. "I'm afraid to tell you that this was not the first time I have been arrested on such charges. In fact, this is the third, and surely I shall be put in jail."

"Oh, Alex, that's horrible! What can we do? Can I get you a lawyer?"

"I'm afraid it's too late for that, too. I'm already a fugitive." He drained the rest of his drink.

"How's that?"

"I escaped from the precinct where they were holding me," he explained dolefully.

"Oh, Alex. Poor Alex," she whispered.

"It was quite easy, really. They left me alone in a room with an open window. I simply crawled out into the alley. I took a bus home, packed a couple of suitcases and came right here."

"Do you think they're looking for you?"

"I don't think there's a nationwide manhunt out for me, if that's what you mean, no. But I'm sure they'll send a couple of detectives to my apartment. After all, they do have my wallet and know where I live. But if you're worrying that I was followed here, I doubt it. And anyway, I came by way of the Port Authority Bus Terminal, where I checked my other suitcase, and if anyone kept track of me, he was Sherlock Holmes."

"What will you do?" Jacky asked, clutching her robe to

her neck against an uncomfortable chill. What she really was asking was: What was he doing here?

"I'm leaving town. Permanently. I'm just a shoplifter; they won't prosecute me across the country. I'll go somewhere. Escondido, maybe, or maybe Laguna and Emerald Beach, where there are available women."

Jacky shook her head sadly.

"Now, now," he said, "don't look so sad. I couldn't very well go off and become a used car salesman at this point, could I?"

Jacky shook her head again.

"Therefore, I must ask your help once again. I intended to leave by bus, but then I realized you could facilitate my trip by plane."

Jacky worried for a second that she might be breaking the law by helping an escaped prisoner, even for shoplifting, but she said, "Of course, I'll get my checkbook."

"Please do," Alex said, "but that won't do for my plane ticket. I'll have no cash, and the airlines won't take your check from me."

Jacky went into the bedroom for her pocketbook. "I might have a few hundred dollars' cash, Alex. If not, maybe the building could cash a check."

"I'd like a check for ten thousand dollars," Alex said flatly.

Jacky, who heard him quite clearly, pretended she hadn't, hoping the subject would be dropped.

"Jacky, I'd like a check for ten thousand dollars," Alex said again.

"Ten thousand dollars? Why so much?"

"I feel I'm owed at least that much."

"By me? Certainly not by me."

"By your mother and, therefore, by you."

"Alex, that's not fair. Mother took very good care of you, and if she didn't leave you anything, it wasn't because she didn't want to; it was because she was broke when she died, as you well know. I had to pay all the bills. Nobody owes anybody anything in this situation. Nevertheless, I feel bad you're on hard times, so here's a check for a thousand dollars. But don't call or write from California expecting more, Alex. I've been more than generous."

"Then maybe we should negotiate for the other nine thousand?"

"Negotiate?" Jacky asked, snapping her pocketbook shut.

"I have two photographs with me that you might like to purchase."

Jacky was too startled to say anything for a moment. She smiled out of nervousness, and then her face grew set and serious.

"What kind of photographs?"

"Photographs of Angela."

"What kind of photographs of Angela?"

Alexander said nothing.

"I don't believe that photos of Momma like that exist. . . ."

"Why not?"

"Because why would my mother take photographs that were damaging to her?"

"At the time we never thought they were damaging. They're Polaroids. We were staying at the Connaught, in London. I think it was the same trip she met Maxwell Pudding. It was late one night, we had been out clubbing, somebody gave us some cocaine and we were drunk and silly. We took Polaroids of each other. It was very innocent."

"I can't believe it."

"I think I should show them to you," Alex said. He purposefully went to his suitcase, snapped the locks open and produced two Polaroid pictures from an envelope. Jacky's heart began to beat wildly as he crossed the room to her and extended the photos.

The first was Angela in front of a mirror, laughing hysterically at something with her mouth wide open, her face ugly and distorted. The top of her dress was down; her breasts, pasty and striated, were hanging forward as she laughed. The picture was all at once disgusting and yet innocent in the moment it was taken.

The second picture was not as innocent. Angela was in bed in the same hotel room but the picture was framed by the front oak poles of a four-poster bed. Angela was propped up against pillows, stark naked with a glass of champagne in her hand, her legs open. She was laughing again but not so hard in this picture. Jacky was overwhelmed with pity for her mother. The poor dear, getting her rocks off by taking smutty pictures. And to be involved with a creep like Alexander! Her poor momma.

"This is hideous, Alex! You're contemptible, to suggest blackmailing me with these. How could you do something like that to Momma?"

"Easy. I'm desperate."

"And what if I call the police?"

"I thought of that," Alex said, taking the pictures away from Jacky. "The fact of the matter is there are four pictures altogether. The two others are in my second suitcase in the locker at the Port Authority. If you call the police, I'll simply call the New York *Post* and tell them which locker to go to to find the two pictures. The other two pictures are more"—he poured himself another cognac—"let's say they leave even less to the imagination."

"And if I give you the ten thousand dollars? Do I get all the pictures."

Alex smiled and shook his head. "No, no, no. I keep the other two photographs as memorabilia."

"To blackmail me with when you run out of money again?" Jacky asked.

Alex sipped his cognac, shaking his head sadly. "Please, Jacky. Blackmail is such an ugly word. Let's just say that this is my inheritance money."

Jacky put her face in her hands and sighed. "And how much will you want for the other two photos?"

"Negotiable at the time. You know about inflation. . . ."

"And how do I know there are only two more? Maybe it'll turn into six and on and on."

"Alas, there were only four shots left in the camera that night. If you don't want to believe me, there's nothing I can do, but the fact of the matter is there are only four photographs."

Jacky sank into a chair and held herself tightly, rocking back and forth. She was full of contempt for Alex and remorse for her mother's life. Poor Angela, to have let herself believe that a man like Alex was really in love with her. It was almost better to be alone than to fool yourself. Her eyes started to tear as she thought about it. It was almost better to be alone.

She stood, stiffened her back, wiped away a tear and went to her pocketbook. She took $200 in cash and wrote a check to Alexander for $10,000. "Here. Take this and get out."

"And you won't call the police?" Alex asked, taking the check and staring at it in amazement.

"Not this time anyway. But I don't know what I'll do about those other two photos. I might call your bluff and have you locked up for good."

"Really, now, Jacky."

"And let me tell you something else, you ugly little wop: You live off people because you're nothing. You're a bloodsucker and a lowlife."

Alex said nothing. He folded the check, put it in his pocket, buttoned his jacket and closed his suitcase.

"You know what else?" he finally said. "I have no conscience. I don't care."

"I don't believe that," Jacky said. "Somewhere inside you you must suffer."

"Why should I suffer?" he asked her. "I made your momma happy."

Jacky looked down at the rug and held back tears. "Leave now, Alex," she commanded in a low voice. She didn't look up again until she heard the front door close.

Lying on the coffee table were the two pictures of her mother, facedown. Without looking at them she took them into the kitchen and burned them to ashes in the sink.

22

As exotic as an orchid forest in Brazil or any journey down the Nile, there is Fifth Avenue on a sunny spring day. The street streams with the excitement of the world's most exciting city. Hundreds of thousands of people traverse the avenue's broad asphalt streets during a single lunch hour, pouring in and out of the glittering array of stores: Valentino, Steuben, Tiffany, Godiva Chocolates, Harry Winston's, Bergdorf's, F.A.O. Schwarz and, of course, the leather and suede emporium of the world, Gucci.

It was from the doors of one of Gucci's many stores that Ken and Alice La France burst, laden with shopping bags full of expensive goodies. Alice held her face up to the warming sun and inhaled deeply as she led the way to a parked limousine. Her hair was piled on top of her head and laced with tiny braids and bells that she had brought back with her from a trip to the Himalayas. The dress she was wearing was an authentic national costume of Lithuania, a colorful, full-cut peasant dress that Alice had made for herself on a field trip years before. Ken was wearing his usual thirties garb: pinstripes, spats, a cane, his hair slicked and pomaded and parted down the middle. They struggled with their packages to a waiting Lincoln limo and threw themselves inside.

"I'm exhausted," Alice said, heaving her chest and kicking off her Louis Jourdan pumps from under her Lithuanian skirt. She put her feet up on the jump seat and groaned, "If I see the inside of one more store, I'll spit." The bells in her hair tinkled lightly as she spoke.

"So spit."

"I guess I'll have to. We still haven't gotten anything for the *grande dame*, Ms. Mellon."

"What? Two grand worth of Gucci goodies, and you didn't buy anything for Jacky?"

"It's got to be something special for Jacky."

"I don't see why we should spend ten cents more on this crap shoot. . . ."

"We can't stop with the gift for the star on opening night, Ken. We're doing it because we're *menshen*. . . ." The bells tinkled slightly.

"We're doing it because you have a fetish for shopping. Over two grand already today. . . ."

"Besides, it's traditional to get your star a gift. Now what could we get her? Aside from Eddie back in her bed?"

"You've got me," Ken grumbled, picking up his copy of the *Post* from the magazine rack in the rear door. He took his blackrimmed reading glasses from his jacket pocket and hung them on the tip of his nose.

"Where to, Mr. La France?" the driver asked.

"Just stay parked for a minute until we figure it out," Alice instructed him.

Ken grumbled through the first two pages of the *Post*. Nothing but decapitation and family murders. He turned to "Page Six," skimmed it, then read Jack Martin. There was a girl in California who announced she was pressing a paternity suit against Dean Martin.

"What about pearls? Jacky would love a strand of pearls."

"What is this, her high school graduation?" Ken barked. There was also an item about Universal's canceling a three-picture deal with an unnamed Broadway director. Who could that be? Ken wondered. He turned to Addison Critch's column and began reading silently.

CRITICISMS
by Addison Critch

A young handsome bartender believed to be the informant who fingered Club owners **Stuart Shorter** and **Sandy Dubrow** on income tax evasion charges has been missing from his apartment for five days. Sources close to the investigation at The Club say both the New York police and FBI have warrants for his arrest in relation to his testimony in the case, and there is some concern for his safety. The bartender, twenty-six-year-old **Tinder Kaufman**, from Houston, Texas, was last seen leaving The Club a week ago after Shorter and Dubrow were seized at The Club and charged with evading more than $2.7 million in taxes over a two-year period.

Other sources claim that Kaufman isn't missing at all and that his disappearance is a ruse by the FBI to ensure his safety while the delicate investigation continues. The special prosecutor for the government is expected to ask the full twenty-year sentence for the nightclub owners. . . .

In another seemingly unrelated occurrence last night, **Richard Loomis**, a twenty-one-year-old busboy at The Club from Canyon, New Jersey, was accidentally poisoned when he mistakenly mixed crystalline rat poison into his drink, thinking it was sugar. The two other busboys who were present in The Club kitchen at the time of the accident say that Loomis reached up onto the shelf, poured two tablespoons of the poison into a protein drink and downed it in front of them. He was reported in critical condition in Bellevue Hospital. And still more peculiar events seem to haunt the ill-fated discotheque. . . .

IN OTHER QUARTERS: The fates seem to bode just as ill for **Jacky Mellon,** but for different reasons. Ms. Mellon took it to involve me and the diners at the Russian Tea Room in part of the drama of her life. Lunching with her boyfriend-director of Hollywood women's lib flicks, **Eddie Bernardo,** Jacky seemed to be in quite a tiff with Bernardo. That very day the rehearsals of her show had been postponed because of *her* illness, but there she was lunching at the RTR. I had just walked into the dining room to join my luncheon partner when Jacky sprang to her feet, hurled a few slang words at me and charged out of the restaurant with her boyfriend rushing after her. Opening night is tomorrow, televised nationally. A real, live disaster movie.

Ken put the paper aside for a moment and took off his reading glasses. "Did you read this business in Critch's column about Jacky at the Russian Tea Room? When was that?"

"I read it. It happened two days ago. What Critch didn't know is that he went home, fucked her and left her again."

"Really? Why didn't you tell me this?" Ken was flabbergasted.

"Jacky told me, and it was, well, girls' stuff."

"I think we should drop in on rehearsals."

"OK. As soon as we buy Jacky her gift. Now what can we get her? It has to be something personal, something special."

Ken slipped his glasses on again, staring at Critch's column. "And did you read this business about missing bartenders and poisonings at The Club? The place is absolutely tainted. Everywhere you go you hear Mafia, murder, missing, poisoned."

"Don't be foolish, Kenny." Alice sniffed. "Stuart Shorter isn't smart enough to have anything to do with the Mafia. He's just a cheating little Jew they caught. Everybody cheats on income tax. He just did it big. Anyway, I love that place. I wouldn't desert it for the world. Who *cares* if it's Mafia?"

The driver looked at her in the rearview mirror. She watched out the window. People walked briskly by the car as they just sat.

"Well, do *something*," Ken hollered. "I can't stand sitting in a parked limousine all day!"

"You're the one who always thinks up the great gift ideas. *Think*."

"Burt Reynolds."

"Don't be snide."

"Maybe we should go to the Pleasure Chest and buy her sex gifts, you know joke things like dildos or those pleasure balls."

"Too tacky. Anyway, she'd probably use them."

"It would keep her off the street."

"Stop it."

"I know!" Ken cried. "I've got the perfect idea! I saw it months ago at Tiffany. I hope they still have it! Driver, away!"

A half hour later the La Frances arrived at the rear entrance of the Janoff Theater and sneaked, unnoticed, into the darkened orchestra. They slipped into the last row and sat low in their seats while they watched a full-blown rehearsal. The entire company was on stage rehearsing the climax of the show. Stage center, atop a Plexiglas cube big enough to encase a tank, Jacky stood with her arms

outstretched, singing her heart out. Behind her, row upon
row of sequined chorus girls in feathered headdresses
emerged from below a milky horizon. The long-legged
girls kicked and pranced out to the bib of the stage,
surrounding Jacky atop her cube, which began to fill
with pastel-colored smoke. The effect was quite dazzling as
the girls were joined by two rows of men in satin tuxedos,
dancing around them, stepping and turning Astairelike to
the disco music filling the theater.

"Step together, turn, *turn*, I said!" Noel Chomsky
screamed at Jacky, who couldn't hear him above the sound
of her own recorded voice being blasted at her from
speakers hidden below the Plexiglas cube.

Eddie sat in the third row of the theater, holding his
face in his hands, glumly watching the stage. Jacky could
make him out there in the light spilling over from the
stage, and she tried to focus elsewhere, executing a sharp
turn and very nearly falling off the cube.

The chorus sang, "Show time! Like no time!"

Jacky tried to sing along with her own voice coming out
of the monitor, but she could hardly breathe. She was full
of water and was a good five pounds heavier than just a
few days before, and the costume was digging into her
waist and biting the hell out of her. With all the extra
weight on her body and the nonstop smoking she could
hardly talk sometimes, let alone sing and dance at the
same time. Even now at the back of the auditorium in a
sound booth a technician was mixing prerecorded tapes of
Jacky in a studio singing the high notes that she couldn't
reach onstage. It bordered on the unethical—the show was
billed as live, and none of it was supposed to be prerecorded—but there was no way around it. Jacky just
couldn't handle the singing.

She lifted her legs as high as they could go in the kick
and remembered to smile out at the empty theater. She
was taking three Tylenol 3 every two hours to kill the pain
in her jaws from her rotted teeth. This was a subject she
hadn't even dared to mention to Eddie; it was as implausi-
ble an excuse for not being up to snuff as it was embarrassing. She had dentist appointments all the next week, a
six-day stretch she regarded like going to the gas chamber;
fourteen cavities, six caps in forty hours in the dentist's
chair.

For a few days after their reunion at the Russian Tea

Room Eddie was gentlemanly, if short-tempered, at rehearsals. But things had degenerated so badly that sometimes Eddie was even siding with Chomsky against her.
She huffed and puffed up on the cube, spinning around so
fast she thought she would faint.

"No more turns!" Chomsky screamed at her, throwing
his hands in the air and turning to Eddie for help.

Eddie stood up and shouted, "Hold it! Hold it!" but no
one heard him over the din of the music.

The Velcro strips on Jacky's costume began to come
apart in the back.

"No more turns!" Chomsky begged.

Dancing fountains sprang up at the rear of the stage,
and Vegas-type show girls descended from the flies on
trapezes.

Eddie walked out to the aisle, down to the orchestra,
bunched up his script and threw it at the conductor to get
his attention. The conductor jumped a foot in the air when
he got hit, and the orchestra ground to a squawky halt.
Everyone onstage turned to Eddie.

"A waste of time!" he shouted, waving at the assembled
cast on the stage. The fountains dropped. Jacky stood still
with her hands at her side. The houselights came up, and
everybody could see Eddie standing in the middle aisle.
"Everybody in the cast knows this number except the
star!"

Jacky put her hands on her hips. "I do know this number, Eddie; all I did was forget one little turn," she said
atop the box.

"You *added* two extra turns!" Chomsky was exasperat-
ed.

In the rear of the theater Alice elbowed Ken and said,
"You'd better do something."

"What?"

"I don't know, but go up there and stop this before
there's bloodshed."

"It's hopeless. It will be the end of my career!" Eddie
yelled at her.

"What career?" Jacky screeched. "You couldn't direct
traffic in an amusement park!"

Ken La France went rushing down the aisle, imploring,
"Please, please, please!"

Eddie turned on his heels and stormed up the aisle,
meeting Ken halfway.

"That's it!" he shouted. "I'm through!" He continued up the aisle and out of the theater.

The cast all started to speak at once. Suie appeared from the wings with a white flannel robe for Jacky, who was drenched in perspiration.

"Come down from there," Alice called to Jacky, waving at her. Two dancers from the chorus rushed to her to help her down from the cube and over the narrow plankway that bridged the orchestra pit. Alice took her in her arms and hugged her reassuringly. "I was here, and I thought you were terrific."

"I don't know how much longer I can take it, Alice, I really don't. Eddie is pulling me one way; Chomsky is pulling me another."

"Poor darling," Ken said, rolling his eyes at her behind her back as Alice continued to hug her. Ken's patience was running low with Jacky; all he really cared about at this point was getting the show opened.

Nancy Beale came down the aisle toward them, and when Jacky saw her, she cringed in Alice's arms. Jacky had taken such an aversion to the girl that the sound of her voice was practically like nails on a blackboard. Nancy seemed to have absolutely gloated over Jacky's estrangement from Eddie. Maybe Jacky had been imagining it, but she always thought the girl was standing off in a corner somewhere smirking at her. And she was indulgent and solicitous, like a psychiatric nurse afraid her psychotic patient is going to go off the deep end any second.

"What is it?" Jacky asked.

"There's a phone call for you."

"Take a message," Alice said.

"They said it was important," the girl announced, holding her ground.

"*Take a message*," Alice insisted. She sounded dangerous.

The girl cocked her head and stood still as a tree trunk. "But it's the *doctor's* office. Dr. Meritt's office."

The La Frances looked surprised. "Oh." Jacky said, defeated again by the girl. "I guess I'll take it then."

"Are you OK?" Alice asked.

"Yes, of course," Jacky said.

"There's a phone in the sound booth," Nancy suggested.

Jacky held her bathrobe collar up to her neck and stomped to the back of the theater with Ken and Alice.

The phone in the sound booth wasn't very private, but it was convenient. Ken and Alice stood on either side of her. Suie made her way up the aisle with a terry towel for Jacky. Jacky pushed the blinking button on the phone and said, "It's Jacky."

"Hello?" Dr. Barry said abruptly. He sounded grave and serious. "Jacky, come see me right away. Today."

"Why, what's wrong?"

"I'd like to speak to you in my office."

"But you sound so *serious*. What's wrong? What's the matter?"

"Nothing terrible. . . ."

"Then what's *wrong?*" Jackie demanded, her voice rising. The La Frances stared at her, gripped with fear.

"I just got back your blood test . . ." Dr. Barry said.

"My blood test?" Jacky repeated. She knew it all along. Just like her mother. Cancer. Death at a young age.

"What's wrong with my blood?" she begged.

"Oh, God," Alice murmured, taking Jacky's hand.

Dr. Barry paused on the other end of the phone. "You have syphilis."

"I have *what?*"

"Syphilis," Dr. Barry repeated. "It's a simple shot, and you'll be fine in a week."

"Omigod," Jacky said weakly. "Omigod." She hung up the phone. "Omigod."

What was she going to tell Eddie?

"What did he say?" Alice asked, her eyes filling with tears.

"VD."

"VD?" Alice softly repeated.

Very quietly: "I have syphilis."

Alice's mouth fell open. "You're joking. Who gave you syphilis?"

There was a moment of silence, and then all three of them slowly turned to the chorus on the stage.

23

Bobby Cassidy stared out the subway window at the labyrinth of tunnels under the city as the D train rumbled swiftly on its noisy journey. He was lost in thought, interrupted only when the pneumatic doors wheezed open and shut at subway stops or when the lights blinked off at power substations and his reflection was lost in the black reflective surface of the grimy window. Behind him in his reflection he could see the newspaper of the Chinese man who sat next to him on the aqua plastic seat, engrossed in the third page of the New York *Daily News*. There was a photograph of Stuart Shorter and Sandy Dubrow taken outside The Club and a headline above it, INDICTED TODAY IN IRS CONSPIRACY.

Bobby focused back on the tunnel outside the train before closing his eyes and resting his head on the subway window. He was drained. Today's arraignment seemed inescapable. The investigation at The Club haunted him as if it were his own investigation. It followed him everywhere, nipping at him, on TV, in the newspapers, people gossiping, until he was able to think of nothing else. And it was the last thing he wanted to think about.

Then why was he on his way there?

Because in some weird way it was almost all he had left.

He felt like a perfectly reasonable man who thought he had taken a beautiful dive off a high diving board into a lovely pool that turned out to have no water in it. His life had seemed to dissolve before his very eyes. Grace one week, Ellison the next and then that very night at The Club—the most horrible night of his life.

The Club was jam-packed that night and had been since the federal arrest. People had rallied there from all over, including judges and senators, to show their support of The Club and its powerful attorney, David Willick. Bobby had not seen either Sandy Dubrow or Stuart Shorter since he had been brought in for testimony that afternoon and had no idea what he would say to them when he ran into them. He had been behind the bar for two hours when he got suspicious that he hadn't seen Shorter even once, not even across the dance floor or rushing about as he usually was. It was nearly one o'clock when a busboy ambled up to Bobby's side of the bar and said, "Stu Shorter wants to see you."

Bobby poured one last drink and climbed out from behind the bar. The kitchen door was only a few yards away, and he reached it just a minute or two after the message was delivered, not more.

Inside there was a ghastly scene taking place. A busboy was lying on the floor in convulsions, turning blue. He was making desperate sounds in his attempts to breathe, but he had no suction, and the foam pouring out of his mouth was thick. Bobby was positive from the second he saw him that he was in his death throes. Two other busboys were kneeling close to him, holding him gently by the shoulders. Both boys were white and crying, "Oh, my God! Oh, my God!"

One looked up at Bobby and cried, "Get help! Get an ambulance!"

Bobby backed out the door and rushed madly through the crowds to the pay phone, where he called 911 and asked for an ambulance. He couldn't bring himself to go back to the kitchen or the bar after that, and he was sitting by himself in the lounge when Shorter appeared in front of him.

"There you are!" Shorter snarled, obviously stewed on Quaaludes. "You're fired!"

"Fired?" Bobby couldn't believe what he was hearing. "Why?"

"Because you're a stool pigeon, and we don't want any fucking stool pigeons around here."

Bobby hadn't been near The Club since. From the next day on he had done nothing but lie in bed all day. He had stopped shaving and jogging and working out at the gym. For the first time in his life he looked pale and sickly. And he was lonely, the worst part of it.

And he worried constantly. About himself and everybody around him. Tinder Kaufman was still missing. The *Post* had reported again that he was being hidden by the IRS, but Bobby didn't believe it. Tinder Kaufman was

dead. Just like the busboy in the kitchen, who died two
days later in Bellevue from accidental poisoning. Accidental poisoning his ass. How anybody could believe that rat
poison would be mistaken for sugar. . . . That kid was
murdered because he had seen something, just as Bobby
had seen something.

The subway stopped at West Fourth Street.

What would Grace think if they killed him? Would she
mourn for him? Or worse, what would she think if he
chickened out and didn't testify? Why couldn't he allow
himself to run away, go back to Miami? Because it was his
duty to stay? He laughed aloud in the train, and he saw in
the window reflection the Chinese man stare at him a brief
second before going back to his newspaper. Yes, that was
the answer, as ludicrous as it seemed. He was moral. He
felt an obligation to tell the truth.

The subway stopped at Centre Street, and Bobby dipped
forward in his seat. He heaved a deep sigh and darted
from the train onto the station and up the concrete steps
into the sunlight, his anxiety growing in quantum chunks
as he emerged into a landscape of courthouses and federal
buildings of downtown Manhattan. He was still a block
away from Foley Square when he recognized the massive
federal courthouse with the sprawling expanse of steps up
the front to a row of fluted Greek columns. On the
sidewalk a cluster of news reporters and a TV location
crew milled about, waiting for the protagonists to arrive.
Bobby avoided them by staying on the opposite side of the
street and crossing diagonally so he could walk up the
steps behind them. He picked a spot in the shade of a
column and wished he had a cold beer. He didn't have to
wait long before a gray Fleetwood limousine pulled up to
the curb. The newsmen rushed to it as the door flew open
and out strode David Willick. Bobby had never seen
Willick before, and he never came into The Club. He was
a short red-faced man with something distantly dangerous
about him. He was smiling, but the smile was sardonic,
and his red complexion made him look as if he were just
on the verge of great anger. He was followed up the steps
by a legal assistant in a three-piece black suit with his hair
pomaded down the middle and an overstuffed briefcase
under his arm. After them followed a bodyguard, conspic-
uous for his powerful shoulders under his gray suit. The

threesome quickly went up the steps with the reporters doggedly following. The assistant kept repeating, "Mr. Willick has no comment."

By the time they had reached the top of the steps another limousine pulled up to the curb, and all the reporters raced back down the steps to the curb, where Stuart Shorter got out of the car with another man who looked like a lawyer and his bodyguard. This time the news corps was raucous and joking. "Where'd you hide the money?" one of them yelled to him, and Shorter laughed good-naturedly. He knew most of them by name and chatted about the weather on his way up. Once at the top he stopped next to a column, where he spotted Bobby standing not ten feet away. Their eyes met, and Bobby thought he detected a small friendly smile on Shorter's face. At least Shorter nodded at him, and Bobby, unsure of what to do, nodded back.

"I have no doubt," Shorter announced loudly to the reporters and cameras, "that these charges will be proven false, that this so-called informant will turn out to be just another sap with sour grapes who has some personal vendetta against me. I'm sure I'll come out of this clean as a whistle. David Willick promises me this, and anything David Willick promises, I believe."

Back at the curb, a third limousine arrived, this one discharging Dubrow and his wife, Ella. He was in a dark blue suit; she, in a gray tweed suit. They solemnly walked up the steps. From behind them in the limousine emerged burly bodyguards Bobby recognized from the Club. With great seriousness and his head down like a criminal hiding from the news photographers, Dubrow stalked up the steps and into the building with the cameramen excluded from the court building. The crowd dispersed, and Bobby finally followed everyone up to the second-floor courtroom.

When he turned through the swinging doors into the courtroom, he was startled for a moment at how small everything was. He supposed he expected a courtroom that looked like the ones in the movies, those big, airy, two-story courtrooms with a judge's bench that looked like one St. Peter might borrow and a substantial jury box, where twelve sensible, middle-of-the-road people would judiciously tilt the scales of justice.

There was none of it. The room was green, clinical, no bigger than an average living room. Fluorescent lights.

The judge's podium was just a desk on a small raised platform with an American and New York State flag behind it. The jury box was just a raised area on the right side of the room with twelve chairs. A small wooden banister separated the defendants and proceeding tables from the viewers' gallery, which was only seven rows deep and five seats to a side. It was already filled with reporters and a few sketch artists, who were busily drawing Stuart Shorter. Shorter sat at the defense table very unhappily discussing something with the lawyer he had arrived with and glowering at Dubrow and Willick, who were standing in the corner instead of sitting at the defendant's table next to him. David Willick's assistant was busily sorting papers at a third table.

At the prosecution table were two young attorneys in their mid-thirties, indistinguishable from the men who had served Bobby with the subpoena and brought him downtown to take his disposition. They sat quietly and confidently, with a row of typed pages neatly stacked before them.

Bobby took a seat in the last row and scanned the room for a friendly face. He found one up front.

It was Grace. She was dressed in a black linen dress and matching jacket and was watching Shorter curiously from behind her big dark sunglasses. She was as beautiful as he dreamed she was, and she looked conspicuously stunning in the ugly courtroom, radiating that same quality of grace and composure she always did.

He could hardly believe it. What brought her to this courtroom?

His attention was drawn from her as he realized that something strange was going on on the other side of the partition that she was staring at. Stuart Shorter had left the defense table and was now talking animatedly with Willick, whose face grew harder and redder with Shorter's every word. Some of what Shorter was saying drifted into the gallery, and the reporters up front were writing furiously in their notebooks. Willick tried to put his arm around Shorter's shoulder to calm him, but Shorter pulled away from him violently and yelled, "You liar!"

Unexpectedly the door behind the judge's desk opened at that moment, and a uniformed bailiff stepped into the courtroom. He held the door open behind him and cried, "Quiet in the court! All rise for Judge Mary T. Hayes, presiding!" Everyone stood and faced front while a black woman in black judicial robes walked out the door and to the bench, where she sat down. The people in the courtroom settled back into their seats as Bobby studied her. She was in her fifties, she had natural salt-and-pepper hair pulled back behind her ears and horn-rimmed glasses. When she spoke, she showed very white buckteeth, which made her look homely and intelligent.

"Court is now in session," she announced in a precise, clipped speech. "I believe, counselors, that we are here to try indictment number three-four-eight-two-seven-six. That's the United States versus Stuart Shorter and Alan Dubrow, defendants. Special prosecuting attorney Melvin Franks and counselor David Willick, would the two of you please approach the bench?"

The two men went to where she sat. For the first time Bobby saw who the prosecuting attorney was. He was young and sharp-looking, dressed in a dark suit that was remarkably similar to the one worn by Willick. Bobby bet that the kid was a good match.

"I would like to say a word about the notoriety surrounding this case before we even begin to hear it," the judge said sternly.

"Your Honor," Willick interrupted, bowing formally and dramatically. The judge looked taken aback, and Willick's blue eyes glittered. "I must ask the Court's pardon, but I cannot represent Mr. Shorter in this matter. It's been necessary for him to find new legal counsel, and before the trial can begin—"

Willick was interrupted by an uproar in the courtroom from the gallery. He turned and smiled for the reporters.

"What kind of prank is this, Mr. Willick?" the judge asked, obviously flustered. "My court will not tolerate this kind—"

"I beg Your Honor's pardon, but this is no prank. This was an unforeseen machination of justice."

"What is that, Mr. Willick?" the judge asked dubiously.

Willick paused, walked to the defendant's table, gave Dubrow a knowing look and then turned toward the press corps in the visitors' gallery. Bobby wasn't even sure the judge could hear Willick, but that obviously wasn't what he was interested in.

"My client, Mr. Dubrow, in the pursuit of justice and

with all credit due him from the court and the prosecuting attorney, is willing to testify in the government's behalf against Mr. Shorter. . . ."

There was another outburst in the courtroom from the gallery.

Shorter's mouth fell open as he stood in his place and stared at Willick and then at Dubrow. "Testify against *me!* You bastard," he yelled at Willick. "You traitor!" he screamed at Dubrow.

"Quiet in the court!" the judge shouted above the pandemonium. "Sit down, Mr. Shorter."

The bailiff yelled, "Quiet in the court!" and slowly the noise subsided.

Willick walked to the bench, smiling again. "We've already discussed this with the prosecuting attorneys, and we'd like to retire to the judge's chambers, if it so pleases you," he asked the judge.

"I'm warning you, Mr. Willick, this is highly unusual. A change of plea should have been submitted to the Court before this time."

"But, Your Honor, I beg, this is not a change of plea; this is a change of charges."

"No more of this in open court, Mr. Willick," the judge ordered sternly. "Let's adjourn to my office." She hit the desk with her gavel. "Court is adjourned!"

The reporters in the gallery jumped out of their seats and rushed up the center aisle toward the swinging doors. Shorter was left standing bewildered in the courtroom with his new lawyer and two bailiffs at his side. Willick was already hustling Dubrow out of sight after the judge.

Bobby was making his way toward the center aisle when his eyes locked with Grace's. She waved to him tentatively, and he nodded back. They met together in the crush of people and walked slowly out of the courtroom together.

"Why are you here?" he whispered to her.

"Why do you think?"

"You've got some interest in the trial?"

"You're my interest in the trial."

They went through the court doors and into the marble hallway in silence. Bobby looked around anxiously to see if anybody had recognized her, but it appeared the reporters were too busy rushing to get the news in about the change

of charges to pay any attention to them. He led her away
from the crowd into an alcove down the hallway where
there was a copy machine.

"Would you mind explaining yourself?" he asked her.

"I heard you were in trouble. I heard that they called
you to testify because you knew something and that you
had been threatened."

"So what?"

"I also knew that you didn't have anybody here in New
York and that Ellison had fired you. I thought you needed
a friend."

"And what if somebody saw you coming to court? What
if people saw you with me?"

She looked down at the floor and hesitated. "I'll have to
live with that. I care for you, for what happens to you. I
don't know if our affair will ever work out. Maybe it's
over already, but that was no reason for me not to come
forward if you needed my help. Damn what the gossip
columnists will say."

Bobby had no idea what to say himself.

"So?" Grace asked him.

He smiled and laughed. "So," he said.

She resisted the impulse to kiss him. Instead, she asked,
"Would you buy an older lady lunch?" And he said he
would.

The judge's chamber was a dreary green office with
wood venetian blinds, bars on the windows overlooking an
airshaft, a large desk with a green blotter and an overwhelming smell of chalk and old books, as if the windows
hadn't been opened in five years. On the judge's desk,
turned just so visitors in the room wouldn't be able to see
it, was a picture of the judge with her three young
daughters and her husband, who had been a postal worker
for twenty years. The man who sat across the desk from
her, Stuart Shorter, was the symbol of everything false and
phony and prejudiced that she and her family had dedicated their lives to ending.

Shorter sat in a chair leaning forward, his arms hanging
between his legs, his mouth slack. The one, two punch in
the courtroom had been too much for him. The only
security he had felt all along was in having Willick on his
side. Not only didn't he have Willick, but the man was
now against him.

Willick stood whispering with Dubrow in a corner. Occasionally Dubrow would rub his face in his hands in deep anguish.

"What are you so upset about, Sandy?" Shorter called out to him. "That you're turning in an old friend? That I have to take your punishment?"

"Turning you in? Why should I have to take the rap for your drug habit? Why should I have to take the rap for your income tax fraud?"

"That's enough of that, gentlemen," the judge intervened. "We are here to discuss a change of charges. What are the new charges, Mr. Franks?"

One of the prosecuting attorneys cleared his throat and spoke for the first time. "Your Honor, the situation is this. We've agreed to prosecute Mr. Dubrow on minor income tax evasion with a maximum six-month sentence."

"In return for?"

"Mr. Dubrow is prepared to testify that Mr. Shorter conspired to cheat the government of over three million dollars in taxes. Also, it seems Mr. Shorter distributed drugs to clients of The Club, some of them very famous in show business, some in politics. Mr. Dubrow's testimony could reach the White House, but that's going to be looked into by a grand jury. . . ."

"Another grand jury?" Shorter gasped.

"That's not all, Mr. Shorter," Mr. Franks said. He dug into his jacket pocket and came up with a folded legal document, which he handed to Shorter to read.

"What's this?" Shorter said.

"It's an injunction we asked Mr. Franks to obtain for us," Willick answered.

"*You* asked him to obtain?"

"Yes, to keep you out of the fucking Club," Dubrow snarled.

"Keep me out! You can't keep me out!"

"Yes, we can, Stu," Willick said in a fatherly tone, "and we had to in order to protect ourselves. We were about to lose our liquor license with the drug charges against you and the new grand jury investigation. Our renewal is still pending, but at least now we can keep The Club open."

"But it's my business! You can't take my business away from me!"

"Nobody is taking anything away, Stu," Willick explained calmly. "You still own it and your share will be looked after by a court-appointed receiver. But until you're cleared of the drug charges, you just can't go inside."

Shorter turned to the judge. "They can do that to me, can they?" he begged her, handing her the injunction.

The judge read it over slowly and nodded. "I'm afraid, Mr. Shorter, that they just did. You're banished from your own club."

Outside the courthouse Grace and Bobby hailed a taxicab and took it just across the Brooklyn Bridge to the River Café, an elegant floating restaurant off Brooklyn Heights with a breathtaking view of the downtown Manhattan skyline. When the cab arrived at the entrance to the restaurant, it dawned on Bobby he had only subway fare home from the courthouse, and they both laughed while Grace had to shell out the taxi fare.

Inside the restaurant the Maître d' recognized Grace immediately and led them to a quiet table by a glass wall overlooking the river. The sun was still high in the sky, and a silver light played off the choppy waters of the Hudson. They ordered bullshots and sat quietly staring at the magnificent skyline for a while.

"Did you miss me?" Bobby eventually asked.

"Of course I missed you," Grace said. "But it wasn't until I heard you were fired from The Club and might be in trouble that I realized how much I missed you."

"Why didn't you call?" he asked.

"Pride . . . probably false pride. . . . I told myself that you needed to be alone and that it was better for both of us to be apart. But when I realized I could find you at the arraignment today, I knew I had to see you."

"But why?"

"Because I still love you," she said quietly. "And I want us to get back together."

Bobby looked surprised. "And what about the press and your public finding out about us?"

"I'll live with it."

"No, you wouldn't. They'd take one photograph of us together, and it would be everywhere. It would make you miserable. I know you, Grace."

"I'll live with it to be with you."

"But your reputation is a sacrifice you shouldn't have to make for me." He put his hand on her arm. "Listen,

Grace, you're very special to me. You're the only nice thing that happened to me in that fucking city." He gestured across the river. "But I don't belong here. They eat people alive in the city. People are always afraid. Afraid of muggings and robberies, afraid of columnists and photographers, afraid of being out or not chic. I simply don't belong here."

It finally dawned on her. "You're leaving."

He nodded.

"Where will you go?"

Bobby shrugged and sipped his drink. "I'll probably stop home in Miami, to see my folks and take some sun, but just for a week or two. Then, Los Angeles. I think I'd like to live in L.A. I need the sun and the ocean and outdoors. . . ."

"But what will you do there?"

"Act. Write. Model. Lots of things."

"They'll love you up out there, Bobby. You'll be very successful," Grace told him unhappily; she was going to miss him terribly. "When will you go?"

Bobby took her hands in his and kissed her lips. "Only after I've spent the most unbelievable week with you."

OPENING
NIGHT

24

Glamorous, garish, honky-tonk and seedy, but always Broadway. A fluorescent nightmare, a million twinkling light bulbs, a broken heart for every one of them, a million flickering dreams light the streets. Up and down the Great White Way the theater marquees sparkle in the falling dusk as the hot orange sun disappears beyond the Hudson. On Eighth Avenue the heroin junkies hover in the doorways of porn parlors and massage shops and souvlaki palaces. The couples from New Jersey, rushing to the Atkinson for the new Neil Simon show, mingle with the black hookers in their omnipresent hot pants. Out the revolving doors at Sardi's early-dinner patrons stroll across the street, to the Shubert, where *A Chorus Line* is in its tenth year.

On Forty-sixth Street a crowd had assembled in front of the Janoff Theater, snarling a jumble of limousines and taxis creeping toward the theater. A crew of TV cameramen waited on the red carpeting for arriving celebrities while a brace of policemen held the crowd back on the street. Above them on the marquee was a silver and red sketch of Jacky's right hand, the fingers curled and grasping in her characteristic way, her name splashed above the title, bathed in hot pink spotlights. Parked directly across the street was a flatbed truck with a 4,000-watt klieg light that searched to and fro across the Manhattan sky.

Jacky Mellon had a royal view of the pageant taking place below her from the large windows in her second-floor dressing room, but she took little notice of it. She had been in her dressing room for three hours and had spent most of the time staring at herself in the mirror, putting on her makeup in bursts of energy and self-determination. When she arrived, she found the room already filled with flowers and fruit and champagne and a stack of telegrams three inches thick. She didn't have the heart to read one of them. She felt unexcited and lifeless.

She studied herself in the mirror. She wasn't so bad. She

261

wasn't a great beauty, but she wasn't any horror either. She was famous and rich. So why was she alone? She still could have gotten Eddie back. She just knew it. All she had had to do was wait until after the show opened and the pressure was off both of them, and she was sure she could have gotten him back. Somehow.

If only she hadn't got syphilis.

She shivered at the thought of it and pulled her pink bathrobe over her shoulders more. What an ugly word it was, syphilis. Even though Dr. Barry had assured her it was all gone and out of her system, she still felt dirty just thinking about it. Thank God for penicillin, and thank God she wasn't allergic to it as her mother had been. The pain of getting rid of the VD was a lot less than the pain of contracting it, Jacky remembered ironically. But neither of them put together would equal the pain of telling Eddie about it.

It was three days since she found out, and she hadn't been able to bring herself to tell him. And she had to; she had slept with him. She swore on her mother to Dr. Barry that she would tell Eddie herself so he didn't have to report it to the health department. The La Frances knew she had broken her promise to the doctor, and it was a secret that hung heavy in the air at the theater. But the La Frances didn't pressure her about it; they knew it was impossible for her to tell him until after the show opened. The disclosure that Jackie had given him syphilis would have pushed him over the edge altogether. His sensitive Italian ego couldn't be expected to tolerate what no one's ego could be expected to tolerate: that in a period of forty-eight hours, when Jacky was supposed to be languishing without him, she had managed to contract syphilis and give it to him the next day!

And whom did she get it from? A chorus boy!

A chorus boy she wouldn't let them fire.

At first she was furious with the kid herself, but the next day he sent her the kindest, most understanding note. It must have taken him hours to compose. He said he was never so relieved to be with anybody in his life and that there was no one he could think of who understood show business and art from the level they did. He asked to see her again and the next day sent roses to her apartment. And after all, he was Helen Lawson's son. And she was sure he was mortified when Dr. Barry had the Board of

Health notify the poor kid. So she would not let the La Frances fire him.

After all, she reasoned, veneral disease is pretty icky, but it was nothing to be ashamed of.

She could *die!* If only she hadn't got VD, she could have reconciled with Eddie. She was sure she could have pulled it out of the fire. Now what could she do? Well, there was one last way out. It was a cheap shot, but she had to take it. And she had to take it the next time she saw Eddie, or it would be too late. She hadn't seen him for two days now. He had disappeared after rehearsal two days ago, and nobody had seen him. For all she knew he might not even show up for opening night, but she couldn't believe that.

"Don't you think you should be finishing up?" Suie called to her from the dressing room adjoining hers. "You've been screwing around at that mirror for hours."

Jacky shrugged and blotted her lips on a Kleenex, drew in her eyebrows just a tiny wisp more, darkened her makeup under her chin so her neck wouldn't look so fat. She sat upright and sighed aloud again. Every time she thought she had it nailed she wound up getting screwed.

There was a sharp knock at the door. "It's Ellison, pussy!"

Jacky got up to let him in. He was dressed in a black satin tuxedo jacket with a stunning white monogrammed turtleneck. His hair was combed to perfection. In his hands he held a gaily gift-wrapped package.

"I don't know when you're gonna get ready with all this socializing. . ." Suie called from the other room.

Ellison glared at her and whispered to Jacky, "I'm not used to having the maid talk to me in that tone. . . ."

"She's not a maid. She's practically a family member."

Ellison shrugged. "How do you feel?"

"Suicidal and depressed."

"Too bad," Ellison said, primping in the mirror behind her. "They're not about to call it off unless they have to cart you out of here screaming and kicking in a straitjacket to Payne Whitney."

"I can't tell you how depressed I am. . . ."

"I must admit, that's a new one on me. I've never heard of you complaining about being depressed. Frantic, anxious, in pain, in triumph and in crisis, but never depressed."

"What's even more depressing is to be depressed on my

opening night, the one night I thought would be special. . . ."

"Well, my God, it certainly *is* special. Did you see the hubbub in front of the theater? It's one of the most glamorous opening nights I've ever been to."

"You know what I meant. I meant with Eddie."

"I don't want to hear it, pussy." He cupped her chin in his hand and looked her directly in the eye. "Listen to me. You are a *star*. A giant, internationally loved star. And do you know why? Not because of your momma, who couldn't get you through the first film, and not because of your director or your costume designer. It's because you are a brilliant talent. Maybe you inherited it, maybe it's in your genes—who knows?—maybe we all just talked it into you. Whatever it is, it's there. And you have nothing to worry about."

There was a sharp knock on the door.

"Jacky? Its Ken and Alice!"

She hugged Ellison in silence for a moment and then called, "Come in!"

Ken and Alice pounced on her, hugging and kissing her and showering her with flowers and gaily wrapped packages.

"You look lovely," Ken said.

"And thin!"

"Stop it."

"I swear! Look, she looks thinner, I swear."

Ellison thought Ken and Alice were superb the way they relaxed Jacky. In a few minutes Jacky actually seemed to be regaining a little of her sense of humor. She even asked Suie to open a bottle of Dom Pérignon.

"Open my gift!" Ellison insisted excitedly, handing her the brightly wrapped present.

Jacky tore off the red ribbon and foil paper to find a shoebox.

"A shoebox full of cocaine!"

Ellison guffawed. "Who do you think you are, Tallulah Bankhead?"

"Ballet slippers!" Jacky cried. There was a beautiful pair of pink slippers in the box. "For Glesnerovsky?" She laughed.

"Naturally."

They all had a hearty laugh.

"Now, something special," Ellison said, producing a tiny box from his jacket pocket.

Jacky unwrapped the package carefully. It was a tiny ring box. Inside there was a green velvet pouch. She turned the pouch over in her palm, and out fell two cloudy uncut diamonds.

"That's us," Ellison explained. "Gems in the raw, pussy."

"I love you, El," Jacky said, hugging and kissing him.

"Now this," Alice said.

Jacky opened the La France's present, a large blue box from Tiffany.

"A carrot!" Jacky gasped.

"An eighteen-karat carrot!" Ken corrected.

"Just don't use this one," Alice begged.

"At least not for the same thing as the other one!"

They all roared again with laughter.

"A toast! A toast to the most fabulous lady in town!" Ken said.

"To success!" Ellison said.

"Come here, look!" Ken called, pointing out the window to the crowded street. "We've got a front-row seat!"

A taxi discharged a distinguished middle-aged man and a young woman.

"It's Rupert Murdoch, the Australian publishing magnate who owns the *Post*."

"He's *awful!*" Jacky yelled.

"He is *not!* He revitalized the newspaper business in New York. I think we're lucky to have him," Ken said.

"Look, there's Shorter!"

"Stu Shorter!"

"Shorter? How'd he get here?"

"I sent him tickets," Jacky said, confessing. They all turned to her as if she were crazy. "I *like* him. He's my friend."

"That's OK," Alice said understandingly. "You're allowed."

"Look," Ken said, "there's Grace Dunn."

Grace climbed out of a Checker taxi and the *paparazzi* surrounded her with cameras.

"Oh, no!" Jacky cried. "I'll be so nervous with her out there."

"Rubbish!" Ellison snapped.

"Who invited her?" Jacky wondered.

"She *wanted* to come," Ken said. "She called our office and said she was a fan of yours and asked for tickets."

"Really?" Jacky beamed. "Is that *true?*"

"My *God!* Look who she's with!" Ellison gasped. They all pushed closer to the window. "It's that boy from The Club, Bobby Cassidy."

"Didn't he work for you?" Jacky asked.

Ellison said nothing.

"She's old enough to be his mother."

"Disgusting."

"Dirty old lady."

"Is that an *affair?*"

Ellison finally broke into a smile from ear to ear. "I'll be," he said. "*She* was the secret girlfriend. . . ."

A white stretch limousine with a sun roof and a television antenna came down the block.

"Look at that limousine," Jacky said.

"It's a real nigger car," Ellison said, then turned to Suie and said, "Sorry, dear."

"That's all right," she said. "I know a nigger car when I see one."

A tall attractive woman got out of the car with Larry Gatsby and Pat Kelly behind her. The woman was magnificent, not in the classical sense, but because she was so angular and striking, her eyes so wide and exotic.

"Who is *that?*" Alice asked. "She's gorgeous."

"She's stunning!"

"Look at those fantastic jeans she's wearing. Those clasps must be real gold."

"Eighteen karats," Ellison said quietly.

"It's Mallorey! In jeans," Jacky realized.

"Who's Mallorey?" Ken demanded.

"My house model," Ellison admitted. "She demanded to be seen, so I got her a ticket to opening night. And she's even going to make her debut as a runway model tonight in the fashion show."

"How uncommonly nice of you," Ken said. "And whatever happened to that dispute you were having with the people who owned your company?"

"It's. . . . settled. . . ."

"How?"

"Jeans. Those are *my* jeans Mallorey is wearing."

"Ellison, you're making jeans!"

For the first time ever Jacky saw Ellison blush.

"Well, they're not jeans, really. They're not denim anyway, and they retail for a hundred fifty dollars and up. They're mostly raw silks and nubby cottons with eighteen-karat-gold studs and zippers. But they're certainly more casual than anything I've ever done. And I never realized how gorgeous Mallorey looked in jeans until I saw them on her in the showroom the other day. And it is a hundred-million dollar business, so I figure what the hell. . . ."

They all laughed aloud. "To Ellison's jeans," Jacky called, lifting her champagne glass in the air.

The toast was interrupted by a sharp rapping at the door.

"I'll get it," Suie offered. Everyone turned to the door as she opened it, but already Jacky knew who would be there.

"Hello, Eddie," she said softly.

Eddie stood in the doorway, unshaved, his white shirt rumpled, his raincoat in his hands. "Hello, Jacky."

"I've got to be off," Ellison said, pecking Jacky on the cheek and rushing off.

Ken and Alice kissed her on both cheeks. "Break a leg, darling," they both wished her. Suie followed them out the door, and suddenly Jacky and Eddie were alone.

"I came to wish you luck, Jacky," he said, his voice deep and tired.

"In the theater . . . we say, 'Break a leg.' "

Eddie lowered his eyes. "Well, yes, of course. . . ."

She stood watching him for a moment. She knew him so well. The texture of his skin, the feel of his body, his warmth, his charm. . . .

"Please don't be uncomfortable, Eddie," she said, trying to reach out to him, to touch him and make him her friend again. "There's no need. . . ."

"Jacky, I'm so sorry for the way this turned out. We've hurt each other a lot in the past few weeks . . . and this night is the culmination of everything good we have meant to each other. . . ."

"Eddie, if I'm any good out there tonight, it'll be for you. . . ."

His eyes darted up to hers for a moment and held her gaze before breaking away in disgust.

"No," he said, in a staccato cadence. "Be brilliant for yourself. Don't blame your success or failure on anybody else. Respect yourself a little. You won't be any good until you're doing it primarily for you, not your boyfriend and not your local gossip columnist."

"Don't lecture me, Eddie! I've had it up to here with lectures," she begged.

He thumped his chest with his palm. "What do you want from me, Jacky?"

"No, the question is: What do you want from *me?* Why were you with me, Eddie? Would you unravel the mystery for me before you go? Was it the show?"

He sneered at her. "Of course not. To pretend it was the show is the biggest insult to both of us. So what if I could never have directed on Broadway without your name? Fuck Broadway. My movies make more money in a week than Broadway grosses all year! What do I need with the small-minded New York intelligentsia! Faggots! You know why I was with you?" He pounded the dressing-room table. "Because you had the potential to be something special. You had talent—"

"I'm sick of hearing how talented I am!" she screamed, covering her ears.

He grabbed her wrists and pulled her arms down to her sides, hissing in her face, "You know why I was with you? Because you were *once in your mother's cunt!*"

Her scream started as a low growl and then shredded into piercing shrieks. "You wop! You low-class, demented wop! You second-class Don Juan! *You gave me syphilis! Do you know that?*"

Eddie was clearly horrified. *"I* gave you syphilis?" he beseeched her. "Not *I!*"

"Well, I have it!"

"But I slept with no other woman!"

"Liar!"

"You fool! It's true! I slept with no other woman!"

Her heart broke as she saw in his face that it was true.

All that *Sturm und Drang* about jealousy and Horay, and he had been faithful to her all along.

"You didn't need *me* to give you syphilis. You think I didn't know how you've been running around?" he shouted. "You and your faggot friends at that discotheque, taking drugs, fucking each other. . . ."

"Get out!" she shrieked." Get out! Get *OUUUUUUUT!*"

The door flew open, and Ken and Alice burst into the

room. Jacky hoisted a wastepaper basket over her head and threw it at Eddie. "Get out! Get out!" she screamed, grabbing a lamp off the dressing table and smashing it on the wall. "Get out, all of you!"

Eddie walked out the door.

The La Frances, white-faced and frightened, slammed it closed behind them.

Alone, Jacky stormed to the dressing table and tried to take deep breaths to calm down. When she managed to compose herself, she rummaged through her overnight case until she found a leather Dunhill envelope. She turned it over on the table and a Baggie of cocaine fell out. Using a little spoon to break up the congealed powder, she spread it out over the counter in clumsy lumps. Then she produced a sterling silver straw from Tiffany hidden within the case and started to snort up large amounts.

Unexpectedly there was someone standing over her.

"What are you doing?" Suie asked, ever so quietly, a whisper verging on hysteria.

Jacky threw her head back and inhaled deeply, glaring defiantly at Suie.

More quickly than she could realize it Suie's hand swept out and smacked her in the jaw with a crack so loud she thought her jaw must have snapped. Her hand went up to touch her face. "Suie, my God!" she managed to say, but Suie's hand went out again and swept the counter clear of the cocaine, showering the crystals all over the blue carpeting. "Stop it!" Jacky screamed too late, falling to her knees, trying to save the cocaine.

"God damn you, young woman!" Suie shouted. "No more, you little fool! No more!"

She flew into the other room and took her coat from the closet.

"Suie!" Jacky shouted, a little frightened. "Where are you going?"

"I'm getting out. I've been through this opening night before, and it doesn't have a happy ending. I'm tired of doing this. No matter how much those people scream for you, you ain't never gonna be happy. I'm goin', Miss Jacky."

"Suie, you can't leave me now. I need you, Suie—" The sound of the door slamming in the other room cut her off in mid-sentence. "Suie!" she screamed again, ragefully getting to her feet and rushing to the door. She ripped it open and came face to face with the stage manager, who was about to knock.

"Oh, Miss Mellon! Ten minutes to curtain!" he said excitedly.

Jacky pushed him aside and caught a last glimpse of Suie as she disappeared down the stairwell and was lost to her forever. Slowly she stepped back into the dressing room and closed the door behind her. She sat before her mirror, her veins streaming with the cocaine she had just inhaled, and watched a play unravel on the black screen, the dressing room and bouquets and telegrams fading into the background. There she was alone in the mirror, all made up for a party.

Momma was there somewhere, too, coming up behind her, smiling, holding flowers in her hand.

"No, no flowers, Momma." Jacky told her. "Don't fuss with my collar," she begged, brushing away her cold, fluttering hands.

"I've got to do something with myself, darling. I'm so nervous for you," Angela said to her.

"I'm OK, Momma, Jacky assured her.

"You're so grown up. I was always afraid to go on. Sometimes it was so frightening—"

Jacky interrupted her. "I remember how frightened you were, Momma."

"I took pills to calm me, but that didn't work either."

"You took too many pills, Momma."

"But there was Maxwell. Now Maxwell could talk me out of the blues in a second, Jacky."

"But I *married* him, Momma, and he was a fag." Jacky turned around in her seat now and faced her mother directly. "I'm not afraid anymore, Momma. I promise."

"All right," she said, reaching out to her, disappearing, fading.

"Momma?" Jacky whispered to her. "I'll do it for you, Momma. . . ."

Two hours and fifteen minutes later the curtain fell on the opening night of *The Performance*. Jacky Mellon, at that moment, was standing atop her Plexiglas cube filled with pink smoke, her arms outstretched, her fingers twisted and grasping. The curtain seemed to fall in front of her at exaggerated speed, a gesture by an inanimate object to make a punctuation point.

There was stunned silence in the theater, as if there were no audience.

Grace Dunn turned to Bobby Cassidy and shook her head, speechless. Two rows behind her Addison Critch noted the expression on her face with great interest.

Stuart Shorter sat dumbfounded, the bow tie crooked on his tuxedo, his mouth hanging open a little.

Ellison turned to the La Frances beside him; they both were weeping. "I'm still holding my breath," he began to say, but the rest of it was cut off by an eruption in the theater, an explosion of cheers and applause like a giant steam pipe exploding. The audience rose to their feet in one sudden move.

Swept along with them, Grace Dunn found herself cheering, "Bravo! Bravo!"

The cheers could be heard out on the streets down to Broadway as the theater ushers opened up the exit doors. But no one budged to move.

Ellison shouted at the top of his lungs with the rest of them. "Bravo! Bravo!"

The curtain rose again, and there was Jacky, alone on the cube in a single spotlight, her hands at her sides. Slowly, ever so slowly, she lifted her big, mournful eyes to meet her praisers. Then she took a deep, well-deserved bow.

25

In Manhattan, the most social of all social places, there are tens of thousands of special events every year, and there would probably be tens of thousands more if there were time to fit them in. Often on any one night there'll be five or six smashing parties and openings, all competing for the glitterati's attention. Yet with this plethora of social and entertainment distraction in New York all of them seem to meld into each other into one very long, not very amusing cocktail party. Only a few galas in the seventies stood out: the New Year's Eve and Academy Award parties at The Club; Diana Vreeland's black-tie events at the Metropolitan; Robert Stigwood's opening-night party for *Tommy,* when Allan Carr and Bobby Zarem transformed the Fifty-seventh Street subway station into a lavish disco and restaurant with $75,000 worth of flowers and lobster and champagne. And Lester Persky's *Hair* opening at which Pier 52 on the Hudson was transformed into Central Park by the actual transporting of full-sized trees and shubbery.

But there are parties and there are parties. And then there was the opening of *The Performance.*

Romeo Schneider pulled at his polka-dot bow tie and grinned boyishly at the minicamera facing him, aware that an international audience of some 40 million people was watching him live. Romeo, when he couldn't figure out what else to do, often grinned boyishly at the cameras. In fact, it was his good-natured, boyish, athletic quality that made him so popular with television audiences. But it also made him a befuddled, apologetic talk-show commentator and a bad choice for an emcee for *The Performance*'s opening-night festivities. According to his press releases, his charm came from retaining his small-town, Ohio humility, but according to Paul Fitzpatrick, the overweight, overworked network unit director who had got stuck directing this turkey of an opening, Romeo Schneider was about as charming as pig shit.

"That *shmuck*," Fitzpatrick said, watching Schneider on the monitor in a giant control booth trailer parked up the block from the doors to The Club. Fitzpatrick pulled a chewed cigar from his mouth and stuck it into the ashtray, a thin line of saliva drawing from his lip. "If that asshole mugs into the camera when he doesn't know what to do one more time, I'm gonna cut to crowd shots all night," he told the tech director.

On screen Romeo Schneider squinted a little as he listened to Fitzpatrick bark orders at him through a transistorized speaker plugged in his ear. Then he said, "The curtain was a little late in going up on *The Performance* this evening, so our opening-night arrivals won't be getting here until just a few minutes more. In the meanwhile, we've got some tape of what it looked like two hours ago outside the Janoff Theater this evening."

Schneider paused while the tape of the opening appeared on the TV screen. There were shots of Stephen Sondheim, producer Hal Prince, Grace Dunn and Bobby Cassidy, Stu Shorter, Liz Smith and Rex Reed. Some pushed by; some smiled and waved to the camera. There was a shot of the marquee and klieg lights and a shot of Ellison, carrying Jacky's gift as he arrived at the theater.

The picture cut back to Schneider. "Here on Fifty-seventh east-bound lanes have been cordoned off for the arriving traffic." The camera cut to a view of Fifty-seventh Street from a camera on top of the mobile control trailer. Hundreds of people were standing in the middle of Fifty-seventh Street, each end of which was closed off by police cars with flashing beacons. As the camera roamed the crowds and up the swooping skyscraper, 9 West Fifty-seventh, across the street from The Club, Schneider's voice continued. "The mayor made available the special entertainment police corps, which is a special force the city keeps in stock for entertainment events like this. This is to show the gratitude of New York City in getting major motion-picture stars like Jacky Mellon or Valerie Perrine or Raquel Welch to appear in Broadway shows. . . ."

"What a *shmuck*." Fitzpatrick sighed. "He has no idea what he's talking about. Those police are probably costing the taxpayers hundreds of thousands of dollars in salaries so these people can throw a party for themselves."

The camera cut to the entrance of The Club. There was a line of gray police barricades holding back the crowd of noisy fans. The *paparazzi* and cameramen, dressed in the obligatory ill-fitting tuxedos, with minicams strapped to their backs on braces wandered about impatiently.

"Of course," Romeo's voice announced, "many local storeowners and restaurants on this block have complained bitterly about the cordoning of the street, and many have objected always to the presence of this famous nightclub on this block, claiming—"

An assistant director on the sidewalk was motioning furiously to Schneider that the first cars were arriving.

"Here's the procession coming up the block now," Schneider said as the camera cut to a sea of limousines and taxis making their way up to The Club entrance.

David Susskind and his wife got out of one of the first cars, waved shyly at the cameras and hurried into the Club.

From the next car Ken and Alice La France, beaming and laughing like teenagers in the midst of a snowball fight, bounded up the sidewalk and over to Schneider. They practically grabbed the microphone out of his hand as he was saying, ". . . . producers of *The Performance*, Ken and Alice La France. Congratulations! We heard from the Janoff it was wonderful. . . ."

". . . . proud, very proud . . ." The microphone picked up Alice's voice momentarily.

"That *schmuck* doesn't even know how to control a microphone," Fitzpatrick said.

"She left everyone breathless," Ken said, warmly hugging first Alice, then Schneider on the screen. "Jacky is truly a star of the firs—"

His words were lost in a burst of cheers from the crowd. The camera cut to an overhead shot of the mob pushing at the barricades as a limousine door popped open and Dustin Hoffman got out, smiling bashfully into the bright lights, giving a half wave to the crowd. Everyone waited breathlessly to see who would emerge from the car after him, but as he started to move up the red carpet, it became clear—he was alone!

"Get Hoffman!" Fitzpatrick screamed at Schneider through his earphones.

On the screen Schneider looked frantic as he pawed his way to Dustin Hoffman, calling, "Mr. Hoffman! Mr. Hoffman!"

"That bush leaguer!" Fitzpatrick screamed.

Dustin Hoffman made it safely by Schneider without a word.

The crowd roared again as Margaux and Mariel Hemingway emerged from the next limousine with their parents escorting them. A production assistant tried to corral them over to Schneider for a quick interview, but Jack Hemingway, the girls' father, shook his head no, and the family proceeded undisturbed to the doors. Margaux did turn to Schneider and the cameras and shout, "She was wonderful!"

In the control room Fitzpatrick could hear the sound of angry yelling coming over the microphone. "Where's that shouting coming from?" he asked the camermen. "Can somebody get me a shot of that commotion?"

From an overhead camera Fitzpatrick noticed a knot of people in the crowd near the sidewalk as some sort of scuffle was developing. A cameraman was wading further into the crowd when suddenly Stuart Shorter broke through, straightening his tuxedo jacket. A policeman moved to push him back behind the barricades, and Shorter yelled belligerently, "I'm Stuart Shorter, and I own this club!"

"This should be good," Fitzpatrick wheezed in the control booth, sending a camera to zero in on Shorter.

At the curb a baffled cop stood back and let Shorter, who was in an advanced state of intoxication, onto the red carpet. From the doors to The Club, two bouncers in dark suits moved up to keep him away.

Schneider, seeing this, rushed into the fray to intervene.

"This is my Club," Shorter announced to the bodyguard, slurring his words, specks of Quaalude foam forming in the corners of his mouth.

"Not anymore it isn't," one of the bouncers told him.

Schneider stuck his microphone in front of Shorter's face. "You must be aware that there's an injunction to keep you out of The Club," Schneider declared.

"Finally, finally." Fitzpatrick sighed.

"Loser!" a voice rang out of the crowd to taunt Shorter.

"Crook! Crook!" a woman's voice screamed.

Shorter turned to face the crowd, weaving a little in place. "I love my life!" he screamed at them. "I love my life and my friends. I don't care if I have to go to jail for six months! I love my life! You should be grateful to me! I invented you! I made standing on the street in front of this club an international pastime!"

"And now you're out on the street with them," Schneider commented.

"Not for long," Shorter promised, "not for long." He began to walk out to the curb, tipped a little unsteadily, and then made it out to a taxicab just as it discharged another passenger. The crowd jeered him the whole way, and the cameras caught his exit into the cab.

"Liz Smith from the *Daily News* has just alighted from her limo," Schneider excitedly announced. "Liz Smith is a great and a warm and charming lady. The aristocrat of columnists. Liz! Liz! Give us a few words on the performance tonight."

Liz Smith smiled her straight, white smile. "She was wonderful," she said happily. "And with what we've been hearing about the show and the pressure of Jacky's personal life it just goes to show that perseverance and talent will out in the end. It was a magic evening in the theater."

The crowd roared again and the camera cut to the curb, where Olivia Newton-John was getting out of her limousine with her manager-boyfriend, Lee Kramer, an ex-shoe manufacturer from England who is younger than she. She flashed her dazzling smile at the crowd, and they oohed and ahhed as she made her way up the red carpet. She stopped for Schneider and in a delicate Australian accent said, "Just wonderful. It was fascinating to watch her perform. I really respect her abilities. . . ."

The camera cut back to the street, now jammed with cars and people and pandemonium. Schneider was saying, "This live telecast from New York is probably one of the biggest events that's ever taken place here at The Club, I would guess . . . Here's the *Post*'s Addison Critch, ladies and gentlemen, Addison Critch. . . ."

The camera cut to Schneider moving in on Critch, who was in an old velvet tuxedo with wide lapels and a yellowing tuxedo shirt. "What was it like tonight?" Schneider asked Critch.

"No comment," Critch said, walking by quickly. Schneider kept alongside him.

"But, Mr. Critch, you've been the most vocal of critics about Jacky Mellon and the show. Certainly you have something to say."

Critch considered it and stopped. "You will have my full report in tomorrow's column, but I'll say this," he intoned. "Many are crying that Christ has arisen and walked on water again. Miss Mellon's performance tonight was not quite as miraculous as that, but if the theater is a birthplace of miracles, let us say that Jacky Mellon's performance tonight was akin to that of a paraplegic who learned to run a mile."

Schneider was baffled. "I would take that as a compliment then," he asked.

Critch smiled enigmatically. "I would say, in terms of a value judgment, that her performance was supernatural. Aside from that the rest of the show was garbage. The direction was flat and nonexistent. The choreography was awful, particularly with that disco music, which was intolerable."

With that, Critch walked away.

"Well, you've heard some of the verdicts," Schneider said.

The shot changed to an overhead of the block, alive with people and cars and flashbulbs going off like the Fourth of July.

"We'll be going inside soon for some celebrity interviews and an inside peek at The Club itself. Coming up in the second half is an exclusive Ellison fashion show of costumes from *The Performance*. But first, a word from your local stations...."

The theater was empty, like the way she felt inside.

She sat in the same row in the same seat she had sat in so many days at rehearsal. She wanted to cry, to have some release, but she only felt hollow and spent. Ellison sat silently beside her, holding her cold hand in his. The curtain was up, and the set looked dark and spooky in the shadows cast by the work light. The maintenance crew had left ten minutes ago, and except for the night watchmen they were alone.

Ellison squeezed her hand gently and said, "Come, darling, we have to get to the party."

"Just a little while longer...."

"It's not healthy to sit in an empty theater, trying to recapture memories of things that never really were, Jacky. We have to get to The Club before the TV special is over. My fashion show is being held up. . . ."

"I can't do it. I just haven't got the energy. . . ."

"Pussy, this is the biggest personal triumph of your life. You are now and forever one of the biggest show business figures in the world. People literally worship you. I bet you even win the Tony Award over Grace Dunn. Now, stop mourning. We're off to your coronation, not your funeral."

Jacky sighed loudly. "The only thing I ever wanted in my life," she said to him, the tears finally rolling down her cheeks, "was to have a boyfriend, to get married. A man was the only thing that I wanted, the only thing to make me complete, a relationship with somebody. . . ."

"Jacky, pussy, don't fret. If it happens, it'll happen. It would probably take a miracle for either of us to sustain a relationship. Faithful to us means not sleeping with more than one man in the bed at the same time."

Jacky started to sob, the saddest, most heartfelt sobbing Ellison had ever heard. He took her in his arms and purred, "That's all right, pussy, cry it all out. Get it all out and you'll feel better. There's someone for you, pussy, I promise. One day you'll find the right guy for you, I know you will. You're too special not to." Ellison thought about his own words, but they didn't sound very convincing.

He stood beside her, pulling himself up to his full majesty. "Now we have to go where we belong."

Still weeping, she stood next to him in the aisle and walked with him out of the theater.

The crowd, restless and angry from waiting for so long, broke into a deafening roar as word spread that Jacky's limousine was finally on its way down the block to The Club. As the car got closer to the marquee, the swell of onlookers got so frantic that a section of the crowd broke through the police barricades and knocked over a policeman.

The TV cameras cut to an overhead view of the block, with Jacky's limousine spotlighted as two mounted policemen cut a path through the crowd to the marquee.

The limousine came to a sharp halt under the marquee, and two policemen blocked it off from the crowd on the street side.

A valet rushed forward to open the door, and a thousand flashbulbs erupted as Jacky got out of the car with Ellison close behind her. She was smiling prettily, holding her head high.

"Jack-y! Jack-y! Jack-y!" the crowd called. They threw roses in her path as she walked up the red carpet, clutching Ellison's arm tightly, mustering the best smile she could for the cameras.

Romeo Schneider, who was all set to pounce on her, backed off as she came toward him, awed by her elegance and beauty and the triumph of the moment for her.

They were chanting her name now, "JACK-Y! JACK-Y! JACK-Y!"

The cameras came in for a close-up, and her eyes were brimming with tears.

She wondered where Eddie was. Maybe he was in some hotel room, or maybe he was having dinner. . . .

"JACK-Y! JACK-Y! JACK-Y!"

ABOUT THE AUTHORS

STEVEN GAINES is the author of *Marjoe*, the biography of evangelist Marjoe Gortner, and *Me, Alice*, the autobiography of Alice Cooper. He has written hundreds of articles on show business, personalities and the pop culture, which he surveyed from his post as "Top of the Pop" columnist for the *New York Sunday News* for five years. His work has appeared in *Playboy, Playgirl, Interview, After Dark, Melody Maker, New York* and *New West* magazines. *The Club* "was inspired by the ten years I've spent on the celebrity circuit. When I first saw Robert Jon Cohen on the disco dance floors of New York, he was only nineteen years old, fresh from Miami. I hoped with my hindsight and his amazing experiences we would have something interesting and entertaining to say about this segment of life."

ROBERT JON COHEN was a college student in Florida before moving to New York and landing a job as a bartender at a real disco, Studio 54. He now lives in Los Angeles.

RELAX!

SIT DOWN

and Catch Up On Your Reading!

☐	13098	**THE MATARESE CIRCLE** by Robert Ludlum	$3.50
☐	12206	**THE HOLCROFT COVENANT** by Robert Ludlum	$2.75
☐	13688	**TRINITY** by Leon Uris	$3.50
☐	13899	**THE MEDITERRANEAN CAPER** by Clive Cussler	$2.75
☐	13396	**THE ISLAND** by Peter Benchley	$2.75
☐	12152	**DAYS OF WINTER** by Cynthia Freeman	$2.50
☐	13201	**PROTEUS** by Morris West	$2.75
☐	13028	**OVERLOAD** by Arthur Hailey	$2.95
☐	13220	**A MURDER OF QUALITY** by John Le Carre	$2.25
☐	11745	**THE HONOURABLE SCHOOLBOY** by John Le Carre	$2.75
☐	13471	**THE ROSARY MURDERS** by William Kienzle	$2.50
☐	13848	**THE EAGLE HAS LANDED** Jack Higgins	$2.75
☐	13880	**RAISE THE TITANIC!** by Clive Cussler	$2.75
☐	13186	**THE LOVE MACHINE** by Jacqueline Susann	$2.50
☐	12941	**DRAGONARD** by Rupert Gilchrist	$2.25
☐	14463	**ICEBERG** by Clive Cussler	$2.75
☐	12810	**VIXEN 03** by Clive Cussler	$2.75
☐	14033	**ICE!** by Arnold Federbush	$2.50
☐	11820	**FIREFOX** by Craig Thomas	$2.50
☐	12691	**WOLFSBANE** by Craig Thomas	$2.50
☐	13896	**THE ODESSA FILE** by Frederick Forsyth	$2.75

Buy them at your local bookstore or use this handy coupon for ordering:

Bantam Book Catalog

Here's your up-to-the-minute listing of over 1,400 titles by your favorite authors.

This illustrated, large format catalog gives a description of each title. For your convenience, it is divided into categories in fiction and non-fiction—gothics, science fiction, westerns, mysteries, cookbooks, mysticism and occult, biographies, history, family living, health, psychology, art.

So don't delay—take advantage of this special opportunity to increase your reading pleasure.

Just send us your name and address and 50¢ (to help defray postage and handling costs).